Informer 3
Bloodshed Never Ends

INFORMER
BLOODSHED NEVER ENDS

RHOAN FLOWERS

THE STREETAUTHOR

* 2021 Rhoan Flowers…
All rights reserved.

No part of this book may be reproduced, distributed, stored in a retrieval system, or transmitted by any means, including photocopying, recording, or other electronic or mechanical methods, without the prior written permission of the author, except in the case of brief quotations embodied in critical reviews and certain other non-commercial uses permitted by copyright law.

First published by:
Tellwell, in 2019

ISBN: 978-1-989995-06-8 (SC)
ISBN: 978-1-989995-01-3 (EC)

Library and Archives of Canada
395 Wellington Street
Ottawa, Ontario

Be advised: since the publication of this novel, websites inserted may have ceased existence or changed.

Dedicated To

The Native victims of unsolved rape and murder cases.
Those who served time for Marijuana possession and those killed during Marijuana related offenses, prior to Canada's legalization in 10/18.

Introduction

While some men lived to become lifelong wholehearted friends, there were those who would sell out their brothers like Judas did Jesus. There were also those who would disown their very parents and family members for the companionship of others, whom they deemed more trustworthy than the people they actually grew with. The most important factors in relationships between criminals were trust and forgiveness, therefore once trusted bonds were broken, could they find it within themselves to forgive? After escaping the clutches of death Kadeem assumed he was done with the criminal lifestyle, until the unlikeliest of persons dragged him back into the furnace. Kadeem had been on both sides of the coin with the people he thought would have his back through thick and thin; and soon found himself the difference between Kevin living or dying.

The Native & Indian Affairs of Canada have fought for decades to get the Government to investigate the disappearance and murders of many indigenous people. Kane the Mohawk Indian uncovered a scheme against his native people, who have been kidnapped and murdered across Canada without justice for centuries. This secretive plot managed to get everyone who knew of it killed; and threatened to extinguish the renegade Indian also. As much as the veteran ragamuffins tried to separate themselves from their past lives of surviving by the gun, there were no other options available against the injustices of certain powerful individuals, who were only consumed with greed and nothing else on Planet Earth. Therefore, somebody had to die!

Part 1

Kelowna, British Columbia

Federal Agent Ross Mohara and three members of his Gangs and Organized Crime Unit, sat inside a Ford Explorer across the street from a funeral possession. Agent Mohara and his crime unit teamed up with west coast agents in a joint operation to uncover more information about the Rough Riders Gang. There were several federal agents at different locations around the cemetery, all of whom communicated with each other with two-way radios. Mohara watched as several bikers blocked off the street and guided traffic, allowing only those invited to their events to enter the burial grounds.

"This trip is turning out to be a waste, we couldn't get the chopper in the air with this bad weather and now this crap," Agent Mohara argued, before he brought a two-way radio to his mouth! "Agent Gibbons has any of your team members been able to infiltrate the grounds?"

Informer 3

"That's a negative Agent Mohara, these bikers are stretched out all around the grounds and most importantly, they got a permit to legally block off the roadways and this entire cemetery," Agent Gibbons answered through the radio!

"Is that shit even legal for these fucking crooks to block us and the local police from entering the burial ground," Agent Mohara enquired?

"I'm afraid this place is privately owned and that permit they have says they legally can," Agent Gibbons stated!

"God damn it! Son of a bitch," Agent Mohara angrily yelled as he slammed the two-way radio on the floor!

The Lakeview Memorial Gardens Cemetery was closed to visitors and most of their staff members, while the B.C Rough Rider gang members held a private ceremony to lay to rest their lost leader, Antoine Hickston. There were over two thousand local bikers, special guests and friends in attendance, but the newest recruits served as guards for the event. Bikers were aligned around the perimeter of the funeral grounds and stopped everyone from entering at the front gate, including family members whose relatives were already buried there and reporters seeking to broadcast the event. The Kelowna Police Gang Squad also wanted to capture pictures of the private members, but were denied entry at the gate and could not get close enough during the church service. The entire funeral procession was kept tightknit from the church service that was held a St. Paul's Cathedral, where bikers kept spectators at bay from a radius of two street blocks.

Antoine Hickston's body was brought back to the place he spent most of his life, for his friends and comrades to mourn and celebrate his passing. The day was rainy and somber, and for as far as anyone could see was a sea of black umbrellas that stretched towards the deceased final resting place. While the preacher spoke to the mass both surviving brothers stood over the grave wearing extravagant dark glasses, which failed to mask the tears flowing down each man's face. There were females in the crowd who sobbed throughout the entire event as if they were martially joined to the deceased; and would be left with children to care for alone. Despite the thundering rain, biker members chose to ride their loud Harleys to honour the fallen tribesman, thus there was an impressive lineup of bikes that stretched from the gate throughout most of the burial grounds.

At the conclusion of the ceremony, all the special guests and out of town visitors began walking by the surviving Hickston brothers to offer their condolences. Kevin was the third person in line and paused by the grieving brothers the longest, while they emphasized their desire to catch the perpetrator who killed their sibling. After offering Kadeem's life as a constellation prize back in Montreal, neither of the Hickstons had any reason to doubt Kevin would find him and have him assassinated for the crime.

"Thank you for coming sir! We would also like to thank you for using your influence to find Antoine's killer," Alex Hickston declared.

"Don't worry we a family now, so no matter where this guy is, I'll find him. I already have someone on his case and I'm sure we should have him in a few days," Kevin exclaimed.

"Antoine would rest easier knowing that we took care of this personally," Adrian Hickston exclaimed!

"As much as I sympathize with you both, Jamaica isn't the type of place where anybody can walk around wherever they please," Kevin warned!

Amber Dickson AKA Miss Cutthroat stood behind Kevin and held the umbrella over him during his brief interaction, before they went directly to their awaiting limousine and departed for the airport. Kevin was the only dignified guest of color, nevertheless he received similar praise and admiration from the attending bikers who only paid tribute to their comrades of higher rank. The instant they entered the rear of the limousine, Kevin instructed his female bodyguard to contact the White Widow who was on assignment in Jamaica. Miss Cutthroat did as commanded and telephoned Fiona, however her cellular rang continuously without a response. Even though Amber wasn't overly concerned about her comrade being abled to look after herself, she continued calling for the next few hours to appease her employer.

***

Thousands of miles away off the Canadian shores in the beautiful West Indies Caribbean, the cellphone being contacted by Miss Cutthroat rang unattended inside an abandoned purse. Instead of being in the owner's possession the purse sat inside her hotel suite on the northeast coast of Jamaica, in the parish of Ocho Rios. It was 5:49 AM locally and the temperature was seasonably warm despite the expectation of a tropical storm later that day, as forecasted by the National Weather Center. Miles away from the tourist resorts of Ocho Rios in the small community of Three Hills, Saint Mary, the sounds of roosters crowing could be heard coming from several residences. Deep in a wooded area was a broken down abandoned concrete house, which had no roof and was being consumed by the surrounding vegetation. Eighteen men formed a line that stretched from outside the residence directly to an old mattress that had been tossed on the filthy floor. The lineup had been drastically reduced from where it was four and a half hours prior, when two employees of Kadeem Kite brought the drugged and unconscious body of Fiona

Pierson, AKA White Widow to the location and temporarily abandoned her. While dumping the female's body, Elroy Akutu and Demitry Rokett overheard music at a nearby party, hence after leaving the Caucasian female they attended the session on a rather peculiar mission. The workers were instructed by Mr. Kite to transport the intoxicated female to a rural location, where it would be easily possible for them to employ impoverished locals to rape her, while they recorded the proceedings. That specific location was selected by Elroy Akutu, who grew up several miles from that area and knew the surroundings well.

When Elroy and Demitry arrived at the party venue they stayed outside the entrance and performed an assessment to determine who might be interested in their proposal. The dance was being held at a local bar in the community, where several street vendors seeking sales sat up their Merchandise Stalls and Pushcarts outside. All the serious party enthusiasts who came on the scene went directly into the session, thus the employees focused their attentions on the young men who lingered outside. After a keen assessment, the employees approached five residents all of whom were rather reluctant to pay the entry fees being demanded. The targeted young men were initially sceptical of the proposal, until Elroy and Demitry offered a hundred American dollars each for their participation. One of the men being contracted offered the services of some other friends for free, then temporarily went off and returned with eleven additional sexually charged associates. By the time Kadeem's employees left the party their registered rapists count had tripled to sixteen, hence they had accumulated more than enough bodies to fulfill their boss' request.

Once they reached the ruins and the locals realized the free pussy offer was an actual valid proposal, the line exponentially grew as nearly everybody telephoned some other associate and notified them. None of the volunteers had ever been with a Caucasian female, therefore everyone grew excited at the chance to sample their first white vagina. Very few of the volunteers in line had condoms, and those without frankly didn't care whether their victim or any of their mates had some venereal disease. Elroy and Demitry recoded several of the men raping White Widow with their cellular phones until both their devices ran out of memory storage, following which they departed the area and made the long trip home. Almost five hours later the line was still extended through the house, when White Widow began slowly regaining consciousness. The Caucasian female was naked with her clothes tossed by the bedside and had a python size penis lodged deep inside her vagina. To ensure his victim was stationary the rapist positioned Fiona on her knees and elbows with her derriere hoist towards him, as he pounded her like a battering ram while the other volunteers either complained or cheered.

The bed in addition to their surroundings was filthy with condom wrappings and used condoms tossed throughout. White Widow had a splitting headache, drool dripping from the corner of her mouth and could barely open her eyes, however she was forced to acknowledge the battering ram pounding inside her with uncontrollable moaning. The last thing the Canadian visitor remembered was walking into Kadeem's suite, where he grabbed her from behind and spun her into his arms. They passionately kissed and explicitly fondled with each other before he walked over toward his liquor cabinet and fixed a pair of drinks, while she made herself comfortable on the sofa. Kadeem brought over the glasses of liquor and passed one to White Widow, following which they toasted to each other and drank. After she finished the entire contents of the glass, the Canadian Hitwoman started fondling with her host's private area to sexually entice him. While caressing Kadeem's genitalia through his pants, White Widow began seeing multiple images of her companion and developed a nauseated sensation. Seconds later she was completely unconscious in her host's arms, after Kadeem unknowingly drugged her drink with a high dose of Liquid Ecstasy. To avoid raising any suspicions an ambulance was used to transport the Caucasian tourist from the resort, by the men employed by Kadeem to sodomize and abandon her far away.

With each aggressive stroke by the rapist, Fiona's level of consciousness and intimate sounds likewise drastically increased. She assumed that the person digging into the pit of her stomach was Kadeem, thereby she attempted to lend her participation and slowly whined on her partner. While cautiously blinking her eyes open to lessen the pain from her throbbing headache, the grungy mattress on which White Widow stooped triggered the first red flag, as she began looking around her surroundings to realize it did not resemble Kadeem's suite. There were murmuring from several of the men in line, who wanted the incumbent rapist to make haste and ejaculate, so they could get their turn. The Canadian Tourist curiously spun her head around to look who was behind her and became startled to note that the person was a stranger. A slight glimpse of the lineup of impatient participants formed from the edge of the mattress, presented Fiona with an overall report of her predicament. The Rapist grabbed a handful of her hair and yanked back the female's head, however she was still too weak to tackle such a physically imposing male in addition to his other mates in line.

"Listen to me bitch, if you try anything you is a dead blood-clatt! You understand," threatened the Rapist!

Instead of arguing or resisting the Canadian Tourist wisely began caressing her clitoris to stimulate an organism, which would likewise energize and regenerate her blood flow. After hours of being flipped and turned in every position imaginable, White Widow's entire body felt numbed and cramped in some areas. To regain sensation and adequate strength back in her paralyzed limbs, the Rape Victim conceded to her aggressor and meditated to control her body. With his victim cooperating fully, the rapist felt comfortable enough whereby he released his tight grip on her hair and began rubbing his hands along her body towards the buttocks. The impactful thrust by her violator in addition to the sight of the used condoms invigorated White Widow, who felt disgust at

Informer 3

the notion that each of those packets represented someone that fondled her.

As soon as the Canadian felt reenergized enough to defend herself, she reached between her legs and began caressing the man's testicles, then abruptly grabbed tightly onto them and squeezed. The Rapist squealed in distress as his victim flipped onto her back and dragged him forcibly to the floor by his testicles. As her tormentor fell to the ground, the rape victim timed his fall perfectly and kicked him with her right knee directly on the bridge of his nose. The male antagonist suffered a broken nose that cracked and fractured his skull as a result, before he also banged his face on the turf and was dead once he struck the ground. None of the men in line thought he was in any danger, until his body laid motionless on the dirt with blood seeping through different parts of his face. White Widow swiftly transitioned onto her feet expecting the rapist's associates to seek immediate revenge, but instead of attacking the lineup of sexually perverted misfits felt dumbstruck at the sight of her voluptuous breasts, shaved pelvic area with a heart design to the right of the vagina and her plump derriere.

After waiting hours in line none of the participants were about to leave without acquiring what they went for, therefore, to intimidate the female two of the men withdrew their Ratchet Knives. White Widow backed up against the wall and pretended as if she was terrified at the sight of the sharp blades. The rapist at the front of the line who had been masturbating to remain erected, checked the vital signs of his bloodied friend on the ground.

"Blood-clatt, the bitch killed Terry," the man exclaimed!

One of the men armed with a Ratchet Knife stepped closer to their intended victim and signalled her to approach him by waving the hand holding the weapon. White Widow shook her head and declined the man's instructions, therein he angrily moved towards her as if he was about to do her harm. The Trained Martial Arts Expert who was exceptionally dangerous in tight quarters, grabbed the man's outstretched hand and twisted it behind his back, then took a hold of the hand in possession of the knife and wrenched the blade from his grip. With one swift move White Widow controlled her attacker's posture, disarmed him and used his own knife to cut his throat from ear to ear.

"Yow, what the fuck! Let's get this blood-clatt white bitch," said the Rapist who checked the first victim!

Following the man's instruction, the nine other volunteers inside the room moved towards White Widow in an attempt to overwhelm her with sheer numbers and brute force. Sex was unequivocally what everyone desired, but the chances of their victim surviving was null after she singlehandedly killed two of their comrades. The naked female held her last attacker upright after slashing his throat, then shoved him at the group of approaching attackers. The body of the deceased rape participant knocked four of his associates to the ground and derailed their advancement. White Widow wisely stumped the leader ahead of two other misfits, who sought to attack from the left side of the men she had knocked to the ground. The Self-Defense Expert kicked the man directly in his chest, which propelled him backwards and thereby knocked two others onto the filthy floor.

With a third of her attackers temporarily incapacitated, the Canadian immediately focused her attention on the three participants approaching from the right. One of the young men was overweight, in addition to being an undisclosed homosexual who only attended to convince the street hustlers he ran with that he was not gay. An opportunity presented itself for the overweight volunteer to rush in and securely grab the victim from behind, but the Caucasian female unexpectedly spun around and stabbed him directly in the neck. Blood began squirting everywhere once the tourist withdrew the knife, leaving her antagonist bewildered as he grabbed for the wound and staggered against the wall. There was no time for remorse considering White Widow was fighting for self-preservation, however she distinctively heard when the young man whisperingly confessed to being gay as he slowly crumbled to the floor.

The loudmouth who shouted the order to attack paused and looked over at his associate, which thereby enabled White Widow to advance and deliver a stunning Spinning Back Heel Kick to his face, that broke his jaw and knocked him unconscious. The next volunteer rapist was also armed with a knife and rushed in with a stab attempt that failed, as his target sidestepped the blade, grabbed his hand and twisted the knife from his grasp. The Caucasian Female confiscated the Ratchet Knife with ease, before falling to one knee and using both knives to slice open a long incision beneath the man's navel. The Rape Participant's mouth fell open and a blank stare appeared across his face as he looked down at the wound in amazement. With his intestines about to fall to the ground, the severely injured volunteer dropped to the ground and tried to hold the wound closed.

The man whose throat had gotten slashed, fractured one of his companion's leg when he got intentionally pushed onto them. White Widow moved towards two of the men who struggled to toss their comrade's dead body aside, then viciously stepped onto one of the man's throat and kicked his comrade in the back of the head. The devastating sound of the volunteer's neck getting broken angered the other participants, who allowed their numbers and egos to delude their thoughts of being victorious versus the martial arts expert. Fifteen-other sex enthused participants from the section of the line that extended through the house, began forcing themselves into the room. Once all the rape participants crammed into the room and both sides stood face to face, the foreigner gripped tightly onto the knives and prepared to be assailed by the locals.

After hours of being sexually molested in addition to being squirted with blood, White Widow resembled a filthy beggar who had not showered in months. The Tourist had blood dripping from the tip of both knives and even looked as if she was crying tears of blood, nevertheless to some of the volunteers she looked extremely captivating.

"Listen guys, if you do not leave me alone; I will be forced to…," White Widow began with her French accent, before one of her antagonists interrupted!

"You can call out or scream all you want, we go chop up you blood-clatt just now," the rapist threatened!

"Wait a minute my youth, I didn't leave my house at this hour not to get some pussy! So, I say we tie up back the bitch, kill her with some fuck, then cut her throat or whatever and burn her," insinuated one of the men speaking Patois!

"You didn't see what this bitch just do you friend? The only thing I want to push inside of her right now is my knife," argued another participant!

"Don't be so hasty hombre, we have all day for that…! Is some pussy me come here for still, so I support the tie back up argument," commented a third rapist!

"Yow dawg bout two years I don't get piece a pussy! And I don't come over here to fuck no dead body," declared a fourth!

Different participants weighed in and gave their opinions, thus when it was said and done most of the men supported the idea to recapture and bind the Canadian Tourist. The island's lingo sounded like an alien language to the antagonized female, therein without comprehension she accepted their unwillingness to depart as a means of aggression. White Widow knew she would have to strike with detrimental precision, as a result she aimed for vital body points that would incapacitate each attacker. With such a limited area with which to operate, the rape victim waited until the first pair were within arms length, then dropped to the ground with an acrobatic leg split and stabbed both men directly in their groin area. The blades pierced through their Genitofemoral Nerve and temporarily paralyzed them both, therein they grabbed for their crotches and fell to their knees.

A third attacker threw a punch that struck the Canadian on the forehead and propelled her against the wall as she pranced back to her feet. White Widow telegraphed the next punch thrown and countered by stabbing her attacker through the soft tendon between the middle and ring fingers. The Volunteer Rapist yanked back his hand as if he had touched hot lava and grabbed onto it tightly, as the pain sent a cramp up his arm and numbed his hand. With a stern stump in the fourth attacker's chest, the Canadian spared herself a few seconds to wrap up a few lose ends, hence she stabbed the kneeling paralyzed men in their necks. Before the man with the injured hand could move away, the female spun with a Spinning Heel Kick to the side of his jaw that knocked him unconscious.

A knife wheeling maniac rushed in with his blade held high and swiped at the Tourist's face. The knife narrowly missed its target and passed slightly above the female's head, as she ducked underneath and pierced one of her blades upwards through his bicep. The attacker yelled loudly in pain and instantly dropped his knife on the ground, thus his victim completed her maneuver by withdrawing her blade and stabbed him in the rib area four times. After Fiona withdrew both her knives, the stunned attacker slowly reached out to touch her beautiful face, before he tumbled to the ground. A sense of doubt was developing in the minds of several of the volunteers, but despite all the killings most them were still unfazed.

Seven of the volunteer rapists looked at each other and shook their heads, then suddenly rushed the lone female and tried to overpower her with sheer numbers. White Widow adjusted the knives in her hands and held the blades downwards, as she braced her right foot against the wall. With the men moving towards her, the female used the wall as a springboard to propel herself forward at her antagonists. The attackers expected the Canadian to cower and fold into a shell to protect herself, therefore her retaliation caught them completely off guard. After pushing off the wall Fiona leapt slightly off the ground and delivered a Knee Kick directly to one of the men's chest. As she crashed to the ground atop of the attacker, the Killing Specialist stabbed both men on either side of her in the pit of their backs. The two injured victims grabbed at the wounded area and tried to apply pressure to relieve the pain and stop the blood flow. Directly after retracting her knives the Tourist swiped her right blade across the first victim's throat, before he could react to being stumped to the ground.

The female's effective and deadly maneuvers stunned her attackers, who initially attributed the prior killings to luck and fright. Three of the volunteer rapists closest to the door casually snuck out, after seeing enough of the female's handy work to realize she was a dangerous opponent. The other four attackers neither of whom had a weapon, simultaneously rushed from different angles. White Widow gripped tightly onto the knives and waited until all four men were close enough, wherein she stooped to their stomach levels and spun in a circle with both blades extended. All four men received incisions across their stomachs and immediately abandoned their cause, as they grabbed for their wounds fearing their intestines might fall to the ground.

"I was trying to say, I will kill all you blood-clatt," White Widow exclaimed with her French accent!

The remaining participants had seen enough to realize that the Caucasian female was a dangerous bitch, therefore they neglected their wounded allies and fled. Instead of killing the men she had severely injured, White Widow left them to mope about in pain and flutter about in pools of their own blood. Despite the valiant stance to save her life, the female victim still had cramps across her abdomen from hours of sustaining some phenomenally sized penises, therefore she tightly squeezed her stomach and knelt on the mattress.

The brightening of the sky eventually cast enough lighting into the abandoned structure for the Canadian to clearly see her surroundings. To cleanse herself the female took a pocket rag from one of the men she had killed and collected four partly devoured bottles of water from about the grounds. White Widow soaked the rag with water and wiped the blood from her skin, before she dressed herself, confiscated money from several of her victims for taxi fare and left. The Foreigner slowly limped through a pathway that led from the bushes to a main road and slightly after emerging she hailed a passing minibus.

When White Widow returned to the resort all the employees were concerned for her health, however the front desk attendant told her of her predicament the day they presumably rushed her to the hospital and provided her with an alternative key to her suite. Fiona was initially suspicious of the resort's employees, but believed the female attendant was genuine in her concerns and thanked her. While passing a terrace on which people often dined, the Canadian Tourist lifted a Steak Knife from a set table and casually continued. The Vexed Canadian marched directly to the room where she recalled being taken by Kadeem and listened through the door before she knocked. White Widow could clearly hear people inside the room and readied the knife to strike at whomever answered.

"Click, click," sounded the door lock!

White Widow was about to stump the door into whoever opened it and decided against taking such action at the last second.

"Hello, can I help you," responded an elderly woman from England?

"Pardon moi, I thought I forgot something inside this apartment," White Widow stated before barging through the door!

"Excuse me ma'am but what are you doing," asked the English tourist?

The Agitated Canadian walked inside and found the woman's husband naked on the bed. The astonished husband quickly grabbed for the blanket and tossed it over himself to hide his wrinkled anatomy and shrivelled penis. White Widow looked around the suite and realized that she was indeed at the right place, but the person she was in search of was nowhere to be found.

"I am truly sorry, I thought I left something important inside this room," Fiona declared as she exited the room!

When White Widow entered her personal suite, she was surprised to find the purse she had in her possession last evening on her bed, with her cellular and other valuables untouched inside. Despite her rugged and tough personality, the Canadian was a woman who had been sexually violated, therefore she sat and wept on the edge of the bed for a few minutes. After moping about for a short time, the first means of business was to check in and inform her boss of what had occurred, thus she directly telephoned Kevin Walsh in Canada. While waiting for the call to connect, the Canadian Assassin felt a sharp cramp in her stomach, nevertheless she started filling the bathtub with hot water, got undressed and prepared to thoroughly soak and wash herself.

"Hello, my dear, I take it you were successful," greeted Kevin.

"I am so very sorry boss, but this guy must have known who I was to put something in my drink. I…I was taken to a place where they tortured me before I escaped. But I must leave Jamaica right away, because I had to kill a few people to survive," White Widow stated!

"Arrangements have already been made. There will be someone downstairs to pick you up in one hour, he will bring you to a small airstrip where a private plane will fly you back to Canada," Kevin instructed.

"I am truly sorry for failing you! Thank you, boss," White Widow responded!

Forty-five minutes later White Widow descended to the front desk where she checked out prior to the arrival of her transport. Precisely an hour as indicated by Kevin, a man pulled up in a Toyota Corolla and asked the receptionist to ring her vacated suite. The receptionist pointed her out to the driver and informed him that she was the person for whom he enquired; thus, the man walked over and introduced himself, then helped to transport her luggage to the car. Before White Widow entered the vehicle, she took one final look at the buildings on the resort and saw Kadeem standing in a window looking at her. The man she had targeted smiled at her and saluted her like a private to an officer, to which she cut her eyes at him and climbed into the car. Kadeem watched the vehicle closely to ensure that it departed the compound without the passenger returning. Once the taxi passed trough the main gate Kadeem received a status report from the guard on duty, who watched the car until it completely disappeared then advised him there of.

Part 2

Montreal's Prosecution Bureau formed a dynamic team of investigators to locate the people responsible for their colleagues' deaths. Members of the Bureau believed they knew the man responsible, however they needed adequate evidence to put him away for a very long time. With the criminal proceeding versus Kevin Walsh being the most high-profiled case on Prosecutor Thompson's workload that day, the focus undoubtedly pointed to him. Even though Kevin was already inside the courthouse when the accident happened, members of the prosecution department believed he was the mastermind behind the killings. The hit and run murders of Gary Thompson and his prosecution team was one of the darkest moments in the bureau's history, nevertheless they were committed to solving the murders. Special Inspector Eric Ruchard and Inspector Emmanuel Ellesbury were placed in charge of the case that begun with a very disturbing crime scene.

To uncover who was behind the steering wheel of the Chevy Yukon that somber morning investigators ran the vehicle's license plate number, which came back unfortunately stolen. They then looked through hours and dozens of videos footage from several businesses along Notre Dame Street, from news reporters' cameras outside the courthouse and other establishments throughout the route driven. After combing through hours of unsubstantiated video footages, the detectives found one camera that caught a perfect image of the driver as he sped through. The image was copied into the National Database, which scanned through the profiles of every documented criminal in Canada and identified the hit and run driver as one, Quail Fromage of 1243 16th Avenue, on the east end of the island.

According to Quail's criminal docket he was already on bail for resisting arrest and violent assault against his landlord, who went by to collect his rent one day when his tenant was entertaining guests. Quail and three of his friends had been drinking Molson Beer, getting high on Crystal Meth, while using Nitrous Oxide or Laughing Gas to stimulate their high. After eighteen hours of smoking Crystal Meth through a glass pipe and inhaling laughing gas from balloons prefilled with the chemical, the four men were stoned beyond their wildest dreams. When the landlord knocked the door, Quail peeked through the peephole and saw that it was him but ignored the interruption and went back to his business. The landlord who was already owed for the previous month's rent, pressed his right ear against the door and listened to hear if anyone was inside, then used his personal key to gain entry. Two of Quail's friends were playing a game on Play Station and a third falling asleep on the sofa, when the landlord took it upon himself to open the door and entered.

The instant the landlord opened the door he knew he had overstepped his boundaries when he saw the gas canister and other paraphernalia across a filthy table. The man tried to explain that he only came in check if Quail had moved out to skip paying his rent, when the tenant charged at him and started punching him. To protect himself the landlord tried to run from the apartment, but the video game players jumped in and helped administering the beating. If the third occupant had not intervened and stopped his friends, they might had killed the landlord without realizing. The man crawled from the apartment and drove himself to the hospital, where police were called in and he gave his statement.

When the police officers went to arrest Quail and his friends, they were still too high and had completely forgotten about what they did to the landlord. Officers quietly approached from the front and rear doors to ensure nobody escaped, then simultaneously kicked in both doors to gain entry. The Caucasian male and his friends fought with the officers to resist arrest, but were all detained and arrested on the same charge.

Two of Quail friends with more severe criminal records were remanded when they passed through court, but the young man who stopped the beating and Quail were granted bail pending their trial. Quail got released with several restrictions and was even ordered to stay at least 150 metres away from his landlord. Down on his luck, Quail who was a wicked graphic and tattoo artist went by the Rough Riders new blues bar located in Verdun. Jim Bartello's main assistant Lil Wasp was a customer of the tattoo artist, thus he went by the bar to try earning some quick money. Lil Wasp had some touch-ups and unfinished work he wanted attended to, therefore they went to the establishment's basement to get the work done. While doing the tattoos Quail enquired if there was any way he could make some extra money and emphasised his willingness to do just about anything. The contract against Prosecutor Gary Thompson had just been issued and knowing Quail's violent history, Lil Wasp offered him the assassination job.

After mowing over Prosecutor Thompson, his team and an innocent bystander, Quail went to hide in Ville Saint Pierre until things calmed down. The stolen Chevy Yukon he used to commit the crime had been destroyed and he assumed the tinted glasses prevented anyone from identifying who he was, therefore, he simply planned on staying out of sight for a few weeks. Quail was paid fifty thousand dollars for the hit and run and warned by Lil Wasp to leave town for a while, but he thought he had nothing to worry about. To avoid being implicated in the crime should anything went wrong, Jim Bartello refrained from any interactions with Quail and allowed his assistant to handle the entire deal.

When the inspectors uncovered who the driver of the Chevy Yukon was, they refrained from publicizing the name, in fear that their wanted man might flee the country. Quail had several specific identification marks such as tattoos from his neck down to his toes, and a few piercings to his lower lip, his ears and nose. The first place a task force went in search of Quail was his designated address in the east end, but found no clues as to his whereabouts. Detectives were apprehensive about letting the public know who this man was, knowing he had biker resources who could help him go underground. Regardless of the concerns the coppers released their wanted suspect on the Crime Stoppers website for the public and hoped there was someone across the city who might had seen him.

Five days later inspectors received a report on their emergency hotline from a woman who said she owned a corner store on St. Jacques Street in Ville Saint Pierre. The woman claimed to have seen the wanted suspect once inside her store buying cigarettes and other items, which was the biggest tip they had received thus far. For clarification that it was indeed Quail Fromage investigator went to the woman's convenience store and watched her surveillance video, which provided the evidence. To locate exactly where Quail was hiding out the detectives acquired half a kilo of Crystal Meth, half a kilo of GHB or Gamma-hydroxybutyrate and six 11-ounce canisters of Nitrous Oxide from their evidence vault. Their plot was to send an undercover detective into the Ville Saint Pierre area with the shipment of drugs and have him use the illegal substances to sniff out their wanted man.

For the undercover inspector to appear credible instead of being considered a law enforcement agent his appearance had to fit the profile, therefore the assignment was given to a Caucasian male with multiple tattoos, long hair, a thick beard with a shaggy mustache and several ear piercings. Inspector Filip Coinburg had all the attributes the investigative team sought, especially the fact he had never worked within the district being targeted. To give Inspector Coinburg some sort of personal history, his superiors loaned him a Ford Explorer with Alberta license plate to make it appear he was from out of town. The officer was also given a fake driver's license and a health care card to help support his argument of being a resident of Alberta. Even though Inspector Coinburg would not constantly be under protective eyes of his team members, he knew they would not be very far away should he call for help.

To get Inspector Coinburg to meet the main drug dealers in the Ville Saint Pierre area, he was appointed a guide who was a well-known street junky from the neighborhood. The junky whose primary drug was crack cocaine had to be assured that his dealers would not get arrested, or that any requital would befall him before he agreed to make the introductions. Even though the crack addict known as Moe had been a reliable police informant for over six years, the team of investigators' biggest scare was whether he might cave under pressure and give away their officer's identity. Moe had no problem offering the police information and did so to keep himself out of jail, but he was initially incredibly uncomfortable with the idea of introducing the undercover to known criminals.

While driving to Ville Saint Pierre, Detective Coinburg noticed that his guide was rather nervous, therefore, to ensure that Moe remained focused and calm regardless the situation, Filip gave the drug addict a small piece of crack cocaine to smoke. Moe who was rather quiet and nervous before he hot gunned pieces of the drug, by sprinkling tiny crumbs onto a cigarette and smoking it, transformed into a talkative and vibrant individual thereafter. Both men finalized some key details such as how they would refer to Inspector Coinburg, and how they came about knowing each other if asked, before they reached their destination.

The neighborhood crackhead first brought Filip to an address on Elm Street to introduce him to Chops, who was the local Rough Rider representative placed in charge of the area. Moe personally knew the area drug boss and his delivery colleagues from their regular dealings and knew that certain types of products were primarily provided by the Rough Riders. Chops ran an auto repair shop as cover for his illegal drug dealings, wherein customers received whatever services they required without raising any suspicions. The mechanic shop was called Chops' Auto Repair and employed four full time mechanics. The building at which they were located had two huge bay doors, with two hydraulic lifts and a tire repair station on the ground floor. On the second floor of the building was a two-bedroom apartment, where Chops lived with his girlfriend Valorie and their two daughters, plus a pair of Rottweilers which protected the yard at nights. There were two 50 ft. trailer containers in the backyard behind the shop where Chops kept spare parts, various sizes of tires and hid his shipment of illegal drugs. Only certain drug dealing customers were allowed at the mechanic shop, thus the boss had a call for drugs line that catered to addicts throughout the community.

When Detective Coinburg and Moe pulled up by the garage's main entrance Chops was finalizing some business dealings with a customer. Moe leapt out of the Explorer the instant they came to a stop, at which his mouth began chattering so quickly that the person to whom he spoke could barely get a word in.

"Yow-yow, my man D what's up dawg!? Yow, you heard what happened to Loo; crazy shit man. I told him a long time ago to leave that fat bitch alone! I always knew she only wanted another welfare baby. Yow, that bitch kicked his ass out the other night in the cold, soon as they came home with that new baby. Yow I told him that bitch only plan to get another few years of free money from the government! Talking bout that love shit, fuck that! Yow l need you to do me a favour dawg? Yow I need to talk with the boss, I got some stuff he's gonna love! Check it my cousin just rolled into town trying to dump some things he brought from out west, and yow I know this is the only place to bring him," Moe exclaimed!

"You know Chops don't fuck with anybody except his own people," whispered the mechanic.

"Yow if I'm going to bring my family here straight, he gotta have some serious shit! Yow I know all that biker club rules bullshit, but Chops could make some serious money off this shit! Yow Just ask him for me and if not, we'll get the hell out of here," Moe remarked!

"OK, what sort of dope your cousin got; and how much of it," enquired the mechanic?

"Yow he's got half a kilo of GHB, half a kilo of Meth and a few canisters of that Laughing Gas shit," Moe explained!

The mechanic's eyes widened at the quantity mentioned, at which he looked at Filip behind the steering wheel, then walked off in his boss' direction. By then Chops had finished dealing with his customer and was walking towards his office. Both men spoke very briefly during which Chops appeared agitated, then stormed off into his place of business. Chop's employee walked back towards the crackhead with a disappointed look on his face.

"The boss said to get the fuck off his property and never bring anybody to his shop in the middle of the day again! If he decides to do business, he says knows where to find you," lamented the mechanic as he went directly back to work!

Moe climbed back aboard the Explorer and drove away. The local crackhead brought Filip to a smaller dealer who lived a few blocks away on Des Erables Street in a five-story apartment building. On their way to the location Moe phoned the dealer and got approval to bring Filip with him into the building. After they were buzzed into the building both the undercover and the crackhead climbed the stairs to the third floor and went to the apartment 309. The residence belonged to a Trinidadian man named Raffie, who secretly sold crack cocaine and marijuana under the bikers' nose. When Filip and Moe brought their proposal to Raffie, the dealer exclaimed that he would have taken some of their inventory had he dealt with such substances, but he declined and thus they left empty handed.

Moments after Moe and Filip left Chops' Garage the owner received a phone call from Quail, who had been partying illustriously on various sorts of illicit drugs for nearly a week straight. Quail had been acquiring his drugs from Chops and was held up in an apartment on Quellette Avenue, with two male friends and four females. The wanted hit and run driver phoned to order an ounce of crack cocaine, some Ketamine and Ecstasy, which were the three main drugs being dealt by Chops at the time. During their conversation Quail enquired when Chops expected to receive some items he had requested, at which the Rough Rider representative thought of Moe and his proposition. To satisfy his customer Chops told Quail that he would send over a portion of his immediate request, then personally drop off a different assortment of treats later that night.

To acquire the products promised to Quail, Chops contacted Moe and arranged a meeting at the addict's residence later that evening, instead of having them return to his place of business. Chops believed that having addicts within the vicinity of his business gave just cause to the police to start a surveillance, thus he preferred any interaction occurred away from his property. There were never any guarantees in the drug trafficking business that one might be dealing with trustworthy individuals, therefore along with three thousand dollars in cash and a digital scale, Chops also shoved an AREX Rex Zero Compact 9mm handgun into a small leather pouch. Before departing his home, the Rough Rider representative played around with his daughters for a few minutes and was about to give his girlfriend a kiss, when his driver pulled up outside the gate and honked the horn.

Moe lived on Government Assistance which covered his rent and provided him with a little money for groceries, although he had very little furniture and absolutely nothing inside his refrigerator. When Moe and Filip reached his apartment building, the undercover inspector only brought a portion of the drugs given to him upstairs. Filip did not wish to have their expected guests see the entire shipment he had in his possession, therefore he wisely brought two canisters of the Nitrous Oxide and a portion of the other substances.

When Chops arrived at Moe's building with his driver they drove around to the back and parked in a vacant parking slot. To deter their hosts from any preconceived notions Chops ordered his companion Kenny to "bring the chopper", to which his driver went to the trunk of his Acura TL and removed a small bag. Both men climbed the stairs to Moe's second floor apartment and knocked the door, which was attended to by the home owner. Moe graciously allowed his guests to enter his single bedroom apartment where Filip was seated around a table watching a hockey game between the Canadians and the Boston Bruins. The room was somewhat cloudy with Moe puffing on a cigarette and his visitor smoking a Marijuana Joint.

"Yow Quail man how you doing? Yow I apologize for bringing my cousin to your shop today, but yow I couldn't disrespect you and try to go anywhere else with this stuff," Moe stated!

"This your cousin? Where is he from," Chops asked?

"Yow of course he's my blood, you see the family resemblance!? He lives out in Alberta," Moe declared!

"What's your name big man," Chops questioned?

"I'm Vince man, nice to meet you," Filip introduced himself and stood up to shake Chops' hand, when he sighted Kenny with an Uzi Assault Riffle guarding the door!

"They call me Chops and that's my man Kenny… So, tell me something Vince, how did you come by this shipment Moe claimed that you have for sale," Chops questioned?

"Selling products is what I do man; but to be honest some of the people that I usually deal with got popped back in Alberta by the police, and I got bills to pay, so I had to hit the road to try and build some new clientele," Filip exclaimed!

"So… this could be a regular thing if I wanted, is what you're telling me," Chops insinuated?

"If your money is always good, I could come through twice a month if you want," Filip argued.

"And just about how much product can I get each order? Plus, what kind of products are we talking," Chops enquired?

"Man, I can get whatever amounts of pills, cocaine, gas, grass whatever you need," Filip boasted!

"Well depending how things turn out, maybe we can do some business. I heard you got canisters of laughing gas, Crystal Meth and GHB with you right now," Chops questioned?

"Yeah, I got some a those! How much do you want," Filip questioned?

"Let me see what you're working with first buddy," Chops emphasised?

Filip was deeply concerned for their safety with an armed visitor carrying an assault rifle inside the apartment. The bag containing the drugs he had brought upstairs was on the floor next to him, therefore he slowly reached down and picked it up. Once Filip took everything out of the bag and placed them on the table, Chops' companion pulled closer to the table to have a closer look at the drugs. The Crystal Meth looked like actual crystals which glistened so brightly that Chops quickly withdrew a small pipe and prepared it to smoke a sample. The Rough Riders' representative blazed up a small piece of Meth, which was so potent that Chops' entire facial expression changed. Watching his boss smoke made Kenny jones for a hit, therefore he licked his lips, pulled up a chair and sat, placed his firearm on the table and took the pipe from Chops. Filip slid Kenny a small piece of Meth to smoke and like his boss, the driver was also instantly intoxicated.

Had it not been for some intrusive customer who began telephoning Chops forty minutes later and continued doing so every two minutes thereafter, the drug boss would not have considered leaving Moe's apartment that soon. When Kenny and Chops departed with the products they attained, an unmarked undercover cruiser followed them to Quellette Avenue. The undercover officer noted that stop which was the only other made by the pair, who stayed at the location until 5:12 AM before they left. An investigation into who resided at that location determined that the lodgement was being rented by two females, described as Rough Rider affiliates by the property's landlord. Plain clothes detectives watched the apartment for two days, during which nobody left the residence and everything the occupants wanted was delivered.

On the third day of their surveillance, undercover Inspectors Ruchard and Ellesbury were parked down the street when Omar who was one of Chops' delivery boys brought a package to Quail and his companions. The coppers pursued the vehicle and stopped it two blocks away from the apartment and out of the view of their suspects. Omar was on his way to make another delivery and tried to appear calm knowing he had illegal substances inside his vehicle. The officers initially had no reason to pull Omar over, but once they approached the vehicle and smelt Marijuana inside, that also gave them cause to perform a search. The driver was detained and placed inside the back of the police cruiser while the officers searched his car, where they found six prepackaged parcels of crack cocaine. With enough evidence to arrest Omar for drug trafficking and distribution, the detectives returned to their cruiser where the detained worker was shedding tears. To show the trafficker that they had found his hidden stash, Detective Ruchard threw the plastic bag container onto the dashboard as they entered the cruiser.

"Well Mr. Copelord it looks like we'll be placing you under arrest for trafficking and distribution of a narcotic substance…," Inspector Ellesbury began.

"Oh god no, please, I'm sorry! I only wanted to make some money to support my pregnant girlfriend! Please I'm begging you don't arrest me," Omar pled?

"You wish to help yourself get out of this mess," Inspector Ellesbury asked?

"Anything please, I'm sorry," Omar cried!

"You just left from an apartment on Quellette Avenue, who are the people inside that residence," Inspector Ellesbury continued?

Omar paused and thought about what was being asked of him. Both of his options were life threatening, thus he seriously considered which would be the lesser of the two evils. He absolutely did not wish to go to jail and was somewhat skeptical of informing against known Rough Rider killers, but then he thought there was no way anyone could find out that he told.

"If I tell you guys what you want to know, are you going to let me go," Omar questioned know exactly who they were after?

"If the information is good and leads to the person we're looking for, we'll consider it," Inspector Ruchard answered.

Omar made a huge sigh and shook his head and said, "Quail is hiding out in there, with some other people!"

The detectives reacted as if their mates unexpectedly told them they were pregnant, as they looked back at Omar in amazement.

"You sure about this," Inspector Ellesbury asked?

"Yes, I'm sure," Omar responded!

"It seems like that might be your lucky get out of jail free card. But if we go in there and he is not there, believe me when I tell you that your door will be the next door we kick in! So, if you leave here and try to warn anybody in there that we're coming, it will be a long time before you see freedom when we catch you! You understand me," Inspector Ruchard threatened!

Detective Ellesbury got out of the cruiser and opened Omar's door, then leaned him against the car and removed the handcuffs. The drug trafficker was given back his delivery package to avoid raising any unwarranted questions from his boss. As Omar was being released from his confines, one of Chops' crackhead customers drove by in a taxi and noticed the incident. To alert and help protect Chops in case the officers were intent on raiding his residence next, the crackhead female telephoned and advised her dealer.

Two hours after that traffic stop transpired an arrest squad led by Inspectors Ruchard and Ellesbury was sent to bring Quail in alive. Investigators hoped to question the hit and run driver and possibly get him to give up the people who paid him to commit the murders, in exchange for a lesser sentence or whatever deal possible. At 11:33 AM, two Ford Excursions loaded with fourteen officers dressed in riot gear, pulled up in front the three-level apartment sectional where Quail and his friends were stoned on several types of drugs. Nobody inside the dwelling had slept in days, hence they all looked like walking zombies with their eyes barely opened. The television light was all that brightened the main room inside the apartment, as all the windows were blocked with either blinds or curtains.

When the officers reached the top apartment where Quail and company were held up, the ram operator moved into position to break down the door. The ram operator was a huge man at 6 ft. 3 inches, 398 pounds, therefore with the door area quite small, his size threatened to create a problem with the invading officers' ability to quickly enter the residence. Detective Ellesbury provided the instructional silent count, before the ram operator swung the metal door buster and knocked it wide open.

"Police officers get down on the ground now," shouted the officers as they struggled to get pass the ram operator, who pressed himself against the wall but still obstructed his comrades!

When the door flew open that momentary pause before the first officer entered, allowed some of the delusional occupants to arm themselves. The police expected to find one or two firearms inside the residence, but they were not expecting to face a full-fledged assault. By the time the first officer entered the lodgement, Quail who had been inhaling Nitrous Oxide from a prefilled balloon, reached for his Glock 45 on the table beside him and started firing in the officer's direction. With the Laughing Gas and other narcotics in his system, Quail found the situation comical and laughed at his actions while discharging bullets at the intrusive officers.

The male across the room from Quail on the sofa was receiving fellatio from one of the females, hence that negated him from quickly reaching his weapon on a side table. Two of the females wearing only panties were inside the kitchen preparing food for everyone, while the fourth female and the Quail's third associate were locked away inside a bedroom engaged in coitus. After Quail fired at the leading officer and missed, the same officer dived to the ground then shot and killed the female and his friend on the sofa.

Informer 3

Everyone inside the apartment were too intoxicated to think rationally, as the ladies inside the kitchen grabbed for their firearms and started a shootout versus the arresting squad. One of the females in the kitchen had an AK-47 Assault Rifle with a Clutch Bag and began scattering bullets at the invading officers, while her friend reached for a CMMG MK9 Luger and participated. The male and female inside the bedroom unexpectedly rushed out naked with automatic handguns and joined the intense shootout. Quail shot the third officer through the door in the left shoulder and twice in his vest, before the pursuing officer shot him four times with his T91 Assault Rifle. The officer who shot and killed Quail was killed by one of the shooters inside the apartment, as they continued their violent assault against the intruding coppers.

The first two officers through the door who were forced to hit the floor before Quail's aim improved, shot and killed the nude lovers who both had the least powerful weapons in the gun battle. Inspector Ruchard who was the best sharpshooter on the team, changed the bullet deployment selector to solo on his T91 Assault Rifle with a mounted distance scope. With the heavily armed ladies inside the kitchen still shooting callously at anything that moved, Eric waited for a pause in their shooting then popped his weapon inside the door frame and shot the female brandishing the CMMG MK9 Luger. The detective expected the last female to surrender after losing all her friends, but instead she only taunted the police and continued shooting at everyone. None of the officers inside the apartment had a clear shot at the female inside the kitchen, therefore they tried to maneuver but she kept them pinned. Detective Ruchard again waited for a pause in the shooting, before he was able to end the standoff by shooting the final female directly in the head.

The mission was considered a failure due to the officers' inability to bring in their wanted suspect alive. As a result, investigators sought to find anyone with information on who initiated the hit and run contract. The order was given to arrest Chops and seize whatever drugs found, in order to pressure him into providing whatever information he knew. The Drug Squad went to Chops' garage and arrested him and two other men on drug related charges. Chops' girlfriend was also taken into custody during the arrests, and their two children handed over to social services. Even the dealer's dogs were taken away to some kennel, while law officials implemented their strategy to transform the dealer into an informant. Much of the treatment awarded to Chops and everyone else arrested was due to the information already gathered, plus what they expected to find during their search. With their raid on Chops' garage a surprise, investigators were certain they would uncover drugs and possible weapons, but were surprised to find absolutely nothing.

The first night while Chops was in police custody, Kenny exited the Lafleur Restaurant on the corner of St. Jacques Street and Gowans Avenue with a paper bag containing food. As he approached his car a white Chevy Cube Van pulled up next to him and two men dragged him into the vehicle at gunpoint.

Kenny was brought to the Bucher in Dorval, where they tortured him for hours by severing multiple body parts, before finally chopping up his body and putting the meat through a meat grinder.

With Quail's case closed, Inspector Coinburg was ordered back to the station for reassignment, therefore he parted ways with Moe and returned to his life. Moe was inside his apartment with a female crack head named Patsy that same night smoking his favourite drug, when three bikers knocked his door. Instead of neglecting the intrusion, Moe who did not have a peephole cracked open his door to see who it was. At the sound of the door unlatching, the men forcibly barged into the apartment and closed the door behind them. None of the intruders were there to engage in small talks, therefore they brutally attacked both occupants with knives and stabbed them to death. The innocent female was stabbed eight-nine times all over her body, while Moe got stuck more than three hundred times. As a message to the police and anyone else who might have considered informing, the bikers cut out Moe's tongue and left it shoved up his anus.

Part 3

Private invitations were sent out via bird service to the newest inductees of Quebec's Undocumented Governing Committee. Every member of the Province's Secret Governing Cult was summoned to their place of deliberation for an important meeting, by the Foundation's Monitoring Division. The Secret Covenant was a complexed institution with multiple departments, millions of members, prospects being scouted daily, students graduating from their technologically cutting-edge schools annually, yet only the Monitoring Division knew of their connection to the Distinguished Club. The Institution only selected specific candidates for their free educational program; persons deemed intellectually gifted whom they would acquire either through Adoptive Services or directly from economically struggling guardians. Every student who went through the Institution was branded as property, furthermore their continued involvement as whistle blowers in whatever field of employment they entered was mandatory.

The two most important functions of the Secret Committee were: to introduce new legislations into law; and second, vote on amendments being proposed by other government officials. With a mountain of extremely sensitive materials being processed daily, it became the Monitoring Division's duty to ascertain which legislations must be voted on by their committee. Monsieur Gilbert Stephano who was also the Hall of Conference moderator, supervised the division that collected the whistle blowers' information and organized their Judges' gatherings.

Quebec's Secret Cult had entered an unprecedented phase where for the first time in their history they had a High Chancellor, who was ranked above everyone else and held the deciding vote on every issue. The Monitoring Division had uncovered news that the Office of Conflict of Interest and Ethics Commission was about to start an enquiry into Prime Minister Mathew Layton's dealing with Kevin Walsh. Such an investigation threatened to expose the cult's existence, therefore the emergency meeting was called for a decision on how to proceed. The Hall of Conference was redesigned, but they maintained the original circular seating concept, with slight changes such as tinted bulletproof glass protecting the judges inside their booths, and a more dignified seating for the High Chancellor.

Almost every replacement representative of the prestigious club was born to a wealthy family and lived exceptional lives due to their riches, nevertheless none of them knew of anything more distinguished or powerful as being a Lord of the Secret Quebec Covenant. While inside the halls or private chambers all members were bound to wear their infamous black gowns, however, the attached cloaks to shield their identities were made optional. Each member arrived through a private entrance that led directly into their personal suites, where they prepared themselves before, they were summoned to their individual booth. At the beginning of the conference every judge was asked to rise for the playing of the National Anthem, before they got down to business and ushered in a new era.

"Judges please take your seats," began Gilbert Stephano the moderator, whose identity was shielded by his cloak? "Welcome to your official gathering. Today we will begin with a brief video that will get you all acquainted with the files on the agenda for discussion. If you could please, watch the screens ahead of you?"

A video screen popped up on the glass inside every judge's booth that first showed their ancestors plotting to get their Montreal mayoral candidate elected into office. In each of the videos watched the Society Cult gained millions in revenue through their business endeavors, therefore they could not afford to be exposed or found guilty on any count. In another video the judges watched as Prime Minister Mathew Layton, after receiving a package containing sensitive documents, contacted Judge Bryere and illegally interfered in an ongoing court case. During the entire presentation of the Prime Minister's video, Kevin stared at the Moderator whom he knew was aware of all the intricate details they neglected to feature.

"Gentlemen, we have several major issues to discuss. Our Canadian Prime Minister will, in the next few days be called before the Department of Conflict of Interest and Ethics Commission for a hearing, which threatens to expose this chamber's very existence. According to our reports this hearing would have been called months ago, had it not been for the fact that the appointed commissioner Mme. Teressa Lablonde had been undergoing breast cancer treatments. It appears that the other electoral groups are heavily pushing for this hearing, so there must be no cancelations of these forthcoming proceedings," Gilbert exclaimed.

"What sort of evidence is there that could expose us," Monsieur Delrose asked?

"According to our reports the Prime Minister may have in his possession a DVD that highlight some of our past members. Where investigating these leads may end; we have no idea, but there can be no loose ends," Gilbert stated!

"If our only chance to save this committee is to have the Prime Minister killed, you gentlemen have my vote," Monsieur Huron declared!

"Killing the Prime Minister at a time when they are threatening to investigate this cabinet will definitely get us exposed for stupidity," argued Monsieur Royal!

"That is how our forefathers handled things for years, if anyone lacks the spine for such decisions, I suggest they resign," Monsieur Huron exclaimed!

"Gentlemen please show respect to your inner circle. We are here to determine how to best manage these sensitive issues, not argue amongst ourselves," interrupted Gilbert!

"Have there been any investigations ordered into our organization by the Ethics Commissioner," asked Monsieur Paneau?

"Mr. Judge so far there hasn't; however, we at the monitoring bureau predict that once the Prime Minister testifies, that order will be given and for the first time in history our secrecy will be mentioned if not exposed," Gilbert responds!

"If Mme. Teressa is the only appointed government official who is legally authorized to investigate these cases, we simply get rid of her discretely," Kevin suggested!

"Monsieur Chancellor, any intentional deaths at this junction could be detrimental for us," Gilbert reasoned!

"We simply get her doctor to give her a more aggressive form of cancer, and while the government figures how to proceed we'll sabotage whatever evidence they have. The next Ethics Commissioner must be appointed by us, and through him we'll get to control what happens with this enquiry... Prime Minister Layton will be losing his position in the up coming election in a few months, so whatever decision needs to be made about his future will depend on the enquiry's outcome," Kevin instructed.

"But Monsieur Chancellor, we must expect that by this point too many other persons have heard of us, therefore we must run the Reboot Program," Monsieur Huron stated!

"You are indeed correct Monsieur Huron, but the Reboot Program will be too excessive. I believe the System Cleansing Program will be more efficient," Kevin directed.

"Brilliant suggestions Monsieur! Is there anyone else who would like to suggest another method or strategy," Gilbert enquired, then awaited a response? "Since there are no further suggestions gentlemen, arrangements will be made to proceed as indicated by our Chancellor... Next on the docket are the Quebec Premiers whom your fathers got elected into office, who are also presently being investigated by the Ethics Commission and the R.C.M.P. Reports have surfaced about some private recordings of Premier Joseph McArthur's business dealing at his office with several of our past judges, where illegal transactions were discussed. It appears now that the Premier has found himself in a bit of a bind where jailtime seems likely, he is seeking immunity for his testimony against this institution since he believes the gentlemen he dealt with are no longer with us."

"The Premier has underestimated the powers of this institution, he must be made an example of before he makes matters worst," Monsieur Huron insisted!

"Gentlemen, we at the Monitoring Center believe that this could potentially affect this institution once investigators start checking into the Minister's business dealings. Have any of you any solutions to dealing with Premier McArthur," Gilbert asked?

"The Premier is worthless at this point, I vote to have him killed," nonchalantly suggested Monsieur Melvick!

"We can't have him turn over whatever information he has, he must be annihilated," argued Monsieur Vitran!

"Premier McArthur will be easily controlled with the information we already have against him in our database. I believe we can also get him to do the job my colleagues are proposing," Kevin lamented.

Informer 3

"Thank you again Monsieur Chancellor," Gilbert exclaimed!

Part 4

Kevin sat inside his private office at the late Monsieur Francois Trudeau's Estate, watching the video sent to him of White Widow being raped while unconscious. The video was vile and graphic in nature and highlighted some of the rapists' identities, considering none of them at the time felt concerned about impending liabilities. While watching skits of the video on his computer monitor, the New Boss peeked over at his television screen on which he was tuned into the Jamaican TVJ Newscast, where a reporter was discussing the pile of dead bodies left in Fiona's wake. According to the local reporter, statements taken by the police from survivors found at the scene implicated rival gang members instead of the embarrassing truth. The rape video was truly disheartening for Kevin knowing he appointed White Widow the assignment, but the undisclosed number of murdered men found at the scene sat his mind at ease.

The Jamaican Rude Boy looked at a picture of Kevin Junior on his desk and smiled to himself at the thoughts of his son's silliness. He then looked at a large portrait on the wall of Francois Trudeau and reminisced on the funeral, where he and Junior spent a few minutes alone with the casket prior to the guests' viewing. There was an array of security screens inside a cabinet against a wall that enabled Kevin to view everywhere on the property. A BMW X6 pulled up at the gate and after inspecting the vehicle the guards rang the house for entry confirmation.

"Beep-beep," sounded the intercom, to which Kevin responded! "Yeah!"

"Sir there is a Mr. Jean-Pierre Patrice here to see you," the guard said.

"Let him in and send him up to the house," Kevin instructed in his Caribbean tone.

"Right away sir," the guard answered!

As Kevin refocused on the rape video his office phone rang, and the display featured a number that contained the 876 Jamaican area code. Before responding however, the Rastafarian picked up his Marijuana Joint from the ashtray and sat it ablaze, then pressed the intercom button on the phone.

"Hello," Kevin answered, while in the background moaning from the video could be heard through the speaker!

"It sounds like you watching your white bitch getting some stiff cock under her blood-clatt," Kadeem joked!

"You think me go make you get away with this shit? You think you see anything yet," Kevin responded?

"Yow I don't intend to spend the rest of my life exposing your mercenaries! So is best you stop send them or else a some body bags I go start mail back," Kadeem warned!

"Until I get back what was stolen from I nothing naw stop," Kevin answered!

"A the second time this you set up somebody to kill me my youth! Don't make me have to fly back up there and personally settle this," Kadeem threatened!

"You only full a tough talk Pussy-Hole! No man dare get close to me with the amount of killers around me daily! It's best you just send me back what's mine, because one way or the next I go get it back," Kevin declared!

"My youth after everything we go through together, a this it come down to," Kadeem argued?

"Friend or no friend you killed my cousin! So, you done know you have to pay for that, and the only payment acceptable is you dead," Kevin sighted!

"Defend your battyman cousin all you want! But any day you make me jump back on one of them iron birds and reach foreign, not even your suck cocky gal them go save you," Kadeem exclaimed!

"Me have some new associates who would love to hear you back in this country! So, jump anytime you feel brave Pussy-Hole," Kevin insinuated!

"No matter what you do you'll never get accepted by them French bikers. And if those cult people ever find out that you killed their fathers then what? You used to be a smart businessman my youth, but it looks like greed turned you into a fool," Kadeem suggested!

"Listen me, don't watch how I conduct my business! You either send me back my memory disk and I'll consider if I should lessen your debt to me, or else something unfortunate go happen to you," Kevin threatened, as someone knocked the door and he thereby disconnected the call!

"Yes, come in," Kevin instructed!

"Jean-Pierre is here Sir," indicated Miss Cutthroat!

"Bring him in," Kevin declared, as he stopped the video and walked to the front of his desk then leaned on it!

Miss Cutthroat showed a short and stout man into the room and walked over beside Kevin.

"Jean-Pierre this is our new boss Kevin Trudeau," Miss Cutthroat declared!

"Pleased to meet you sir," Jean-Pierre stated!

Both men shook hands at which Kevin pointed his guest to a chair. Despite Jean-Pierre's wide frame, he dressed quite elegantly in a suit, plaid shirt without a tie, leather shoes, slicked back hair and was clean shaved, but most importantly smelt terrific.

"A man who cares deeply about his image. Dresses well, smells good, I like that," remarked Kevin, who was also properly attired in his suit vest, buttoned shirt with a tie and leather shoes!

"Like you, I only wear the finest fabrics sir," Jean-Pierre boasted!

"Would you like a drink, a joint, a line, or anything before we begin Jean-Pierre," Kevin asked?

"I sure would like a drink sir, some Scotch if you please," Jean-Pierre answered?

"Anything for you Mr. Trudeau," Miss Cutthroat enquired?

"My regular thank you," Kevin stated!

Miss Cutthroat went over to the liquor cabinet and prepared the requested drinks while the men proceeded with their discussion.

"Miss Cutthroat informed me that you have always handled certain delicate matters for Francois," Kevin exclaimed.

"As we all know certain things require the right person, and I'm the right person for those things Mr. Trudeau," Jean-Pierre said.

Miss Cutthroat brought the drinks and gave the glasses to both individual. Kevin collected the glass and took a sip of its contents, before putting it down to grab a picture from his desk. Just before he could show the photo the guard at the gate again buzzed the intercom for approval, hence he excused himself and attended to the call.

"Yeah," Kevin answered!

"Sorry for disturbing you sir, but your lawyer is here to see you as well," indicated the guard?

"Let him head up to the house," Kevin directed, before returning to his discussion! "You know who this is Jean-Pierre?"

"But of course, I am very sorry to hear what he did to Monsieur Trudeau," Jean-Pierre indicated!

"I want him found like yesterday you understand," Kevin instructed!

"You did not have to request for me to do this sir. I have already made it known to my people that he must be found for, how the English say, bite hand of master that feed you," Jean-Pierre declared!

"As you are aware Jean-Pierre, Monsieur Buchard is a very dangerous man who will identify any threat to his life and possibly take them out before they can get to him. He has a Black Belt in Karate and is extremely skilled in all the other martial arts disciplines, in addition to his pinpoint accuracy with a weapon. So, we would prefer if whoever finds him, just report his location and try not to alert him." Miss Cutthroat instructed!

"Let me know as soon as you find him Jean-Pierre? My lawyer is on his way up and I must speak with him, so keep me informed," Kevin stated, to which they shook hands then his visitor followed Miss Cutthroat out!

Moments later the female returned with Mr. Logan Duntroon, who came by to discuss the status of Kevin's criminal case. Kevin met the lawyer at the door where they greeted each other and shook hands, then signalled Miss Cutthroat to allow them privacy and ensured they weren't interrupted. Both men had several prior meetings, therefore Kevin knew not to offer any form of alcohol to his guest, who often refrained from liquor consumption during work hours. Logan Duntroon wasn't an eccentric lawyer who obtained his clothing from a tailor but would purchase off the rack suits from local merchants, nevertheless he was always very meticulously dressed. They sat together on a sofa where Logan withdrew several documents from his briefcase and passed them to his client.

"This new prosecutor on your case Monsieur… Maurice Lamour initially is behaving more like the former prosecution representative. I have spoken with him and so far, he refuses to negotiate a better deal in your favor, therefore pending no further litigations the government will be ready to proceed with their evidence early this spring," Explained Mr. Duntroon.

"Can we get an extension on the court date? I have some unfinished business I must see to before I can attend to this," Kevin enquired.

"I'm not too sure how possible that will be with this pushy new prosecutor. The court believes that this case is taking too long to reach trial, and there are several highly ranked people who are interested in the outcome. So, pending a miracle I believe that we're scheduled for April tenth," Mr. Duntroon stated.

Kevin angrily tossed the papers on the floor and jumped up off the chair. "Right now this is all a waste of my fucking time! Why isn't the case thrown out of court already if they lost all their evidence? All this is some witch hunt business to put a face behind this city's biggest embarrassments. Listen me, until them bring a no jail sentence deal to the table, I'm not stepping one foot inside them courthouse!"

"Please do not be upset Monsieur Trudeau, whatever they try to claim we are ready to argue our case, so don't worry sir," Mr. Duntroon said.

"Is the new prosecutor's personal information written on any of these pages," Kevin asked?

"Yes sir, if you check either the first or last page, I believe his name is written somewhere about there," responded the lawyer.

"If you believe this prosecutor boy going to be tough to deal with, we go have to just demand that them assign someone else to the case," Kevin stated!

"I wish we could just snap our fingers and have him changed, but fact of the matter is we're going to have to beat him and his team in court. What happened with the last prosecutor Mr. Thompson was a freak of luck, but I don't expect lightening to strike twice in our favor. It's bad enough that these investigators believe that you had something to do with his killing, another accident like that could cast more unwanted doubts against you," Mr. Duntroon argued, not knowing that Kevin intentionally had Mr. Thompson killed.

"In business, you have to always get your competitor to negotiate on your terms. How about the judge, you believe we need another shake up," Kevin questioned?

"I think we have the right judge in place Mr. Trudeau. And don't worry about this prosecutor, the government have a strong climb to prove their case with no confessions or physical evidence," Mr. Duntroon exclaimed!

"So, what type of evidence does the government have," Kevin asked?

"Presently their most compelling piece of evidence is a video footage they acquired through the media, that only shows you men on the scene. They also have a few arresting officers and doctors to discuss your appearance and so forth at the time of your arrest. However, without any actual evidence it will be left up to the judge to determine if any liabilities should be accessed. But you're right about the prosecution team out for blood, because they boasted about their case and the evidence so highly that they must prove without a shadow of a doubt what they said about you, or risk losing credibility in their department," Mr. Duntroon explained.

"I've gotten word that the Prime Minister is being investigated by the Ethics Committee for his involvement in my friends being released from jail, in addition to my extraction from U.S custody. Will any of this affect my trial," Kevin enquired?

"I have heard no such news about the Prime Minister being investigated for this, but I will check into the matter for you sir. If there is nothing further, I must get back to the office, and I will keep you informed if there are any further developments," Mr. Duntroon stated.

"Thanks for coming by Logan! Call me in a few days and let me know if the prosecution department assign someone more negotiable," Kevin declared.

The defense lawyer had been asked by several reporters about his client's involvement in the unsolved hit and run killings, yet had never given serious thought to the possibility until that moment. Both men again shook hands, following which the lawyer departed and got shown to the front door by Miss Cutthroat. Kevin went to the widow and watched Mr. Duntroon climb into his vehicle and drive away, as snow flurries fell from the sky. Miss Cutthroat returned after showing the lawyer out and immediately began picking up the scattered papers from off the floor. While Miss Cutthroat assorted the documents, Kevin returned behind his desk and finished his drink, then waked over to his liquor cabinet and refilled the glass.

"You see the chief prosecutor on those documents, I want him to experience some sort of fatal accident," Kevin instructed!

Miss Cutthroat walked back to the desk and sat comfortably, before scrolling through the documents to find the person her boss referred to.

"Are you referring to this Maurice Lamour," Miss Cutthroat asked?

"Exactly, he's looking to play handball and we don't have time for that shit! Just make sure it looks like a complete accident," Kevin exclaimed, as he picked up his cellular phone and scrolled through the numbers, then placed a call!

"I'll see to it that everything goes as you instructed sir," Miss Cutthroat answered!

The sound of a male's greeting could faintly be heard through the receiver, to whom Kevin responded, "I have a job for you and the boys! Twenty-five grand up front and the other half when you return!"

Part 5

Yves Buchard went to the only place he could possibly find temporary safety, which was in Val-d'Or, Quebec, a small little town northwest of Montreal. The town of Val-d'Or had one dominant biker gang known as the N.W Rough Riders, who were affiliated with the ruthless Montreal crew. The Val-d'Or biker gang was created by a former member of the original bikers who rode with Martain Lafleur's uncle Yves Lafleur. In the second year of the Rough Riders' existence they went to war versus an Irish mobster known as Sagetini Breathnach, over control of the underground liquor racketeering business in Montreal. Yves Lafleur had a vicious and short tempered second in command known as Bruno Dawkins, whose methods of settling altercations kept them constantly bickering. The Rough Riders had another member whose real name was Dennis Girard, who resembled Bruno to the extent that strangers assumed they were brothers.

The war began when Yves Lafleur and his associates decided to begin taxing certain criminal enterprises that were previously untaxable. Yves and four of his biker comrades caught Sagetini off guard at his favorite Irish restaurant having supper with a beautiful French model. Sagetini's guards were stationed outside the establishment, when the bikers pulled up with their weapons drawn and easily overpowered them. As soon as the bikers entered the restaurant a huge commotion unfolded, when the host behind the reservation desk attempted to stop them from advancing. Bruno reached over the desk and grabbed the female host by her ponytail and smashed her face onto the desk. The forceful impact bloodied the host and knocked her woozy, whereby she fell back onto the floor as the intruders passed and went directly to Sagetini's table.

When the bikers reached the table, Yves sat down across from Sagetini and poured himself a glass of wine and drank it down before he uttered a single word. The Bootlegger knew not whom the bikers were but had heard rumors of their troublesome exploits throughout the city, therefore he simply listened to Yves' dictation. The Biker Leader was not one for much chatter, hence he informed the Irishman of the price for continued business in the city and stipulated the offer was none negotiable. Yves gave Sagetini a piece of paper with his phone number written on it and advised him that, "he would be waiting for a verbal agreement," before they exited the establishment! The Irish Mobster was embarrassed in a place where everyone else revered him, so to save face and show he wasn't intimidated he lit the paper ablaze and watched it burn on top of the food on his plate.

Three days later the bikers hijacked Sagetini's next shipment of bootlegged liquor and hid the two trucks in a storage facility in L'Acadie. Sagetini was inside his taxi warehouse awaiting the deliveries when the unharmed drivers of his trucks arrived in a taxi with the devastating news. The Bootlegger was furious and began throwing a tirade, during which the office phone rang with Yves on the other line.

"If you want back your trucks with the contents, you first must agree to our arrangement and make the first payment," Yves exclaimed!

"I would suggest that you boys return what is mine, before it's too late to apologise," Sagetini warned!

"I am a businessman Sagetini, if you don't want the booze, we could always sell it; and the arrangement still stands," Yves threatened!

"Now wait a minute don't be too hasty! OK, you got a deal! Bring the trucks to my warehouse," Sagetini said!

"In one hour, I make two drivers drop off your trucks. Have the money ready to pay your bill," Yves instructed!

An hour later the trucks were delivered, and the drivers collected the requested payment. Sagetini was furious that he was being blackmailed but had no other choice at the time with his clients awaiting their products. Yves placed Bruno in charge of collecting the extortion funds from Sagetini, who had no intentions of continuing the imposed sanctions. A week later when the next shipment arrived Bruno telephoned Sagetini to inform him that he would be coming by to collect the dues. When they finished conversing the Irishman assumed, he had disconnected the call and began 'professing his intentions to kill every biker once he discovered their primary whereabouts'.

Bruno brought two associates with him to collect the extortion payment at Sagetini's warehouse. The two men he brought along were Dennis Girard and Alain Bal, who were both armed with Mini Teck 11 beneath their jackets. Sagetini's office was located up a flight of stairs at the back of the warehouse, which was also the location from which he ran his taxi service. The three extortion collectors entered through the main hanger door and walked through the warehouse towards Sagetini's office, where the boss and four of his goons awaited them. While passing through the warehouse the bikers could sense the hatred towards them from the employees, who stared at them with disgust. The beautiful model who was seated across from Sagetini at the restaurant was also present inside the office, seated on a double sofa in the corner.

Dennis and Alain first walked into the office and stood on either side of the door, following which Bruno entered and stepped to the desk. A paper bag containing the payment was on the desk, so Bruno looked inside the bag then picked it up and turned around to leave when Sagetini said, "tell your boss I want to have a meeting with him!"

"No need for that you can talk to him right now," declared Bruno, who pulled his handgun, spun around and shot Sagetini three times in the chest.

The French model began screaming with fright as Alain and Dennis withdrew their weapons and killed the bodyguards before any of them could fire their handguns. Dennis pointed his weapon at the terrified female and threatened to kill her unless she stopped screaming, thus she covered her face and crouched up on the chair. Sagetini's armed associates gathered outside the office and began spraying the structure with bullets, which forced the extortionists to seek shelter and return fire wherever possible. Bruno had prearranged plans in place for such an event and thereby used his cellular to summon fifty backup bikers, who were only three street blocks away. With such a loud distraction being caused by Sagetini's gunners and Bruno's team, the camouflaged backup bikers easily slipped into position behind the Irishmen and killed them all.

Following the slayings police had very little evidence to prosecute most of the bikers involved, after they were cautious to conceal their faces and license plate numbers. Investigators retrieved video footage of Bruno and his peers' entrance into the warehouse but had no footage of what transpired after they entered Sagetini's office. For an idea of what happened inside the office investigators questioned the lone survivor, who was the model that was inside the office when shots started firing. When provided with a mugshot book for her to identify the person who killed Sagetini, the distraint female who could only remember the face of the man who threatened to kill her, pointed to Dennis as the shooter.

Within six hours of the killings police arrested Dennis Girard at his apartment on Longueuil Street in Notre Dame, and were in search of Alain and Bruno for whom they had active warrants. Two months after Dennis' arrest Alain was taken into custody, when his girlfriend's mother phoned the police and informed them that he had been hiding out there. The eradication of Sagetini's mob paved the way for the Rough Riders to take over a major distribution in Montreal's bootlegging industry, therefore Bruno gained credit and got promoted for the new enterprise. Bruno got offered a lucrative deal to expand the biker club in Val-d'Or and moved there to avoid getting arrested and charged in connection with Sagetini's killing. The former Montreal biker who was second in command to Yves Lafleur, lived using false identification and kept out of trouble for nearly thirty-five years, before he was arrested and charged with the decade's old crime.

Before Bruno went to prison, he gave control of the NW Rough Riders to his son whose name was also Bruno Dawkins II. When Yves Buchard chose to hide out in Val-d'Or he went to the home of a long-time friend named Franco Demerit, who lived in a basement apartment at 86 Lafontaine Street on the corner of Cadillac Street. Franco was also a Rough Riders member who knew of the situation back in Montreal, therein he was obligated to report Yves to his commander or risk being considered a conspirator. Yves expected his friend to obey the codes of their gang and report him to Bruno, but moreover he believed that the Biker Leader would show him leniency for his past services to the club.

It had been years since Yves and Franco saw each other, therefore they embraced then sat inside the kitchen over a bottle of Canadian Whiskey and caught up on old times. Almost an hour later while they drank, a knock sounded at the front door to which Franco responded and allowed the visitors to enter. Even though Yves assumed that he would be allowed to hide out in Val-d'Or, for precautionary reasons he placed his weapon on his lap underneath the table and began fiddling with his knife. Bruno Junior and his driver Hymus walked into the apartment and headed directly to the kitchen, where Franco introduced them to Yves who reached over the table and shook their hands.

Both visitors removed their jackets and sat around the table, hence Franco retrieved another pair of glasses for them to partake of the alcohol. Bruno Junior had heard stories of Martain Lafleur's exploits that involved Yves and past members, therefore he saw the Montreal gangster as more of a hero and was excited to be in his company. Yves was granted permission to stay in Val-d'Or for as long as he chose, but he still knew he wasn't completely out of danger. For the next three hours, the local bikers listened to past stories of the Montreal clan, while they drank, smoked Marijuana and popped Ecstasy Pills. By the time Bruno Jr. and his driver departed it was well pass 2:00 in the morning, and a short time thereafter Franco went to bed.

There was already a Chevrolet Suburban XLT filled with an eight-men assassin team on route to Val-d'Or from Montreal, after it was revealed that Yves had fled there. Bruno Junior was with a lady friend when Franco called to inform him of Yves' arrival. After Bruno Junior left with his driver the young lady began gossiping to friends about what she had learnt, thereby news eventually got back to the people who wanted Yves Buchard killed. Jim Bartello sent the team of killers to bring back Yves' body, as proof that he was indeed killed.

When the assassins reached the location given to them, they parked in a vacant guest space close to the three-story residence, that had six total apartments included. While the address given to them was correct, the apartment number was false which was the second blunder in their plot. Yves was urinating inside the toilet and looking through a small window in Franco's bathroom when he saw three armed men scurry pass. Unlike Franco and their other departed guests Yves did not consume as much alcohol and was far more alert, therefore he shook off whatever fatigue he felt, put away his sexual weapon and armed himself with the genuine prototype.

Yves quickly snuck to the front door and stood behind it expecting the assassins to kick in the door and rush into the apartment. While standing behind the door Yves could hear the men whispering outside, but it sounded as if they were concentrating on the adjacent apartment. To see what the men were intended on doing, Yves snuck a peek through the peephole and saw four bikers counting down from five before they barged into the dwelling. As the assassin who signalled the entry timer showed three fingers, Yves unexpectedly opened the door and shot them all in their backs. The killers who intended to surprise the residents and assassinate their primary target, got surprised and killed before the indicator signalled one finger. Franco soundly slept through the loud gunfire explosions after passing out intoxicated, however his neighbors whose apartment was being targeted awoke from their sleep.

The other half of the assassin team were about to enter the residence through the rear door when the shots rang out. Believing their timing was slightly off, the bikers barged into the dark apartment where they expected to find their comrades in control of the situation. The couple that resided in the apartment was awakened by the eruption of gunfire, before the displacement of their back door convinced them there was a serious incident. The male resident owned a firearm and retrieved it from his night table, while his scared girlfriend positioned herself behind him for safety. They could hear people whispering inside their apartment which stipulated there were intruders inside, although they were clueless why anyone would want to rob them.

Yves went through the building's front door and snuck around to the rear entrance used by the bikers to enter Franco's neighbors' apartment. As Yves snuck close to the door, he saw two of the intruders inside the kitchen with their backs turned towards him, while the other pair stood by a doorframe that lead into another room. When the assassins entered the dark apartment and saw no signs of their comrades, instead of flicking the electrical switch to turn on the light and see what was happening they took up strategic positions and stupidly tried to verbally communicate with their associates. The Wanted Biker shoved his weapon into his waist and pulled his knife, then snuck up behind the first two assassins, grabbed and covered each man's mouth from behind and wiped his knife across their throats. Yves cautiously brought each deceased biker to the ground instead of allowing them to fall, which would alert their friends to his presence.

The darkness allowed Yves to maneuver with stealth coverage, therefore he crawled up behind the third assassin and covered his mouth, then rammed his knife into the man's ribcage three times. The terrified female resident began shouting that 'they were armed and are calling the police', which muffled the sound of the Yves' victim who gasped for oxygen as he died. Fearing that something happened to their comrades in addition to the mention of police, gave the last assassin reasonable doubts to abort the mission. Yves was poised to pounce on the last killer when suddenly the man began backing away from the doorframe. As the assassin drew closer with his sight focused solely from which he came, he began signalling for those behind him to backup, thus Yves simply stood his ground and made the assassin back onto his blade.

After executing the entire assassin team, Yves went back to Franco's apartment and grabbed his belongings. Before leaving through the door the Wanted Biker went into Franco's room and aimed his weapon at his friend, but lowered it shortly thereafter without shooting. Yves hurried from the apartment and closed Franco's door, but as he passed the dead bodies he stopped and stole one of the man's wallet. While driving away from the location, Yves looked in his rear-view mirror and saw police and ambulance converging on the scene, so he removed the magazine from his weapon and restacked the bullets.

Yves felt somewhat betrayed and drove to the local NW Rough Riders' biker tavern, which was closed at such a late hour, but the caretaker lived above the establishment in a bachelor's pad. The caretaker was laying on his bed watching television with a bottle of Molson Beer at hand when Yves knocked the door. The instant the man opened the door Yves stuck his weapon in his face and forced him back inside, where he shoved the caretaker onto his bed.

"You know who I am," Yves asked?

"Yes sir Mr. Buchard, word is… you were in town," the caretaker stuttered to say!

"Where does Bruno Junior live," Yves demanded?

"He lives slightly out of town on Giguere Street, southwest of here. You can't miss it he got a big ole ranch out there with horses and stuff," explained the caretaker.

"Nothing personal old timer," Yves declared, then shot and killed the caretaker.

At such an early hour of the morning the town was as silent as a lamp. To satisfy his ego Yves drove to Giguere Street and strolled southwesterly by the houses heading out of town. When he came across Bruno's house, he had no objections he found the right place as previously indicated to by the caretaker. Bruno Junior was so proud of his heritage and his biker brotherhood that he had three flags hoisted on poles in his front yard, which were of the Canadian National Flag, Quebec's Provincial Flag and the Rough Riders' Insignia on a black flag. Without hesitation Yves turned onto the property and drove up to the house, where Bruno Junior had two humongous Pitbull dogs inside his home.

The dogs began raising a huge ruckus as Yves stepped to the front door and knocked, then stepped back a few feet to avoid further distressing the animals. The Revenge Seeker looked around to ensure he wasn't being watched then withdrew his firearm from his waist and held onto it inside his jacket pocket. Had there not been any dogs on the premises Yves would have kicked the door in and entered, but there was absolutely no way he would survive versus the massive pit bulls. A few minutes thereafter Bruno's lady answered the door and immediately recognized their visitor, thus she offered to lock away the dogs inside a bathroom. Bruno Junior was still sound asleep, but he neglected to mention to his lady that arrangements were made for Yves' assassination, thus without any prior knowledge she graciously allowed him to enter. The instant Yves entered the house he placed his weapon to the female's head and grabbed her mouth close.

"To the bedroom," Yves whispered in her left ear!

When they reached inside the bedroom Yves snuck right up to the bed before he shoved the female to the ground and woke Bruno Junior with a gun butt to the face. A wound busted open and blood began gushing all over the bed, as Bruno jumped up and realized there was a gun being held to his head.

"You set me up to get killed," Yves exclaimed!?

"No, no, wait," Bruno Junior begged?

"Bam, bam, bam," sounded the firearm!

Bruno Junior's lady began screaming at the sight of his lifeless body motionless on the bed. Yves grabbed the female by her hair and dragged her from off the floor and jammed the hot weapon's tip against the side of her head. The woman screamed in pain as the hot metal burnt her skin, therein Yves knew he had her undivided attention.

"Where is the money stashed," Yves demanded?

Without any arguments, the female walked into a room and opened a huge safe that was designed on the exterior to resemble the furniture. There were piles of money, jewelry and deeds inside the safe, therefore Yves filled a huge Duffle Bag and threw it over his shoulder. As he exited the room Yves spun around with his weapon aimed at the female and shot her three times. The Wanted Biker walked out of the house and looked around to see if anyone heard the blasts, before he tossed his belongings into his vehicle and left town.

Part 6

Jim Bartello met privately with Gilbert Stephano, who was given instructions by the secret French cult to transfer. Both men met under extreme secrecy in a back room at the illustrious Restaurant Europea, located in the heart of downtown Montreal. The place chosen for their rendez-vous was ideal, as Jim and his associates' attire would have negated their entry into the fabulous five-star restaurant. Gilbert was already at the location when Jim arrived with his seven men entourage, who all guarded the door and surrounding perimeter during their leader's meeting. There was a specific reason for which Jim got hired by the Rough Riders instead of appointing an existing member, and he was fast discovering exactly why that was.

"Mr. Stephano, it's a pleasure sir," exclaimed Jim as he walked up to the delightfully assorted table, behind which Gilbert was partaking of his supper!

The room was wonderfully designed with golden crown moldings and trimmings, priceless artworks, and in the center of it all sat the spokesman behind the lone table, which was covered with a Peruvian white laced tablecloth.

There was an expensive vintage 1940 bottle of Chateau Montrose red wine being chilled to the gentleman's preference, in addition to abundant fruits and food. The spread was fit for a king and had a single chair placed directly across from Mr. Stephano, who merely looked up and nodded his head in acknowledgement to Jim's introduction.

"You may have a seat Mr. Bartello," stated Gilbert as he pointed to the chair.

A beautiful waitress knocked the door and walked into the room, then went directly to the biker boss. "May I fetch you anything sir?"

"Yes, you may; some Cognac please," declared Jim?

"Would the XO be fine sir," asked the waitress?

"I guess it would, and so would your phone number," Jim exclaimed.

The female giggled to herself and gracefully exited the room, but ensured she closed the door behind herself.

"Mr. Bartello thanks for meeting with me, I won't beat around the bush but rather get to the reason you were summoned here today! There used to be a time in the Province of Quebec when your department produced nearly twenty million dollars in revenue monthly, from the sales of guns, drugs, extortion, prostitution and every other business affair that you gentlemen pursue; but today that figure has been significantly reduced! So…the people who we represent believe that is purely unacceptable and insist that your payments be drastically increased," said Mr. Stephano!

"With all due respect sir, the times and the streets have changed, so production in those numbers will be impossible Mr. Stephano. There are too many pipelines flowing into the city right now, so too many opportunities for workers in the hustling industry to get whatever product they supply," Jim explained!

"Then I suggest you gentlemen go back to regulating the streets with the Rough Riders old version of martial law; and start closing these other sources to up your revenue…," began Gilbert before a knock sounded at the door.

"Excuse me gentlemen," interrupted the waitress who brought the glass of cognac on a small tray, then ensured everything was satisfactory before departing?

As soon as the waitress exited the men returned to their candid conversation, wherein the spokesman continued reiterating the directives given to him.

"As I was saying before we were interrupted; any means necessary to regain total control of these street markets. At this point all options are on the table, even if that includes informing your old friends at the police bureau to get rid of some of these nuisances," instructed Mr. Stephano!

"We are going to need more inventory if we are to take back this entire city as you envision," Jim suggested.

"A shipment had already been sent and should be here in a few days. Until then I suggest you start eradicating the garbage and make way for change," instructed Mr. Stephano!

"Whatever you gentlemen require of us, will be taken care of," answered Jim!

"There is one other pressing issue Mr. Bartello; it appears we have some unpaid dues that must be resolved. All the information you require is inside this envelope," Mr. Stephano emphasised as he slid a manila envelope across the table.

The Biker Leader ripped open the envelope and slightly extracted a picture of Agent Ross Mohara of the Canadian Federal Agency. There was a paper attached to the picture with information about the agent, which revealed where he lived and other valid details. A brief peek at the contents told Jim all he needed to know about what was being demanded, so he returned the documents into the envelope and finished his drink. Following their meeting Jim Bartello went directly into the kitchen and sought out the captivating waitress, whom he hoped to personally get to know better. The female was rather busy and argued against 'getting in trouble or losing her job', therefore the Biker Boss wrote down his phone number and gave it to her, yet refused to leave until he got her name. After trying desperately to put an end to Jim's consistent nagging the waitress' supervisor walked into the kitchen, thus, to avoid getting fired she introduced herself as Carolin to quickly get rid of him. Carolin was accustomed to serving the restaurant's wealthy and elite clientele and aspired to marry one of them, therefore she knew what rich looked like and Jim did not fit the profile.

The moment Jim returned to his chauffeured transport he instructed Vincent Leguerre AKA Lil Wasp, that 'he intended on holding an emergency club meeting later that night.' Lil Wasp immediately notified two other important members of the unscheduled gathering by sending them coded text messages, which featured the destination and a time. Word then immediately circulated amongst the other higher ranked members of the biker gang, who were the only personnel invited to the meeting. With law enforcement personnel ramping up their efforts to infiltrate their gang and learn about their illegal operations, it was imperative that their communications and business dealings not get intercepted. Their meeting was scheduled for 11 PM at Jim's new bar located on Wellington Street at the corner of Conde Street, in the Verdun sector of the island.

The location at which Jim's Rhythm & Blues Bar was situated, had a commercial plaza with several other businesses such as a beauty supply store, an insurance broker, a pizza parlor, a jewellery store, and a small Pakistan grocery market. Jim's bar would open at 11:30 AM for lunch and remain open until an hour after it was legally permitted to stop serving alcohol. The bar had a sexually erotic atmosphere wherein the waitresses wore skimpy tight shorts with revealing alter tops, in addition to having mandatory huge plump breasts to enticed male clientele. One of the main attractions at the bar was their live performance shows, where they would highlight live bands from across the country. That night was the night on which Karaoke was scheduled at the bar, thus they customarily had more female customers present than any other day of the week.

All the bikers invited to the meeting arrived before the scheduled time and sat throughout the establishment drinking, conversing, and critiquing the amateurs. The lights inside the venue were dimmed and it was incredibly difficult for anyone to identify the customer seated across from them. There were locals from the crowd in attendance going on stage to perform their favorite acts from a Karaoke machine, while they read the words for the songs from a television monitor. Jim's bar had a huge basement where they stored inventory, had the employees' lounge, a locker area, an employees' toilet and an additional wide-open area where the owner contemplated opening a tattoo parlor. Twenty minutes before the meeting was scheduled to start each biker began sneaking away from the crowd and secretly made their way to the basement.

While Jim Bartello was assigned the main leader of the gang, their organization realized the importance of overseers in each zone and thus appointed area managers to serve beneath him. There were twelve top ranked Rough Riders members invited to the private meeting, each of whom oversaw the business affairs in different sections of the city. Each zone across the island had three overseers, who were given the task of collecting the club's monthly income and bringing it in. None of the bikers saw Jim before or during their time inside the bar, nor were they aware whether he was on the premises, nevertheless they were eager to find out why they were summoned. At 11:04 PM Jim and his sidekick Lil' Wasp walked into the basement, where the biker leader greeted each of his comrades, then stood amid those gathered.

"At the pinnacle of our dominance in the city the Rough Riders controlled every major underground market from selling pussy to illegal drugs! If a street hustler made a dollar, thirty cents of that money was guaranteed payment to us! Businesses paid to keep their doors open and if not, they would get burnt to ashes! Cops knew to turn their heads and look the other way whenever they saw us doing business, and if not, they too would get visited that same night. Civilians would never think of giving a statement or identifying a biker, much less testify against any of us! Whatever Rough Riders wanted they would just take and there was nothing anyone could do about it... I'm talking about the good old money days boys; when everything and everybody got taxed! Those are the days we are going to bring back starting now; we seize all shipments coming into the city, nobody buys anything unless it's provided by us, we will again control of the drug market, liquor and weapons distribution," Jim exclaimed!

"What about the cops and their new initiative to get rid of local gangs," G-Stack asked?

"Our initiative to regain control of the streets is all you need to concern yourself with! If or when we get to the legal issues, we'll deal with it. Until then we start by announcing our new ways of doing business in this city to every street corner dealer, urban community hustler and suppliers to the rich and powerful! Then we are going to close every other pipeline coming in and get every worker in every industry to only buy from us! Anybody who gets in your way get the same treatment, you understand," Jim lamented!

"Yeah," cheered everyone in attendance as they pumped their fists in the air!

The bikers' level of excitement pleased Jim who displayed a cynical smirk, despite the knowledge that his orders meant the streets would thereby get painted with the blood of their enemies as well as uninvolved citizens.

Part 7

The television program W5 aired a special report where they concealed the identity of the female being interviewed. Megan Riviera, a reporter went to Saint-Casimir in Quebec, where she sat and spoke with Lyzette Cormier who recently lost her husband. To protect Lyzette from retaliation from the bikers, their location and the names used throughout the story were kept confidential. The story began and ended inside a house, where Lyzette wore sunglasses and a baseball hat to disguise herself, regardless of the W5's employees' insistence that her face would be blocked. Even though many other families had similar experiences, fear protruded much of them from speaking out, knowing that the Rough Riders would annihilate everybody should they return.

Megan Riviera began the interview by discussing the premiers' office and talked about unfounded allegations of how the magical duo of McArthur and Blanc came into existence. Both premiers were always known as individuals with different agendas towards the handling of the province, therefore Megan wanted to uncover how and why they united. Following her short introduction speech, Megan introduced her interviewee as Jane Doe before listening to the woman's incredible story.

"My husband and I are dairy farmer, so most of the milk we get is sold for us to make a living. We raised three children on this farm and never once dreamed of selling it, but now with my husband gone I have no choice but to. Our family have been lifelong supporters of the Party Quebecois, and a few years ago we started getting more politically involved around election time. Anyhow during the last election, I was inside my kitchen one morning; my husband, our youngest son and the helper were working inside the barn, when I looked through my window and saw six people riding Harleys towards the house... Seemed a bit strange, but I finished what I was doing and was about to walk out to the yard when this biker woman walked into the kitchen holding a gun, and ordered me to sit down."

"While me and her had tea, her five male friends went to the barn and started trying to persuade my husband that he should vote for the Liberal Party and start convincing other people to do the same. My husband was a very proud and stubborn man and would not be told what to do, so the bikers threatened to kill our son and the helper and put guns to the back of their heads. Obviously, my husband agreed to their demands, but to further embarrass my husband they made him strip naked and have sex with one of our cows while they recorded it! They told him that they would put the video all over the internet; and that broke my husband! My husband stopped doing everything that he loved doing, and even didn't leave the house for months. Our doctor diagnosed that he had developed a severe case of depression, which caused him to finally put a gun to his head and take his own life, while we were at church one Sunday," Lyzette exclaimed, as she wiped away the tears.

"How has all this affected your son," Megan queered?

"He is lost right now... We all are in a sense," Lyzette softly answered.

"So, do you believe that these bikers were working for Monsieur McArthur and Monsieur Blanc," Megan asked?

"Those are the people that they wanted us to vote for, so of course who else would they be working for," Lyzette stated!?

"Do you know of any other families that were approached and threatened by these bikers," Megan enquired?

"Not exactly because this isn't the type of story that folks gladly talk about! It killed my husband inside knowing that these people around here knew what happened to him! Plus, most of these people around these rural areas are scared shitless of those bikers! They know how long it takes for the police to get out here; sometimes hours and by then them bikers could have killed everybody and left," Lyzette declared!

"Did your family finally vote for the Liberals, if you don't mind my asking," Megan asked?

"Those people threatened to kill us all if we didn't do as they said, what do you think!? Of course we did," Lyzette answered!

Montebello, Quebec

The same night that the W5 program aired Lyzette's story, a convoy of forty all-terrain 4x4 and SUV trucks drove into the small town. It was quite late into the night and most of the town's folks had turned in, but a handful of locals still lurked about. As the impressive line of new trucks from companies such as Ford, Chevrolet, Toyota, Dodge, Nissan and Hyundai passed along Notre Dame Street, the locals on the street watched with awe. The truck convoy drove directly to Montebello Hotel which was one of the largest structures in town and parked all throughout the parking lot. Each vehicle carried at least four Rough Rider occupants, all of which were heavily armed with assault rifles. The owner of the hotel was a tough mid-age woman named Monica Hamon, who was said to have boasted publicly about defying the Rough Riders who threatened her to vote Liberal.

It was a cold evening, but the bikers came prepared with four large drums that were stacked with firewood, which they immediately sat ablaze. Six of the armed bikers most of which were females rushed into the hotel, as guests inside their suites began looking through the windows. Jim Bartello was present with his bikers; who all began consuming beer while they listened to loud music provided by a Chevy Silverado, that had a huge sound system with eighteen-inch speakers installed. When the front desk employee saw the armed bikers outside on the surveillance monitor, she quickly telephoned the police and made a complaint, then alerted the owner. Miss Hamon who owned the hotel only lived four minutes away, therefore she arrived on scene before the police. There was nowhere on the property to park, so Monica left her Cadillac along the side of the road and walked towards the hotel.

The Property Owner was unsure of what to do but saw a police cruiser approaching and thought the lawman would be able to disperse the gunmen. At the sight of the huge drums engulfed with flames only metres from the building, Miss Hamon panicked and started making her way to voice her objections. The lone officer who answered the call drove up along Notre Dame Street and paused for a few seconds, before the cruiser continued its way. Before Monica realized she had no backup she was already shouting at everyone to disperse and get off her property, even though none of the bikers paid her any attention. The petit five-foot three agitated hotel owner made her way to the bond fire where Jim Bartello, his new girl friend Carolin from the restaurant and several of their associates were keeping warm.

"Which one of you dumbasses built them fires and started making all this racket," Monica argued?

"Who wants to know, you old bag," Carolin asked?

"I do you little tramp, this is my hotel and I want you all gone off my property this instant," Monica declared!

"Oh, Miss Hamon its you… The boys have been looking all over for you," Jim stated!

"And what do you want with me," Monica demanded?

"You were given some instructions you forgot to follow Miss Monica," Jim implied.

"Nobody is going to tell me what to do Sunny! I'm not scared of any of you," Monica declared!

Jim simply snapped his fingers then spun a circle with his Index finger and several of the bikers circled Miss Monica. Once the lengthy bikers surrounded the mouthy owner, it became difficult for hotel spectators inside their rooms to clearly see what was occurring. The bikers bounded the female's hands, mouth and legs, before Lil Wasp and others pilled some fire wood on her, then took a container of gasoline and poured it over the hotel owner. Without any remorse the bikers sat Miss Hamon on fire, then drank around the flames as if they were at a bond fire. Following the W5 interview the bikers sought to send a message to anyone who may have thought of joining the female whistleblower's campaign, and they departed Montebello thereafter knowing they had accomplished their mission.

***

The two most controversial premiers appointed to the Quebec office, Joseph McArthur and Richard Blanc were constantly under scrutiny. Months after their attempt at dividing the country through their referendum process, and the Mohawk crisis that cost the province and private sector millions in revenue; wherever the premiers went thousands of angry Canadians would protest. The large crowd of protesters was always peaceful and would call for justice and the firing of both men. The mayor of Montreal was one of several incumbent politicians across the province who supported the premiers' bill to transform Quebec into its own sovereign country. While many in government assumed that the premiers fought to change the country's landscape for the preservation of the French language in Quebec, no other group except the Rough Riders understood the advantages they would have gained had this new country been created. Both Premier Blanc and McArthur would thereafter find themselves in legal troubles, when allegations surfaced of punishable infractions committed by biker enforcers, who had intimidated many voters to select the Liberal/French Independent political ticket. Law officials from the Royal Canadian Mounted Police who had been investigating both premiers, made an unprecedented acquisition in the forms of arrest warrants for both elected politicians.

The highly scrutinized premiers received word of the impending arrest the same night the warrants were issued. Premier Blanc and his legal team discussed strategies at his house until 11:35 PM; while his co-accused and his lawyers did the same until 2:24 AM. Joseph McArthur and his legal team listened to several recorded conversations which he intended on bargaining with for a lesser punishment. Despite the severity of his expected charges, his testimony and corporation in exposing the Secret Cult would have liberated him. At 2:30 AM after Joseph's lawyers went home following a strenuous discussion on how they would proceed, a private caller rang the premier's cellular phone. McArthur's mind was worrisome with his impending problems and negated him falling asleep, therefore despite the late hour he answered.

"Hello," Premier McArthur answered!

"The cops will be at your front door by 7:00 AM! Until then I suggest you seriously reconsider your strategy to turn over those tapes and burn them! Your life and those of your entire family depends on your actions from this moment forth," said a muffled voice before the phone went dead!

When the call ended the premier received several pictures of his wife and children doing their daily chores, but what was most disturbing was the fact the photographer in every picture stood directly beside his relative. For the remainder of the night Joseph who was already anxious could barely stay off the toilet, given he had made the choice to embark on a life-threatening path. The morning after the arrest warrants were issued, special agents accompanied by mounted police went to the homes of both premiers and arrested them. Montrealers who assumed their elected officials were obeying every letter of the law were surprised to witness their incumbent premiers being led to jail in handcuffs. While inside the jail facility Premier Blanc and his co-accused were given the opportunity to speak with investigators, which could have helped their case in court.

Joseph McArthur stunned his lawyers and investigators when he declined to help the agents, piece together their case and instead chose to rely on his legal council's expertise. Even though Ex-Premier Blanc's legal charges carried less time than Joseph McArthur, the thought of five years imprisonment if found guilty innerved him, therefore he decided to cooperate with the R.C.M.P agents. Ricard Blanc knew he could be vindicated if they proved he was only a victim, hence cooperating with investigators was his last available chance. After a few hours of incarceration where they signed declarations to appear before a magistrate on a certain date, both men separately left the central jail's main parking lot in their private limousines, to a crowd of reporters and paparazzi attempting to get answers and capture photos.

Opposition leaders for the Party Quebecois and the People of Quebec National Party, leapt at the opportunity to capture the premier's position and demanded that another election be held immediately. The core members of the French Independent Party and the Liberal Party ousted their disgraced political leaders and forced them to resign. Never in the history of Canada had any public servant holding such a high office been arraigned while serving their term. Both political parties following the dismissals began searching for replacements who could lead them into a new era, and eventually restore the public's trust in their organization. Neither Richard Blanc nor Joseph McArthur argued their electoral committee's decisions and gave their individual resignation speeches, where they apologised to their bases and thanked their friends, families and supporters.

Despite all the legal ramblings, no other families assaulted by Rough Rider members came forward and provided law enforcement with information. The investigators who checked into Ex-Premier McArthur's dealings, found no direct evidence where he had any interactions with gang affiliates, thus even though they knew he was guilty they could not distinctively prove the bikers were acting on his behalf. It was believed that Minister McArthur had made some sort of business deal with Martain Lafleur, who was deceased and therefore clouded the investigation. R.C.M.P investigators even checked the minister's personal finances to determine if any money transactions transpired between, he and any known criminal element, but found none. Richard Blanc's documented testimonials about Joseph McArthur became a key factor in prosecuting the former Quebec Premier, who came close to changing the entire Canadian demographics.

With the upcoming election set to transpire in eleven months, the Liberals selected Monsieur Gyslain Demarre from amongst their party constituents to be the next leader. Gyslain was born in the small town of Stittsville, Ontario, but had been living in the province of Quebec for nearly twenty years. The minister was a resident of Quebec City, where he had a wife named Elene and two sons. Following the disastrous leadership term of Premier McArthur's government, Gyslain understood that he would have to go above and beyond any expectations to restore his party's dignity.

After a long, careful, and tedious process the French Independent Party also selected their next leader from amongst their members; and named their first female Minister Maxine Poivre to the position. Madam Poivre was an environmentalist whom the party hoped would bring a different vision and steered them away from the dark cloud created by Ex-Premier Blanc. Unlike Gyslain Demarre who relocated to the province, Maxine was a Montreal native who never moved away from the city and loved Quebec. Both Maxine and her retired husband Tod were career-oriented people who had no children, nor were they ever interested in producing any. The excitement that surrounded the choices made by the Liberals and the French Independents only came from within their respected camps; considering Quebecers were still adamantly angry with the political parties.

Most political economists predicted that Minister McNeil would be victorious during the next Quebec Premier election, as preliminary poles had him slightly ahead of his opponent. However, to set himself apart from every other politician and try to appear tough against corruption, Minister David McNeil of the People of Quebec National Party, sat off a windstorm when he called for an enquiry into Prime Minister Layton dealings with Nicholas Henry. Gerald Lavoie of the Party Quebecois realized that with both the Liberals and French Independent Parties under investigation, the race for the premier's office would mainly be contested between himself and David McNeil. While Minister McNeil chose to chastise Prime Minister Layton, Minister Lavoie steered his attacks at the People of Quebec National Party leader, by airing several negative personal Ads of the minister's own misconducts throughout the years.

Part 8

Kane Esquada who was considered a radical Indian by the Frenchman, spent two months living with Kevin. Despite their different nationalities both men had developed a mutual love for each other throughout the years, however with greater responsibilities and power Kevin changed drastically. The ancestors of the businessmen with whom Kevin dealt were the original organizers of key legislations that the Canadian Governments implemented to oppress the Indian people, hence the environment at the Trudeau's estate eventually became stifling for Kane. The Native Indian was against Kevin's decision to harm Kadeem who was a proven loyalist, thus he took no part in the betrayal and walked away. After the entire ordeal unfolded Kane abstained from voicing his opinion, because he understood the hurt in losing a family member, even though he believed Kevin was defending the person who was at fault. Kevin was extremely gracious to Kane nevertheless, and purchased him the most technologically engineered prosthetic arm, compensated the physicians for his physio therapy and gave him a new Ford

Bronco. They parted ways as brothers even though Kane knew at heart that he would abstain from visiting, however if ever Kevin needed him for anything, he would never hesitate it come.

The Mohawk Indian went back to his reservation with thoughts of returning to the peaceful lifestyle he once enjoyed. Kane expected a huge commotion whenever it was revealed that he had survived the fall, therefore prior to the excitement he felt he had obligations to fulfill. There were a few locals with whom he had developed a close friendship and thought to reveal himself to them first before word got out. The first-person Kane went to see was Steve Nagutenai, who was one of the rebels that helped with the Pont Mercier Bridge seizure. Before turning onto Steve's property from the main road, Kane noticed a young female standing at the bus stop approximately twenty yards away. Trusting the bus would be along soon on such a deserted stretch of roadway, the Warrior Indian drove up to his friend's house where a domesticated wolf could be seen through the windows patrolling the residence. The home owner was a taxi driver who shared the use of the vehicle with another taxi operator, therefore even though his vehicle was not parked in the yard Kane still knocked the door to make certain he was not home. After determining that Steve wasn't in, the visitor climbed back into his truck and drove to the main road where he looked down the street and saw a man from inside a Honda Ridgeline, attempt to drag the young Indian girl inside his vehicle.

Kane started blowing his horn and sped out onto the roadway towards the horrific incident. The male occupant inside the truck noticed the Bronco approaching and released the female, then sped away to flee the scene. Immediately after being released the scared young girl ran towards her house, which was on the property next to Steve's. The young female recognized that she owed a debt of gratitude to whoever the Bronco driver was, therefore as he sped by the young lady caught a glimpse of his face. The Warrior Indian speculated that the girl was forcibly being pulled into the vehicle and continued after the perpetrator, instead of first questioning the girl to check if his assumption was correct.

It was a briskly cold and snowy winter, and as the trucks sped along the slippery countryside roadways their chances of losing control after hitting a patch of black ice steadily increased. The chase continued for several miles before Kane drew closer to the Honda truck, which was a vehicle model five year older than the rereleased Bronco. While in pursuit of the Ridgeline Kane got the opportunity to verify the nationality of its driver and noted that he was of Caucasian descent. The Indian Nation had lost thousands of their children to murders and theft, either by individuals or by the government itself, which displaced these kids predominately into white homes. To force the Honda off the road Kane rammed the bumper, causing the vehicle to swerve along the asphalt before the driver steadied it and regained control. Images of abducted native females molested, killed and dumped, flashed through Kane's mind where he envisioned the person, he chased committing some of the crimes.

With rage and disgust for such offenses fueling his actions, Kane pressed on the gas and again struck the back of the Ridgeline. The vehicle swerved along the roadway and drifted towards the right shoulder, where it slid on panes of black ice and flipped multiple times before crashing in the ditch. When the pursuit began the Honda's driver panicked and forgot to fasten his seatbelt, as a result he was thrown from the truck and collided against a tree. Kane stopped momentarily and looked over at the wreckage and thought to check on the driver's status, but as he exited the Bronco, he noticed a semi-trailer approaching and changed his mind. Returning home to unsubstantiated murder charges was not how Kane envisioned moving forward with his life, hence he drove to his old place, packed a bag with essentials and waited until nightfall to leave the reservation.

The driver of the Honda Ridgeline was a fifty-four-year-old businessman from Quebec City named Maurice Leduc, who died on the scene before medical technicians could arrive. The driver of the semi-trailer noticed the wrecked vehicle that came to a halt on its roof and stopped to see if he could help. Once the man saw Maurice's predicament after checking to verify if anyone else was inside the vehicle, he simply alerted the medical dispatcher for them to send an ambulance. It was obvious that there was nothing he could do for the victim whose body was contorted around the tree, hence the tractor trailer driver waited inside the warmth of his vehicle until emergency personnel arrived.

A Mohawk Reservation police cruiser was the first emergency response vehicle on the scene. Officer Tim Pitchu followed procedure and checked the victim who appeared visibly deceased; then blocked off the accident area with Emergency Flare indicators. The trailer driver had a scheduled delivery south of Montreal for which he was already late, so Officer Pitchu took his statement and personal information during which he found out about the Ford Bronco. The deliverymen described what he saw from his vantage point and indicated that the Ford deliberately struck the Honda, then fled the scene without attending to the injured conductor. Despite such intricate details the semi-trailer driver neglected to capture the Ford's license plate number, which would have made finding the vehicle much easier. After receiving the information Officer Pitchu sent a message to his dispatcher for her to put out a regional search for the Ford Bronco, with presumably 'a damaged front grill and bumper'.

Instead of returning to Kevin's luxurious estate, Kane opted instead for a change in scenery and began driving towards the Shamattawa First Nation Reservation, located east of Manitoba. When Kane was a teenager in high school there existed a native arts program that enabled participating students to travel to different provinces across Canada, where they would interact and showcase their artifacts amongst native students from other regions. During a field trip to Edmonton, Kane befriended and bummed a cigarette off Eshanwai Mahawuka and Ojasuk Hallumahe, who were amongst a group of students from Manitoba. The three youths snuck away from their individual Arts Fair group and found a place where they could hang out and smoke. Throughout the years since they seldom remained in contact, although they swore to a binding agreement which provided a place of sanctuary, should any of them ever need somewhere with which to escape.

Kane expected the Tribal Police to post a cruiser by each exit leaving the reservation, so he waited until the officers on-duty changed shift at 7:00 PM, before he attempted to leave. Once off the Mohawk Reservation, the Outlaw Indian filled his gas tank in Montreal to avoid getting himself or his vehicle tag caught on a service station surveillance monitor within his hometown. After filling his tank Kane jumped onto Autoroute-20 and drove to the Sainte-Anne-de-Bellevue exit that enabled him to transfer onto Autoroute Trans-Canada-40. Following a short distance of approximately six miles the highway divided into Autoroute-417 and the Autoroute-401, hence he selected the 417 which brought him west through Ontario into the Province of Manitoba. The Mohawk Indian had never visited the Shamattawa First Nation and had no idea where it was located, thus he had to depend on the directions provided by his GPS, which indicated the distance was over 2,000-km.

When Kane got close to Sudbury, Ontario, it was almost 2:00 AM, so he decided to refill his gas tank and find a place to take a short nap. There was a Petro-Canada Service Station with a huge resting area just off the highway that appeared open. Despite the late hour, the Trans-Canadian Highway was still quite busy with huge tractor trailers traveling in both directions. Inside the service station worked a twenty-three-year-old female, who had the features of a First Nation Native but was been raised locally. After Kane refilled his gas tank and entered the store, he fixed himself a cup of coffee and grabbed a carrot muffin, then stepped to the register to pay his bill.

"You are Kane Esquada, aren't you," surprisingly asked the service attendant?

Kane looked at the female's name tag that read Nancy, then checked over his shoulder to see if anyone else was inside the store. Once he noted that the store was empty, he turned back around and slightly grinned at the attendant.

"What business is it of yours who I am," asked Kane?

"I'm Nancy Fawfakuk, I'm sorry but I saw your pictures in the papers, plus you have one arm, even though they said you're possibly dead! I just think you're fucking awesome! I mean, what you did for your people and all," exclaimed the female!

"Is it free to rest up for a bit over in the parking area," Kane exclaimed then paid his bill?

"Yes, it is but if you give me a ride home, I'll give you something way more comfortable than just a place to sleep; and maybe even breakfast in the morning," Nancy declared, as she flirted with a dazzling smile!

Kane thought about the offer for a second, then said, "what time does this place close?"

"I'm supposed to stay open until my replacement gets here at 5:00 o'clock, but if you'll give me a ride I'll close up right now," Nancy insisted?

"OK, let go," Kane insisted!

The Mohawk Indian waited until Nancy went through the painstaking ordeal of shutting down the business sign lights, the cash register, the gas pumps, and several other appliances before they departed. As they closed the establishment three separate travellers pulled into the station to purchase petrol and were rather disappointed. Immediately after entering the Bronco Nancy turned on the radio and tuned onto her favorite station, lit a cigarette and released her long hair from the Elastic holding it. Nancy directed Kane onto the Kingsway, Autoroute-55 which led towards Sudbury, but after a few miles they exited left onto Autoroute-74, commonly known as Moonlight Avenue. The female was quite the talker and asked several questions before blurting out everything about her troubled life, which involved an on and off boyfriend, whom she claimed loved their sexually promiscuous cat more than her.

"Where are you heading," Nancy asked?

"Shamattawa Indian Village," Kane responded.

"That's where my father is from. My bigger sister still lives there, she is some bigtime psychiatrist down there. My father moved away when I was five; said he did so for us to have a better chance to survive and yet my sister moves back there years later to work! Funny, isn't it? Let me write down my number for you before I forget," Nancy stated.

Kane could barely get a word in and didn't care to after they smoked a Marijuana Joint; furthermore, the mere mention of a troubled boyfriend sparked his disinterest, whereby he could not recall much of what she said thereafter. They drove down Autoroute-74 and turned left onto Claude Street, which continued for a few metres before they went around a curve and the street's name changed to Ridgemount Avenue. The gas attendant lived in a bachelor apartment near the end of the road, which was amongst five other apartments inside a huge house.

Kane grabbed his backpack with some of his essentials to take a shower in the morning before he got back on the road. Nancy had mentioned that her boyfriend was in Toronto for a few days, nevertheless Kane took his Glock 22 Semi Auto Pistol from his armrest compartment and shoved it into his bag. When they entered the apartment, Nancy offered Kane a beer and provided the television for his viewing, then ran off into the bathroom for a few minutes. The Mohawk Indian placed his bag on the side of the sofa and sat back drinking the beer, when suddenly the female's cat jumped up onto the back of the chair. The black cat startled Kane, who pushed the animal off the sofa back onto the floor. Following a few more sips from his bottle of Bud Light, Kane placed the beer onto the center table and relaxed into the sofa with his eyes closed.

Nancy emerged from the bathroom wearing nothing but her G-String Panties and slowly walked over to Kane, then climbed on top of him. When Kane opened his eyes, he was shocked at the sight of Nancy's firm and voluptuous breasts, in addition to her smooth and radiant skin. Their lips clashed in a lava of passion as the Renegade Indian clutched her tightly into his grasp, before he began kissing her neck down to her pointed breasts. While caressing Nancy's tender skin, Kane filled his mouth with one of her breasts and succulently sucked on it as if he was enjoying a delicious fruit. The sexually enticed female began sucking on her partner's left earlobe, which further influenced him to remove his clothing. As Kane unfastened his shirt buttons, Nancy undid his jeans and removed them then proceeded to perform oral sex. Despite feeling extremely fatigued after hours behind the wheel, Kane was reluctant to refuse the intimate advancements made by the very desirable Female.

For Kane, the entire experience was fantastic until he climbed onto Nancy and stuffed her head into the sofa and began pounding her from the rear. Without fair warning, the female's weird cat leapt onto the sofa and sat watching them without any intentions to move. Kane fanned his hand at the cat to chase it away, but instead of fleeing the animal started licking itself continuously. That was the strangest and frankly most disgusting act that Kane had ever seen, therefore, to remain in the moment he looked away and tried paying attention to Nancy. Regardless of his endeavors Kane felt provoked being watched by the cat, thus he could not avoid seldom sneaking a peek at the distracting animal to ensure it didn't advance any further.

Nancy's passion and energy revived Kane's youthful senses, hence he felt like a young buck at work. After surpassing his greatest performance timing ever, the Outlaw Indian was still inspired to perform another Marathon, when suddenly he heard a key being pushed into Nancy's door lock. The Female also heard the doors key and jumped off Kane, then instinctively ran into the bathroom and locked the door. A split second later the boyfriend opened the door and walked into the apartment, where the first thing he saw was some naked Indian standing there. Before Kane could utter a word, the angry boyfriend ran to the kitchen and armed himself with a knife, therefore he withdrew his

Glock 22, grabbed the cat from off the sofa and stuck his gun to the animal's head. The angry boyfriend stopped in his tracks and dropped the knife, following which he fell to his knees and began begging Kane not to harm the cat. Kane calmly got dressed and collected his belongings, while holding the animal as hostage to keep the boyfriend civil.

"Your cat is going to follow me to my truck, then I'll release him you understand! Don't let me have to kill you or your fucking cat," Kane threatened, as he left the apartment with his belongings!

Kane walked out to his vehicle with Nancy's boyfriend a few paces behind, climbed aboard the Ford Bronco and started the engine, then released the cat as he drove away. The Renegade Indian went back the way he came on Moonlight Avenue and made a right onto the Kingsway, Autoroute-55, along which he had recalled passing a lounge area with a restaurant. When Kane got back to the location, he pulled into the lounge area where several other overnighters were stationed, parked between two trailers and went to sleep. The sounds of honking car horns and other noises awoke him at 7:22 AM, therefore Kane stepped out of the vehicle and went into the restaurant where he first visited the restroom. After relieving himself and freshening up a bit, the Mohawk Indian bought himself breakfast and ate his fill before he got back on the highway.

Kane had always been somewhat of a superstitious individual and therefore refrained from contacting either of his friends to inform them of his visit, until he was five miles away from their reservation border. When he contacted Eshanwai to advise him of his visit, the Manitoban First Nation Indian sounded depressed yet invigorated to hear his voice, hence Kane was left rather skeptical on whether to visit. Following such a physically taxing drive Kane stopped along the side of the road and pondered over proceeding but decided against turning back and advanced on faith.

Eshanwai and three other men were at the Shamattawa First Nation entrance to welcome Kane, whose initial concern was if he was about to get arrested as he drove up. His childhood friend flashed a huge smile once he saw it was truly Kane, thereby lessening his concerns and encouraged the Mohawk Indian to approach without skepticism. Both Eshanwai and Kane embraced tightly like long lost brothers, following which Kane looked closely at the other individuals to see if he recognized his other friend.

"My friend we are truly happy you have come here, but today is a very difficult day for the people of my village! Last night another four of our youths committed suicide, which now makes nine over the past few months. But this is the chief of our village Kenu Shomittaroua, this is Mukaii, Divyansh and Shann, who all insisted that they come to welcome you in person," Eshanwai declared!

The Shamattawa Indians were all elated to meet Kane, however, while shaking the chief's hand he could see the emotional hurt on the man's face.

"We have heard of the great things you have done for your people, and across these lands your name is beloved and well respected! I beg of you to help guide our youths, so they may stop this insane act," Kenu declared?

Kane shook his head in acceptance but was rather encouraged by the comment that he was considered infamous. When returning to their reservation, Eshanwai rode with Kane while his companions all piled into Chief Shomittaroua's Hummer.

"Where is Ojasuk," Kane asked, as he followed the Hummer's lead?

"My friend, like you Mohawks we too have many problems of our own. For centuries, we have experienced the theft and killings of our people, many unsolved deaths and unmarked graves, yet still no enquiry or investigation by the government! Our dear friend Ojasuk's youngest sister went missing, and when he found out that a local officer was the last person seen picking her up, he went to have a word with the officer. During the conversation Ojasuk was shot four times, and the officers who committed the murder claimed that he started making trouble and threated to kill him, before he pulled a knife! I spoke with Ojasuk before he walked up there, and I tell you he had no knife," Eshanwai exclaimed!

"What is this officer's name," Kane demanded?

"His name is Jack Quiere, and the other shooter was Rvyan Hartwell," Eshanwai answered.

"I see many signs of our people losing their way. Why do you think these kids are killing themselves," Kane enquired?

"The system, where they see these crimes occurring and no one gives a fuck! They watch on TV how these investigators find out who killed other people, but here at home anyone can go missing, and even if you find the graves there is no one to investigate, no autopsy, nothing! These kids see no hope in the world they are to live in, because there is nobody to defend their rights," Eshanwai lamented!

"Persecution against any of this country's first people is persecution against us all! Never forget my friend, as long as I breath the air of our ancestors, I will always defend the rights of my people," Kane fired back!

Part 9

Kadeem sat in the rear passenger's seat of his black Range Rover, Sport, that was being driven by Elroy. Seated across from Elroy was the second of Killa's two sidekicks Demitry, both of whom did most of his dirty work in addition to his personal security duties. The three men had been partying heavily at a house party in Ocho-Rios; and departed slightly after 1:00 AM for a reggae stage show that was being held in Clarendon. The live performance concert was stacked with huge performers the likes of Capleton, Chronixx, Damian Marley and many others; thus, the music lovers despite the late hour left for the event. Elroy and Demitry loved working for Kadeem, who would often go out on exciting excursions that basic Jamaicans could hardly afford. Killa was no typical employer and would often hire multiple whores to his private getaway in Santa Cruz, where the females would strip, dance and entertain them all. Whatever either man wanted was of no significance once they remained loyal, which was an expensive commodity in a society of impoverished people.

The party enthusiasts drove to Highway-2000 and headed southbound to their destination. When they departed from Ocho Rios two separate Juta buses began following them, however, with passenger transports leaving practically every other minute for different parts of the island, it was difficult to ascertain they were being pursued. Aboard the first Juta bus were four Columbians sent to Jamaica by Manuel Lagarza on a mission to kidnap and return Kadeem to Columbia. Through the first twenty minutes of the voyage the Juta bus carrying the Columbians remained approximately fifty yards behind the Range Rover, which was also being trailed by a second Juta bus that had five Haitians aboard. The Haitians were mercenaries employed by Kevin and sent to exterminate Killa, who lived a quiet life and was only seen on occasions. The second Juta Bus maintained a ten-yards separation between them and the first passenger transport, which initially jeopardized the Haitians' mission. Inside both Juta buses were occupants loading and readying their automatic rifles for an assault, against a man they were all prewarned would be armed and dangerous.

With the second Juta bus refusing to speed up and pass the first, the Columbians were somewhat tentative to start their attack, knowing the spectators could ruin their plans. Following days of searching for their target, the Haitians on the other hand believed the time to strike was then and thus, threw caution to the wind as they decided to attack. The second Juta bus sped up pass the first, then cautiously drove up alongside the Range Rover. As the Juta bus pulled up beside the Range Rover, two of the assassins prematurely opened windows at which their rifle nozzles could be seen. Realizing what was about to occur and knowing they could not fail; the pursuing Columbian driver began flashing the vehicle's high beam lights.

Elroy noticed the headlights flashing behind them through the mirror and said, "why this guy flashing his high beams all of a sudden!?"

Kadeem looked over his left shoulder through the back window and saw the flashing signals, then withdrew his 45mm hand pistol without hesitation and held it on his lap. Demitry out of curiosity spun around to look through the side window, as the Haitians began opening fire at the Range Rover's occupants. Killa responded by firing three shots through the shattered rear door window across from him, which smashed one of the Juta bus's window and subsequently forced a shooter to move. A bullet struck Demitry directly in the face and killed him instantly, at which Elroy ducked his head and veered the vehicle off to the right, where they crashed into the guardrail.

"Them fuckers killed Demitry," Elroy yelled as he withdrew his firearm, unbuckled his seatbelt, and quickly exited the vehicle!

The Juta bus came to a halt a few feet away as its passengers dismounted while reloading their weapons, then moved towards the crashed SUV. The Haitians believed they had the advantage and sought to finish the job, meanwhile the survivors of the initial attack sought to even the score. Once the Range Rover crashed and stopped, Kadeem ripped the leather covering from behind the driver's seat ahead of him and removed two AK-47 Assault Rifles from their storage position, then quickly exited the vehicle on the opposite side.

It was pitch black along Highway-2000 aside from the light being shone straight ahead by the mercenaries' Juta bus, thus the scenery drastically aided the outnumbered and outgunned Jamaicans. One of the hired mercenaries could be heard barking instructions at his comrades in Creole, before two of them separated from the group and the other three got into a tight attack formation. The group of three overwhelmingly-confident mercenaries started destroying the Range Rover with bullets as they approached, expecting Kadeem and Elroy to possibly still be inside the wreckage. After tossing his companion a rifle Kadeem signalled his intentions to circle behind their attackers, then leapt over the guardrail and crawled back towards the Haitian's Juta bus.

Elroy stooped on his knees behind the wrecked SUV and awaited his opportunity to return gunfire, in addition to offering Killa enough time to get into position. Neither of the Jamaicans had any idea how many shooters they were up against or what their attackers' motives were, but they were certain the gunmen were out to kill them; hence it was either kill or be killed. The three Haitians soon emptied another clip and started reloading simultaneously, nevertheless Elroy refrained from returning fire not knowing his boss' situation. The hired mercenaries had heard a great deal about Kadeem and thus had grave respect for his talents, therefore they readied their weapons and emptied another clip into the vehicle.

There was no denying the fact the Haitians were there to eradicate everyone inside the Range Rover, as they again completely emptied another magazine and started reloading. The Nervous Bodyguard could hear their opponents' empty magazines being dropped on the asphalt and knew he may not be given another chance, therefore he mustered the courage and leaned against the hood of the SUV then fired several shots at the mercenaries. The group of attackers were at arms length from each other which should have made executing them an easy enough task, but the Haitian to the furthest right was dressed completely in black and had such dark complexion that Elroy could not identify him under the darkness of night.

Once Elroy began his defensive output and opened fire, Killa stopped advancing along the guardrail and looked to support his lone assistant. As he turned his assault rifle in the direction being fired by his associate, he overheard the two gunners who separated from the group whispering a few feet away on the opposite side of the guardrail.

"I am telling you, he is the only survivor," whispered on gunner!

"Ok, ok! He is a dead man," answered his companion!

The Haitians were seconds from shooting and killing Elroy who had no idea he was aligned into someone's shooting scope, thus Killa had no options but to shoot the unsuspecting mercenaries who had no inkling he was there either. Due to Kadeem's body positioning on the ground it was difficult to use his assault rifle against the mercenaries, thus the Rude Boy withdrew his 45mm pistol and shot them dead. The hand weapon discharge startled Elroy, who took his eyes off his downed targets and looked off in the direction from which the shots erupted.

Seconds after killing the two Haitians Kadeem heard one of their opponent's weapon disburse, following which Elroy yelled out in pain and dropped back behind their wrecked SUV. Once Elroy got taken out the mercenary immediately turned his weapon in Kadeem's direction and fired several shots that were blocked by the metal guardrail. The lone surviving mercenary realized that his crew members were all killed in what he perceived was an ambush, and thereby started running back to their Juta bus to escape. Killa was not about to allow their antagonist to simply get away without paying a penalty, therefore he grabbed for his AK-47 and fired several shots at the fleeing Haitian. As the mercenary neared the Juta bus, a bullet struck him in the right leg and he tumbled along the left side of the bus. The Haitian revelled in pain as he quickly pulled his belt from around his waist and tied it around the wound, then hopped onto the bus bleeding and quickly started the engine.

The Columbians had stopped a safe distance away from the altercation, but were in amazement at the developments right before their eyes. Killa and his peers had thus far proven they would have been a challenging opponent for any opposing force, but they were especially happy they did not have to combat the Jamaican. Even though they were instructed to kidnap Kadeem and return him to Columbia, Manuel's abduction team knew that should they offer any further assistance their target may become suspicious of them. It had been nearly four minutes since the gun battle erupted and the foreign spectators hoped that nobody came along who might inform the police.

The fifth hired mercenary yanked the gear shifter into drive and stepped on the gas, which started the vehicle moving. As the mercenary's hopes of escaping increased, Kadeem vanquished all his aspiration by shooting out both back tires. When the last surviving Haitian realized that the bus was decommissioned, he grabbed for his weapon and started looking around frantically not knowing from which direction Killa would attack. The Jamaican Bad-man picked up several rock stones off the ground and started hitting different areas of the Juta bus. The injured Haitian inside who would not get very far on a wounded leg without transportation, began shooting at every startling sound until his rifle ran out of bullets. Once his weapon was empty and the assassin searched for additional clips with no success, the disappointed man sat back on the driver's seat and stared through the windshield, until Killa came along the opened door and shot him several times. Kadeem looked at the man with disgust as he fell forward onto the steering wheel, before he ran back to check on his bodyguard's status.

Elroy had gotten shot in the upper right shoulder and was bleeding profusely, nevertheless he was still alert and conscious. The bodyguard was in immense pain and could hardly gather his weapon to fend off any adversary that came along, hence he was delighted to see Kadeem after hearing numerous shots fired. While Killa attended to his associate the Columbians drove up in their Juta bus and stopped to aid.

"Hello! Amigos we come in peace. Anybody need help," declared Ricardo who was placed in charge of the expedition?

Kadeem held tightly onto his 45mm gun handle and looked what type of inquisitive passengers dismounted the transport bus. Once the suspicious Jamaican noted that travellers were of a completely different race, his jittery eased and he shoved the weapon into his waist.

"How can we help you my friend? We saw everything, we can even tell the police what happen if you want," Ricardo offered!

"Thanks for the offer, but for now I just want a ride to bring my friend to the hospital," Killa asked?

"That will be no problem my friend, come I help you," Ricardo answered!

"What's your name by the way," Kadeem asked?

"Me, I am Ricardo, and this is one of my friends Marquez," stated Ricardo!

"Nice to meet you Ricardo, I'm Kadeem and this is my bodyguard Elroy," Killa responded!

Kadeem and the Columbian helped Elroy off the ground and brought him to the Juta bus, where they climbed aboard and drove away from the scene. Even though Killa wasn't suspicious of the Columbians he brought along both their AK Rifles instead of leaving them for the police to recover. When they fled the crime scene Kadeem sat in the middle of the vehicle attending to Elroy, whose vitals were stable and appeared he would recover. A few miles away from the horrific scene Kadeem began looking through the windows to ensure the driver was heading in the hospital direction. When he noticed that they were driving in the wrong direction Kadeem alerted the driver and exclaimed that 'they should make a U-turn and return to the closest medical center in Ocho Rios'. The instant Killa made that assumption the entire ambiance inside the bus changed, as three of their hosts surprisingly pointed handguns at their heads. One of the Columbians bounded their hands, disarmed them and confiscated their weapons, to which Kadeem argued Elroy would die should he not receive immediate medical attention. The Columbian seated in the front passenger seat pointed his weapon closer to Kadeem's face, before switching to Elroy and nonchalantly shot him in the forehead. Killa could not believe the man deliberately shot Elroy and started turning his head to look at his companion, when the Columbian behind him dragged a blindfold sac over his head and everything went blank.

Part 10

The appointed Commissioner for the Office of Conflict of Interest and Ethics Commission of Canada, Mme. Teressa Lablonde began an investigation into Prime Minister Mathew Layton's involvement in the Government's legal case versus Kevin Walsh. The recommendation for the Commissioner to investigate was made by the leader of the People of Quebec National Party, Monsieur David McNeil several months prior, following the release of the initial story. When Monsieur McNeil made the original request, the Ethics Commissioner was indisposed due to a medical absence, however once she returned to work the case was made a priority.

Mme. Teressa Lablonde was appointed the head of the Ethics Commission some five years prior under the Parliament of Canada Act, and had two additional years remaining on her seven-years term. Mme Lablonde's personal assistant was Juliette Jolicoeur, whose entire schooling was sponsored by the elaborate Secret Cult's Academic Institutions. On the morning scheduled to announce publicly their intentions to question the Prime Minister, Juliette received a phone call from a private caller who said before disconnecting, "We want no mention of our institution in this enquiry!" The Office of the Conflict of Interest and Ethics Commissioner is an entity of the Parliament of Canada, along with the House of Commons, the Senate and the Library of Parliament. The duties of the Ethics Commissioner involved the production of two annual reports: one on the Office's activities under the Conflict of Interest Act and one on activities under the Conflict of Interest Code for Members of the House of Commons.

It was up to Mme. Lablonde's department to ensure that the Conflict-of-Interest-Act, was followed by all public holders such as Ministers, Ministers of State, Parliamentary Secretaries, Ministerial Staff, Governor-in-Council appointees, and Members of the House of Commons. The Office administrates these two regimes through a variety of activities. These include providing confidential advice to public office holders and elected Members of Parliament about how to comply with the Act and the Members Code. The Office also reviews these individuals' confidential disclosures of their assets, liabilities and activities, and is tasked with making publicly declarable information available through a public registry, investigating possible contraventions of the Act or Members Code, and reporting to Parliament. The Commissioner is also mandated to provide confidential advice to the Prime Minister about conflict of interest and ethics issues.

When the Prime Minister's office received the formal request to attend the enquiry, they released a response calling the investigation, "A late political witch hunt without merit!" Later when asked by reporters how he felt about the probe, Prime Minister Layton repeated the same sentiments shared by his Public Relations Team. The Office of Conflict of Interest and Ethics Commissioner disputed the Prime Minister's claims and explained that the reason for such a delay in the proceedings was due to Mme. Lablonde's medical absence, after her doctors discovered a lump in her right breast for which she thereby underwent a vasectomy. Following her cancer treatment, the Ethics Commissioner was skeptical about returning to work, but thought it was her obligation to the office to fulfill her duties. The Ethics Committee requested a hearing with four of the Prime Minister's employees, whom they believed could corroborate their corruption case.

To prepare for his testimony the Prime Minister met on three separate occasions with his private council to discuss how they would proceed. On the second of such meetings his lawyer Mr. Laurence Finkelbaum requested that he provided whatever physical evidence he had in his possession, for them to evaluate how to best proceed. The meeting was held in Prime Minister Layton's office, where they went over all the national condemning materials received during the biker slaughtering debacle. Once Mr. Finkelbaum inspected the evidence, he became confident that the Prime Minister operated with the country's best interest at heart, therefore he felt confident they could provide a compelling argument to the Ethics Committee. Prime Minister Layton knew that his entire case depended on the files sent to him by Kevin, thus he chose to hold onto the files until their final meeting a day prior to the hearing.

During their final meeting both men went over the manner with which they would approach the P. M's testimony to ensure he did not politically harm himself by his responses. Mr. Finkelbaum advised his client that 'should he find himself uncertain how to respond to any question, then immediately correspond with his council before proceeding'. It was imperative that Prime Minister Layton exited the hearing without any questions looming to silence his critics, or his oppositions leaders would have feasted on his caucus until he was removed from office. There was already several other M. Ps, Ministers and Senators that were already being reprimanded for illegal conducts while in office, and Mathew wanted to avoid being added to the list at all cost. As a result, Mr. Finkelbaum had to not only calm the Prime Minister's nerves with assurances of victory, but also convince him that the Canadian public would not allow his sacrifices for country to be distained without proper praise.

By the end of their meeting Mr. Finkelbaum had the Prime Minister so mentally prepared and confident that he handed over the evidence to be inspected by the Ethics Committee to his legal council. To ensure that his lawyer reached home safely with what he believed was his most compelling means of vindication, Prime Minister Layton arranged a police escort to accompany the lawyer home. Regardless of his renewed confidence Mr. Layton had daunting concerns about the people associated with the organization behind the documents and how the proceedings would affect his political future. That night Mathew had a nightmare wherein he dreamt that four thieves robbed his lawyer of the evidence at gunpoint, thus he awoke at 1:41 AM and phoned Mr. Finkelbaum. Following their brief conversation Prime Minister Layton found it difficult to return to sleep and stayed up for the remainder of the night watching television.

On the morning of the Ethics Committee hearing Mr. Finkelbaum got picked up by a limousine service at 8:45 AM for their 10:00 AM appointment. They first drove to Laurence's personal assistant's apartment building located in the Byward Market, where they picked up a female named Giselle Lamont then proceeded to their destination. Giselle brought Laurence an unexpected medium cup of his favorite Dark Coffee and ensured they were prepared for the day's challenge by asking, "if he had brought the necessary documents?" Even though he was confident that the desired evidence was inside his briefcase, Laurence opened the case to assure his assistant.

The hearing was scheduled to take place on Parliament Hill in Ottawa and news coverage was denied inside the chamber, nevertheless that failed to hinder nearly every news organizations from appointing their reporters to cover the event. Mr. Finkelbaum arrived ten minutes before Prime Minister Layton and as he emerged from his limousine a wave of questions was shouted at him from the reporters, who were kept at a safe distance. Instead of responding to any of the questions, Laurence waved to the crowd like a rock star then walked into the building with Giselle.

While he waited for his client to arrive Mr. Finkelbaum went into the men's room to urinate and freshen up for a long a dulling day. There were Senators and Civil Servants all throughout the hallways of the building and inside the restroom, where a helper offered to hold Laurence's briefcase while he used the urinal. Knowing his briefcase was locked the lawyer did not give a second thought to foul play and handed it to the colored gentleman. The instant Laurence turned his back the bathroom helper opened the briefcase with the correct code and stole the Prime Minister's evidence inside. Once Laurence finished, he stepped to the sink and washed his hands, before being given a paper towel to wipe them dry. After he was through using the facility, Mr. Finkelbaum collected his briefcase from the helper and went back to waiting for the Prime Minister.

The presiding leader of Canada arrived a few minutes later to the cheers and hollers of both spectators and reporters. Prime Minister Layton refrained from answering any of the questions shouted at him, although he spent more time than others at the entrance of the building smiling and waving at his fans. When the Prime Minister entered the parliament building his lawyer was the first to approach and shake his hand, following which they climbed the stairs to the designated private chamber on the second tier.

Prime Minister Layton and his personal council entered the hearing chamber where Mme. Lablonde, the stenographer and her Ethics Committee handlers awaited them. The Prime Minister was given a table to sit while his legal team were awarded chairs that were placed a few meters behind him. There was a bottle of water along with a glass of ice placed on the table for the P. M's consumption, hence he sat and laid his personal notes on the table ahead of him. A clock on the wall behind the committee members showed there was two minutes before the hour of ten o'clock, when the meeting was scheduled to begin. Neither the committee members nor any of the Prime Minister's associates acknowledged each other prior to the beginning of the meeting, which led to somewhat of an uncomfortable silence.

"Good morning everyone, Mr. Prime Minister welcome to this enquiry we have several questions to ask of you. On the committee panel with me today we have Monsieur Cristophe Janvievre, Monsieur Henry Scrotton and Monsieur Kellen Marchand, and I am the Ethics Commissioner Mme. Teressa Lablonde. Before we go any further, I should advise you Mr. Prime Minister that this entire enquiry will be recorded, therefore you may answer at your discretion. We ask that you be truthful in all your responses to the best of your recollection and if at any time you require the assistance of your personal council, you may go ahead and ask whatever it is you wish of them. Today we two scheduled intermissions where we will be breaking for lunch and a second intermission later this afternoon, but we have a lot to cover so let us get started!... Mr. Prime Minister if you have any opening remarks or would like to introduce your legal team at this time, you may go ahead and do so!" began Teressa at precisely 10:00 AM.

"Good morning to you also Mme. Lablonde, as well as your distinguished colleagues. Today I'm here with my legal council Monsieur Laurence Finkelbaum and his assistant; and I will respond as truthfully as I can to all your questions," Prime Minister Layton answered!

"Very well! Prime Minister Layton do you know of a Mister Kevin Walsh also known as Nicholas Henry," Teressa asked?

"Yes briefly," Prime Minister Layton answered.

"In what capacity is Mister Walsh known to you," Teressa questioned?

"Well Mme. Commissioner Mister Walsh became known to me after he was arrested and arranged to have a package sent directly to me through a private parcel service...," began the Prime Minister.

Laurence Finkelbaum opened his briefcase and began extracting his notepad and file folders from within. The folder that contained the Prime Minister's main defense was missing, hence the lawyer turned his briefcase upside down in search of the document. A disgraced look fell over the lawyer's face as he tapped his client on the shoulder and interrupted his response.

"Sir I seem to have misplaced the documents we should be entering into evidence," whispered Mr. Finkelbaum.

"What," yelled the Prime Minister, before he gestured his apology to the panel!?

"I must have left it in the restroom downstairs! I'll run down and retrieve it at once sir," Mr. Finkelbaum stated, before excusing himself from the chamber!

"You better find that file," whisperingly threatened the Prime Minister!

"Are you prepared to proceed Prime Minister Layton," enquired the Ethics Commissioner?

"Ah, yes I believe we are, my council seem to have left an important file containing most of our evidence in the restroom, so if we can have a brief intermission, he should be right back with it," Prime Minister Layton declared.

There was a different black attendant inside the restroom when Mr. Finkelbaum returned. The lawyer as a result became more convinced that the first attendant may had stole the file, therefore he went to the attendant's lounge to search for the individual. Unsuccessful at his endeavor the lawyer sought out the attendant's supervisor and enquired about the man's whereabouts. When the Prime Minister's lawyer heard that the attendant had returned home ill and might be back at work the following morning, he grievously contemplated bringing charges against the employee, but thought better of it. With everything he had learnt and experienced about the mystery organization, challenging such a dangerous entity might be hazardous to his health. Mr. Finkelbaum knew that they could still argue the Prime Minister's case without the files, therefore he disgracefully returned to the enquiry and informed his client.

When the bathroom attendant Omar Delly left work that morning, he walked south on Metcalf Street for four blocks until he reached Laurier Avenue, where he turned left and headed east. There was a Bentley limousine parked half way down the block, which he climbed into as if they awaited him. Inside the back of the vehicle was Monsieur Gilbert Stephano, to whom he gave the package as the chauffeur drove them to the Rideau Mall bus transit. Mr. Stephano handed Omar a Manilla Envelope filled with a hundred and fifty thousand dollars in U.S $100 bills, before they stopped and allowed him to exit at the bus station.

Back inside the Parliament Building Prime Minister Layton and his legal team spoke in a private room about what happened and how they would proceed. Mr. Layton was initially furious at his lawyer for loosing the documents and was overheard shouting profanity, before he settled down and listened to his legal council. The absence of the documents meant that they would have to rely solely on the disclosures of their witnesses, who could fully corroborate the Prime Minister's story, but his government would be in peril without factual documents to counter the impending attacks from his political opponents. While Giselle's boss strategized how to deal with the Ethnic Committee, his personal secretary received a phone notification from her bank that stipulated she had funds available for direct deposit. Miss Lamont secretively checked her email statements then logged into her internet banking system, where she inserted the proper code to collect the funds and retrieved her payment. There was a hundred thousand dollars in the transaction paid to the secretary's account for providing her boss' briefcase code, which nobody knew she had obtained. With nothing but long faces and tension inside the room, Giselle quickly abandoned the smirk that materialized across her face and returned to the business at hand.

Part 11

When White Widow's chartered flight landed at Dorval International Airport in Montreal, she exited the Customs Department to find Miss Nutcracker waiting patiently for her. Fiona was elegantly dressed as they customarily were and wore a huge Dior Sunglasses that covered half her face, while pushing her Louis Vuitton luggage on a baggage cart. The females of the Pigeons of The Order prided themselves on presenting a tough image at all cost, thus they simply greeted each other with the traditional French smooch on both cheeks. Miss Nutcracker's Range Rover was parked inside the airport garage, hence they found a meter and paid for the time before going out to the vehicle. After the ladies loaded up the Range Rover and sat inside, Fiona broke down in tears and was immediately consoled by her friend.

"I hate to say it, but you know this sort of shit comes with the occupation," Miss Nutcracker exclaimed!

"Cherie, right now it is not about getting raped; I fucked up enough of those bastards to sleep well at nights! I think those big dick motherfuckers fucked up my insides! Just please carry me to the hospital," White Widow declared?

Miss Nutcracker drove her girlfriend to the Lakeshore Hospital, where following a few test doctors admitted her and decided to operate to repair internal damages. After the surgery, the nurses prescribed that Fiona remain in the recovery ward for an additional seven days while they determined if she was mentally fit to return home. For the first two days, White Widow rarely slept and would awake herself from dreams due to her violent outbreaks. The doctors and nurses believed that Fiona was gang raped and wanted her to speak of her ordeal to law enforcement, but she refused and insisted that nothing criminal occurred.

During Fiona's second day inside the hospital Kevin went by to visit and brought her a huge bouquet of assorted rose and flowers. When the Jamaican Rasta walked into the room and surprised his employee, he caught her smiling and chatting on the phone, however she rudely disconnected the call without alerting whoever was on the other line. White Widow was still receiving fluids and had a monitoring machine attached, so the boss had to be careful when hugging her. There was a nurse checking the monitors and documenting the results, who smiled at Kevin and finished her duties before exiting the room.

"You didn't have to get off the phone because I come to visit. I'm in no rush," Kevin insisted!

"It was only my mother, I will phone her later," Fiona responded.

"I called and told the nurses to make sure they give you the best treatment possible. How you feeling, I hope they sending you home soon, Kevin declared?!

"I, I, I am OK, they treat me very good! Thank you," Fiona answered!

"That's good, make sure I get the bill and you can stay off from work as long as you want! Just make sure you back to a hundred percent before coming back," Kevin instructed.

"Thank you, Mr. Trudeau; and again, I did my best to get your property back," Fiona argued!

"And I already told you to forget about it! I know the type of jungle that I send you to, and I know how vicious them gorillas from the garrisons can be. So, I'm happier you back safe than anything else," Kevin stated!

"Well, I must thank you for visiting me, I surely never expected this," Fiona said.

"Anybody who puts their life on the line for me have my support! So anything you want just let me know," Kevin offered.

"You are too kind Mr. Trudeau, already I think you have done too much just for coming," Fiona suggested!

"After this is all said and done one day, I bring all you girls to Jamaica and we really enjoy the entire island," remarked Kevin.

"I will surely look forward to that trip," accepted Fiona.

Kevin and White Widow spoke for several additional minutes before he gave her another hug and left. Fiona was initially nervous when Kevin entered her room without any of his female guards and thought that he intended on killing her for failing, thus she was left suspicious of the visit after he departed. Even though Kevin never expressed any ill-sentiments towards Fiona, she assumed that his visit meant his disapproval, hence there would have been an assassination placed against her. Moments later White Widow began detaching the medical devices connected by her nurse, before she located her clothes and slowly got dressed. The nurse whose care Fiona was in came rushing into the room and was shocked to find her patient getting dressed but could do absolutely nothing to stop her. The patient had checked herself into the hospital under her own free will and could legally depart once she was well enough to do so. To deter White Widow from leaving the nurse summoned the doctor on duty, still Fiona ignored them all and started exiting the ward. Instead of remaining in the hospital as prescribed, White Widow checked herself out that very same evening and was brought to the front entrance in a wheelchair by her nurse. A taxi was summoned to bring the rape patient to her destination, hence she climbed aboard, and they drove away.

Even though her friends would have taken her to her residence for free, Fiona did not feel confident in any of them at that point. Miss Nutcracker had dropped off her luggage just inside her condominium door and brought her some personal items in a smaller bag. As she entered her dwelling White Widow callously tossed the bag containing her hospital apparels beside her other luggage and closed the door. The instant Fiona entered her residence she began sniffing about as if she smelt a specific aroma in the air. She walked over to her liquor cabinet and picked up a glass, then opened and poured a half glass of Xo Cognac inside. Fiona began removing and dropping every piece of clothing from her body, as she walked into her bedroom on route to the bathtub.

Yves Buchard was hiding behind the door and crept up behind her, then grabbed her around the neck and squeezed tightly. Fiona could hardly breathe yet neglected to react violently, as she took a gulp of her drink and passed the remainder over her shoulder to the intruder. Yves spun her into his arms and gave her a long sensuous French kiss, however as his hands gravitated towards her mid section, she grabbed a hold of it and stopped him.

"The doctors said I won't be abled to for a while," Fiona warned.

Yves developed a puzzled look as he stared into the female's eyes. White Widow pulled herself away and went into her bathroom where she began filling her tub in preparation for a warm bath. Seconds later Yves walked in and hugged Fiona from behind, but it was evident she was not her usual self.

"Did you get the data in Jamaica," Yves questioned?

"Is that all you care about? They raped me and fucked up my insides and that is all you want," Fiona argued?

"What! Why didn't you tell me," Yves demanded?

"It does not matter now! But no, I did not get the memory file, and Kevin came by the hospital to see me. I feel he was poking around to find out something," Fiona answered.

"Does he know about us," Yves asked?

"I don't know, I don't think so! Maybe he would already be at the door, I don't know," Fiona insisted!

Yves Buchard dropped to his knees and hugged Fiona around the legs. "Damn it! I'm sorry baby, but I promise they will all pay for this!"

"Nobody has more to lose than me! And I will put a bullet through your head if you ever try to fuck me," threatened Fiona!

The female assassin ran her right hand through her lover's hair and stroked his cheek. She then walked into her bedroom and retrieved a folder from her drawer and gave it to Yves. There was a photo of a beautiful woman inside the first page, followed by additional documents with information about her.

"I was doing my homework and I think there is one person we can get to help our cause, but even the introduction could be dangerous," Fiona lamented!

"Who is this person," Yves enquired?

"Mme Madelaine Royal aka Queen Rich Bitch of Hempstead, who is the only person funding a secret investigation into who killed her father. Her younger brother Daniel sits in the seat once held by their father, and she had been very vocal about the fact she should be the one seated on the council," Fiona declared.

"Mme Madelaine Royal sounds like the perfect ally to get me in the council seat that I deserve," Yves connivingly whispered!

Part 12

Maurice Lamour, the new prosecuting attorney assigned to argue the Canadian Government's case versus Nicholas Henry, was a brash and pompous young Frenchman who was born and raised in Quebec City. Maurice had similar morals, ambition and character as his predecessor and sought to propel his career with a signature win over Kevin's legal team. The head of the Prosecution Department and several members of the government wished for Kevin to be punished to the full extent of the law, thus Maurice was instructed not to consider any plea deals that would substantially benefit the defendant. Kevin's attorney made three attempts to reach an out of court settlement, but each time Maurice refused his proposals.

Miss Cutthroat at the request of her boss spent several days studying the lawyer's profile to learn more about his habits, and thereby develop a plan to execute her orders. Throughout that time, she followed Maurice, took pictures and watched him during his daily interactions. While the prosecutor was at work, Miss Cutthroat received regular updates from a security guard at the front desk, who would alert her every time the prosecutor exited the building.

Whenever Maurice went to court Amber had him watched and recorded at times, to determine whether he had any bad habits.

Maurice was unmarried and dated females from an online couples' website. He would at times spend up to three nights weekly doing leisure activities such as playing basketball and poker with his friends, in addition to dining at his Aunt Myra's house every Sunday. The lawyer lived in a very secure and private condominium suite, loved riding his bicycle around the downtown sector and owned a droptop BMW Z Coupe. If Kevin had not requested that the murder look like an accident Miss Cutthroat would have simply put a bullet through Maurice's head, but what was demanded required more preparation and a subtler approach.

One of Maurice's favorite restaurants to take his dates was a quiet Italian/Canadian cuisine located on Ontario Street West. The restaurant was situated in the basement of a three-story building beneath a cellular phone sales center and two apartment suites. The food was excellent at the establishment and being a regular meant that Maurice received special perks, therefore the prosecutor loved impressing his dates at the local eatery. There was a private backroom for reservations only, thus the restaurant's servants would judge Maurice's level of interest in his dates by where he chose to sit. Quite a number of other rich and important clients ate at the establishment, thereby the prosecutor always felt within his element. Maurice was at the time dating a beautiful red hair female name Monique Doriel, whom he had tried diligently to impress on many occasions. While determining how to go about killing the prosecutor, Kevin's hitwoman discovered that the restaurant was amongst his favourites and deemed it a perfect location for a plan she had conspired.

Restaurant Le-Decosta was a forty-year-old establishment that was being ran by second generation family members. The restaurant would open for lunch daily and remained open until their final customer left that night, even though they advertised that they closed at midnight. Each day three handlers of the restaurant arrived at 9:30 AM to accept deliveries, prepare the restaurant and cook certain types of food. A second chef arrived by 10:00 AM to help in the kitchen and two other waitresses arrived at 11:30 AM to help with their busy lunch rush. Crystal Cerris was one of the two waitresses employed by the restaurant on a full-time basis. On her way to work one morning, Crystal was walking two blocks away from her destination when an Aston Martin, Vanquish S two door sports coupe pulled up beside her and the window rolled down.

"Crystal Cerris," Miss Cutthroat shouted!

The female stopped and curiously walked over towards the vehicle expecting it to be some former schoolmate. As Crystal stepped close to the car door and realized she had no clue who the woman was, Amber showed her a picture on her cellular phone of her parents seated inside their living room and said, "Get in if you want to save their lives!" Crystal felt scared and frightfully looked around, before she built up the courage to enter the vehicle.

"Why do you have my parents on your phone," Crystal asked?

"You never met me, and this conversation never happened, you understand," warned Miss Cutthroat before showing a picture of Maurice to Crystal! "This man occasionally visits your restaurant. The next time he visits I want him scheduled inside your private room and inform me when the reservation is made! Here is a list of the items I want you to provide to him and enough money to cover the bill."

"Why are you doing this," Crystal enquired?

"Believe me when I tell you that I will have both your parents killed, then I will find and kill you and that puppy of yours if you don't do exactly what I say! There is a number to call on the back of the paper, make sure you follow the instructions. Fuck this up and I will put a bullet through your head!... I have been watching you and I know you have a lot of bills to pay, so play your cards right and you just might make some money," Amber instructed, as she removed a Walter PPQ M2 9mm handgun from her armrest and placed it on her lap!

"Please, I can't," Crystal argued?

"If you want to live, you will do what I said! Get out of my car," Miss Cutthroat advised, to which the waitress obeyed!

The Prosecutor was oblivious to the fact that he was being targeted and the person intent on harming him had arranged for an employee at his favorite restaurant to betray his trust. Crystal had no idea what the female she spoke to had planned, but she was certain Miss Cutthroat wasn't planning some surprise birthday celebration. Still despite her uncertainty the waitress refrained from mentioning anything about her weird encounter, even though she had physical evidence such as a phone number and the list that specified what Maurice's meal should be that evening. There was also a stipulation that Maurice and his guest be given a free bottle of Champaign plus whatever else they desired. Three days later the restaurant received a reservation call from Maurice, at which Crystal immediately telephoned and informed Miss Cutthroat. When Mr. Lamour and his date arrived for their dinner, the instant they entered the private dinning room the waitress brought in a bottle of Crystal that was already being chilled on ice.

"Wait, wait a second, I didn't order that," Maurice declared!

"Sir this a gratitude bottle from our management for you and your lovely date this evening," said the waitress!

Before Maurice could dispute Monique picked up the bottle and looked at the crest with a huge smile glistening across her face. "Wow, these people really appreciate your business," she exclaimed!

"It's obvious they know who helps to keep this place running," Maurice boasted!

"Plus, your meals are also complimentary tonight sir. Our chef would like to prepare for you a succulent Oyster Dish, which is a favorite meal of his," stated the waitress?

Maurice looked down at the menu and scrolled down to the dish being offered, before sneaking a peek over at the price. "Holy fuck that is a hundred and twenty-dollar plate they offered me for free," thought the prosecutor to himself, before nonchalantly responding! "How exactly does he prepare it?"

"Sir you are in for such a treat, the chef uses this ancient technic from Italy where he tenderizes and does such wonderful things to the Oysters, I guarantee that this dish will become your favourite and each time you return you will order this," said the waitress!

The waitress' faint yet alluring description of the seafood dish sent a desiring sensation through Maurice's date. Hence, she licked her lips and reached for her glass of Champaign, then quickly swallowed the contents and shoved the glass towards their server for a refill. While both customers dealt with the waitress, Miss Cutthroat surveyed from the next room and awaited her chance to pounce. The prosecutor was sold after such an incredible sales pitch; therefore, he handed his menu back to the waitress and sat back while she attended to his date. The thought that they could both enjoy a fabulous expensive meal with champagne and whatever else they desired was reassuring to Maurice, who lifted his glass and admired the sparkling bubbles before partaking of the gratitude.

"I think this is one of the best restaurants I've ever been! I mean they actually treat you like a Rockstar, I could really get used to this type of living," Monique exclaimed!

"You haven't had noting yet, just wait till you taste the food! Only the best joints round town with me baby," insisted Maurice!

Monique loved the taste of the champagne so dearly that she drank two and a half glasses before the food arrived. They had amazing hors-d'oeuvres on the table for consumption while their customers awaited their meals, which delighted the female who had been enchanted by the ambiance. Shortly before the main courses were brought out, Monique excused herself and rushed off to the restroom. Seconds later Miss Cutthroat dressed as one of the restaurant's waitress brought in the meals and presented Maurice with his Chef's special, which smelt so delightful that the prosecutor instantly picked up a fork and tasted the Oysters. As Maurice began swallowing the seafood, Amber unsuspectingly passed behind him and used a Mini Portable Stun Gun to electrocute him to the back of the neck. To avoid leaving any distinguishable marks that could be uncovered during an examination, the female assassin pressed the Stun Gun against the prosecutor's shirt collar before shocking him. Maurice fell forward onto the hot plate of food shivering as if he had suffered an epileptic attack; hence the assassin pulled him back against the chair and placed him in a lethal chokehold.

Monique returned from the bathroom thereafter to find her date faced down on the plate of hot food and screamed out loud in fright. Restaurant employees and others rushed to their aide, wherein another waitress immediately began performing CPR on the customer. By the time employees attended to Maurice he was completely lifeless, nevertheless the waitress pumped his chest and continuously blew air into his mouth. When the 911 dispatcher received the phone call the name of the victim was not made known, therefore only two regular police street cruisers and a supervisor got sent to the call. Upon their arrival the first officer on scene took over the CPR administration and kept at it until the paramedics arrived and relieved him. The head paramedic hopelessly performed CPR for another seven minutes before he final ceased trying. The ambulance technicians speculated that the prosecutor might had suffered a heart attack after choking on the Oysters, but all that would be determined through an autopsy. The paramedic's speculation deterred the officers from pronouncing the case a homicide, which would have led to them sealing off the area and calling in the forensic team.

Throughout the entire ordeal Crystal was scared shitless, however, she was far more terrified of Miss Cutthroat's threat and thus burnt the paper with the information given to her. When the waitress returned home that night, she was visibly shaken believing she had something to do with the killing. Despite her foul mood the joyous temper of her dog's excitement to see her brought a smile to her face, hence she removed her snowy boots and hung her jacket on a coat hook. The nervous female went to refill her dog's water and food bowls; but was surprised to find them half empty. Instead of speculating that someone may had refilled the bowls that were typically empty whenever she got home, Crystal only assumed her dog ate less than normal and ignored the warning. As a result, she picked up the animal and went to sit on her sofa, where she grabbed for her television remote and turned on the tele.

Miss Cutthroat was unknowingly hiding inside the closet and watched the female for another six minutes, while she sobbed and soothingly caressed her dog. The female assassin was dressed in an all black outfit, with a thin mustache, tam down to her eyebrows, black gloves and a hooded jacket. Once Crystal had gotten comfortable, Amber snuck from the closet and crept across the wooden floor, where the dog which had gotten accustomed to her did not even bark. Instead of putting a bullet through the waitress' head, Miss Cutthroat snuck up with a piece of fishing wire and wrapped it around the female's neck.

"Sorry kid, no loose ends," Miss Cutthroat stated as she strangled Crystal who struggled briefly.

Before leaving Amber picked up the dog and pulled her hoodie over her head, she did not want to kill Crystal but had no choice. There was no sense in letting a full bag of dog food go to waste, therefore she grabbed it on her way through the door.

***

Three weeks before Kevin's trial was scheduled to begin his legal team received word that a new prosecutor had been assigned to the case. The pathologist who did the autopsy had not yet published their findings, thus, Mr. Duntroon and the entire city were on edge to hear whether some preposterous claims would be made against Kevin. Once it was revealed that Maurice Lamour's death was not being considered a homicide, each member of the defense team knew they had dodged a bullet with the deaths of two prominent prosecutors, which was the most peculiar case they had ever undertaken. The police had recently botched their ability to gain priceless information about the hit and run murders of the first prosecution team by killing Quail Fromage. As a result, Mr. Duntroon and his legal team knew the government would be highly motivated to make their client the scape goat.

When Logan Duntroon phoned Kevin to inform him of the lawyer change, the only thing his employer wanted to know was if the new lawyer was more willing to negotiate? The defense attorney had not entertained the thought that the first prosecutor could have been murdered by Kevin's goons, however a second death even though already determined accidental stirred controversy. Attorney Duntroon advised Kevin that the third prosecutor was behaving like his predecessors who drove a hard bargain and wanted extremely stiff penalties. Instead of reacting annoyed as he did the previous two prosecutors, Kevin simply told his lawyer "to forward him the prosecutor's information" and disconnected the call.

The third prosecutor assigned to Kevin's case was a young man of color who was born in Canada to Caribbean parents. Jamaal Rickson's mother legally migrated to Canada from St. Vincent and his father was initially a Jamaican farm worker who abandoned his duties during a work trip. When Kevin received Jamaal's profile and saw that he was a black man, he smiled to himself and wondered if the government believed appointing someone of color would deter him from murdering them if necessary. After scrolling through the prosecutor's profile, the defendant being charged passed on the folder to Miss Cutthroat, who had done an amazing job at eliminating obstacles thus far.

"How would you like this handled sir," Miss Cutthroat asked?

"Some type of accident... One where someone else gets blamed for whatever happens," Kevin stated.

"I will personally see to it sir," Miss Cutthroat declared!

Jamaal Rickson's personal life was much different from Maurice Lamour, considering he had been happily married for six years and had two children. The Dark Complexion Attorney had been a prosecutor for seven years and was married to a Caucasian French Canadian from Gatineau, Quebec named Violet. Amongst the attorneys inside the prosecution office Jamaal was considered one of the best, but would often get excluded from career propelling cases despite his exemplary win and loss record. With two attorneys deceased prior to arguing such a huge controversial case, other lawyers throughout the bureau had begun condemning the case as bad luck and vowed to refuse it if they were awarded the task. When Jamaal got presented with the challenge, he boldly accepted the case, despite the concerns of his wife Violet and other friends.

Jamaal would drive to work every morning and often took the same route, unless there was some sort of detour along his journey. The court prosecutor would leave from his home on De-Lavigne Road in the Mont Royal area and travelled east along Sherbrooke Street. When Jamaal reached Mansfield Street he would turn right and followed the road, which brought him down to the Old Montreal sector. Miss Cutthroat spent several days studying the lawyer's habits and followed him around to conceive a plot that would fulfill her boss' instructions. On her first day touring the quiet neighborhood in which the prosecutor lived, the female assassin observed that their house was on the side of a hill with steep inclines all throughout. There were renovations being done to a home partly destroyed by fire four houses away from the lawyer's, therefore at certain times of the day huge dump trucks would pass along the road.

On the day chosen by Miss Cutthroat for Jamaal's assassination, the lawyer left his house at 7:35 AM for the office. Depending on the traffic the ride typically took twenty-five minutes, which left Jamaal with approximately an hour to prepare for court at 9:00 AM. Jamaal drove to the main entrance to his street and turned right onto Atwater Avenue heading in the direction of Sherbrooke Street. There was usually a higher volume of traffic along Atwater Avenue each morning, but that morning almost no vehicles were heading southbound. A dump truck filled with waste materials drove off from the house being repaired as soon as the prosecutor turned onto the main road, and slowly drove down the hill to the stop sign. Atwater Avenue had a menacing curve while descending a steep hill that caused most commuters to nervously hack their brakes. It initially seemed peculiar that there was not a higher volume of traffic, but Jamaal them noticed signs indicting Road Work being done atop the hill.

The court prosecutor reached the red traffic light at Sherbrooke Street and stopped for the green amber, while listening to his favorite morning talk show. Jamaal watched several vehicles pass through the intersection then turned his focus to the indicator countdown that alerted pedestrians the light was about to change. To the left of him a public transit bus took off from the bus stop just as the lights turned yellow, hence the driver quickly sped up to avoid blocking the intersection. Mr. Dickson who drove a manual transmission automobile, sunk the clutch and placed the shifter into first gear, then slowly lifted his right foot off the break expecting to proceed as the lights changed.

Suddenly the dump truck rammed into his vehicle from behind with such force that his car propelled forward and slammed into the transit bus. The entire front end of Jamaal's vehicle was pushed underneath the bus, which caused the transport vehicle to tilt onto the left tires. The dump truck compressed Jamaal's vehicle to half its regular size and trapped the prosecutor who was killed instantly. Loud screams could be heard coming from passengers inside the bus who had gotten injured, when they were thrown from their seats onto the floor and onto other unsuspecting transit users. A few seconds after the accident occurred the wobbly driver of the dump truck stumbled from the truck's cabin in fright at the destruction he had caused.

Within two minutes an officer arrived on the scene and immediately rushed to help those who were still trapped on the bus. The female passenger who was seated across from the bus driver got propelled onto the transit employee and fractured the man's shoulder. With the bus tilted and the woman pressed against the driver, it was initially difficult to open the doors, plus the conductor did not want any of the passengers to sustain further injury while exiting. The first officer on the scene tried to locate another way for passengers to exit the bus, but the only two doors were both a least three feet off the ground. Realizing that he had very few options available, the officer attended to the morning traffic and waited until members of the fire department arrived. Other police cruisers pulled up thereafter and cordoned off the area to clear bystanders away from possible danger.

When the Police Supervisor Noland Weise arrived on the scene and ran Jamaal's license plate number, he immediately notified his dispatcher before confirmation was even made that it was indeed the prosecutor. The special investigations team led by Detective Emmanuel Ellesbury and Detective Eric Ruchard that was formed to investigate the deaths of Attorney Gary Thompson and his prosecution team, as well as Attorney Maurice Lamour got sent to the crash sight to gather information. Even though Supervisor Noland emphasized that the person responsible had been detained, his instructions were not to interfere with the crime scene until the investigators arrived. Hence the injured and distressed bus passengers were forced to wait an additional thirteen minutes before anyone got taken off the bus. There were many severely injured passengers crying for attention and nearly everyone had to be taken to the hospital, however emergency employees also had to stabilize the bus before the rescue could take place.

The dump truck driver was Giovani Marza, a fifty-three-year-old husband of two who worked for La Cite Cement Company, which belonged to a member of Kevin's secret fraternity. Mr. Marza was held for questioning and taken to the police precinct on St. Catherine Street, where Detectives Ellesbury and Ruchard showered him with questions. The construction employee had advised authorities on the scene that his company's truck brakes failed and maintained his account of what happened even through tough questions. Any formal charges against the truck driver were withheld until the detectives completed their investigation, hence Mr. Marza was released until the government decided how to proceed. Officers received several statements from witnesses and victims who all described the same occurrence, therefore investigators had to rely on mechanical evidence to determine if what happened was indeed an accident. After inspection of the truck a few weeks later it was determined that the brakes were intentionally interfered with, thus Mr. Marza was then charged with manslaughter.

Part 13

The crime and violence levels in the city of Montreal reduced for several months, which led to the outright praise by every political party leader to their chief of police for a magnificent job. Criminal activity statistic polls illustrated that crime across the board was significantly down, due to a stronger police presence and more enforcement of the laws. The politicians' assumption was that the increased police manpower in addition to the newly appointed organized crime unit had curved the thoughts of criminals, but they could not have been further from the truth. Federal Agent Ross Mohara received two citations for his undercover work against gangs and organized crime, but even he would be quick to testify that the law enforcement did not know enough about the bikers and organized crime. The Federal Bureau did not have an undercover agent operational inside much of the criminal organizations, thus they were completely oblivious to the manner with which certain groups operated.

Many foreign traffickers benefited from the Alliance Crew defeating Martain Lafleur and his dominating biker regime, one of said nationality was the Japanese who became the biggest importers of heroine and the fourth largest illegal drug importer behind the bikers, the Chinese, and Sicilians. To begin their operation the bikers investigated which other groups were importing illegal products into the country, what were their methods, where were the products brought and how were they distributed. Jim's bikers found out that the Sicilians were fast becoming the biggest suppliers of cocaine, through their distribution deals with the Albanians, Ukrainians, Slovenians, Lithuanians, Lebanese and the Greek. The Sicilians had an arrangement where they acquired up to a tone of cocaine from Afghanistan or other parts of the Middle East, had it transported to an industrial factory in Indonesia where it was transformed into figurines, and packed into a shipping container before exported to Canada. Unlike the Japanese and Chinese who only sold their products to the Frenchman, Germans, Italians and Russians, the Sicilians ran the biggest distribution market and the bikers wanted control.

Prior to the Sicilian's drug pipeline's availability in Canada, they smuggled their merchandise to countries such as the United States, South Africa, and several other countries throughout Europe. The smugglers had several ways of camouflaging their products, however a cutting-edge technology was used to create the inventory that was being shipped to the Canadian market. The Interpol Agency learnt of the international drug trafficking ring when a routine inspection of a container's inventory uncovered that the products within were made of illegal substance. Once it was discovered that cocaine was the substance used, the International Police Agency sought to arraign the main players involved and assigned four investigators to the case. Franchesco Marrianari who was a Spaniard that spoke four languages and Titouan Gaspe from France, were given the task of following the shipment to its destination, while the second team investigated the people who sent the container. Franchesco and Titouan were sent along on the voyage to track Container 597, which was secretly carrying the half tone of illegal cocaine.

The name of the cargo ship was MIXXIM-IV and the Interpol agents' duties aboard the humongous freight carrier were as security detail, responsible for keeping the vessel safe from sea pirates and other dangers. Before the ship docked in the Montreal Harbour, Agent Marrianari placed a small tracking device onto the container to track its whereabouts once it left the port. Within three hours the container was picked up by Sergio Capuchelli, who was employed as a driver for a furniture store. Sergio brought all the proper documents to get the container released and loaded onto a semi, which he then drove to a warehouse on Boulevard Beaconsfield in Baie D'Urfe. Both Interpol agents followed the container and pulled up in a rented vehicle across the street from the warehouse, where they watched the front entrance and the tracking monitor. The driver of the semi Sergio Capuchelli drove the trailer into the warehouse where Paolino Salvatore, Andray Serchivoli, Benji Carrousel and Filippo Alessandro were awaiting his arrival.

"Any problems," Paolino enquired of the driver, as he dismounted the cabin?

"No boss, everything went smooth as usual," Sergio responded!

"Alright Benji you guys get those crates outta that trailer and be very careful! Let me have that manifest Sergio; and give them a hand will you," Paolino instructed!

Benji Carrousel was sitting on a Forklift and drove up close to the rear doors of the trailer. Sergio leapt onto the foot stand and opened the door, then went into the trailer and unfastened the straps holding the crates. With the merchandise prepared for removal, Benji used the Fork Lift to extract the crates from the trailer and placed them on the floor. Paolino, Andray and Filippo all gathered around the first crate while Benji and Sergio continued unpacking the other merchandise. Andray used a crowbar to pry open the crate, before gently unmasking the magnificently created statues. The statues looked like they were made of Porcelain, some of which were two feet tall and done with extraordinary craftsmanship, and thus easily fooled anyone visually.

"Wow look at those beautiful art pieces! It's a pity we gotta destroy them," Paolino remarked.

"Yeah, you right boss," Filippo agreed!

Franchesco and Titouan were trying to remain incognito and collect information when a black Chevrolet Yukon pulled up in front of the warehouse and four heavily armed men wearing ski masks jumped out. The men all formed a line and without hesitation began showering the warehouse with bullets. None of the Interpol agents were armed nor could they have interfered in the violent assault occurring in front their faces. All the shooters emptied two clips without any response from those inside the warehouse, who were overwhelmed with the barrage of bullets being dumped into their establishment. The shooters were not intent on killing as much as they wanted to disrupt the European's business, therefore as soon as they heard sirens coming, they seized firing, boarded their vehicle and fled the area.

Once the bullets stopped and the sirens drew ever closer, the only thought that occurred to the traffickers was to flee. Paolino and his associates exited through a side door that led to their vehicles, thus they quickly fled the scene to avoid arrest. Police officers arrived in force seconds later and blocked off the entire area while they investigated. The Interpol agents were the officers' best source of information considering they watched the entire ordeal. The drug bust became one of the biggest in Canadian history and fascinated law makers with the ingenuity of smugglers, who have always found none-conventional means to transport their products.

Within hours after the drugs was discovered police officers raided three homes and arrested De'angelo Riviera, who owned the warehouse, Maria Benligavi and her husband Ben Benligavi who rented the warehouse to store extra merchandise, and Sergio Capuchelli who transported the drugs to the location, on several counts of drug trafficking. With everyone else from the warehouse keeping a low profile the following morning, Paolino Salvatore went to his favorite café three blocks from his house for his daily coffee. While reading the day's newspaper and enjoying his warm beverage at the same table, in the same seat where he routinely did, Jim Bartello walked up and sat across from him. Paolino's bodyguard was standing beside his car and did not expect Jim to interfere with his boss, therefore he began walking towards them.

"It was essential that as your newest business partners we got rid of your old products," Jim stated.

Paolino looked over at Jim and held aloft his hand to stop his approaching guard. The bodyguard turned around and walked back to where he was.

"Instead of having to rearrange business dealings with the people who already buy from you, we are going to supply you and have you continue to both breathe God's air and making money," Jim instructed!

"I provide a significant amount of products to my clientele, what makes you think you can fill that order," Paolino enquired?

"We could have simply taken your products and sold them back to you. But we want your foreign investors to publicly see their investment burn. I don't think you believe I would be sitting here if I couldn't provide whatever it is that you require," Jim said, then slid a piece of paper to Paolino and got up and left!

***

Agent Mohara and four friends from the Federal Bureau went out to play pool on Saturdays whenever possible, at a popular billiards hall within their residential community of Laval, Quebec. The hall was located on Boulevard Cartier West, along the main strip where numerous companies sold their products. There was the live showing of an MMA pay per view event that evening and Quebec's favorite fighter Georges St. Pierre was fighting on the card, thus the agents stayed until closing. The five agents shared two vehicles none of which were driven by Mohara, therefore he got fairly plastered off alcohol and beer while enjoying the evening.

Agent Mohara drove with Agent Russel Maire and Agent Kyle Laroach, who both occupied the front cabin of their Ford Taurus. Despite being out off duty all the agents were armed with their service pistols and carried their official badges inside their wallets. The evening was enjoyable and culminated with a victory by the fighter everyone went to watch, needless to say the massive left in good spirit. The entire parking lot was nearly empty by the time the group of agents left the billiards hall and walked to their vehicles, which were parked a few spaces from each other. As Ross and his mates approached their car, two females driving a Chevrolet Corvette pulled up in front the Taurus.

"Jenny, I told you it was Ross," excitedly shouted the female seated in the passenger seat!

"Oh, shit it is! Hi Ross, how have you been," yelled the captivating Caucasian female driver!

Agent Mohara was near intoxication and believed he knew the females, so he began staggering towards the Corvette. Agent Kyle Laroach wanted to get introduced to both ladies and thereby began following his co-worker, whose face brightened the closer he got to the car. When Ross got within three-feet of the Corvette the passenger who was seated the furthest from him, brought up a RTS-ZK-S-12 Gauge Shotgun and blasted him directly in the chest. With Agent Mohara airlifted a few inches off the ground his companion tried to retrieve for his weapon, but the female assassin selected another bullet and blasted at him. Agent Laroach was forced to dive for the turf to save his life, as the female driver sped off like a professional racer. Immediately after hitting the ground Agent Laroach withdrew his service pistol and struck the fleeing vehicle twice. Agent Maire managed to withdraw his firearm and discharged several bullets at the Corvette, before both he and Kyle ran to Ross' aide. Due to the extra flow of adrenaline Agent Laroach didn't realize that he had gotten shot in the arm until he was busy attending to his injured co-worker, wherein Agent Maire pointed out that there was blood on his arm.

While their comrades attended to their injured mate the two agents who shared the second vehicle climbed aboard their car to give pursuit. The male driver started the car and yanked the gear shifter into drive, but the vehicle barely moved from the parking slot. Confused about what could be hindering their progress the agents got out of the car to inspect and found that their rear tires had been intentionally slashed. There was no way to pursue and locate the Corvette at that point, therefore both men ran over to their friends to check their status.

***

Cheng Lo was a Chinese nationalist who managed to develop a very sophisticated drug operation, wherein he imported his drugs through Mainland China.

Like the Sicilians Cheng trafficked his drugs in shipping containers, however the drugs were built inside the wood carvings of high-priced furniture to avoid detection. Once the furniture cleared customs in Canada and was brought to his storage facility, the pieces containing the drugs were demolished and the drugs removed, before they burnt and destroyed the damaged furniture. Mr. Lo had several different residences from homes, duplexes to apartment buildings, and owned four businesses that included a restaurant, a nail treatment facility, a furniture store and a grocery market.

With all the homes and businesses owned by Mr. Lo nobody would have thought that his biggest income came through his illegal drug trafficking, which brought in millions each year. The Chiney K Gang members worked with Cheng and sold most of his products to their customers. As a result, Mr. Lo and all his establishments throughout China Town were very much protected, despite the mischief caused by the gang members against other business owners. Mr. Lo would pretend he took a stand with the Chinese business owners who fought against the troublesome gang members, when in fact he would often utilize the Chiney K members to eradicate competition.

The bikers got word that Mr. Lo had five hundred kilograms of cocaine stored inside one of his many residences throughout China Town. Jim and his associates would have loved to confiscate all the merchandise and reap the profits but challenging the Chinese in the place where they were most dominant would have been suicide. With every scenario taken into consideration the bikers decided that if they could not forcibly take the drugs then nobody should have it. It was impossible for the Rough Riders to decipher exactly where the drugs were been stored; and Cheng did not make the options any easier by housing residents in every lodgement that he owned. In every residence were pregnant females, children and elderly folks, nevertheless Jim ordered his gang members to burn all of Cheng's establishments to the ground.

To avoid any alarms being sounded or unexpected interruptions from community residents, the Rough Rider members decided to conduct all the arson attempts at the same time. During the night was agreed upon as the best time to strike, however getting into the residences unquestioned to ignite the fires would be easier accomplished during the daytime. Mr. Lo had nine separate residence all in close proximity to each other around China Town and likewise were all his businesses. To acquire entry into each of Cheng's residences the bikers used their cunning and pretended they were employees of the Metro Gaz company, who were conducting routine inspections. In order to give the impression, they were actual employees of the gas company, the bikers attained similar uniforms and bought advertising magnets that featured Metro Gaz logo, which they attached to their 4x4 trucks. The exact time for each of the arsonist to enter their assigned dwelling was 10:30 AM, with ten minutes given to find either an electrical junction box or the gas line and set their disruptive mechanisms. By 10:45 AM each of the arsonist were expected to have exited the residence and leave the area, without alerting anyone to what they have done.

Cheng Lo left for his restaurant at 8:00 AM each morning and would stay there until 8:40 AM when two of his helpers arrived, at which he would then head over to his nail treatment store and opened for 9:00. Cheng's wife Kim Lo would leave their home around the same time as he did each morning and went to open their grocery market, while their eldest son departed much later to attend to their furniture store. When Cheng's son Ty Lo was leaving for work the morning of the arson attack, he passed the imposter Metro Gaz employee at the front of their residence. Ty's grandmother who lived with them allowed the fake worker to enter and showed him where the boiler room was located. The grandmother was a sweet old lady who made the repairman a cup of coffee and kept it waiting for him once he was finished. The biker went to the boiler and found a gas pipe, used his wrench to crack open a connector and placed an ignitor with a timer close to the exiting fumes.

When the biker got through in the basement, he sought to leave quickly but the old woman stopped him with the cup of coffee. Jim had instructed all the arsonists to maintain the illusion of who they portrayed, therefore the biker sat for a few minutes to partake of the coffee. The imposter thought that the granny was alone until three other occupants appeared from other places in the house and quickly grabbed snacks prior to departing. With the clock ticking closer to the residence going up in flames, the biker began getting agitated yet did not want to concern the old woman. Matters got even worst when an alarm sounded, and the sweet old Chinese lady got up and walked over to the microwave, insisting that she had warmed two Cinnamon Buns for them. The pretending Gaz employee peeked at his watch and without any explanation took off running for the front door, where he even abandoned his shoes and left the door ajar as he ran from the home.

The old woman found the serviceman's actions strange and went over to close the door when the phone rang. Cheng called to enquire if his other children had left and after answering his question his mother told him about the weird service employee. The ignition contraption that the biker placed inside the basement sparked a flame and created an explosion that blew away much of the house. Mr. Lo's mother was tragically killed in the explosion that shook the homes of neighboring residence and immediately disrupted their phone conversation.

Phone calls began pouring into emergency services as other gas explosions and deliberately set fires began popping up throughout the China Town region. A national alert had to be sent out to every fire department in and around the city, which proved devastating for some of the fires as emergency personnel were stretched thin. Cheng was in shock and redialed his home to a dead phoneline, at which his cellular and other phones lines began sounding. By the third call received Mr. Lo knew he had been marked but had no clue who could have done such a treacherous thing. Even though his mother was killed inside the explosion at his home, the first demolished property that Cheng went to personally inspect was a building he owned on Brady Street, which was where he stored his cocaine reserves. Mr. Lo wept when he saw the building engulfed in flames and had to be restrained from approaching by police officers on the scene. With fire crews stretched to their capacity due to so many detrimental fires at the same time, only a small crew operating with two hoses connected to street hydrants could be afforded to tackle the blaze. Nearly sixty percent of the residence targeted by the bikers were destroyed; and due to remarkable strategy, they managed the feat without surrendering any lives.

Three days later Mr. Lo went to open his restaurant and left the door unlocked for his helpers to enter whenever they arrived as he customarily did. There was no reason for Cheng to work as hard as he did, but he had to maintain the facade for investigators and moreover was addicted to hard work. Cheng walked into the kitchen and started a pot of Herbal Tea, then took some plastic containers from inside the refrigerator and placed them on the counter. After washing some rice, the boss put some to cook on the stove, and walked into the dinning area where Jim Bartello was seated at one of the tables.

"I am sorry sir, but I'm afraid we are not open yet," Cheng stated!

"That's fine with me Cheng, I'm not really here for the food. Why don't you just bring over that pot of Chinese Tea with two cups, so we can discuss our new business arrangement," instructed Jim, who wore a suit and looked like a businessman.

"I don't quite understand you sir," Cheng answered.

The stranger began playing a video on his cellular and placed it on the table; that showed Cheng's workers removing the imported items from a container, before they proceeded to carefully extract the drugs and destroyed the remaining furniture. "You can call me Jim… and may I be the first to inform you that that video you just watched was sent to the Chinese Customs Department. Now with that said, you can only continue doing business in this city if we provide you with the products, or shop just closed permanently!"

Cheng did as advised and sat across the table from Jim. Both men poured themselves tea and sipped from their cups, all while staring directly into each other's eyes. "So, who are you and what makes you think you can handle the size of my business?"

"I wouldn't be sitting here wasting either of our time if I couldn't! As a sign of good faith, I believe this might help you to understand the range of our business capabilities," Jim said and slid Cheng a folder containing several documents.

Mr. Lo looked at the pictures and documents inside the folder, which were of a trusted employee. "How did you get this information?"

"Your cousin Dong Si Lang has been compromised. The local police know that he cannot return to China, so they used this to pressure him into working for them," Jim exclaimed.

"I can't believe; my own fucking relative! Who are you," enquired Cheng?

"My name again is Jim Bartello and who I represent is no concern of yours! Secondly, I'm sorry about your mother; but in our business collateral damage is to be expected! And you would not want the same thing to happen to Kim or any of your other kids, now would you?... It's quite simple Mr. Lo, you are going to secretly start buying from us from now on! My number can be found on the card inside the folder; and I expect to hear from you pretty soon Mr. Lo! You have a fine day," Jim exclaimed before getting up and leaving the restaurant!

***

The Japanese had a decades old Heroine and Opium arrangement with the Rough Riders that went unmanaged since the death of Martain Lafleur. The terms of the deal allowed the Japanese to sell their products in Quebec's illegal drug market, at a pre-negotiated continuous rate. The funds were paid directly into one of the Secret Cult's many private offshore accounts, which were checked once every five years by a private accountant. Due to the death of Martain Lafleur the bosses in Japan considered their deal with the bikers void and stopped issuing payments to the overseas account. One of the people Jim was instructed to speak with was Jingsu Sakahaushi, who had recently been appointed the Montreal representative for the Japanese Mob.

Jingsu Sakahaushi was a large sized man at six feet three inches, four hundred and fifty-five pounds. Strangers would often mistake him for a Sumo Wrestler, but those who knew him knew that he was nobody to fuck with. Mr. Sakahaushi was born and raised in Japan and spent the first twenty-four years of his life there, until a job opportunity caused him to relocate to Canada. His father ran one of the main gangs in Japan and had two sons before Jingsu, therefore taking the old man's position would not be possible so he requested the Montreal position when the incumbent headman died. Throughout his childhood years Jingsu admired his father and wanted to be just like him, so with the blessings of his entire family he moved.

Jim Bartello brought along one sole helper the first time he saw Jingsu at the park down the street from his house, walking his pet bulldog with his bodyguard. At the sight of Jingsu's massive body frame, Jim reconsidered his approach and drove away, knowing he would need much more help to subdue the huge Japanese. Jingsu owned a traditional Japanese restaurant where he often spent his evenings, prior to completing his nights at his after-hour whore/gambling house. The private event was held in the basement of a popular downtown nightclub called Discotheque Tokyo, where only certain patrons were allowed entry. Most of the club attendants were Orientals nevertheless to avoid being recognized and foiling their plans, Jim sent one of his companions to keep an eye on Jingsu once he entered his nightclub. The Japanese boss travelled by personal chauffeur and was always with Joe his bodyguard, who was as massive as he was.

Inside the club was lit with party enthusiasts dancing, drinking and doing all sorts of cosmetic drugs openly. To enter the gambling and whore house visitors to the nightclub would have to walk downstairs to the toilets on the level beneath the dancefloors and pay a fifty-dollar entry fee to the guards. Unlike the discotheque inside the secret establishment was an absolute marvel, with half naked ladies walking around servicing their clients, while they gambled at games from slot machines to card. Jim's spy took a seat at a Blackjack table, from which he could watch the door to Jingsu's main office. The Japanese Boss stayed at his gambling house until 6:00 AM, when the door to his office opened and he again materialized. That night was Jingsu's birthday and he was in a celebrative mood, therefore the mistress who handled the whores brought and presented him with two newly imported Japanese females prior to his departure.

Jim and his associates followed Jingsu back to his home on Phillips Avenue in Senneville, on the western coast of Montreal, where the Japanese boss dismounted his limousine with both females and brought them inside, following which his chauffeur drove away with his bodyguard. The team of four bikers gave their target ten minutes to settle in and get comfortable, before they began making their way towards the house. Jingsu lived on a quiet street in an old suburb just meters from the River of Two Mountains, where once the river froze fishermen brought their huts onto the ice and fished. There were no cars or neighbors going about the dead-end road, so the bikers walked decisively to a side entrance at the Japanese's residence. Jim Bartello used his lock picking tools to open the door and entered the house, where they could hear Jingsu advising the young ladies what to do. The floors throughout the house were done either with tiles or wood, which allowed the bikers to sneak close to the room without being detected.

"I just told you how I want my balls licked, now do it properly you whores," threatened Jingsu, who then slapped both young ladies on top of their heads!

Jim snuck a peek through the door and saw their target laying back on his bed while the ladies licked on his genitals. There was a handgun on the night table to the left of the bed, but Jim doubted that Jingsu would be stupid enough to reach for it. With his 360 Ruger Handgun at hand Jim walked into the room with his companions behind him and stood at the foot of the bed. When the intruders walked into the room Jingsu passionately had his eyes closed, until one of the ladies noticed them and sighed out-loud. The Japanese boss was furious at the sight of the intruders and shoved the females aside, as he turned away from his weapon on the opposite nightstand and exited the bed to his right. Both females were unsure if they would be killed and held tightly onto each other, while Jingsu picked up his rob and slowly put it on.

"What do you men want inside my home," Jingsu demanded?

"According to my bosses, you fellows have not been paying your bill, so I'm here to collect what's owed with interest," Jim stated!

"You obviously have the wrong house," Jingsu warned!

"Nope, I'm in the right place. All we need you to do is contact your people back in Japan, so we can clear this whole matter up," Jim instructed!

"My people in Japan don't talk to peasants," Jingsu argued.

"Is that so? Then if I carve you up like a turkey, do you think they'll listen to me then," Jim asked?

Jim shoved his 360 Ruger hand pistol into his waist and walked over to a collection of exquisitely designed Japanese swords that were mounted on the wall. As he removed a sword and twirled it in his hand, Jingsu who already felt threatened charged at his companions without any fare warnings. To ensure he had enough muscle to counter the Japanese beast, Jim brought three physically muscular bikers who all clashed with the psychotic Japanese. Jingsu punched the first biker in the chest with such force that it lifted the dude off the ground and sent him crashing against the wall. The Japanese martial arts expert grabbed the second biker who was bigger than he was with one hand around the neck, picked him up off the floor and choke slammed him. With their target down to one knee, the third biker jumped on Jingsu's back and tried to render him unconscious with a choke hold. The effect of the maneuver was not being felt and as Jingsu started rising to his feet, Jim rushed in and kicked him in his private area, which sent him crashing to the ground in pain. All three muscular bikers then regrouped and confined the Japanese, before they proceeded with the business for which they came.

An international call was then made to Tokyo, Japan, where the thirteen hours time difference made it much later in the evening. The video phone call was placed to a Mr. Chinzu Zingawju, who was the business correspondent with whom Jingsu dealt in Japan.

"Good day to you, Young Master," Chinzu greeted, at which he saw Jingsu forcibly being held with his head exposed for decapitation across a stool, while Jim held the sword aloft!

"You have ten minutes to gather all the main family heads and call back, or Jingsu here dies," Jim warned!

"Hai, I will at once," Chinzu answered, before the line went dead!

Within eight minutes the phone rang with all the family heads required for key decisions. Jingsu's father was one of the men participating in the joint discussion, therein the sight of someone holding a sword to his son's neck was way more taxing for him.

"What is the meaning of this insolence," Mr. Sakahaushi Senior demanded?

"You gentlemen have not been paying your Quebec bill, and I have been authorized to collect all past due amounts with a five percent interests! It seems as if you Japanese forgot what will happen if our custom agents start looking in the right places," Jim declared!?

"Why is there interest being added," Mr. Sakahaushi Senior asked?

"Inflation, plus the disrespect," Jim lamented, as he lifted the sword and prepared to decapitate Jingsu's head! "You gentlemen have ten, nine, eight, seven, six, five, four, three!"

"Enough, whatever is owed will be payed within the hour; and you may advise your employers that everything will return as it was," Sakahaushi Senior insisted!

"Thank you, gentlemen it was a pleasure doing business," Jim said, as they released Jingsu and left the premises!

Jingsu was embarrassed and felt he had disgraced his family and thus bowed his head to the floor while pleading for forgiveness.

Part 14

Kane observed that the Indians of Shamattawa were peace abiding people unlike some renegades in other indigenous tribes across Canada, therefore whatever actions he took had to be taken with consideration of the ramifications that could follow. Like many other native tribes, the people of Shamattawa had a love hate relationship with their local police force and governing leaders, whom they believed had done very little to stop the injustices done against their people. First Nations' Officers Jack Quiere and Rvyan Hartwell were at the top of the hatred list, for their involvements in the persecution of locals who had nowhere else to turn. Numerous complaints to exterior government agencies had resolved nothing for the people of Shamattawa, who continued to disappear without trace as if captured by aliens. For those whose bodies were found, natives experienced the agonizing reality of those murders going uninvestigated and unsolved.

Eshanwai sat with Kane inside his home and told him everything he knew about the two most corrupt cops working on the reservation. There was something unsettling about the officers that none of the Indians knew, but the fact that Jack Quiere a decorated thirty-two-year veteran had to meet with a psychiatrist twice monthly raised added concerns. Most of the local Indians also knew that Officer Quiere lived a double life, wherein he had two homes, a wife with a cat and a sweetheart with two dogs. Jack and his with Emily had raised four remarkable children none of which still lived at home, but they remained quite close. Even though Eshanwai and many others knew of the adulterous husband's extra marital affair, nobody ever disclosed the information to his wife regardless of their hatred towards him. There were concerns over where the officer got the money to pay for both homes on a regular police salary, but everybody who ever dared to challenge certain officers turned up dead or missing.

Officer Jack Quiere was a half breed born on the Shamattawa Reservation to a female who had moved away for school and returned for the final five months of her pregnancy. His mother Jhunna left him to work in Alberta and was raped and killed one year later, thus he spent the next four years living with his grandparents until his Caucasian father showed up with signed court papers that claimed him. His father Samuel was a Frenchman who raised him in Saskatoon, Saskatchewan, where he later trained to become a police officer. Due to his half native heritage, Jack got the opportunity to transfer to the Shamattawa Reservation and serve his mother's people, therefore as a local product the people were initially excited to have him join their police force. While the Shamattawa people felt proud of him, Officer Quiere detested his native heritage and his mother, whom his father led him to believe was a street working prostitute.

Kane did a bit more investigating and uncovered that the name of the psychiatrist Officer Quiere had been seeing for over six years was Natnah Fawfakuk. The last name sounded familial to Kane, who later recalled how he came about knowing it and ran outside to his van. The Mohawk Indian searched inside his glove compartment for the female's number whose cat he held hostage in the weirdest standoff he had ever been in. Nancy Fawfakuk was at the service station working and became excited to hear Kane's voice, whom she never expected to ever hear from him again. The Bad Boy Indian asked Nancy to arrange a private meeting between himself and her sister Natnah, and without any fears or concerns the female responded yes. Within an hour Nancy phoned back Kane with a location, date and time to meet with her sister, who requested that their meeting take place in a very secluded place.

The following night at 11:00 PM Eshanwai and Kane met with Natnah at the bottom of Main Street close to the pier at Echoing River's edge. Natnah arrived in her Toyota Rav 4 mini SUV and parked just off the side of the road where most fishermen seldom left their vehicles. The men she went to meet with had already arrived on two snowmobiles and rushed her aboard, before they rode out onto the frozen river in the dark of night. They rode their snowmobiles onto the frozen Echoing River and stopped half way across, where they unpacked beer, stools, a spacer heater, assembled a small tent, cut open a hole in the ice, pulled out fishing poles and cast their lines into the water.

Neither Kane nor Eshanwai were remotely worried about the place they chose to conduct the meeting, but Natnah was convinced the police could still eavesdrop on their conversation. Natnah was terrified beyond her control and had to be reassured they were at a location that was believed to be safe, because officers only went on frozen rivers to conduct rescues. With her associates relaxed and calmly fishing Natnah eventually calmed down, then began disclosing whatever information she had about Officer Jack Quiere. Before she uttered a word the thought of what she knew brought tears to the female's eyes, but she knew her story had to be told.

"Nothing I say to you gentlemen must never come back to haunt me, or else I will lose my license and my practice; and possibly even my life! The only reason I'm telling you this is because my little sister seems to believe that you are the only person who can do something about this! God knows for years I've been listening to this officer's new and old stories of murder and abduction; but am obligated not to disclose these secrets by profession. I'm so scared that they will do the same to me; but one day if only to silence me, they will kill me like the others. About seven years ago Officer Jack Quiere suffered a nervous breakdown due of the stress of his work. He was placed on medical leave and ordered to start seeing a psychiatrist if he was to return to the force... The thing is both he and his partner and several others in our police force have been receiving healthy payouts from people in our medical field to provide the bodies of healthy indigenous people. To people of this world organ transplant has only been known for a few years, when in fact the practice has been around much longer than that. In 1950 when it was believed that the first kidney transplant took place in the Little Company of Mary Hospital, Dr. Lawler the surgeon who directed the procedure knew that a few other doctors were far more advanced than they were, and one of these doctors was a Dr. France Liechtenstein who defected to Canada from Germany." Natnah took a cigarette from her pack and lit it, then unzipped her jacket zipper halfway down and drank some beer.

"When Dr. Liechtenstein came to Canada nobody would fund his projects until this rich Canadian Ben Hargrove got diagnosed with a heart problem and needed a new heart. Nobody thought that it would be possible and then again where were they to get a strong and healthy heart; and so, began the harvesting of our native people for our organs. They also preyed on black people, but white racist motherfuckers would refuse to have any colored organs inside them; and turn to the next best choice which are natives. Everything I have said to you was told to me by Officer Quiere, who has been one of these collectors who found out which youngsters amongst us best match those seeking donors, then abduct and kill them. Throughout the years they have kidnapped many first nation people, most of which were never found, and even those found dead had organs removed, but without any form of autopsy those things will never be proven!"

Neither Kane nor Eshanwai asked any questions or added any comments following the shocking story. They sat and fished thereafter for another forty minutes, with tension so thick one could slice it with a knife. Eshanwai was not a man of violence, yet even he felt angered by the actions of those assigned to safeguard and protect them. They later brought Natnah back to her vehicle and made sure there was nobody around to see them together before dropping her off.

**

Officer Quiere made his wife Emily believed that on Saturdays and Wednesdays he went out target shooting and tactical training with other officers, when in fact he spent those days with his side-chick at his second house. To avoid being seen Jack would use his remote to drive directly into the two-car garage and often remained indoors, but should they go out he would take her car. His sweetheart Shakara knew of his family life and graciously accepted the terms of their relationship, though not even his children knew of his adulterous second life. As long as Jack paid the bills and provided whatever his sweetheart desired, Shakara kept their relationship a secret and protected the crooked officer.

The following Saturday morning after Jack kissed his loving wife goodbye and drove away, he came across a beautiful native female named Linnora, who appeared to be experiencing car trouble approximately three miles away. Jack had been in several encounters with Linnora who was Chief Shomittaroua's eldest daughter, and worked for the Indian's Health & Welfare Services, which would often clash with police over the ill-treatment of natives. The female's vehicle was parked along a lonely stretch of roadway that only led to the officer's residential area. Officer Quiere was driving his personal Dodge Ram 4x4 instead of his police cruiser, therefore as a precaution he threw on his four-way flashers. It appeared as if the female was alone, so Jack left his service firearm on the passenger's seat and went to assist the stranded motorist.

As the officer approached the car from the rear the driver stepped away from the engine compartment with a huge Remington 44 Magnum handgun pointed at him. Jack began backing away from the female when her car truck flew open and Kane popped out with his Glock 22 at hand. The officer immediately threw both hands into the air to surrender and began instructing his antagonists to remember that "he was a lawman". Kane grabbed Jack by the shirt collar and held his weapon to the back of his head, while the female searched him to ensure he was not armed. The Mohawk then dragged the officer back to the rear of the car, where he shoved him into the truck and locked it. The female accomplice ran and jumped in the officer's 4x4 truck and drove off ahead of Kane, who still needed directions to get around.

Officer Quiere was taken to a small cottage deep in the woods, where they stripped him naked and tied him to an old armless chair with both hands underneath the seat, and his legs stretched across onto another chair. There was a second piece of rope used to secure his legs to the chair, but his captors found no reason to bind his mouth and allowed him to talk, scream or whatever he chose to. As nervous as Jack was, he tried to remain calm and reason with his abductors, who left him for the first few minutes after securing him to both chairs. Kane and Linnora went back to her vehicle to collect several items and engaged in a small conversation, wherein the Indian bad-boy offered his accomplice the opportunity to reconsider proceeding to the next stage. When Linnora initially overheard Kane's suicidal plans being recited to her father, she chose to participate without any fear of retaliation, thus it was somewhat obvious that she had a personal vendetta to settle with the officer. After declining the offer both abductors returned to the cottage, with items such as a baseball bat, a portable hand torch, a pair of needle-nose pliers, a tape recorder and a bird feather.

"I'm sure you realize that it will be hours before you are even considered missing; seeing your girlfriend will only assume that you stayed home today, and your wife trusting you are wherever you claimed to be, won't start getting worried until at lease an hour passed your regular arrival time! By that time, you might be buried so deep they won't be abled to find you, like the hundreds of natives killed and placed in unmarked graves across these lands," Kane threatened!

"What the hell are you people going to do with that stuff? Believe me they will never let either of you out of prison when they catch you, so I advise you to let me go before this gets pass the point of no return! Linnora whatever you and your friend think that I did is not true, so cut me loose," Officer Quiere yelled!

"What we want to know is how much more of your people are you going to torcher and kill for the white man? You are going to tell us what happened to my friend Ojasuk's sister and why you killed him?" Kane instructed?

"I am an officer of the law, I protect and serve the people of this community and it is my duty to maintain law and order! Ojasuk's sister like much of these young girls and boys run away from the reservation, Linnora you know this," Officer Quiere stated!

"I was there that night you know; June twenty first many moons pass. That night when you and your friend arrested Moyra for public intoxication, before she was found five days later murdered and raped. Many elders have spoken of the tragedy we keep living, but I never believed it until that day they found my friend's body. When we saw your cars coming that night, to avoid us both getting taken away Moyra told me to hide and stood right there unafraid. I watched you lie through your teeth on the news that you released her and had no idea what happened to her after that, but I know you fuckers raped and killed Moyra," Linnora exclaimed!

"Now calm down Linnora, whatever you may think happened never did! We got an emergency call a few miles down the road and kicked her out of the cruiser! Believe me Linnora, we searched days for that girl and I still can't wait to find the person who did that to her," Officer Quiere argued!

"Don't worry Officer Quiere, we found the person. Are you ticklish Officer Quiere," Linnora asked?

"What the fuck are you talking about? Get away from me! You just need to get your friend here to understand there is nothing bad happening around here," Officer Quiere declared!

Linnora walked over and used the bird feather to tickle the officer's foot bottom like they were playing a kids' game. Jack began laughing uncontrollably while repeating that "he had done nothing wrong", however the female made him laugh until tears began running from his eyes. Kane stood back and watched until he had heard enough, at which he walked over with the baseball bat and clobbered Jack across his stomach. The officer's mouth and eyes flew wide open as he blew mucus all over himself, then unexpectedly expunged a loud fort. It was as if Officer Quiere deflated once he received the blow then fought to catch his breath.

The Mohawk Indian paused and waited for the blow to simmer, before he pounded Jack several more times across the chest, stomach and thighs. With every blow Officer Quiere yelled out in distress, before Kane passed the bat to his female counterpart for her to release some of her anxiety. The abductors beat their captive until he was black and blue, wherein he couldn't even stand due to the massive swelling on both feet. The thrashing that Officer Quiere received softened him up enough, that when Linnora retrieved the pliers and clamped onto his right toenail, he was none-hesitant to corporate. Kane turned on the tape recorder and began recording their examination.

"Do you have anything to tell us about these missing native women and the killing of our young warriors," Kane asked?

Officer Quiere spoke slowly due to the internal wounds received. "Some members of our government believed that if we exterminate the young or kill their incentives to want to survive, then your people will fail to exist in the future. There is an experimental project known as the Cana-Study Embargo, which was created by physically depleted rich white people who wanted to lengthen their life expectancy. Because of this medically approved experiment, doctors have since needed human Ginny pigs to work on and where best to acquire subjects than on these poor reservations!? Through this experiment doctors have gained the ability to use these subjects as organ donors and pay generously for young healthy organs."

"Where is your sense of Indian pride? Why do you help these fucking people," Kane questioned?

"Indian pride? My mother was a whore who died at the hands of some pervert paying for sex, and it was my white father who rescued me from this shithole, so don't talk to me about Indian pride! That shit doesn't exist," Officer Quiere boasted!

"That's a lie, your mother was killed by a drunk driver after she finished her second job and was walking home, with toys she had bought for you at some toy store," Linnora stated.

At that point Linnora had heard enough and lost her temper, and thereby tore out the officer's toenail. Jack screamed in immense pain and kicked like a mule as the female who had made him laugh like never before, made him bawl in pain like never before. Kane held him steady while the operation was being conducted, after finally understanding why Linnora chose to help him abduct Officer Quiere. The Rude-boy Indian thought that his accomplice would only remove the single toenail, but she angrily removed each nail from his ten toes. By the time she started ripping out the third toenail Jack fell unconscious under the duress and felt assured that they would certainly kill him.

Part 15

Senior Manuel Lagarza and his worker Ricardo exited his chauffeured limousine convoy and walked towards a small house that was surrounded with trees and thick vegetation. Manuel was elegantly dressed as customary in a colorful Versace shirt and a white linen pants, while his guards including Ricardo all wore their basic soldier's uniform. As they walked towards the structure, six heavily armed guards carrying automatic rifles circled them and constantly looked around to ensure their boss' safety.

"I don't give a shit why this guy killed Damian! The fact is Damian was going to kill my adversary and unknowingly pay for the crime once we told the local police about him," Manuel said.

"Don't forget what Damian did to that lovely senorita Stephanie before leaving Columbia. I know a lot of wicked men, fuck, I am one of the worst; but if anybody ever hurt my bambinos, I would take my machete and chop them up like stakes; and feed them to my dogs," Ricardo stated!

Manuel paused for a few seconds and reminisced on that one magical time he had coitus with Stephanie inside his vault, at which a slight smirk appeared on his face. "Damian was already paid to do the job."

"They call this guy Killa; and fuck what you heard about him hunting Damian and his friends, we saw him in action against some assassins who tried to kill him! This is the man you want doing the job," Ricardo exclaimed!

"Ricardo, why else do you think I brought him here? If I wanted him dead, I would have told you to do it in Jamaica," Manuel remarked!

As they drew closer to the small house, they could hear someone inside singing loudly. "That's all I ever had… Redemption songs, these songs of freedom, songs of freedom!"

They entered the small structure and left the armed guards protecting their surroundings. The place was used to store Plant Fertilizer, seeds and other gardening equipment and was miles away from any form of civilization, therefore Kadeem was allowed to roam about the interior freely. When the Jamaican Rude Boy got captured, he had a sizable plastic bags containing Marijuana inside his pocket, thus while waiting he rolled himself a joint and enjoyed himself. There were two of Manuel's personal soldiers standing inside the door, none of whom spoke English nevertheless the Rasta-man had them both intoxicated off his supply. Even though Kadeem had no idea where he was, the locals' Spanish, the hot climate and the sounds of jungle habitation around him, assured him that he was not back in Canada. The instant Manuel entered the structure both guards stood at attention and stopped integrating with the prisoner, who needed no introduction to realize that the well-dressed individual was their boss.

"Have a seat for me Mr. Kite. Do you know where you are," Manuel asked, as Kadeem followed the instructions given and sat on the only chair available?

"Your guard over there said Columbia," Kadeem answered.

"And did he mention who I was," Manuel enquired?

"No, his English wasn't as good as yours," Kadeem said.

"Do you speak Espanola Mister Kite," Manuel questioned?

"Not at all," lied Kadeem.

"The fact is you are here because you killed your old friend Damian; and Damian was employed by me to do a job. So now you have inherited that task," Manuel explained!

"You just kidnapped me from Jamaica, so I'm sure you have a few capable people around here to do whatever you want," Kadeem insinuated.

Informer 3

"You doing this job is the only thing keeping you alive right now, so unless you agree to take your friend's place you really are of no use to me," Manuel took Ricardo's side pistol from its holster and aimed it at Kadeem! "I paid handsomely for this job, and if you don't accept, I'll just get someone else to do it, but you have three seconds to decide!"

"What you want done," Kadeem questioned?

"The killing of the Columbian Presidential Candidate in Montreal, during his visit there in a few weeks," Manuel exclaimed.

"That is all you want, just another dead body?!... I will deal with that for you, but after it is done consider us even," Kadeem decreed, to which Manuel nodded his head in agreement!

"You made the right choice! Now you can come with us; tomorrow I arrange everything you need to get back into Canada," Manuel explained!

The less than hospitable treatment changed for Kadeem from that moment on, when Manuel brought him back to his estate where he received the royalty treatment. Kadeem was given a room and soaked in a long hot bath, but thereafter exited the bathroom to several pieces of new clothing on his bed. Both he and Manuel were somewhat similar in body frame, therefore his host estimated his size and sent him several pieces of boxer shorts, pants, shirts, socks and slippers, in addition to personal hygienic items. Manuel even sent his guest a carryon bag and a larger suitcase to transport his belongings to Canada. The Columbian Drug Lord's house was the largest residence that the Jamaican had ever visited, however like most guests he was absolutely captivated by the range of wild animals in Manuel's personal zoo. Even though most of the Columbians spoke English, Kadeem observed that whenever they were around him and didn't want him to understand they would revert to their native language, thus he continued acting as if he didn't comprehend Spanish although he comprehension was very little. That night Manuel had two business partners over for drinks, and as Kadeem walked pass them enjoying the scenic view while smoking his Marijuana Joint, he overheard their conversation.

"So, this is the guy who is to replace the first man you paid that five million," asked Senior Diaz in Spanish?

"Yes, that is him," Manuel said!

"We all have everything invested in this! Are you sure you will make it so none of this comes back on us," Senior Baracha stated?

"I am absolutely sure my friends! This fool has no idea what he is heading into," joked Manuel, as they drank from their liquor glasses and laughed!

Kadeem stood there looking down at the valley and pretended as if nothing they said bothered him, knowing they were looking for him to be the assassin as well as their escape goat. After another two minutes of cringing his teeth and tightening his fists, the Jamaican politely looked over at the drug lords and said, "You guys have a good night!"

The next day Manuel brought Kadeem into town, where once the little children saw the drug lord's convoy passing, they ran alongside his limousine cheering his name. Ricardo was seated beside Kadeem across from Manuel, and as the Recruited Assassin looked through the window at the shoeless children he reminisced on his own childhood. Kadeem pretended as if he was fascinated by Manuel's popularity and began complimenting him to gain his confidence. Instead of recognizing the trickery Manuel revelled in the praise, as he was convinced that without his drug empire the locals would have no employment and stave. To appease his captor the Jamaican then proceeded to discuss the assassination at length and enquired where would Manuel prefer the Presidential Candidate getting shot, to which he was advised to "just scatter his blood across the pavement"!

Manuel gained the impression that Kadeem had become more engaged and would fulfill his obligations, and thus discretely responded to each question asked. The Drug Lord brought his abducted guest to a photo gallery where the photographer took passport pictures of Kadeem, after which they visited a lawyer's office down the street and gave him the pictures. By the time they reached the lawyer's office both men were in a friendly heated quarrel over who they believed was the best soccer player on the pitch today. With his companions more at eased around him Kadeem begged Manuel to borrow his phone to place a call and inform his family members in Jamaica that he was ok? Once Manuel became focused on his dealings with the lawyer, Kadeem pretended he was doing otherwise and took a picture of his companions inside the room, mailed it to his personal email, erased the picture and dialed Aunty P's phone number.

After leaving the lawyer's office Senior Lagarza telephoned a travel agent and booked a late morning flight for Kadeem and two of his employees the following day. That evening was Kadeem's most enjoyable time in Columbia, wherein Manuel hosted a pool party with almost fifty ladies, three of his male friends who flew in earlier that day from Spain and Kadeem. It became a memorable night that included alcohol, drugs, pills, marijuana, dancing and sex, thus when Kadeem got awakened by a maid with two naked females on either side of his bed, he wished he could relive the last evening. The Jamaican Rude Boy thought that Manuel was being rather presumptuous about receiving the travelling documents in advance of the early flight, however there was a female immigration officer awaiting him downstairs with his valid Columbian Passport. Before the immigration officer departed, she sat Kadeem down and made him sign a Customs Declaration Form that was already filled in, then gave him specific instructions on what to do when going through both airports.

With everything arranged Kadeem, Ricardo and Marquez were transported on Manuel's helicopter to Rafael Nunez International Airport, where they individually checked onto the same flight to Montreal, Canada. Even though Manuel felt confident that his assassination plot would come to fruition, to ensure there were no incidents on the plane he positioned his guards ahead of and behind their Jamaican companion. Kadeem passed through both Rafael Nunez International Airport's checkpoint and Pierre Elliot Trudeau International Airport's Immigration and Naturalization Services, by simply presenting his travel documents to whomsoever Manuel's I.N.S contact advised him to. Neither the airport official nor the immigration officer asked any questions of the only peculiar passenger on the flight, whose identity was not identical to the information inside his passport. The male I.N.S employee who saw Kadeem in Montreal stamped his passport and welcomed him to Canada.

Ricardo, Marquez, and Kadeem reunited at the luggage carrousel, where they collected their belongings and chartered a taxi to bring them downtown together. Manuel had also arranged adequate lodging at a three-bedroom condo on Rue de Bullion; and briefly after settling in Marquez and Kadeem left again to pick up a rented Cube Van from Thrifty Car Rentals. Once they got the vehicle Kadeem made a pitstop by a marijuana vendor on Metcalf Street where he bought a half ounce of Purple Cush Hydroponic, before they visited a grocery store to purchase food and alcohol for the condo.

At 10:40 PM that evening a Columbian male came to the door with his ten-year old daughter and eleven-year-old son. The visitors introduced themselves as Pedro, Marcus and Silvia and were allowed entry by Ricardo. Kadeem and his roommates had been drinking, therefore there were Corona Beer bottles, Hennessy Liquor and glasses across the kitchen isle. Pedro brought a huge Duffle Bag that he sat down on the floor beside the center table inside the living room and opened it. The bag was filled with an array of firearms, bullets and assault knives, nevertheless Kadeem was more fascinated with the children who assisted their father with the display. Kadeem initially thought that the men were all old friends and dismissed their choice to speak Spanish, when in reality they were conducting a gun transaction paid for by Manuel and didn't want him knowing the details. Ricardo and Marquez inspected the merchandise and selected a pair of 9mm handguns, two AR-15 Assault Rifles and a Barrett Model 99 Sniper Rifle with enough bullets to slaughter a herd of buffalo. Before the visitors left Pedro removed a specially hidden envelope from his weapons' bag, that contained the Presidential Candidate's itinerary while in Montreal and gave it to Marquez.

Marijuana was not a drug the Columbians smoked often, but the Rastafarian had them puffing like amateurs, wherein they coughed with each inhale and found everything on the television hilarious. Even though the Columbians were now armed the Jamaican Rude Boy had numerous opportunities where he could have confiscated a weapon and kill them both, however they found him once therefore he had to play this through. Kadeem waited a few minutes after the weapons dealer left to begin teasing his companions with visions of personal wealth.

"If anybody told me that your boss gave Damian all those millions to kill this politician guy; believe me I would have robbed that motherfucker before I killed him," Kadeem lamented!

"It could not be too much money? We all know the boss only spend money on his bitches," Ricardo joked!

"Five million U.S dollars… Senior Lagarza is not the type of man who gives away money like that without getting something in return," Marquez responded!

"But he was paying for the assassination, Marquez," Ricardo argued!

"The boss has people working for him almost everywhere. Why would he pay so much when people who owe him are willing to do this for free?" Marquez reasoned.

"Well I'm sure Damian didn't bring the money to his grave with him, so I'm sure if I snoop around, I can find it," Kadeem insinuated!

"Five million dollars, wow," Ricardo whispered!

"That's US dollars, at least one point six million each." Kadeem added.

"Tomorrow I will call Senior Lagarza's old accountant Guiermo and ask him about the money. Even so we must stay focus, because we here to do very important work for the boss; but I think we can find time to look," Marquez agreed!

The first-person they went to see the following morning was Tank at the Bordeaux Correctional Institution. The Columbians had to wait in the van while Kadeem entered the facility and kept their eyes on the front gate to ensure that he did not slip out undetected. Although Tank had been locked up for almost two years, Kadeem knew that his knowledge of the streets was thorough and visited him for valuable information. While inside the waiting area Kadeem saw a newspapers front cover that read, 'Third Prosecutor Killed in Nicholas Henry Case', which he picked up and read. Both Tank and he were allowed a booth visit, where they spoke on telephones behind a glass to avoid any possible transfer of narcotics. Tank was elated to see his friend and first placed his fist against the glass before sitting, to properly greet his comrade at arms with a fist-bump.

"How you do mi general," Tank declared?

"Not too good right now my friend; under pressure to be back in this furnace because of King Kev's cousin's deal with some Spanish Cartel," Kadeem stated.

"OK, because I know you would be a mad man to freely come back to this country right now with all these white dogs starving to get a bite off you especially! If I'm not mistaken them bikers have some reward out for anybody who put you beneath earth, so don't trust a sole," Tank warned.

"Only thing any boy try bite go get is gunshot! How you stay in here," Kadeem enquired?

"Come on man, you know we run anywhere we go! But I go need for you to rescue the payment that same fool collected? Give me a digit where I can make someone text you some information," Tank boasted?

"Down by my place on the rock, remember the three girls we did meet at four o'clock by the seven eleven, two of them want to fuck you for nothing," Kadeem responded and covertly transferred a Jamaican telephone number!

Tank nodded his head to signify that he understood and said, "when that thing went down over on the other side of the train tracks, four of them people with D were the...," The prisoner used his right Index Finger to simulate someone pulling a gun trigger. "Guys who him get to do the job that you inherit. Luckily for you one of them still above ground, a youth name Delvin from Trinidad. He opened some store over in Saint-Laurent with his cut! I heard he is on Halpern Street somewhere." With a slight twist of his body to shield his hands from the camera, Tank then used numeric signals to transfer the address.

"So, who running the streets right now," Kadeem enquired?

"This youth name Lass, you probably don't know him still! Damian used to sell to him and his people from Saint-Laurent," Tank declared!

"How much longer before these people free you up," Kadeem enquired?

"In about eleven months I should be back on the road," Tank said.

"What's this I'm reading about Uncle Kev," Kadeem asked?

"That pussy-hole is a traitor! How you go work for the same people them who want to put you in a pine box? I did hear how him give you up to them white boys after all the shit we done together! Is straight bullet that traitor must get," Tank recited!

"I feel you on that! Him even send few mercenaries to lick off my head...," Kadeem exclaimed.

"Ha-ha-ha-ha-ha," laughed Tank! "I heard how you made some donkey cod dudes nearly kill some white assassin bitch with fuck!"

"Huh, it a go take much more than some pussy to get me out! Keep up your head till you touch road and I'll make sure your canteen gets maxed out! Until we link again, bless," Kadeem promised, before they again fist-bumped against the glass and ended their visit.

"One love general," Tank remarked!

Kadeem had no idea if Ricardo and Marquez were co-conspirators to their boss' plan, but he needed to convince them that they could return home should they chose to with undisclosed wealth. It was obvious that both Columbians got sent to keep an eye on him and possibly exterminate him after the assassination, moreover he knew that he was expected to be sacrificed and framed as the killer to avoid implicating Manuel Lagarza and the members of his drug cartel.

While leaving the facility a prison orderly named Rene Wamblay, who was mopping the floor inside the officer's working station saw Kadeem and could not believe his eyes. The orderly was a Rough Rider affiliate serving an eighteen months sentence for domestic assault and resisting arrest causing officers bodily harm. Visitors to the prison would have to collect their personal items upon departure and as Kadeem received his belongings the attending officer asked, "if the rented Thrifty van was his", before advised him not to park where he did should he return in the future. Rene pretended as if he was only doing his job and mopped close enough to the officer to sneak a look at the license number written in the log book. The instant Rene returned to his range while everyone else was still locked down, he used his orderly privileges to telephone his brother Xavier Wamblay, whom he told about the Rough Riders' most sought-after man.

The Jamaican returned to the van oblivious to the fact that he had been spotted and sat for a quick chat before proceeding. Ricardo who had lived a very impoverished life despite being in the employment of one of the richest men in Columbia, was quick to enquire what Kadeem uncovered during his visit.

"What, what, what did your friend say?"

"I think I know where to find one of the assassins Damian hired to kill this Presidential Candidate," Kadeem exclaimed.

"What this guy has to do with the money," Ricardo asked?

"This guy might possibly know where Damian hid that money," Kadeem answered.

"OK then my friend let's go," Ricardo stated!

Montreal was a far cry from the Columbian Jungle and the streets looked like an endless maze to the foreign visitors, therefore, Kadeem was forced to drive wherever they went. The address given by Tank was only twenty minutes away from the prison, but as they went along Kadeem could see the increased anxiety growing inside his companions. The man they went to see had opened a weave and hair extensions store, which was at a fabulous location and had a steady stream of customers. Marquez accompanied Kadeem into the store and left Ricardo with the vehicle behind the facility, to watch for any suspicious black males attempting to escape unnoticed. Both men went directly to the cash register and asked the cashier for the owner, who was helping customers find whatever they sought. The attentively engaged female cashier pointed to a gentleman who was attending to a customer in isle number two.

The business owner who had his back turned, spun around and saw Kadeem's face and panicked, with the assumption that the man who had critically injured returned to finish the job. Delvin turned to race for the rear exit, when he tripped over his customer's merchandise basket and fell to the floor. Marquez and Kadeem rushed over and helped him up by both hands, at which the Jamaican whispered in Delvin's ear. "These are the people whose money opened this store; now you either gonna fulfill your obligations or them go burn this bombo-clatt to the ground and still kill you and your whole fucking family!"

Delvin's legs wobbled beneath him and he was forced to grab hold of both men for support, then immediately began apologising to everyone for his irrational behavior and asked another employee to finish attending to his client while he dealt with the visitors. The three men entered Delvin's office following which he closed the door and blinds to ensure that they could not be seen or heard. The Trinidadian thereafter felt quite intimidated, as he sat amongst the Columbian and Jamaican and could barely look in either man's direction, thus he stared more at their shoes throughout the conversation than anywhere else.

Throughout that day Kadeem tried to gain the Columbians' trust, but it was obvious that they were still a bit skeptical about him. That night at the condo Kadeem prepared his own meal and was eating in front of the television with Ricardo, while Marquez chatted on his cellular with his wife back home. They had a huge window at the front of their condo, which was located on the second floor of a three-story building. While conversing with his wife Marquez walked over to the window and looked down at the street below, where people walked by up and down the sidewalk.

"This place is so different; the people are so nice! It is like there is no crime, but the only problem is outside is freezing cold! I miss back home but I want you and the children to come and visit Canada. Maybe even move here if I can make some extra money. Live a normal life finally." Marquez said in Spanish as he watched a car park below, of which five suspicious men exited and cautiously looked around before placing assault rifles beneath their long jackets. "I must go now, I love you!"

The Columbian continued speaking in Spanish and alerted Ricardo, although he did not feel threatened as if they were the men's intended targets. Despite the Spanish spoken Kadeem was the first to jump off the sofa and rushed over to the window, where he caught sight of the Caucasian gunners who moved towards their building entrance.

"Those guys are coming up here to kill me and everybody in here," Kadeem shouted!

"I tell you before this guy is trying to play tricks with us! You can not believe anything he say about money or anything else Ricardo, because he only try to fool us so he can escape! The boss told me this would happen," Marquez emphasised then pulled his weapon and aimed it at Kadeem! "Maybe these are the guys he arrange to help free him this morning at the jail!"

"Listen to me Ricardo, those guys are Rough Rider Bikers, and they are going to come up here and kill all of us if you don't listen," Kadeem declared; however, Ricardo followed his partner's advice and aimed his weapon at him also!

The leader of the crew of bikers was Xavier Wamblay, who was Rene Wamblay's younger brother. When Xavier received the news about Kadeem instead of alerting higher ranked bikers such as Jim Bartello or any of his zone generals, he wanted the reward and thus found out which location the van was rented and payed the store a visit. At the rental location, Xavier and his four friends locked the front door and held the employees hostage at gun point, until they disclosed everything they knew about the van renter.

None of the bikers had any interest in bringing in Kadeem alive, therefore once inside the building they raced up the stairs like vigilantes. Kadeem stood frozen over beside the window and could hear the bikers approaching the front door, as he and the Columbians turned their heads and looked at the entrance.

"Bam-bam-bam," one of the bikers shot out the locks and the door flew open!

The first biker who ran in was astonished other people were present, yet, aimed his weapon specifically at Kadeem who was forced to dive behind a love seat. Two other bikers raced in behind him and frightened the Columbians who quickly turned towards the intruders, while gunshot rang out from the first biker. The Columbians' realized that the bikers were indeed intent on killing the Rastafarian and opened fire at them, striking the two first men to enter the condo. Marquez connected with a head shot and killed the first biker, who managed to squeeze off a few rounds at Kadeem. Ricardo shot his target directly through the neck and critically injured the biker, who dropped to both knees and grabbed for the wound.

Kadeem began crawling towards the sofa which had a hide away bed built in, that could possibly offer him better protection than the wooden framed love seat. The pinpoint accuracy from both Columbians commanded the bikers' attention, therefore the three remaining intruders were forced to deal with them first. After roughly forty seconds of sucking for oxygen while pressing against the wound, the biker who was shot in the neck feel dead on his face. None of the bikers anticipated a gun battle, but they found themselves smack dead in the middle of one and had no choice but to fight for what they came. The fourth biker ran into the condo and hid behind the kitchen counter for protection, while Xavier remained by the front door from which he also disbursed his weapon.

With only a pair of handguns versus automatic rifles Kadeem knew that it would only be a matter of time before the bikers overpowered them and killed them all. The thought of running and jumping through the window crossed his mind, but that would have to be a last resort should everything else fail. As he slid the sofa away from the wall the Rude Boy noticed one of the AR-15 Assault Rifles duct taped against the back of the sofa. The Jamaican had no idea that the Columbians were that crafty as to hide the weapon in plain sight, and thereby smiled to himself as he ripped it off the chair and readied it to fire. While his associates exchanged bullets with the Columbians, Xavier turned his weapon in Kadeem's direction and blasted several shots at the sofa. Ricardo in response fired his last two bullets at the front door that forced Xavier to retreat momentarily, however with an empty weapon amongst both Columbians they began to fear for the worst.

All the bikers assumed that Kadeem was unarmed, therein Xavier shouted at his accomplice closest to their target for him to move in and exterminate. With the order issued, Xavier and the other assassin pinned the Columbians behind their hiding places with rapid gunfire, while their companion climbed onto the kitchen counter and moved closer towards Kadeem. When the biker caught a peek at Kadeem his eyes widened with fright as bullets from the AR-15 Rifle tore away half of his face. Xavier and the last assassin paused and watched their companion propelled backwards onto the kitchen floor, with half his face torn away which meant a sealed casket funeral. Marquez shot the biker behind the support beam in the left shoulder, which caused him to reposition himself and in so doing exposed a portion of himself to Kadeem, who shot him dead. Once Xavier realized that his accomplices had all been killed, he turned and raced down the stairs to the building's entrance, where he hid his firearm underneath his jacket and fled in their vehicle.

The Columbians and Kadeem turned their weapons onto each other after Xavier retreated, but the Rude Boy quickly dropped his weapon to defuse the situation. Kadeem already knew what the police response team was like in Montreal, therefore he understood they only had seconds to exit. It wasn't until then that Ricardo realized he had been shot in the left arm, with blood seeping down his hand but there was no time to attend to the wound.

"Yow we have to go now; the cops gonna be all over this place soon," Kadeem exclaimed!

They all ran to their individual quarters and collected all their belongings, retrieved the hidden weapons and looked to flee through a rear door. While everyone else hustled around, Kadeem noticed a cellular phone slightly sticking from one of the shooter's pockets and stole it. There was a fire escape ladder that led down to their vehicle in the building's parking lot, so to avoid any altercations with the police entering from the front they exited accordingly. As they drove away from the scene and looked back at the huge commotion, the Columbians were fascinated with the police's quick arrival time, plus the number of officers that responded to the alert.

"Now I'm gonna make myself as clear as I can fucking be! If you motherfuckers think that you can do this job and get away without my help, then kill me right now! But you see in this country, there is a fucking bullseye on my back, so anybody even seen with me will automatically be on these bikers' shit list! I didn't sign up for this job, I was selected; so, the next rass-clatt time I say danger is coming! Make sure all guns are cocked and ready to blood-clatt buss! Understand," Kadeem yelled in anger!?

"Yes, my friend, you are absolutely right! We will listen to you next time. So, who were those guys," Marquez calmly responded?

"They are called the Rough Riders! Before I moved to Montreal those guys controlled all the weapons, cocaine, pussy, whatever hustlers' business you can imagine; but me and my friends helped to change how things run in this town. Long story short, I ended up killing one of their main bosses and since then they have me on some sort of wanted list," Kadeem explained.

"What are we to do now Marquez," Ricardo asked?

"I don't know, we have no choice but to phone the boss," Marquez answered, before using his cellular to phone Manuel.

A block and a half away from the condo Kadeem unknowingly drove by Xavier who was parked by the side of the road in his older model Toyota Camry. The biker waited until a few cars passed then began pursuit and followed the foreigners to their next choice of stay.

Part 16

Marolina Veronovichi was the first offspring born to Bethany and Raymond Demerit, and would have been the legal successor to her father's seat on the Secret Council, had not her parents conceived two other sons. Monsieur Raymond Demerit was an eccentric billionaire who loved unconventional sports such as hunting rare animals for trophies that he stored in his games room, however out of all his children Marolina was the only child with her father's passion for such bloodthirsty thrills. Their family owned the first major prescription drug company in Canada and made millions in profit before the government finally regulated the industry. Marolina married a wealthy Frenchman named Samuel Leguerre at the age of twenty, spent eight years with him and bore him two sons, before divorcing him and leaving with a handsome settlement of one hundred and five million dollars. She would thereafter marry a wealthy Australian banker name Arnold Shepherd two years later, whom she spent five years with and bore one daughter, before divorcing and getting awarded ninety-three million dollars. A year and a half later and with both ex-husbands still paying high child support premiums,

Marolina married an Italian named Andrea Veronovichi, whose family owned one of the largest clothing distribution company in the world. Andrea and Marolina had a son they named Valentino, whose conception nearly cost the lives of both mother and son, therefore she tied her tubes thereafter and did away with child bearing.

When Raymond Demerit got killed his eldest of two sons Marceau Demerit took his seat on the Secret Council. There was a list of special requirements sworn to by each member of the private cult, and with the most important being 'brotherhood before all,' Fiona and Yves could have been killed for approaching Marceau. Nobody else knew unquestionably that Kevin had the entire governing body of the secret club killed; and depending with whom they shared the knowledge meant either riches or death.

When Kevin and company killed Raymond Demerit in the most high-profiled unsolved multi murder case in Canadian history, Marolina was one of the family members who publicly vowed to one day find those responsible and execute them, therefore White Widow believed she would be the perfect person with which to disclose their information. Marolina like many other wealthy individuals travelled everywhere with her personal bodyguard, who was a former MMA light heavyweight champion that retired due to a knee injury. Both Fiona and Yves knew that it was impossible to simply get an appointment with Marolina, thus they exploited the only means available to them.

Yves Buchard drove White Widow to the Dream Spa in Dorian, which was an establishment regularly visited by Marolina Veronovichi. Le Spa Du Reve as commonly known in French, was the most expensive body treatment facility in Quebec and a place you were guaranteed to encounter entertainment stars. At five hundred dollars per treatment, Yves was shocked at the number of clients entering the spa as they sat down the street and watched the building.

"How did you even find out about this place," Yves asked?

"I'm a woman, it's my priority to know this stuff!... But the Old Man used to give us special presents and he sent me here a few times for a deluxe treatment. Trust me this place may be costly, but you leave here feeling like a million bucks," Fiona answered!

"Are they sure Marolina is coming today," Yves enquired?

"The secretary said she is here every Wednesday morning from ten," Fiona said.

"With this weather she is probably home sick in bed," Yves argued.

"You spoke too soon, here she comes," Fiona declared after sighting Marolina's car driving up!

Marolina's chauffeured Bentley pulled up at the entrance and dropped her off before proceeding to the parking lot, where the driver and her bodyguard waited until she was finished. Moments later Yves did likewise but left the area afterwards and drove to a nearby Tim Hortons where he awaited Fiona's call. The White Widow entered the spa's doors, where the delightful treatment immediately began with a glass of whatever beverage the client chose. Fiona requested some chardonnay and received a 2009 bottle of Marcassin Sonoma Coast Chardonnay from their wine cellar, which was exclusively hers throughout the duration of the day.

There were several packages available to clients and Fiona ensured that she scheduled herself to participate in whatever treatment sessions Marolina had prearranged. Patrice the instructor was happy to see Fiona walk in minutes after Marolina arrived, considering they both had the same curriculum arranged. Marolina immediately recognized Fiona from an earlier session they did together and pleasantly greeted her, but it became obvious thereafter that her mind was preoccupied with other affairs. To begin the ladies went to the changing room where they got undressed and changed into assigned robes. They then left their clothes and belongings inside a donated locker and reported to the massage area, where a pair of professional masseuses awaited them.

Before they left the changing room Marolina tucked her earphones into her ears and began playing music from her phone; then logged into her email account on her tablet. Throughout the next two pampering sessions Marolina refrained from any interactions with Fiona and responded to several business emails and phone calls, which led the White Widow to wonder if they would get the chance to converse. Fiona also did not wish to appear too invasive and thus fully subjected herself to the relaxation being provided.

At lunchtime, the ladies were brought to the facility's five-star restaurant where a renowned chef prepared whatever dish they ordered. Marolina chose to sit by herself and dived into a novel she had brought along called Mama Devow, while Fiona sat at a separate table and scanned through the daily newspaper. After their half hour lunchbreak both ladies had facial treatments scheduled, which was a session that included cleansings, facial masks, massages, creams and wrinkle-free ointments. Twenty-seven minutes into their lunchbreak after Marolina finished eating and absorbed herself in the novel she had brought, she unexpectedly stopped and walked over to Fiona's table and sat down.

"I heard what happened to your former boss, and I'm very sorry for your loss. I really couldn't make it to the Old Man's funeral, but I was sure to pay my respects by sending a bouquet. It's funny because I remember talking with you about the murder of my father here a few months ago, only to basically have the same thing happen to Monsieur Trudeau," Marolina said?

"Thank you for your condolence, I really appreciate it," Fiona answered!

"Any word yet on where his killer is hiding," Marolina asked?

Fiona looked over her shoulder to ensure there was nobody close enough that could hear their conversation and whispered. "The Old Man was killed because he changed the laws of this province's overseers and injected a colored man in the Trudeau seat. Kevin blackmailed Francois in order to get the position, plus the Old Man even though they believed he was sane, had been slowly losing his memory. The person who did this, did it out of love for the greatest institution!"

"Well, my brother and company seem to believe otherwise! Rumour has it that this Buchard killed Monsieur Trudeau out of envy," Marolina declared.

"Yves Buchard found out that Kevin Trudeau killed your father and the rest of the former overseers, then used the information he stole to blackmail the Old Man," Fiona exclaimed!

Marolina was dumbstruck by the news and stared at White Widow with an increasingly vindictive snare. Their main instructor walked up to the table at that point and said, "I hope both you ladies enjoyed your meals and if you guys don't mind following me to your next session, we are ready to begin!"

"We will be along in five minutes," invigoratively stated Marolina, to which the instructor did as indicated and walked away!

To calm her nerves Marolina reached into her pocket and removed a pack of cigarette, extracted one and lit it ablaze. There was a huge No Smoking sign directly ahead of her on the wall, nevertheless she ignored it and callously puffed away. Although several of the employees witnessed her blatantly disobeyed the rules, none of them went over to protest and allowed Marolina freedom to smoke.

"Does my brother know of this," illiterately asked Marolina?

"No, he does not, and even if he did…," Fiona began.

"Yes, I know; their brotherhood would prevent him from taking any action against their Grand Chancellor. But I am not my brother, nor am I a pussy! You gave me this information now for a reason, what is it that you want," Marolina interrupted?

"The same thing you do; revenge, power and money," Fiona lamented!

***

After years of home-schooling Kevin Junior was initially nervous about entering a classroom, but enjoyed the experience once he did. Due to Kevin Trudeau's criminal exploits and ongoing legal battle, which was one of the most aired news stories across much of Quebec's airwaves, his son became a Rockstar at school. L'École De Queen Victoria was a French Catholic private school where the young Jamaican descendant was one of only three students of color on the entire school's roster. The catholic school employed two guards to help protect and watch the children, most of whom came from famous and influential parents. Some of the children thought Junior was only able to attend such an elaborate and expensive school because his father was a drug dealer, while others high-fived and fist-bumped him every time they encountered each other.

To prevent dangers and stop enquirers such as reporters and the paparazzi from molesting his son, Kevin Trudeau advised Junior not to leave the school grounds at any cost, despite him wanting to purchase lunch elsewhere or accompany friends. Kevin also arranged for the females of the Pigeons Of The Order to pickup his son, who requested that the ladies do the honors when he noticed the attention he received. Aside from Junior's personal safety Kevin also had the Trudeau's Estate to manage, hence he seldom arrived home late whenever he went in to work. Francois Trudeau had taught him how to run the business before his death, therefore he was quite capable of handling whatever was required.

Following Fiona's coming to terms discussion with Marolina Veronovichi, the couple believed they were ready to progress to the next level where their intent was to ruin Kevin Trudeau. Yves Buchard and White Widow drove to Junior's school during his final afternoon class period and parked outside the facility. Fiona knew that once she attempted to abduct Kevin Junior, she would be branded a traitor and hunted by her own peers, therefore she took a few seconds to gather herself before exiting the vehicle. White Widow walked up to the door and rang the buzzer, before she was then granted entry by the secretary. There was a security guard speaking with the secretary behind the desk as Fiona walked up and asked, "if Kevin Junior could be released early"? The secretary temporarily argued that she had not received any phone calls from Mr. Trudeau; but eventually advised Fiona to sign Junior out while she searched what grade he was in. When the secretary found Junior's listing, she contacted the teacher and requested, "that he be allowed to leave for the day?"

The guard had never seen Fiona before yet pleasantly smiled at her, then looked away at the security's monitors of video feeds from around the school grounds. The man was accustomed to Junior's female chauffeurs riding solo in ridiculously expensive vehicles, and an Acura TL with a male behind the steering wheel did not exactly fit the profile. As Fiona stepped away from the desk to waited for Junior, the guard whispered and told the secretary to phone Mr. Trudeau for confirmation. The female secretary made the call that got answered by Kevin's assistant, who begged her to hold while she transferred the call. While they waited for the call to get connected, Kevin Junior came walking down the hallway and saw White Widow whom he had not seen in weeks. The young lad started running towards the female and leapt at her with a huge hug, which led the guard and secretary to assume all was well.

"Hello, hello, hello," Kevin Senior answered!

"I'm sorry to disturb you Mr. Trudeau it's Liz from Queen Victoria, I was just calling to confirm the female you sent to pick up your son," said the secretary!

"What female? I did not send anyone to pick up my son," Kevin shouted!

"This woman your son seems to know is about to leave with him," exclaimed the secretary!

"Leave with my bombo-clatt...," Kevin Senior could be overheard shouting through the receiver!

The security guard had heard enough of the phone dialect at that point and sprung into action. The man hurried around to stop Fiona from leaving with Junior, but as he reached out to grab a hold of the boy White Widow spun around brandishing a 9mm Luger 3.1 Semi Auto. At the sight of the gun the unarmed security guard backed up and threw his hands in the air, hence Fiona jammed the gun underneath his chin and shoved him back behind the secretary's counter. Liz dropped the phone from her hand and raised them both above her head, as Junior curiously looked on without fear. White Widow shoved them into a small supply room behind the front desk and used a Duct Tape from atop the secretary's desk to bind their feet, mouths and hands. As Fiona looked to leave the secretary's station, she could hear Kevin threatening to start World War lll, thus she hung up the receiver and left with Junior.

Part 17

The Ethics Commission Office drafted plans and filled documents to reprimand Premier Joseph McArthur and Premier Richard Blanc; but retracted their legal motion when they discovered criminal charges had already being laid. While the Ethics Office could have pursued their obligations to discipline the disgraced Quebec Premiers, criminal indictments by the Royal Canadian Mounted Police on charges of Collusion and Defrauding Government would have superseded them. In addition, their investigation into whether Prime Minister Layton broke the law was still ongoing and took precedent, therefore they left the Mounties to deal with the premiers. Even though the Ethics Bureau decided against proceeding, to punish both politicians who had been ousted from their political parties, Mme. Lablonde and her Commissioners issued their severest penalty ever, by expelling both men for life from government.

Ex-Premier Joseph McArthur was under house arrest after being indicted on several criminal charges. McArthur was allowed to stay home throughout his trial date and wear an ankle bracelet that tracked his whereabouts, and could only attend religious services, lawyer visits, medical appointments and court appointments. Joseph became fixated on his television and would watch news feeds about the latest developments in his case from dusk till dawn. The Ex-Premier had employed one of the best law firms across Canada and was being represented by their best attorney Monsieur Lloyd Kazinski, nevertheless he discovered more important facts about his case from news anchors before hearing from his own lawyer. The day before Joseph received the registered mail that was sent by the Ethics Committee, he was watching the CBC newscast when they broke the news that he had been expelled for life from government. Even though the expulsion was not as dreadful as a prison conviction, watching everything he had worked for get taken away was completely demoralizing. The anguish and sorrow after going from the clouds to the basement frustrated Joseph, who threw his remote control against the television and broke the screen.

Contrary to his co-accused Richard Blanc refused to watch television or listened to talk show on the radio, with their continued negative rhetoric against Joseph McArthur and himself. The former premier was also under strict house arrest rules, which imposed sanctions that forced him to wear an ankle bracelet and restricted his travels to religious services, doctor appointments, lawyer visits and court appointments. Monsieur Blanc had entertained very few visitors since his release and even refused to open his door to certain associates who dropped by. The day the Purolator deliveryman arrived with the package from the Ethics Commission Department, he rang the doorbell for over three minutes awaiting a signature before he could leave the mail. With news reporters camped outside Monsieur Blanc's house, the disdained Ex-Premier abstained from answering his door fearing it might had been one of them seeking an interview. When Richard finally answered the door, the deliveryman who knew he was home was about to walk away, but they took care of the formalities before he departed. Richard locked his door and ripped open the envelope and read the letter, which brought tears to his eyes knowing he would no longer be allowed to serve his community, province and country.

***

Mme Teressa Lablonde and her Ethics Commission team interviewed Prime Minister Mathew Layton, and everyone tied to her investigation. The Prime Minister's most compelling piece of evidence was never retrieved and passed onto the Ethics Commissioners, therefore they had to rely on the testimonies from government aides and the Cabinet Ministers with whom Monsieur Layton corresponded prior to making his decision. The Ethics Commissioner found it difficult to believe that some common person off the street could

Informer 3

have in their possession such highly classified documents, with information that was not even known to historians or ranking officers of the highest court. The Commissioners spoke with all the witnesses who the Prime Minister claimed saw the documents that were sent to the him by Nicholas Henry, and each witness recounted similar stories. The entire questioning portion of the enquiry took twelve days, following which the commissioners reviewed the evidence for an additional two weeks before they rendered their judgement.

Five days before the Ethics Commission's verdict in Prime Minister Mathew Layton's case was revealed, Terresa Lablonde went for a routine checkup at her personal physician's office. Doctor Deborah Spooks had been Terresa's family doctor for over twenty-five years and helped immensely during her Cancer treatments. Mme Lablonde had decided to compete in the following year's Cancer Survivors race that was held in Ottawa and wanted her doctor to put her on some sort of diet or nutrition enhancement to build her body up for the challenge.

"Madam Lablonde, Doctor Spooks will see you now," instructed the secretary, at which Terresa walked into Deborah's office!

"Hi Terresa, how have you been!? Please come in and have a seat," greeted Doctor Spooks!

"I'm good Deborah, nice seeing you," stated Mme Lablonde as she too a seat!

"So how is the family," Doctor Spooks questioned?

"Everybody is great down to our dog Kirby! And yours," Mme Lablonde remarked?

"Good, thanks! What going on any pain of sickness," Doctor Spooks asked?

"Not at all, I've been thinking about doing the Cancer Survivors race in Ottawa and would like you to put me on something to help boost my Immune System," Mme Lablonde explained?

"Well, that's a great idea and we can surely put you on a diet and give you some Vitamin shots that will help! Take off your blouse for me and let me check you first, then I'll prepare and start you on those Vitamins," Doctor Spooks said?

With Terresa laying comfortably back on her examination table, Doctor Spooks checked her heart rate, her vital signs and took her blood pressure. The Doctor documented everything on Terresa's medical chart, before leaving the room and closing the door for a few minutes. Doctor Spooks returned with a Syringe that was already filled with fluids, however she carefully hid it from her patient and documented something else on Terresa's medical chart.

"Ok Terresa, today I'm going to give you a boost of Vitamins to help strengthen your bones and build up your raspatory system for that long run," Doctor Spooks exclaimed.

"How many of these injections are you prescribing," Mme Lablonde enquired?

"It all depends on how your body reacts to the medication, but no more than two sessions," Doctor Spooks explained.

The Ethics Commissioner detested needles and turned her head in the other direction to avoid seeing it injected. The Doctor at that point prepared the Syringe, used an Alcohol Swab to clean an area on her patient's upper left arm and injected the fluid. After Deborah administered the injection instead of disposing of the Syringe in the Medical Waste Container, she replaced the needle cover and placed the Syringe inside her doctor's coat pocket. Terresa sat up and got dressed, then collected her next appointment sheet from Deborah and politely left the office. Following that visit Doctor Spooks immediately took a break and went behind the office building to smoke. The female doctor was terribly shaken following her actions and noticeably shook as she brought the cigarette to her lips. There was a huge garbage container along the side of the building, and Doctor Spooks made sure nobody was watching before she tossed the used Syringe inside. Deborah then took out her cellular and checked her pockets for a piece of paper that contained a phone number, which she called and had a brief conversation.

"Hello Doctor Spooks," answered a male's voice!

"What you ordered me to do is done," Doctor Spooks stated!

"Thank you, doctor," said the male's voice!

"I could lose my license and practice for this, then what," Doctor Spooks argued!

"You have nothing to fear doctor, either way you will be a very rich woman," disclosed the male before the phoneline went dead.

Part 18

When Kevin arrived at his son's school all the classes had gotten excused for the day and the students were heading to their respective residence. There were police officers all throughout the property already coordinating their efforts to find Junior. The large media presence meant that officers had to moderate the traffic and ensured that the other children went home safely. As Kevin's chauffeured Bentley drove up to the school the slow advancement due to the high volume of vehicles innerved him, thus he jumped out without alerting his driver and ran up to the school. The sight of other children returning home knowing that his son might not be sleeping in his bed, vexed the rude boy who neglected anyone who called to him and went directly into the facility.

An officer inside the main school doors stopped Kevin and enquired, "what do you want sir," to which he responded, "he was the father of the kidnapped child." The officer at that point called one of his colleagues down the hall and informed him who Kevin was, before advising him where to bring the child's father. Kevin followed the officer to the principal's office, where the two detectives assigned to the case spoke with Principal Madam Vivika Crenard. The Principal recognized Kevin and rudely excused herself to open the door for him and allowed him to partake in their conversation.

"Monsieur Trudeau I am so very sorry for what happened to your son Junior; but we have the identities of the people who took him, and the police assured us that they will find him," Madam Crenard emphatically stated!

"How the hell does something like this happen in a private school with on duty security guards," yelled Kevin?

"Sir we do have security guards but remember they have no weapons. This woman came in here armed and took your son by force, there was nothing anybody could have done," Madam Crenard responded!

"So, what happens from here on," Kevin demanded?

"Mr. Trudeau, I am Detective Merton St. Louis and this in my partner Detective Lucas Rickston and we will be the main officers working this case. Sir presently the teachers here at the school are working to provide photos of the male and female suspects who took your son. We intend to pass those photos around to get the public's help, so we can bring your son back home soon. I understand from the school secretary that your son knew who this female kidnapper was and went towards her of his own free will," Detective Merton exclaimed.

"Yes… she was under my employment, but I recently paid for her to travel abroad on vacation and she got unfortunately raped while there; so, I guess this could be some sort of revenge on her part," Kevin answered.

"And how about her male partner, do you know who he is," Detective Merton asked?

"I doubt that I know whoever is helping her," Kevin proclaimed.

The secretary knocked the principal's door then barged in with three stacks of photographs. "Here are the pictures you gentlemen asked for, these are Junior's and those are the pictures we captured from our security cameras of the kidnappers!"

Detective Merton picked up two photographs of Yves Buchard and White Widow and passed them to Kevin, "That is the gentleman I'm referring to sir."

Kevin stared at Yves' picture with disgust for a few seconds, which led the officers to presume he knew who the person was, before he calmly said, "sorry, but I have no idea who he is."

"Mr. Trudeau the police and I are going to show these pictures when we speak with the media people outside and ask for the public's help to find Junior. If you wish you can come on with us and plead with these people to bring back your son," Madam Crenard emphasised.

"Pleading is not my style Madam Crenard; but I am definitely going to get back my son," Kevin lamented as he moved to exit the office!

"Before you go Mr. Trudeau, this is my card if you think about anything that could help this investigation; and I will be in touch with you if we get any leads or locate your son," Detective Merton stated as he handed Kevin his business card.

While exiting the Catholic School, Logan Duntroon telephoned to remind Kevin of his upcoming trial date and to inform him of the new details regarding the prosecution team. Before responding Kevin stepped outside the school doors, where the entire scenery had changed after the children vacated the premises. There were four officers at the bottom of the stairs holding a line that restricted the reporters from advancing, as they were all eager to report the developing story. The instant the reporters sighted Kevin they began shouting questions at him, however he threw on his sunglasses and walked directly to his car, got in and his chauffeur drove away.

"Drive to White Widow's place now," Kevin instructed, before attending to the call! "Mr. Duntroon, what news have you?"

"Hello Mr. Trudeau, it appears that Prosecutor Jamaal Dickson has been killed in a car crash," Attorney Duntroon declared.

"Who is his replacement," Kevin callously asked as if the prosecutor was of no significance?

"At this point I am not sure, but I also received a request to have your case postponed by the Prosecution Office, due to his death. They are requesting the delay on grounds that their new attorney will need time to get up to speed with all the details pertaining to your case," Attorney Duntroon stated!

"That's their problem! I want to proceed and get this done with; if they can't make their case get a dismissal," Kevin instructed!

"It's a possibility the judge could side with them and give them more time due of the circumstances," Attorney Duntroon exclaimed.

"Mr. Duntroon right now my head is not in such a good place; so, don't make yourself the next blood-clatt lawyer I have to kill! Get this fucking case wrapped up the next time we step into court," threatened Kevin!

Logan was dumbfounded at what he heard, following his presumptions that the deaths of two of the three prosecutors killed were accidental. The defence attorney had no idea that Kevin Junior had gotten kidnapped, hence his client was in a depressed mood after getting his son captured for a second time.

"As you ordered Monsieur Trudeau, I'll either request that the case proceed or ask the judge for an immediate dismissal," Attorney Duntroon declared!

"Have yourself a good evening Mr. Duntroon," Kevin insinuated following which the phoneline went dead!

Logan Duntroon came off the telephone with Kevin and sat back in his leather chair. Never throughout his professional career had he received a threat with such profound vigor, that it shook his very core knowing his client had the capability to backup his statement. There was a strange phone number calling on Logan's cellular, which he ignored as his thoughts drifted away on Kevin. As Logan reminisced, he thought back on several conversations he had with Kevin, where his client had projected interests in the type of prosecutors assigned to his case. Their lawyer client agreement protruded Logan from informing law enforcement about Kevin; moreover, despite his personal feelings he was still legally obligated to defend his employer to the best of his ability.

Logan's assistant knocked the door and walked in. "Your client Monsieur Trudeau is all over the news, it appears as if they have kidnapped his son!"

"What!"

***

Kevin loosened the tie around his neck and unbuttoned his shirt collar, then opened the weapon's stash that was built into the backrest of the front seat passenger's chair and selected a loaded pair of Honor Guard 9mm Luger. When his chauffeur came to a stop outside of White Widow's condominium, Kevin sprang from the car and ran up towards the building. The front door was closed but unlatched, therefore the Jamaican Rude Boy turned the doorknob and slid it open, but shielded himself behind the side of the wall. After sneaking a peep into the condo and ensuring the coast was clear, Kevin moved inside but again hid behind another wall from which he could clearly see the kitchen area and the days room section. Pete who was Kevin's newest chauffeur entered the condo behind him and kept his back against the opposing wall. Once both men determined it was safe to proceed, they cautiously searched the entire residence, but found nothing that would indicate where the youth had been taken to.

As they wrapped up their search, the sounds of police cruisers and emergency vehicles echoed outside, therefore they concealed their weapons underneath their shirts and slowly exited. The arriving officers surrounded the residence and were preparing to enter the condo, when one of the lawmen shouted with his weapon pointed towards the residence, "freeze, get down on the ground now!" The officer's superior recognized who Kevin was and leapt ahead of the constable, who obeyed orders and lowered his firearm. Detective St. Louis walked over to Kevin and accompanied him and his chauffeur to their vehicle.

"Monsieur Trudeau it really would be much safer if you left this search up to the professionals," Detective St. Louis stated!

"I expected to find this place already searched when I reached here; and you fellows just arriving, so that is a bit slow where my son is concerned," Kevin declared!

"So, if you knew this was the female's address, why didn't you tell us at the school," Detective St. Louis asked?

"None of you guys asked! Plus, I'm not here to do your job, I'm here to find my son," Kevin answered as he opened the car door to climb in!

"We did not kidnap your son Mr. Trudeau, we are only here to help you find him," Detective St. Louis insisted!

"You got kids detective," Kevin enquired?

"Yes, I do."

"Well, while yours comfortably in bed tonight my son could be getting tortured," Kevin decreed as he entered the vehicle and closed the door!

There was no further need for the assault team to clear the condo, therefore the Forensic Team went into the residence to search and determine if they could uncover any new information that might lead to the boy's recovery. News reporters clogged the exit area and tried snapping pictures of Kevin as his chauffeur slowly drove pass them. During the ride home Kevin felt so stressed that he poured himself a drink of XO Cognac and smoked his Marijuana Joint and tried earnestly to relax. The bright lights of the big city made him to think of Junior, to whom he had promised his empire once he retired. His cellular rang and again displayed his lawyer's number across the screen, but Kevin was in no mood to converse and ignored it. Moments later the phone rang again displaying a long distance 416 Toronto number, and after ringing several times, Kevin who was apprehensive at first to respond finally answered.

"Hello," Kevin said!

"Dad, dad I don't know why they doing this to me," Kevin Junior cried before Yves grabbed the phone away!

"Junior, son I promise I'll...," Kevin shouted!

"You not in any position to promise shit right now! I know you have court in a few days…," Yves commented!

"If anybody touch a hair on my boy's head, them fucking dead you understand me," Kevin threatened!

"If you think of sending anybody after us, remember that your son will be the first one in line of fire. You have court in a few days, let your criminal lawyers do what they do best, and we will be in touch soon with our demands," Yves instructed before the line went dead!

Part 19

With a large fraction of the city's illegal drug enterprise back under the Rough Riders control, the bikers pressed to widen their underground market across the entire island. There were small pockets of Caribbean hustlers who were complicating their efforts to control areas such as Notre-Dame-de-Grace and Cote-Saint-Luc. To resolve these issues the bikers ran a campaign intended to induce the main supplier of these hustlers to purchase solely from them or risk losing his life. It was a well-known fact that some of these groups particularly the Jamaicans, were free spirited people who had proven their resilience by toppling the previous biker regime. Regardless of their past failures the bikers believed they had reconquered the Montreal's landscape, hence Jim Bartello met with some of his area leaders to expand their organization.

To help solve their issues in the Notre-Dame-de-Grace and Cote St. Luc areas, Jim spoke secretly with Chops and offered him the distribution job if he was successful at recruiting the supplier into their organization. Chops had been struggling to get his family back together after his latest arrest, where the officers failed to uncover any physical evidence yet initially charged him for suspicion of drug trafficking. When the Prosecution Office reviewed the case, they decided to drop all charges against Chops due to the lack of evidence, in addition to the investigators' failure to arrest Quail. Because of the arrest, Chops and his girlfriend had to undergo hours of family therapy to prove they were competent parents, to get their children back from Social Services. The couple also had to get documents from the investigators on the case to reclaim their dogs from the kennel, but inspectors were in no mood to comply after being embarrassed.

Inspector Ruchard and his team were angry with the handling of Chops' case and wanted him behind bars at any cost, especially after finding Moe's mutilated body and not being abled to locate Kenny's, following his missing persons report. Even though the Quail's case resulted with the police killing the wanted man they sought, investigators knew the decision to arrest Chops and recover their drugs caused the death of their informant. Despite being morally at fault for everything that happened to his family, Chops filed a lawsuit against the police department for his misfortunes. When Chops left the courthouse with his attorney Logan Duntroon, they spoke briefly with the media and badmouthed the investigators who had provided him with the drugs they tried to charge him for.

To uncover who this supplier was Chops questioned one of his crackhead clients named Molly, who was unsure who the dealer was; but knew of someone who would know the person. Molly pointed Chops to someone whom he had no prior idea about, and the Rough Rider representative was none too excited to learn of the person's existence. After passing on the requested information the crackhead female thought that would be all that's required of her, but Chops had other ideas. The female was forced to bring Chops and three of his crew members to the man's apartment building, where they led her to the residence and made her knock the door. The bikers hid on both sides of the door to avoid being spotted by the resident who first looked through the peephole. As Raffie began opening the door to Molly, the three bikers and Chops barged into the apartment and held him at gunpoint. There was nobody else inside the apartment at the time, so the bikers brought Raffi into the kitchen where it was impossible for anyone in the adjacent building to witness.

"Is who you people be? What is this Molly, who these people," frightfully asked Raffi?

Two of the bikers held Raffi's hands and forced him to his knees, at which Chops walked into the kitchen and surprised him. Raffi knew who Chops was and immediately fell silent, knowing that it was a costly violation for anyone found selling in Rough Riders' territory.

"I'm not even going to discuss you selling to my customers in my zone, but what I want to know is who do you get supply from," Chops exclaimed!

"Listen man I don't want no trouble, but what y'all going to do to me if I tell y'all," Raffi stated?

"What's your name Raffi? Tell me something, what kind a dope you been selling around here," Chops asked as he walked around the kitchen opening cupboards?

"I sell a little weed," Raffi answered!

"But Molly here only smoke crack," Chops declared.

"I'm sorry boss, I do sell a little crack sometimes," Raffi frightfully recounted.

"Where is it," Chops demanded?

"There is a loose tile behind the toilet in the bathroom, I keep it there," Raffi instructed, at which Chops shook his head at his third companion who went and checked!

The biker could be heard dismantling the stash spot inside the bathroom before he emerged with a plastic bag. The items from the bag were thrown onto the kitchen counter, at which the biker used Raffi's scale and weighed the small amounts of crack and powder cocaine. After weighing the products, the intruder went into Raffi's bedroom and confiscated his money, valuables such as jewelry and a large Ziploc bag filled with Marijuana. Chops picked up a 5 grams piece of crack from the table and gave it to Molly, then escorted her to the door. While walking to the entrance Chops placed the hand holding his firearm around Molly's shoulder and whispered in her ear, "if you ever mention anything about this incident you are fucking dead!" Molly felt a nervous shock jolted through her entire body, as she left the apartment and refrained from looking back.

"You still haven't answered my question! Who did you buy this shit from," Chops demanded as he returned to the kitchen?

"I just do this to make a little extra money man, I don't want no..." Raffi began, before Chops picked up one of his kitchen knives and stabbed him in the right shoulder. The Caribbean hustler screamed so loudly that Molly overheard him at the end of the hallway, but fearfully continued her merry way.

"They call he Lass, and he base up on Mariette Avenue close to Monkland," Raffi responded instantly.

"Sounds like we understand each other! Now exactly where on Mariette do I find this Lass," Chops asked?

"I'm not sure the exact number, but he building is the third down on the right-hand side from the corner. Apartment 1B in the basement," Raffi quickly explained.

"Now Raffi or Taffy whatever your fucking name is, what makes you think you can hustle in my fucking zone, without my fucking permission, huh," Chops demanded, as he picked up the knife and moved towards the mobilized dealer?

"Me really sorry please!" Raffi confessed, but to no avail as Chops who used the knife and slit his throat.

***

Under pressure to find the area's biggest drug supplier and arrange a meeting for Mr. Bartello to discuss business, Chops and his three companions went to locate Lass. There was a winter storm advisory in effect and the Local Meteorologist had forecasted forty-one centimetres of snow throughout the Montreal region over the next twenty-four hours. Regardless of the frigid -25 Degrees Celsius temperature that felt closer to -41 Degrees with an 86-mph wind-chill out of the Northwest, Chops neglected all warnings and rode out with his associates. Chops typically did not drive and was normally in the back seat, however he decided to take the helm and hopped into the Hummer's driver seat. The blunt of the snowstorm had not yet struck the city, but the blowing snow was slowly increasing in magnitude.

Unlike Raffi who lived in the apartment from which he trafficked his drugs, Lass resided in Pointe-Claire and used his Mariette Avenue residence mainly as a trap-house. The two-bedroom apartment was rented under someone else's name to steer any possible criminal charges away from Lass. To refrain from raising their neighbors' suspicions, the crew of hustlers only entered the building through the emergency rear entrance, used excessive amounts of air fresheners to combat their Marijuana smoke and followed the building's rules thoroughly. It was also beneficial that the janitor was an undercover crack smoker, who would inform them should he uncover anything troubling. Lass had a call for drug line system that was similar to Chops', which allowed him to employ three Jamaican men named Lazy, Slim and Ranger, who all delivered wherever their customers were. The drug trafficker had a fourth worker called Sammy, who attended to their customers who visited the apartment, but was only there on certain days at specific times.

With a snowstorm developing the crew of hustlers started gambling at Poker and ignored the business phone, while Sammy prepared food for them all and chatted on his cellular. None of the Jamaicans expected any visitors, but with a dope outlet there was always the potential of some random visitor stopping in. The building provided minimal security wherein visitors had to be buzzed in by residents, but Lass had a personal video system installed at both the front and rear doors. When Chops and his three associates rang the door buzzer, Sammy unknowingly watched them inside the lobby and advised his companions. Typically, visitors to the trap-house went alone to minimize the traffic, therefore it was indeed concerning to see four Caucasian men seeking entry.

The Jamaicans first concern was who the men were, having partially ruled out the police knowing that they would most likely find their own entry into the building, then kicked in the front door instead of buzzing. There was also the chance that they could be corrupt cops or many other assumptions, so to find out who they were Sammy and Ranger went across the hall to the janitor's apartment with their illegal products, two assault rifles and four automatic hand pistols. Lass kept his firearm and taped it beneath the table, then telephoned Ranger's cellular and left the phoneline open for them to listen in on their conversation. With most of the incriminating evidence taken from the apartment, Slim then pressed the buzzer and allowed their visitors entry.

A short time later Chops and his three companions arrived at the door, where they requested to have a word with Lass. Slim had sent away his hand pistol but would never be caught without a weapon, hence he kept one hand on a knife inside his pocket and held the door with the next. After showing the men in Slim pointed them towards his boss and callously left the door unlatched. The Caucasian males were nonaggressive and appeared rather timid, thereby Slim felt unthreatened but walked up and stood within arms length of their visitors. To avoid being shot in the back in case their associates had to charge in shooting, Slim stood to the left of the bikers and rested his back against a wall. Chops who sounded rather discrete at the door, became far less reserved once he came face to face with Lass.

"You guys have any idea who I am," Chops asked, at which Lass shrugged his shoulders and shook his head? Believing his hosts were intimidated by his presence, Chops continued his overly aggressive attitude. "This whole area is back under Rough Riders territory, so that means you guys are going to start buying your products from us or close up shop immediately!"

"And, who are you," Lass angrily asked?

"Don't worry about who I am, I'm the man telling you what is going to happen from now on," Chops declared as he unzipped his winter coat and showed off the Remington Automatic 45MM hand pistol on his hip! The bikers who accompanied Chops all placed their hands on their weapons as a sign of intimidation.

"So, you think that some nobody like yourself is going to…," began Lass at which the apartment door flew wide open. Sammy and Ranger rushed in unexpectedly carrying a Beretta ARX100 Assault Rifle and an Uzi Pro with the Laser Guided Scope mounted and aimed at the visitors! Slim withdrew his knife and held it to the closest man's throat, before he could mange to withdraw his weapon. The crash at the door startled Chops and made him take his eyes off Lass for a millisecond, however when he spun back around, he was staring down the barrel of an automatic weapon.

"…walk into my base and try tell me how to run my business," concluded Lass!

Chops' tone changed instantly as he tried to backpedal on his previous statements. "Please, do not take what I just said as any disrespect, but that was what my boss tell me to say to you!"

Lass gestured for Chops and his companions to raise their hands, thus they slowly followed instructions with unknown fears. Lazy got up from his seat and confiscated each of the biker's weapons and placed three of them on the table, before returning to his seat with a FN-FNX-45 Semi Auto Pistol that fascinated him.

"Well, the next time you boys see your boss; kindly tell him I have no need for his services and my business naw close! At a matter a fact, take off those fucking clothes and leave all your shit where it is! And don't let me see any of you fuckers back around N.D.G," declared Lass, to which Chops' associates quickly began removing their clothes! Chops was initially timid because he was not wearing any underwear, but a rifle butt to the back of his head encouraged him to obey orders.

"Yow Brav, you are the whitest motherfucker I have ever seen," joked Slim, after Chops got undressed and stood with both hands covering his genitals! Lass and the others broke out with laughter before the boss signalled for them to be taken away. Sammy and Ranger led the bikers to the rear exit at gunpoint, where they were sent out into the storm which had fully energized with howling winds and heavy snowfall.

Without a cell phone the bikers were incapable of calling anyone, and with most residents locked down due to the snowstorm, the roads were like a desert covered with increasingly fallen snow. It was a three and a half blocks walk to the Ultramar Service Station at the corner of Sherbrooke Street, but in such treacherous conditions that walk seemed like an eternity. With their feet sinking into 3 centimetres of snow on partially frozen sidewalks, every step was brutal for the bikers whose first wish was to not get spotted by the police. Should an officer of the law come to their rescue there was no doubt that they would receive the proper medical treatment needed, but the rescue would also come at a cost. Law enforcement meant an investigation and providing identification, from a group of men between which there were two warrants and an ongoing lawsuit versus the city.

When they reached Monkland Avenue, the bikers were so cold that they coupled together to create body warmth and walked in the middle of the road to stay off the uncleared sidewalks, which had icy conditions beneath the snow in some areas. They could barely see fifteen meters ahead with the blowing snow, but as they were about to cross the road Chops looked up Monkland Avenue and saw what he believed was the bus coming. Seconds later the 162-City Transit bus came slowly driving down the road, therefore the men hobbled to the closest bus stop while frantically waving their hands to attract the driver's attention. In such a treacherous snowstorm it was difficult for the bus driver to see passengers at the designated stops, but the bikers were willing to lay in the middle of the street if necessary and rushed aboard the first chance they got.

There were three other passengers on the bus, but it was the driver's responsibility to report all incidents, so he placed the bus in park and moved to ignite the Emergency Alert Signal. Chops grabbed onto the man's hand and begged him not to turn on the alert, then offered him $500 cash for the ride, his silence and a quick phone call. It was evident by the red flareup on the bikers' outstretched limbs that they had suffered the effects of frostbite, however, each man seemed more willing to tolerate their discomfort than involve emergency personnel. The sight of four undressed males during a winter storm was not something one saw regularly, therefore the passengers initially wondered if they mentally ill.

The driver and passengers felt compelled to help nevertheless and temporarily loaned them their jackets, which was a gesture kindly accepted by the shivering bikers. Knowing that he could lose his job if the passengers informed that he accepted a bribe instead of reporting the incident, the driver shrugged his head in their direction then continued slowly driving. To ensure that none of the passengers recounted what happened to anyone, the injured bikers forcibly took their identification and recorded their personal information, before returning the items. Chops telephoned his girlfriend Valorie from the driver's personal phone and arranged for her to pick them up eight stops away from where they boarded, with the payoff promised and clothing for them all to wear.

Part 20

To avoid murder charges should they find Officer Jack Quiere deceased due to hyper-thermal caused by the cold, an unidentified caller telephoned the 911 dispatcher and informed them where the kidnapped officer could be found. When Jack's peers found him, they immediately transferred him to the hospital by ambulance where he was examined and awarded treatment for his injuries. Investigators were eager to uncover what happened to their associate and questioned the officer at the first opportunity. While collecting Jack's statement, the four officers present casted everyone else from the room to ensure no sensitive information was capture. Jack revealed everything to his comrades and identified Linnora as an accomplice but could not identify her male associate. Once Officer Quiere revealed that his abductors had recorded him, his co-workers wished him a quick recovery and sat out on a manhunt.

Should the information revealed by Jack Quiere get into the wrong hands, it threatened to ruin the lives of many corrupt officers and their illegal organ harvesting project. When Jack's peers left his hospital room, they went to the back of the hospital where they had parked their vehicle. Constable Chief Durohn Takieshna was furious that Jack revealed their secret, but sternly emphasized the need to silence everyone who was made aware. To contain the damaging information, Chief Takieshna, Officer Rvyan Hartwell, Officer Samuel Shakahoshi and Officer Nate Baxwally climbed aboard their Chevy Tahoe and drove directly to Chief Shomittaroua's residence.

***

When Kane and Linnora abandoned Officer Jack Quiere confined, she drove him to Eshanwai's house where he had been staying. Before exiting the vehicle, Kane advised Linnora to leave town for a while until things settled down. Kane expected it to take some time before the police found their missing comrade and knew there would be hell to pay whenever they did. The Mohawk Indian also planned on leaving Shamattawa; but thought he would have enough time to address the tribal council before he left. Such a meeting could be arranged within minutes, thus once Kane entered Eshanwai's residence he asked his friend to contact Chief Shomittaroua and inform him. When Eshanwai spoke with the chief he learnt that three of the council members were away attending an event in Vancouver, however with the council gathering impossible Chief Shomittaroua asked Kane to come and discuss his findings.

Chief Shomittaroua was at his brother Manny's grocery store, which was the villager's only means to acquire imported food, personal hygiene products and other essentials. The store was located in the middle of the village and was readily accessible to each resident. When Eshanwai and Kane drove to the store in the Ford Bronco, they parked a small distance away from the building to hide the vehicle from customers commuting there. Both men then walked through pathways and bushes and came upon the structure from behind, to which they then secretly entered. After ensuring that it was safe to converse, Kane then relayed everything he had learnt from Officer Jack Quiere.

***

The team of officers drove directly to Chief Shomittaroua's home, where he lived with his wife Falling-Snow and Linnora. Each of the officers could be implicated in the organ trafficking scam, therefore they were strictly out to silence everyone who had learnt of their illegal enterprise. Chief Shomittaroua had other children who lived elsewhere with families of their own, but Linnora was his renegade daughter who was more concerned about the welfare of her people than raising a family. Once Linnora returned home from her escapade with Kane, she could hardly conceal what she had discovered and told her mother. Out of fear for Linnora's safety, once she went to her room Falling-Snow secretly telephoned the 911 dispatcher and told them where the kidnapped officer could be found. Falling-Snow knew that Linnora would be tortured and possibly killed should the police uncover evidence she was involved in Officer Quiere's death; thus, she thought it best they rescued him before anything unforeseen happened.

Linnora was packing her belongings into a suitcase inside her room, when Police Chief Takieshna and his associates kicked in the front door and barged into the house. When the coppers broke in, they slammed Falling-Snow on the floor, then searched and found Linnora in her bedroom and threw her against the wall with her right hand in an excruciating hurtful armlock. While Officer Baxwally twisted Linnora's arm, Constable Hartwell punched her several times in the ribcage for what they did to his partner.

Linnora was brought out and placed on a chair to sit inside the kitchen. None of the officers bothered to recite their detainees' legal rights, which were being violated with the officers' illegal entry without a signed warrant. The police chief had several questions to ask of Linnora, who was confused as to how they knew of what happened so soon.

"Who is the man that helped you to kidnap Officer Jack Quiere," Police Chief Takieshna enquired?

"I don't know what you are talking about," Police Chief Takieshna who was directly in front of Linnora, slapped her across the face with an open palm!

Linnora's mother screamed out in protest and said, "tell them what they want Linnora, before they seriously hurt you!"

"I don't know what you are talking about," repeated Linnora as she looked up at the police chief with hatred in her eyes!

"Forgive me Linnora, but I cannot have them kill you if they find your fingerprints or something, when they investigate the officer you kidnapped! So, I called the dispatcher and tell them where they can find him," sobbed Linnora's mother.

With Falling-Snow in handcuffs while being held by Officers Shakahoshi and Baxwally, Police Chief Takieshna aimed his weapon at her forehead and asked.

"I'm not going to ask you again! Now, who is this man who helped you to kidnap and torture Officer Quiere," Chief Takieshna threatened?

It was evident by Linnora's stare that she would not surrender the information easily and Chief Takieshna was not in the mood to play around. The police chief waved both his men away from Falling-Snow, then callously shot the Indian chief's wife directly in the forehead. Linnora screamed out in anguish as her mother's deceased body crumbled to the floor.

"This is your last chance to tell me what I need to know?"

"I hope you and people like you rot in hell," declared Linnora as she spat on the police chief!

Chief Takieshna angrily pointed his weapon at Linnora's head and shot her as he did her mother.

"Why did you kill her? How are we supposed to find out who this guy is," Constable Hartwell exclaimed?

"Who do you think this guy would be telling his story to right now?... Chief Shomittaroua you idiot! Find out where the chief is and that's where we are going to find this guy," Police Chief Takieshna shouted as he went over to the stove, ignited a burner and placed a cloth that would burn directly to the window curtains!

The house was partly engulfed in flames when the officers drove away from the Indian chief's residence, without even informing the fire department of the developing catastrophe. The bodies of Falling-Snow and Linnora were burnt inside their home and later recovered after the fire had been doused by the volunteered firefighters. Constable Nate Baxwally found out Chief Shomittaroua location from an informant who had seen him inside the community's grocery store. The informant was not present when Kane and Eshanwai arrived at the store, but the coppers were sure their person of interest would turn up sooner or later.

Kane and Eshanwai met Chief Shomittaroua, his brother Manny, Mukaii and Divyansh inside the community's only grocery store. The Mohawk Indian had most of his Shamattawa brothers at awe with the information he was able to uncover, but Manny and Mukaii argued they needed evidence of their own before they believed such rubbish. For the none believers to hear for themselves, Kane suggested bringing them to Officer Quiere whom he thought was still in captive. Even though there was still an hour to closing, Manny decided to leave early, and they all began heading towards the store entrance. The Indian chief's truck was parked out front with two other vehicles, therefore when the coppers rode up on the scene, they knew the informant's tip had paid off.

"Chief Shomittaroua, it has come to our attention that you are harboring a wanted criminal who abducted one of our officers and tortured him! I assure you that anything said by my officer under pressure while he pleads for his life is just that; a plea for his life! Now I'm not going to stand out here and get into some loud shouting conversation over this loud speaker! You and everybody inside that grocery store are going to start coming on out one by one! Let's start with you Chief; come on out," instructed Police Chief Takieshna!

"Chief Shomittaroua if they believe you know their secret, they are going to kill you," Kane stated!

"My people make the laws in Shamattawa, not the police! They do what we…," began Chief Shomittaroua before his cellular rang and interrupted him.

The caller was the 911 dispatcher who lived in the community and was a close friend to the chief's family. The instant Chief Shomittaroua looked at the phone number he knew there must be some disaster, hence he quickly responded to the call.

"Hello!"

"Chief Shomittaroua moments ago I received a call from a witness who claimed that the police sat your house on fire; but the officers did not advise me of the incident! I dispatched the fire department to your residence and they have since reported that there was nothing they could do to put out the fire! I'm sorry for bearing bad news, but I must go!" the dispatcher exclaimed.

"Wait, what did they say about my family," asked Chief Shomittaroua?

"I'm sorry, but I don't know," the dispatcher answered.

"Thank you for telling me," declared Chief Shomittaroua, whose hand began shaking so badly he could hardly press the button to hang up the phone. "There will be no need to seek out Officer Quiere, this man speaks the truth. As I stand here now my house burns; and I was told it was done by police officers. What weapons do you have here my brother," declared Chief Shomittaroua!

"Not much, just the old Buck Shot behind the counter," Manny responded.

"While we distract them get out through the back! These stories must be told; or I fear all may be lost," remarked Chief Shomittaroua!

The Chief went behind the store counter and grabbed the weapon with the box of bullets next to it. While everyone scattered about and looked through the door and windows to pinpoint the officers, Kane armed himself and moved to the back door with Eshanwai. With only one shotgun amongst them there were very little options available to the Indians.

"Chief you have thirty seconds before I send my officers in there," Police Chief Takieshna warned!

"Like you did at my house Takieshna; or were you man enough to actually go in," Chief Shomittaroua argued!

There were witnesses gathering and Police Chief Takieshna could not afford for others to learn of the news they fought to conceal. To quickly end the controversy the chief instructed his officers to advance and raid the store, believing everyone inside the store was armed. Officer Baxwally had gotten sent to cover the rear exit and ensured that nobody escaped. Chief Takieshna remained behind the protection of their vehicle and supported his valiant officers, who were intent on killing everyone inside the store. Officer Hartwell and Officer Shakahoshi both converged on the store with their high-powered rifles aimed at the windows and door of the structure. As the officers got close to the front door, Mukaii who was the best shot of them all pulled the door open and shot Officer Shakahoshi point blank. The blast lifted the officer off the ground and threw him on his backside, as his companions began shooting recklessly at the structure.

Everyone inside the store had to dive on the floor as bullets bored through the walls and destroyed the shelved items. Kane and Eshanwai opened the back door and checked if there was anybody laying an ambush. With bullets clashing into everything around them, Eshanwai got overzealous and took off running towards the bushes to escape. Officer Baxwally who was crouched behind the left side of the store, shot him in the back as he ran for safety. Kane took off after his friend and dispersed several bullets at Officer Baxwally, who was forced to hide behind the wall as gunshots struck the building. When Kane reached Eshanwai and flipped him onto his back, he realized his friend had gotten killed and thus continued into the bushes.

Manny sold all sorts of items which included dangerous chemicals such as Propane and Lighter Fluid. While dousing the store with bullets the officers struck a Propane Tank, which caused a huge explosion and sat the structure on fire. To ensure that nobody escaped the cops continued shooting at the structure as the fire spread and engulfed the entire store. Chief Shomittaroua and everyone inside the store were killed in the destruction, which proved costly for the community that was without any means of acquiring essential living apparels. With the community's only firetruck in use at the chief's residence, Shamattawa lost two main structures on that day, in addition to their inspirational leader and others. Kane escaped and ran to his Ford truck, before he fled the community then the province altogether.

When word of what happened reached Natnah Fawfakuk, the physician grew scared and gathered all the notes she had kept on Officer Quiere and placed them in a Manilla Envelope. The psychiatrist addressed the package to her sister Nancy with instruction on what to do, then brought it to her mailbox and mailed it. The mailbox was down the street from her home and after posting the package, Nancy was walking back when a black car appeared from nowhere and ran her over. After the hit and run incident the driver who was

Bloodshed Never Ends

Officer Rvyan Hartwell, stopped by the postbox and used a Crowbar to force it open, then removed Natnah's package and drove away.

Part 21

Manuel Lagarza was furious when he got word that his plans had to be altered due to the shootout between Xavier Wamblay and his assassination team. The cartel boss had everything prearranged before Kadeem and his gunners arrived in Canada, so the last thing he wanted was for them to attract any sort of unwarranted attention. Their target was slated to give a speech at the infamous McGill University within five days, which would be their only opportunity to perform the deed. Following Marquez' explanation of who their attackers were and why they got targeted, Manuel instructed him to do whatever they sought necessary to complete the mission. To emphasize the extent of his disappointment should the mission fail, Manuel threatened Marquez and told him, "they better find another country to live if the Presidential Candidate wasn't killed"! Once off the telephone with Marquez, Manuel telephoned his problem solver Vincent El-Santiago, whom he had sent to Montreal weeks earlier to handle some sensitive business.

"Yes Captain," Vincent responded in Spanish!

"I want you to keep out of slight; and watch our new arrivals for me. I text you their location soon," Manuel instructed and disconnected the call.

***

Following their shootout, Xavier followed Kadeem and the Columbians to a small bed and breakfast motel on Laval Avenue, which was close enough to the university, but a slight distance from where they had the altercation. Kadeem and the Columbians knew that the cops would be looking for them as a group, so Marquez rented the suite and snuck his companions in through a rear door under camouflage. Once they entered their room at the posh Gingerbread Manor Bed and Breakfast Motel, Manuel again contacted his boss and gave him their location as instructed.

Xavier noted the new location that Kadeem and his associates moved to, then drove by and left the scene to find other serious thugs brave enough to join his quest. The Rough Rider thug who was insistent on collecting every penny promised for the reward of Kadeem's body dead or alive, went to check Drastic who lived on the north side of Montreal on L'Archeveque Avenue. Drastic was addicted to prescription pills and would pop anything from Percocet to GHB, which ever was readily available. As Xavier parked along the street, he could overhear Drastic arguing with his old lady Shannon, which was a regular occurrence for them both. Xavier buzzed the doorbell and got let in by Shannon, who also opened the door for him to enter. The visitor politely greeted Shannon who returned to her seat, before fist bumping Drastic and his cousin Jagz who was also present. The previous argument begun when Drastic accused his girlfriend Shannon of smoking the last piece of Crystal Meth; and continued even after Xavier interrupted and sat down.

To terminate the petty quarrel, Xavier told Drastic to phone up his dealer and offered to purchase $100 worth of Crystal Meth. There was already a half a bottle on Smirnoff Vodka on the table and a few beers in Drastic's fridge, so the liquor was already covered. Xavier knew that once he had gotten Drastic properly intoxicated, he could convince him to fly to the moon if he wished. At the mere mention of free drugs Shannon was on the phone contacting their dealer, who only lived four blocks down the street. Within twelve minutes the dealer was at their apartment and brought specifically what was requested of him. Shannon dealt with the dealer at the door area to restrict him from seeing Jagz, who owed him money and did not have it to repay. When Shannon brought the drugs in, Drastic used his Razor Blade to chop up small pieces of the sparkly substance, then passed the first hit to Xavier for his kindness.

Within ten minutes they were all blazed to the extent that they sat quietly and watched an infomercial on the television, where the actors tried to convince their viewers to purchase their product. None of them spoke a word or moved as if they were all pasted to the chairs on which they sat. Nearly half an hour later Xavier realized that Drastic and Jagz appeared poised to be conned, thus he leaned forward and made his proposal.

"Yow, you guys interested in making some easy money," Xavier questioned?

"Right now I'm so broke I could rob a bank man! What do we have to do," quickly responded Jagz who seemed ready for whatever?

"You guys ever heard about some reward for the guy who killed Antoine Hickston," Xavier asked?

"Yeah, some black guy shot him and left the country or some shit like that," Drastic added.

"Well… that black guy is back in Montreal, and I'm the only one who knows where to find him," Xavier exclaimed!

"Fuck we need to phone the rest of the gang and let them know," Drastic suggested!

"Are you fucking crazy? Then what do we get? Nothing, probably a few drinks and an eight ball," Jagz declared!

"Baby Jagz is right, you guys have to bring him in yourself to get that reward," Shannon indicated!

"Count me in! Where do we find this fucker," Drastic said?

"We are going to need some guns to get this guy. He has two guys with him and I think they have some heavy machinery," Xavier suggested!

The recruiter neglected to mention his previous unsuccessful attack, knowing Drastic and his people were not fans of the news and thus would not have heard of the incident. Xavier also knew that there was a great chance the police were looking for him, hence, telling them of the shooting may alter their decision. Both Drastic and Jagz thought long and hard of a person from whom they could get high powered weapons on consignment, without having to mention their intentions.

"The only person who is going to loan us anything is probably D'Works," Shannon suggested.

"Oh no way, I owe that man money for over a month now! He is going to fucking kick my ass," Jagz cried!

"Who else are we going to get them from at such short notice," Shannon argued?

"Phone him back," Drastic stated!

Shannon again called their dealer who was not too enthusiastic about returning there simply to talk, but he eventually agreed and was back in thirty minutes. The instant D'Works walked into the apartment and saw Jagz he moved to attack, before Xavier exclaimed that he would certainly get paid what was owed and more. The drug dealer poised himself and listened to Xavier and Drastic's reason for summoning him, then sat and thought about what was mentioned. Instead of simply loaning his weapons, D'Works wanted a bigger piece of the pie knowing personally exactly how much money had been offered for the reward. Xavier and his new teamsters had no option but to accept their new partner, who donated a pair of Teck 9 Mini Assault Rifles and a 357 Magnum handgun to their cause. D'Works kept one of the Teck 9 Rifles for himself and gave the second to Drastic, before hesitantly passing the handgun to Jagz. Xavier wanted Drastic to bring Shannon along to help them easily acquire information from the motel handlers, but his newest partner rejected the implication of involving his girlfriend.

***

The bed and breakfast motel at which Kadeem and the Columbians stayed offered complimentary breakfast, free WIFI and several other amenities. While the Columbians enjoyed the motel's attraction which they described as luxurious, Kadeem took a lengthy shower but spent most of his time in the bathroom conducting business. The relationship between he and his abductors had drastically improved, though none of them knew that he had the communication device. Kadeem was extremely lucky that the moron who owned the cellular phone he stole, used the factory code of 0000 to unlock the device. When the Jamaican rude-boy successfully opened the phone inside the bathroom, he used it to retrieve his messages and contacted two people. The date for their mission was close at hand and it was either Kadeem tried to help himself or he knew what was to become of him.

The caretakers at the motel provided everything for their guest's comfort, therefore the assassination teamsters ordered their liquor and whatever they needed without having to leave the room. Throughout most of the next day they all remained indoors despite the Columbians' urge to walk around and tour the city. As a result, it was quite difficult for Xavier and his new gang to keep an eye out for their rented vehicle departing the property. Nearly every building around the surrounding area had their personal guards and security cameras, so simply loitering would not be tolerated. To avoid being spotted by Gingerbread Manor's security cameras and others around, the Rough Rider thugs continuously circled the location at a distance and switched who kept watch on the vehicle. Every twenty minutes the four thugs would rotate and maintained a close eye on their only ticket to acquiring the man they sought.

It wasn't until after it had gotten dark around 8:00 PM that Jagz who was the person keeping watch, phoned his associates and told them their targets were preparing to leave. Several seconds after Kadeem and his crew pulled away, a Hyundai Sonata picked up Jagz and gave pursuit. Following a long and conflictive day where the bikers argued continuously over theories that maybe the vehicle had been abandoned etcetera; everybody became excited at the thought of collect their humongous reward.

They followed Kadeem and his companions onto Walkley Road in the Cote Saint Luc area, during which they maintained a four cars length to avoid being spotted. It was extremely dark without the aid of the streetlights and with multiple glares from other traffic it was impossible for Kadeem and friends to notice they were being pursued. The wanted Jamaican parked a block and a half away from their actual destination to show the visitors what basic neighborhoods looked like, as their pursuers did likewise but walked along the opposite side of the street. There was a store at the corner of Somerled Avenue and Walkley where they stopped and purchased a small flashlight, before continuing on their way. Even though relations had improved between Kadeem and his captors, the Columbians were the only persons armed which did not bother the rude-boy.

The temperature was mild at 0 Degree Celsius, but the Columbians felt that outside was always frigid cold regardless. While Kadeem felt comfortable in his T-shirt and winter jacket, his companions were bundled up in turtle neck sweaters and many other layers of clothing. As they drew close to the cordoned off building that was slated to be demolished, Kadeem looked around to ensure they were not being watched. Under the assumption they were not being watched, the visitors snuck their way into the building one at a time through a rear entrance. It was obvious that the building had already been evacuated, with all the doors removed and window panes broken out. Along with his Columbian associates Kadeem made his way down to the boiler room located in the basement, where he shuns the light against a back wall then began removing several bricks from a specific section. While Kadeem removed the bricks both Columbians drew increasing excited as they solely focused on him and provided the lighting.

"Ouuuuuu-weeee," cheered Ricardo who could hardly control himself!

There was a huge compartment built behind the wall where Damian stashed money, drugs and a few weapons. A bag containing four hand pistols with extra magazines and two boxes of bullets was the first parcel Kadeem removed from the stashbox. As he laid the bag on the ground and opened it to reveal its contents, Xavier and his comrades crept up behind them and caught them off guard.

"You fucking boys get your hands in the air," D'Works ordered, to which everyone complied!

"What do we have here," exclaimed Jagz who walked over and picked up the bag with the guns?

"I told you fellows I would produce," celebrated Xavier who aimed his assault rifle at the Jamaican!

"So, who are these two foreign looking motherfuckers," Drastic argued?

"Police officers," Kadeem stated!

"Fuck what are we going to do now," Jagz shouted!?

"Get on your knees and latch your fingers behind your heads," Xavier instructed, to which their captives complied!

"What we doing Drastic," Jagz continued?

"We going to kill them all; then chop off his head and take to collect our reward," Xavier declared!

"Fuck, I don't want nothing to do with killing no cops cousin," Jagz cried!

"You want some of this reward? You all have to kill these men to get it," Xavier decreed!

D'Works, Xavier and Drastic had no second thoughts about doing what needed to be done to collect their biggest payday ever. With their targets knelt before them, Jagz and his thugs held their weapons poised to execute the three foreigners. Sensing he was about to die, Kadeem looked over at his associates and only glimpsed flares of light sparking in the dark behind them. Xavier and his three comrades crumbled to the ground, thereafter, leaving the praying Columbians and a bewildered Jamaican still breathing. Kadeem reached for the flashlight that was closest to him on the ground and used it to shine in the direction from which the bullets hurled. From the darkness stepped Vincent El-Santiago, who used a Glock 9mm with an attached silencer to shoot the Rough Rider thugs.

Ricardo was praying so intensely that he flinched and nearly got a heart attack when Vincent touched him on the shoulder to indicate they had been liberated. Marquez was exceptionally happy to see Vincent, after closing his eyes in anticipation of being murdered.

"What are you doing here," Marquez asked after emotionally hugging Vincent, whom he had known since childhood?

Informer 3

"After the shooting at your last location the boss told me to watch over you. What are you guys doing here anyways," Vincent stated?

"Just getting some guns to do the job," Kadeem declared, as he shuns the light on the bag of guns.

"What about the weapons you got from Pedro," Vincent questioned?

"We had to leave some behind," Marquez answered.

"Come on, let's get out of here," Vincent instructed!

"You go ahead; we are going to hide the bodies back in the hole and seal it up, so they can't find them for now," Marquez suggested!

Vincent agreeably shook his head and accepted the compliments from his peers, before he backed into the darkness and disappeared. The bag containing the money was a black backpack and after retrieving it with several other items, Kadeem and friends crammed the dead bodies into the compartment and resealed it. Nobody throughout the neighborhood had any clue there was a disturbance, hence the foreigners snuck from the condemned building and walked back to their vehicle. Vincent was parked half a block away up the street from them and watched as his countrymen and Kadeem returned to their vehicle and safely drove away.

The recovered cash amounted to 5.3 million dollars; 4.8 of which was the American currency paid by Manuel. Kadeem also took the drugs, the four handguns and the biker's 357 Magnum, which he knew were worth a hefty price on the Black Market. Regardless of such wealth, none of the men in possession of the money even contemplated running off with it, knowing Senior Lagarza would have them found and killed wherever they went. The money however could offer the Columbians freedom from a life they dreaded, but they understood they would have to first complete Manuel's mission. With the Columbian Presidential Candidate dead and their obligations fulfilled, Marquez and Ricardo hoped that Senior Lagarza would allow them to defect from his regime, but there were never any guarantees with such a ruthless drug lord.

During the final few days the assassination teamsters brought Delvin to a distance shooting range twice to practice. Devlin was never included in any factor of the planning stages and had no clue when or where the assassination was supposed to take place. To eliminate all chances of their plans getting disclosed, the exact location selected for the incident was also kept from Kadeem and Manuel's enforcers. Two nights before the scheduled assassination Vincent El-Santiago who was assigned to acquire the floor plans for the Pollack Concert Hall, where the Columbian Presidential Candidate was scheduled to give his speech, invited his co-workers and Kadeem for drinks. Vincent had a fabulous suite at the Ritz-Carlton Hotel and wanted to show-off his accommodations, which was elegantly designed and befitting for a king. The view of Montreal from Vincent's Royal Suite's, Living Room on the twelfth floor of the hotel was spectacular, but the room itself was breathtakingly decorated and bigger than most average hotel suites.

Before they began socializing, Vincent brought his guests over to a table on which he had the Pollack Hall's floor plans laid out. To accomplish such a mission required precision, skill and mastery of the escape, thus he also gave them workers' identification passes, uniforms and keys to the establishment. There would be an array of guards surrounding Dominguez Martel who had a huge list of followers in Canada, that were expected to show up and cheer his name as he made his way into the building. They would have no opportunity for a clear shot outside on Sherbrooke Street and may only have the chance at a definite kill with Dominguez standing on the stage. Vincent illustrated through which entrance they could enter the hall and provided a few photos to show the interior design. Kadeem listened while the assassin explained how he would go about accomplishing the task, trusting he would leave the specifics he had drawn on the paper.

After they discussed the plans everyone got offered a cigar and whatever liquor they desired from the adequately stacked bar, then they sat about talking crap as if they were all old friends. The old Scarface movie was showing on the television in French, but Vincent claimed he had seen it more than a hundred times and wasn't bothered by the language. Kadeem had already figured that Vincent was sent by Manuel to ensure nothing got tied to the Lagarza Cartel, thus he was content with the pretense although he knew they were all expendable at that point. Moments later the Jamaican went to the bathroom where he urinated and programed his stolen phone to record, before exiting with the device hidden against his palm. As the Columbians conversed and neglected Kadeem, he secretly made a video of the Pollack Hall's blueprint and his captors, who had no clue they were being recorded. While all three men served Manuel, Ricardo and Marquez got paid far less than Vincent, who was their boss' number one assassin. With trained killers such as Vincent in Manuel's employment, Marquez thought it strange their boss would pay the price he did to have Damian kill the Presidential Candidate. To get more information on the money they recovered, Marquez tried to trick Vincent into disclosing what he knew of the arrangement.

"The boss should have paid you all that money to do this job! Then he would be sure this would get done no problem," Marquez teased!

Vincent who thought of himself as the most efficient killer on Earth, smiled at the compliment knowing the truth of the story. "Senior Lagarza does nothing without a reason. That money he paid Damian to kill Dominguez was also meant to embarrass the United States Government, and have others believe that they paid for the assassination. It is well known that the present American government prefers our current president; and so does Senior Lagarza, but the cartel must do what we must to preserve this Columbian government. If the assassination was successful, I was to let the authority know where to find Damian and the money, but then your friend here messed everything up."

"Do you know where this money is? Did you not go and try to find it," Ricardo enquired?

"No time to concern ourselves with that now, we have a job to do," Vincent snapped!

***

The Columbian Presidential Candidate Dominguez Martel was leading in the electoral poles and projected to win the election by a wide margin. Senior Martel's new approach to tackling some the country's oldest problems had gotten strict criticism from his opponents, but voters saw his approach as a drastic change from the normal corrupt politics. Prior to his speech at the university Dominguez had a fundraising event to raise money for his campaign, therefore he arrived in Montreal the evening before his main event. The fundraising gala was scheduled in the ballroom at The Holland Hotel, Downtown Old Montreal and had an impressive list of guests from entertainers to business moguls.

While Senior Martel entertained his guests, an uninvited female arrived at the venue and asked the security at the door to speak with the Presidential Candidate. The Canadian guard advised the black woman that she was not getting in without an invitation and pushed her to the side, yet the woman refused to leave and sat in the lobby. A few minutes later one of Dominguez' personal guards walked out to check how things were, at which the guard told him about the uninvited female. The bodyguard then walked over to the female and asked what she wanted from Senior Martel; and the woman told him that 'her information involved Senior Manuel Lagarza'. At the mere mention of Columbia's largest drug lord, the bodyguard brought the female upstairs to a room and had her wait a short while. After a few minutes passed the female began wondering if she had made the right decision by voluntarily entering the room, but there was liquor available, so she fixed herself a drink to settle her nerves. Ten minutes later the guard returned with two other men and thoroughly searched the room plus the female for weapons, before Dominguez Martel entered and his guards exited.

"Would you care for something to drink, Senorita...," offered Dominguez?

"Marlene McDonald; and yes, you can fix me another Cognac," said Marlene who had helped herself to couple of drinks by then!

The Columbian Presidential Candidate passed Marlene the drink and sat across from her. "Why are you doing this Senorita Marlene?"

"There is someone who is mixed up in all this by accident; and he is the person who sent me here today," Marlene stated!

"What do you know of Manuel Lagarza," Dominguez enquired?

"I know he plans to kill you tomorrow during your speech at the hall," Marlene exclaimed, then showed him the information Kadeem sent her on her phone.

"Julio," yelled Dominguez, at which his guards busted into the room as if their boss was being killed!

Senior Martel passed his head of security the phone that contained the information Kadeem recorded, which highlighted the entire assassination plot. Dominguez immediately wanted to cancel the speech, but Julio did not think that would be necessary and convinced his boss that they needed to catch the assassins in the act. It was later agreed upon by the Columbian Presidential Candidate that if the men were in custody before he went on stage, he would proceed with the event. With a ballroom filled of adoring fans, Dominguez had to return to his fundraising event but whipped out his personal checkbook and wrote Marlene a thank you check for ten thousand dollars. Understanding the length to which Marlene went to save his life, Senior Martel also gave her his personal number and told her if ever she needed a favor just call.

***

There was considerable tension between Kadeem and the Columbians as they drove to Delvin's house on the afternoon of the assassination. Their shooter had no knowledge that day was the day he had been practicing for, but the instant he entered the vehicle he sensed an uneased vibe. Delvin was given a security uniform and changed into it before they reached the venue downtown Montreal. Security around the event was beginning to tighten some five hours before the actual start, wherein city employees were putting into place the barricades needed to keep traffic from entering the concert hall zone. A block away from the hall they came across their first checkpoint, where an officer stopped them then allowed them to proceed after realizing they were members of the Pollack Hall's security team. As they approached the service entrance where the two guards did a thorough search of every transport that proceeded them, Ricardo nervously gripped tightly onto the handle of his holstered firearm. When Kadeem brought the vehicle to a stop at the checkpoint, Marquez rolled his window down to speak with the guard who had an unpleasant look on his face.

"Are you friends of Senor Lagarza," surprisingly asked the guard in Spanish?

"Ah, yes," Marquez answered in Spanish!

Without any further questions the guard signaled his partner to open the gate and allowed them onto grounds. Delvin was fascinated by the reach and influence of the Lagarza Cartel, but Manuel's capability to gain resolve was nothing new to his associates. The security jackets and hats they wore made it hard to distinctively identify who they were, still there was a great chance they could get found if they were not cautious. There were caterers and other service employees bringing different items into the hall, thus Ricardo and Kadeem snuck the disassembled long rifle into the building and hid it inside a room. Over the next few hours they posted themselves at the front gate and the back entrance to abstain from interacting with any of the security team members, who would recognize they were not a part of their crew and have them arrested.

As the hour for the speech drew closer and the crowd enlarged the noise level slowly increased, until groups of spectators started yelling the Columbian anthem and cheers. With several officers protecting the barrier that kept the crowd at a distance from the dignified guests and celebrity performers, limousines and chauffeured cars began arriving. There were loud cheers for many of the special guests who were invited, but the loudest cheer of the evening was undoubtedly given to the guest speaker upon his arrival. Senior Dominguez exited his limousine into the protective circle of his bodyguards, who immediately rushed him into the building without allowing him to recognize his screaming fans. There were many dignitaries and representatives from McGill University waiting in line inside the building, who Dominguez shook hands with before he was taken into his waiting room.

Wherever foreign nationals and political dignitaries assembled in Canada, the Royal Canadian Mounted Police was guaranteed to provide some sort of security detail. Therefore, when local officers posted at the Sherbrooke Street's eastern gate saw a RCMP supervisor's marked 4X4 approaching, they simply allowed him entry after only glaring at his identification. Inside the marked cruiser that freely passed through each checkpoint before getting on the grounds was Vincent El-Santiago dressed as the supervisor. When Vincent drove up to the venue's back entrance and the same guards who allowed Kadeem's crew entry saw him, they immediately allowed him in without checking his ID. Once on the grounds Vincent illegally parked close to the back entrance, then switched the onboard radio from RCMP dispatch onto the channel being used by the Pollack's security team.

The short program provided featured two Spanish artists before the main speaker, although Senior Martel was not about to leave his suite until the assassins were arrested. The assassination plot was for Delvin to climb up to the raptors above the projection room, which was located on an upper tier to the back of the hall. Ricardo was posted in the corridor below Delvin and both Kadeem and Marquez were supposed to station themselves at the base of each staircase that led up to the projection and sound rooms. When Kadeem entered the hall and started moving to his station, he noticed a group of men speaking amongst themselves and caught a glimpse of two automatic rifles being concealed. Instead of moving to the assigned position, Kadeem lingered about and watched to see what their next move would be.

Suddenly the group of a dozen men separated into two groups and took off towards both staircases. Kadeem had no doubt their plans had been intercepted and began moving towards the rear exit. Vincent was listening through the security's radio connection and heard when they stipulated that they had taken one into custody. The hitman exited the cruiser and bumped into Kadeem just inside the concert hall's rear door, as he was about to run up to the projection level.

"Follow me," instructed Vincent, as he rushed to the stairs!

Kadeem who was more concerned about his freedom and the recovered items they left inside their rented suite, found himself moving to help two men who abducted him and would have killed him if ordered by their boss. Both Marquez and Ricardo were getting a quick tutorial of the machinery inside the audio and video room by a technician, when the team of specialists ran up on them and easily overpowered them. Delvin who was already positioned up in the rafters could slightly hear the exchange, but he was completely unaware of what was taking place. When Kadeem and Vincent reached the top of the stairs and the arresting officers who had Marquez and Ricardo down on their knees with guns aimed to the back of their heads, saw the RCMP uniform and badge they returned their attention to their teammate, who was in the process of retrieving the shooter.

Delvin looked at the audience below and became reassured there were no issues with everyone still calmly seated, so he went back to patiently waiting for his opportunity to shoot Dominguez Martel from his ambush point. The officer climbing the ladder towards him slipped and gave away his surprise advantage, after Delvin had excused the disturbance he heard prior. Even though the officer paused and waited a few seconds before proceeding, Delvin had sensed there was a problem and pointed his handgun towards the ladder as he whisperingly called out to see if it was one of his associates. The officer on the ladder had no clue where exactly the shooter was positioned, so he tried using a small mirror to pinpoint the assassin. Delvin noticed the small mirror as it slowly elevated then turned towards him, thus he opened fire and shot it from the officer's grasp. The assassin's Beretta APX Compact 9mm discharge told the officer exactly where the shooter was positioned, but Delvin gave him no opportunity to aim his assault rifle at him as he continued blasting his firearm in the ladder direction. Loud screams erupted from the crowd below as patrons began scattering for the exits to avoid getting injured. To return fire at the assassin the officer on the ladder withdrew his service weapon and callously fired off a few rounds without exposing himself.

When the gunshots erupted Vincent saw his opportunity and took full advantage of it. The Columbian assassin knew that the officers wore bulletproof vests and began shooting them with laming bullets to their arms and limbs and kill shots to the head. Kadeem noticed two of the officers reactively turning towards them and dispersed his firearm killing both men before they retaliated. Officer Jerome Leclerk who was standing the furthest from the shooters, tried to escape the mayhem by backing away and shooting, but with his tumbling comrades blocking his pathway he could not get off a clear shot. Kadeem struck Jerome in the groin and dropped him to the ground, but his second bullet struck the officer's vest. There was a corner around which a water-fountain was attached to the wall, so to save his life Officer Leclerk crawled behind it. To Keep the assassins at bay Jerome fired several shots in their direction and remarkably struck Ricardo in the shoulder, as he and Marquez made their way towards their rescuers.

The officer at the top of the ladder gruesomely shot Delvin in the stomach and injured him, but with his teammates under siege he had no choice but to offer them support and neglected the assassin. As the officer began turning his weapon towards their attackers, Vincent shot him directly in the head and thus killed him as he dropped to the floor. Injured and afraid, both Delvin and Officer Leclerk continued firing off an occasional shot to keep their antagonists at bay, even though the remaining assassins had aborted the mission. There were two engineers inside the projection room who both hid beneath a desk and did not move until officers rushed into the building and later rescued them.

The Columbian Presidential Candidate was one of the first people rushed from the hall and scurried into his limousine, before his motorcade drove away and left the scene. With patrons pouring through the exits it was impossible for armed officers to immediately storm the building, therefore Kadeem and Marquez concealed their weapons and began pretending they were helping the guests escape. With several emotionally terrified older females clinging to authority figures, both assassins eventually exited the building affectionately carrying vulnerable survivors. Directly after the guests and other employees vacated the hall, Vincent brought out the injured Ricardo who clutched his bloodied shoulder.

"The shooters are still up there, three or four of them! Go, go, go," Vincent shouted at the entering officers as he brought Ricardo to his marked cruiser and had him sit on the back seat!

It was dark outside and seemed as if there were hundreds of police officers and EMS workers. Marquez and Kadeem led the ladies they carried out into the arms of ambulance technicians, who had to provide warm blankets for much of the attendants who had to flee without their jackets. In all the madness both assassins slowly disappeared into the crowd and made their way back to their motel. The imposter RCMP supervisor had Ricardo sit in the back of his cruiser, then gradually drove away as if he was bringing the injured employee to an awaiting ambulance just outside the service gates. Instead of bringing Ricardo to the ambulance technicians, Vincent neglected to stop and slowly drove by as they made their escape.

Back inside the Pollack Concert Hall, Officer Jerome Leclerk fired off several more shots then realized he was fast running out of bullets. All the officers who entered the building cautiously climbed the stairs that led to the incident, not knowing exactly what they would be up against. It had been a short while since any of the assassins returned fire at Jerome, but the officer thought they might be trying to trick him and continued firing callously in the same direction. Neither Delvin nor Officer Leclerk were shooting at each other, but both men knew what the other symbolized. Officer Leclerk expected his peers to provide support and rescue eventually, hence he simply had to keep himself alive until they got to him. Still, there was nothing more reassuring than when he heard the rescuers shouted, to find out the status of their fellow officers. Only then did the injured officer stopped shooting and allowed his peers to move in, which gave the assassins time to escape.

Delvin had crawled to the ladder's edge, where the chilling sight of the deceased intervention force members scattered across the floor below. As he contemplated his next move, Delvin could hear the rescuers attending to Officer Leclerk and knew his time was soon. Nearly five minutes had passed since his peers abandoned him and with a bullet to the stomach his options were limited.

"You up in the bleacher, throw down your weapons and come out with your hands visible" shouted an officer below!

"Fuck y'all! Come get my scunt if you feel you bad," Delvin shouted!

With their comrades lying about the floor deceased the responding officers were in no mood for games, therefore, they sent a sharpshooter down to the ground floor and another across the hall with hopes one of them might get a clear shot at Delvin. The sharpshooter who went across the hall found an area from which he caught a glimpse of Delvin, who had his attention focused on the coppers below the ladder. A green light to take out the target was already issued, therefore the shooter ended it all with one bullet to Delvin's head.

Marquez and Kadeem left the scene before Ricardo and Vincent, whom they were extremely worried about during their trip back to the motel. To vacate the area around the Pollack Concert Hall, both men caught a taxi two blocks away and drove to Berri Metro Station. Once inside the station they caught a train to Square Victoria, where they exited the metro and took a taxi back to their motel. Both men were extremely worried about Ricardo and Vincent, not knowing if they had made it out successfully. When they entered their suite at the bed and breakfast motel, Kadeem and Marquez were surprised to find their other teammates already there. Ricardo had the bullet in his shoulder and needed medical attention, yet Vincent's first concern was informing Manuel, which was exactly why he was on his phone.

The backpack containing the money and other items was inside the open closet, which led the late arrivals to wonder if the assassin had snuck a peek. Kadeem expected swift retribution for their failure and got himself a drink from the liquor cabinet, all the while keeping an eye on Vincent who paced across the living room floor. Marquez tried attending to his partner who sat at the kitchen table and tried not to get his blood splashed against any of the furniture. Vincent stopped pacing and stared at Kadeem from across the room, before he turned his attention to his fellow countrymen. As nervous as Kadeem felt he knew that drawing his weapon would only lead to a one against three scenarios, therefore he picked up his drink and cuffed a steak knife against the side of his other arm and walked over to Ricardo and Marquez.

After Vincent was through speaking with his boss he went into the bathroom, at which Kadeem walked over to the mini fridge just outside the restroom door. Inside the bathroom, Vincent turned on the tap water then changed the magazine in his weapon; before he flushed the toilet, fixed his hair and finally shut off the tap. Marquez went over and collected some alcohol swabs and bandages from his bag and was bringing them to clean Ricardo's wound, when Vincent charged from the bathroom like a murderer on a rampage. Ricardo was the first-person Vincent laid his eyes on and dumped three bullets in the center of his chest.

There was absolutely nothing Marquez could do to avoid being killed second with both his hands carrying medical supplies. Seeing Ricardo with blood spitting from his mouth was all the confirmation Marquez needed to determine what Manuel ordered, hence he turned to look in the eyes of his childhood friend. Kadeem appeared from nowhere and used the knife to stab Vincent through his hand holding the weapon. The Columbian Assassin dropped the weapon in pain then reactively kicked Kadeem with a roundhouse strike across the side of his face. Vincent grabbed the knife handle and was about to extract it when Marquez came barreling at him and struck him with a punishing shoulder tackle to the stomach. Both men crashed to the floor and started grappling, during which Kadeem slowly rose to his feet and tried to shake out the cobwebs.

"Pussy-hole nearly break mi jaw," Kadeem quarreled, as he exercised his mouth to put things back in place!

Vincent was beginning to gain an advantage over Marquez and had him in a chokehold with his body pressed against the floor. Manuel's assassin had his buttocks slightly arched in the air, thus Kadeem lined him up like a penalty kick during a soccer match; then raced in with a powerful kick directly in Vincent's crotch.

"Agghhhh," screamed Vincent as he released Marquez and grabbed his groin in pain!

"Goalllll," Kadeem cheered, as Marquez reversed the chokehold and strangled Vincent to death in anger!

Marquez was beside himself after killing Vincent and had no idea where to go from that point. There was no sense killing Kadeem who had saved his life and was his only trusted ally on Canadian soil. With the Columbian crying like a baby knowing Manuel would have his entire family killed for his failure, Kadeem confessed that he helped to foil the assassination plan, then gave Marquez an offer he could not refuse. Knowing that Marquez could not only help himself, but solve both their problems by testifying against Manuel Lagarza, Kadeem incited him to help Senior Dominguez Martel and the Columbian Government with his condemning information. Kadeem also offered to purchase the tickets necessary for Marquez' family to flee Columbia to whatever country they chose. Following their arrival, the Jamaican promised to provide them with enough money to survive and placed the remainder of the bodyguard's share in a safety deposit box at a notable bank, then presented the key to his wife Esmenina. There was no other option available and Marquez trusted the rude-boy Jamaican, so he accepted the offer and contacted the Columbian Presidential Candidate.

With their business arrangements settled both men shook hands and hugged, before Kadeem left with the money and several other condemning items. Marquez remained inside the suite and waited for the arrival of the federal agents designated by a unified agreement between Senior Martel and the Canadian Government. There was a huge circus of reporters outside the bed and breakfast motel when the officers brought Marquez out in handcuffs with a jacket covering his head, before they escorted him to an undisclosed prison facility. News of the Columbian assassins' discovery went global immediately; however, when the drug-lord found out who the only reported survivor was, he knew that he had made a grave mistake.

Over the next two days Manuel tried to locate where Marquez was being held, but it was as if his former guard had fallen off the planet. If a trial was necessary to have Manuel convicted, Marquez would get transferred back to Columbia on a private charter under heavy guard, but until then the decision was made to keep him in a private facility in Canada, where he stood a greater chance of not getting killed. On the third day following Marquez' arrest, the Columbian Government launched a huge military operation that involved 250 soldiers, with orders to bring to justice one Manuel Lagarza. There was an international arrest warrant issued for the drug-lord, on serious charges for attempting to assassinate a government official on foreign soil.

To issue their warrant, the soldiers first engaged in a huge gun battle versus Manuel's trusted guards at his house. Most of Manuel's elite guards were murderers, rapists and thieves who thrived under the ruthless drug-lord, therefore they were willing to die for him. Senior Lagarza escaped the initial manhunt through tunnels built beneath his home and disappeared without any clues where to find him. For a month and a half, the search to find the cartel boss revealed nothing until the mother of one of his many girlfriends phoned the rewards line with information regarding his whereabouts. The woman's name was Josephine Sanchez and her daughter were Manuel's ninth girlfriend named Elaina.

To rid her family of the pestilence she accused Manuel of being, Josephine advised government officials where they could find the wanted cartel leader. The following morning at 5:10 am, a team of a hundred and twenty soldiers went to the location provided, where they surrounded the residence and found Manuel hiding inside a hidden room built underneath the house. Many residents actually cried when Manuel was taken into custody, under the lights and cameras of reporters for the world to see. The Canadian Government wanted Manuel Lagarza extradited to Canada to stand trial in their courts, but the Columbian Government had desperately wanted to imprison the cartel boss for years and thus rejected the request.

Despite being in prison the loyalty attained through corruption continued for Senior Lagarza, who got word on who informed on him from a police official. Manuel was so furious about the disloyalty that he sent several men to visit Josephine that same night. When the killers sent by Manuel arrived at Josephine's home, the mother was celebrating after she received the rewards check for providing the criminal's whereabouts. There were twenty-four other family members and friends inside the house, when the killers pulled up in two separate vehicles and rushed into the residence, where they sprayed the entire interior with bullets and slaughtered everyone.

Part 22

Marolina Veronovichi went to see her brother Marceau at his mansion on Ile-Bizard, located southwest off the coast of Montreal. Despite her status as a member of the family, Marolina still had to endure the security protocol at the front gate before being allowed onto the property. The house was huge and sat on a fifteen acres property, with your typical pool, hot tub, sauna, basketball court, tennis court, theatre, gym, games room, eight cars garage and even a private nine holes golf course. Marceau was enjoying an expensive Cohiba Esplendido Cigar, with a glass of vintage Gran Duque d'Alba Reserva Brandy, inside his relax lounge when his elder sister came storming in. When it came to his bigger sister, Marceau knew she had a flair for the mellow dramatic at times but tolerated her antics out of respect.

"Our father will be avenged," Marolina yelled as the maid showed her into the lounge!

"Marolina, you make yourself so scarce I barely see you my sister," Marceau greeted, as they hugged each other! "Would you like a drink?"

"I'll have a glass of red wine," Marolina responded, at which her brother signaled the maid to prepare the drink.

Before proceeding with their discussion Marolina waited until the maid brought her the drink and left the room, not wanting the female to overhear what she had to say.

"So, tell me, how are the kids," Marceau asked?

"Everybody at home is fine, you need to drop in and pay us a visit. But I'm here to discuss the man who killed our father, and how we're going to make him pay," Marolina stated!

Marceau paused whilst bringing the glass of brandy to his mouth and looked flabbergasted at his sister. "Who, and who are the people behind it?"

"Your Grand Chancellor, Montreal's newest adopted son Kevin Lafleur," Marolina declared!

Marceau dropped back into the chair behind him with fright and developed a vengeful look on his face. His sister who thought she had him contemplating revenge, took out a cigarette and set it ablaze while sipping on her wine. After an uncomfortable stretch of silence, Marceau chugged his liquor then went over to fix himself another drink.

"This will be the last time we speak of this; and noting bad is to become of Mister Lafleur! Even if I wanted to do something about that I can't, because noting comes before loyalty to the brotherhood and service to country! Not some pussy, nor material gains, nothing, so you will take this to your grave," Marceau surprisingly exclaimed!

Marolina walked over to her brother and stood staring down at him, before she slapped him across the face with her right hand.

"I always knew you were a pussy! Maybe if you had my balls you would be a bigger man! You fucking coward; I'll deal with it myself," threatened Marolina, who broke the glass on the floor and stormed back out!

"You will do nothing! You hear me Marolina; if you know what's best move back to Europe and stay out of this," Marceau shouted!

***

Marceau Demerit went out to dinner three weeks later at the extravagant La-Cuisine-de-Grande-Chef, located downtown on Cathcart Street. It was his wedding anniversary and he and wife Elise chose one of their favorite restaurants to dine, along with their daughter Adriana. Morgan Demerit who was Marceau's youngest brother was also invited, although he was running late as he customarily did at events. Unlike his brother, Morgan was unmarried yet had a girlfriend named Angela Porter who was accompanying him. When Marceau, Elise and Adriana exited their limousine at the venue, their bodyguard Spencer guided them into the restaurant, while their chauffeur brought the vehicle underneath the Galerie Place Ville Marie building for parking.

Spencer would customarily remain within proximity to his boss, but he decided to smoke a cigarette outside and moved away from the entrance. There was a female jogger running along the sidewalk heading west, who Spencer caught sight of but then returned his attention towards the restaurant. A rider on a Can-Am Spyder Motorbike pulled up in front the restaurant and although the roads were dry enough to ride, Spencer found it highly strange anyone would brave such cold. As he watched the rider who stayed on the bike as if he was awaiting someone, the jogger slipped and fell about five feet away and began hurling in pain. The bodyguard looked up and down the street and realized there was no one approaching to help the female, therefore he moved forward and gave assistance.

With the bodyguard's attention disrupted, the bike rider walked into the restaurant wearing his helmet. Marceau had his head focused on the wine list given to him by their waitress, when the rider walked into the facility and withdrew a Ruger 360 handgun. Not even the loud screams uttered by female patrons were loud enough to drown out the thundering bangs, as the rider shot Marceau four times in the chest and stomach areas. It was obvious that the assassin was there for Marceau, as he waved the weapon to frighten other customers then scampered towards to exit.

Morgan and his date had just caught a parking space across the street from the restaurant and were about to cross the road when the shots fired. The rider expected Spencer to probably attempt to hinder him, so he exited the doors with his weapon pointed in the bodyguard's direction. Spencer drew his weapon and tried to move towards the explosions; but slipped as he attempted to run off and fell back onto the sidewalk. The assassin aimed at the bodyguard and fired twice in his direction, which forced Spencer to roll between two parked cars for cover. As the assassin leident atop his Can-Am Spyder he caught sight of Morgan across the street and pointed his weapon at the couple. There was a Chevrolet Cube Van passing along the roadway moving eastward, inside which the driver was completely oblivious to want had happened. Both shots fired at Morgan struck the van and frightened the driver, who lost control and crashed into a parked car when his windshield shattered.

The endangered Demerit brother knew it was impossible to climb back aboard his Range Rover and escape, so he took off running west towards McGill Street. The assassin assumed Morgan would run into the Galerie Place

Ville Marie building behind him to escape and abandoned his Spyder Motorbike, thus picking up the chase on foot. Through all his antics the assassin kept on his bike helmet to conceal his identity, as he chased after Morgan who was deceptively fast despite his matured age. Angela found protection behind Morgan's vehicle and began screaming, not knowing if the shooter would still target her or chase after her date. Once Spencer realized the coast was clear he raced into the restaurant to check his boss' status, not knowing who the targeted victim was. There was a doctor already present inside the restaurant having supper, who rushed to Marceau's aid and was fighting to save his life by applying chest convulsions and CPR. At the realization that his boss was the intended target, Spencer thought to himself that the jogger might had been the decoy used to hinder his response; and rushed back outside in time to watch the female turn the corner and ride away.

Morgan Demerit continued running along the sidewalk and broke for the other side of the road once his antagonist crossed over fully. Instead of running into the Galerie Place Ville Marie complex that was more cramped with less escape options, Morgan decided to run directly to the police station west on Saint Catherine Street. Knowing that the assassin would have a greater difficulty of shooting him in a crowd, plus the likely chance he could run into an officer along the way, compelled Morgan to take the route he thought offered him better option. As the terrified victim was about to turn the corner onto McGill Street, he narrowly missed bumping into a group of joggers, who all had ear-bugs in their ears and were completely oblivious to the impending dangers. At that specific moment the assassin ran clear of several parked vehicles along Cathcart Street and thought he had an excellent opportunity to shoot Morgan, and thus took aim and fired three shots. None of the bullets fired connected with their intended target, but two of the runners dropped to the ground instantly with serious gunshot wounds. After realizing what happened to their peers the other joggers frantically scattered and tried to get out of harm's way, by racing down Cathcart Street towards La-Cuisine-de-Grande-Chef Restaurant.

In contrast to his pursuer who in addition to the biker helmet, wore heavier clothing such as a leather jacket, bulletproof vest, steel toed boots and jeans, Morgan could maneuver much easier due to his lighter attire. While fleeing for his life the younger Demerit brother tried to keep some sort of object between himself and the assassin; but had no idea of his date's condition or how many people had gotten injured. An ambulance request had already been made for Marceau and even though Morgan could hear the loud sirens, he did not glimpse a flashing light until he was about to turn onto Saint Catherine Street.

With most of the pedestrians crossing the intersection of Saint Catherine and McGill Street inquisitively looking down towards Cathcart Street, the assassin shoved his weapon inside his jacket to avoid being branded as the possible threat. Following several shootings incidents within the downtown core, tourists and locals alike were on high alert even though most pedestrians were unsure whether the bangs were actual gunshots. The assassin was granted another excellent opportunity to shoot Morgan in the back as he approached the intersection, however, the sight of a police cruiser a block and a half away coming straight down the road on McGill changed everything.

There were hundreds of people walking along the sidewalk, which made it difficult to maneuver along quickly. Both Morgan and the assassin fought to swindle through the unyielding crowd, although they were similarly winded due to the intense chase. Motorists along the street were parting the roadways to allow emergency personnel through, hence the endangered victim contemplated whether he should run out in the middle of the street. Fear of being shot by his pursuer or accidentally ran over by police or ambulance technicians, traumatized Morgan to the extent he opted for the station instead. Regardless of how tired he became the victim bumped and banged his way through the crowd, while continuously looking back to ensure he maintained a slight distance between his helmet wearing antagonist and himself.

By the time Morgan reached Crescent Street he expected the assassin to have abandoned the chase, but whoever the maniac was did not receive the memo. The terrified victim had no idea why he was being chased, nor was he about to stop and enquire. Whoever the shooter was seemed determined to assassinate him, thus Morgan continued pressing forward encouraged by the fact Station 20 was only meters away. The traffic light was red when Morgan reached Bishop Street, where he found himself behind four pedestrians waiting to cross, however as he looked down the road, he noticed the motorbike that he saw parked by the restaurant. Just as the light turned green the female to Morgan's left used a knife and stabbed him in the abdomen twice, then walked away casually as if nothing happened. There were officers leaving and returning to the station across the street, thus Morgan staggered to the other side and fainted in the arms of a male officer. The helmet wearing assassin walked to his awaiting transport and climbed aboard with his female accomplice, then rode away from the scene while emergency personnel attended to their last victim along the sidewalk.

White Widow telephoned Marolina with their report and said, "the people on your list have been erased," before disconnecting the call!

A huge smile glistened across the vicious female's face as she hung up the phone. Marolina was home at the time having a drink and a cigarette; and turned on the television to the local news station to watch for any coverage on the incident. While turning on the television she used her cellular to phone Elise, who had just gotten to the hospital and did not respond on the first call. When Elise finally answered she was in a panicked state and simply kept repeating the same statement.

"They shot him---!"

"Whoever is responsible for killing my brothers is going to pay...," Marolina stated!

While speaking with Marolina ambulance technicians burst through the emergency doors across the hall with Morgan, who already had tubes connected to his arms and an oxygen mask over his mouth and nose. Elise's brother-in-law appeared lifeless on the gurney as doctors rushed him directly into an awaiting emergency room. The concerned female passed her daughter the phone and went over to enquire about Morgan's status with their bodyguard, from the nurse at the registration counter. Adriana who remained seated in the waiting area, took the phone and spoke with her aunt who was still ranting about revenge for her brothers.

"But Aunty Marolina dad's not dead; the doctors are operating on him! But they just wheeled Uncle Morgan in, so mom and Spencer went to check on his status," Adriana exclaimed!

Marolina went silent as her hand slowly fell holding the phone before all Adriana heard was the dial tone.

Part 23

The employees and their superiors at the Montreal Prosecution Bureau were stunned to hear of a third colleague's death, after that person had gotten assigned to the Nicholas Henry's case. Because of this, no other prosecutors in the bureau wanted to prosecute the case, which would have been a huge career advancement for that person. A concern for their personal wellbeing even led one out of the three most qualified available prosecutors to abruptly leave work and went on a two-weeks' vacation. The most qualified prosecutor left with the lightest workload was Emma Larake, a nine-year veteran who had worked hundreds of cases and had an impressive winning ratio. Amongst her colleagues Emma was at the end of another case, where both sides had made their final arguments and awaited the verdict from the jury's deliberation.

Emma had not studied the facts of Kevin's case, but there was hardly anyone in the city who had not heard of the story described by news technicians as, "the most unprecedented trial in Montreal's history". The government's case against Kevin was extremely positive without their destroyed physical evidence, hence they were willing to press on and fight for a guilty verdict. To begin Emma spoke with the inspectors charged with looking into whether Kevin had anything to do with her colleagues' murders, but their investigation was inconclusive at that point. Detective Ruchard and his partner Detective Ellesbury told Emma that all the deceased prosecutors were indeed murdered, but with Quail killed by police, the truck driver in custody and their only person of interest from the restaurant strangled, they had run out of leads to pursue. According to their findings the inspectors believed that the truck driver had some significant gambling debts and killed the prosecutor as payment, although none of that could be corroborated.

After losing a record of three prosecutors on one case, the government was not about to permit any atrocities to befall their latest replacement. Prosecutor Emma Larake was appointed her personal security detail, which brought and accompanied her wherever she went. To ensure that they did not lose the case due to preventable occurrences, even Emma's two personal assistants were guarded and followed during the case proceedings. Following the hit and run murder of Prosecutor Gary Thompson, both Jamaal Rickson's accident and Maurice Lamour's heart attack got more attention and eventually listed as questionable incidents. Nevertheless, the inspectors on the case were unable to tie any of these incidents to Kevin Walsh, whom they knew had somehow to do with the killings yet were without proof.

The morning of the trial was another grand spectacle in front of the Palais-Du-Justice Courthouse, with dozens of reporters, cameramen and protestors eager to get at Kevin. With his new chauffeur clearing the way through the mayhem, the accused flanked by the lovely Miss Nutcracker and Miss Cutthroat walked into the building. Regardless of the insulative and judgmental comments being shouted, the Rude Boy held his head confident as he entered the establishment wearing sunglasses with his dreads flowing; and dressed in a long black leather trench coat buttoned to the top, with a scarf warming his neck. They proceeded directly to the courtroom without answering any questions or giving any statements, as paparazzi snapped pictures as if he was a superstar.

Logan Duntroon and his assistant met Kevin outside courtroom 305, where they were scheduled to appear before Judge Steinberg. While speaking with his attorney Kevin met eyes with Emma Larake for the first time, at which he shot her a short smirk and a wink. The female prosecutor was in no mood for pleasantries and thus cut her eyes at the defendant, whom she aimed to lock away for a very long time. By 8:55 AM everybody began making their way into the courtroom which was scheduled to begin at 9 AM. When Kevin walked into the courtroom everyone who mumbled amongst themselves seized chatting as if the presiding judge himself had entered.

"Everybody please rise, the Honorable Judge Steinberg presiding," the court clerk declared at precisely 9 AM!

The judge walked into the courtroom and sat on the bench, following which everyone returned to their seats. "Good morning everyone," declared the judge at which the clerk began reading the case assessment to the court. With the case on the way Judge Steinberg allowed the prosecution to present their opening statement, thereby Emma Larake took the floor and began her presentation.

"Good morning your honor, ladies and gentlemen. As a prosecutor my job is to lock away criminals, and that is exactly who Mr. Nicholas Henry is. Canadians watched in horror as this man killed in cold blood, Mr. Martain Lafleur who I will be the first to admit, wasn't the most upstanding citizen; nevertheless, he did not deserve to be slain like an animal on national television! Our evidence will undoubtedly show that Mr. Henry deserve to be locked away for this and many other murders which occurred at that same incident! This man in my opinion should be deported from this country, for one being an imposter, because he was not born as Nicholas Henry, but because he is a career criminal, he has acquired false identity to escape his troubled past! We will provide witnesses to give an account of the brutality they observed in this provincial park, by Mr. Henry and his companions. By the end of this trial, you will all see the barbarian that Mr. Nicholas Henry is; and I will give you the proof that you need to lock him away for a very long time," Emma Larake decreed!

"Thank you Madam Larake, Monsieur Duntroon you may begin," Judge Steinberg stated!

The defense lawyer took a drink from his glass of water, then got up and walked to the middle of the courtroom. "Thank you, your honor, and good morning to you ladies and gentlemen! Now I've sat and listened to Madam Larake paint her picture of my client and no he is absolutely not some fairy prince, but he none of these things that the prosecutor wishes to say that he is! Madam Larake mentioned that she has inconclusive video evidence and witnesses to corroborate her story, but we will prove that her facts are absolutely incorrect and none of her witnesses can definitely testify to seeing my client harm anyone. The prosecution team would also like to convince you that my client is not trustworthy and frankly some bum off the street, but we look forward to challenging all her evidence and proving exactly who the defendant truly is! Thank you!"

Emma Larake could hardly wait for the chance to present her case and leapt to her feet once Judge Steinberg gave her back the floor. With her arms crossed as if she was being evasive against the defense attorney's comments, the prosecutor stood up next to the prosecution desk and called, Officer Denis Challor to the stand. Officer Challor was the operator of one of the helicopters on which the joint task force of the American FBI Agents and Canadian Law Enforcement flew; and had the best view of what had transpired. The court officer brought over a bible on which Officer Challor placed his right hand and raised his left hand high.

"Do you swear to tell the truth, the whole truth and nothing but the truth," court officer asked?

"Yes, I do," Officer Challor responded!

"You may be seated," instructed the court officer.

"Can you please tell the court your name and what it is that you do sir," Emma Larake asked?

"Yes, my name is Denis Challor and I'm a police constable with the Montreal helicopter division, of which I am a pilot," Denis answered.

"Officer Challor on the date of this biker brawl incident, can you tell us what you witnessed," Emma enquired?

"Well, our department had formed a joint task force with agents from the American Federal Bureau of Investigation who came up here with a warrant for Mr. Henry over there. They received information that Mr. Henry and a bunch of his friends were engaged in some brawl to the death incident over in the Jean-Drapeau Park, so we all packed a few choppers and headed out there," Officer Challor began.

"Tell us what you witnessed when you reached the park," Emma questioned?

"When we got close, Mr. Henry had a weapon to Martain Lafleur's head…"

"Objection your honor, move to strike the witness' last comment from the record," Attorney Duntroon stood up and shouted!

"On what grounds Mr. Duntroon," Judge Steinberg demanded?

"Your honor Officer Challor could not definitively know it was my client from their standpoint," Attorney Duntroon stated!

"Mr. Duntroon your objection was noted, however, if you have an issue with the witness' statement do take it up on your cross-examination! Objection over-ruled, Officer Challor you may proceed," Judge Steinburg directed.

Prosecutor Larake smirked at Nicholas and everyone at the defense bench, as she turned back to her witness.

"When Agent Carbonelli got on the loudspeaker and began telling him to drop it, he shot and killed him," Officer Challor declared.

"Was there any known friction between Martain Lafleur and Mr. Nicholas Henry," Emma questioned?

"Law enforcement was aware of the gang war between both parties. They were both wanted for questioning regarding that huge shootout that occurred downtown St. Catherine Street, where dozens were killed and injured. We also know they were responsible for many other murders and abductions across the city, which we are still adamantly investigating." Officer Challor responded.

"Your honor I would like to enter into evidence this DVD video that was filmed of the incident when the officers came on scene. Also, with your permission we would like to show this video to the court for them to witness exactly what Officer Challor described." Emma exclaimed as she walked over to a DVD player already prepared and placed the DVD inside the machine.

"You may proceed Madam Larake," Judge Steinburg responded.

Emma played the recording made from the helicopter of the incident, during which everyone inside the courtroom appeared to struggle to clearly identify Nicholas. A majority of the video was shot from behind Nicholas as the choppers approached and were inconclusive from the side and front angles, due to the filth pasted on the rude-boy's face. When the shooter on the video callously shot Martain, almost everyone inside the courtroom exhaled a huge sigh at the savagery. Having received the reactions she sought, the prosecutor declared that she was through with the witness and confidently returned to her seat.

"Mr. Duntroon you may cross examine the witness," Judge Steinberg exclaimed.

Logan Duntroon was unimpressed by the prosecutor's display and went directly to attacking the officer during his questioning. The defense team had a strategy for each of the prosecutor's witnesses, with their sole intent being to create any form of reasonable doubt.

"Officer Challor would you say that you had the best view of what took place," Attorney Duntroon asked?

"Apart from Agent Carbonelli who was in the seat across from me, I'd say yes," Officer Challor answered.

"And approximately how far away from these combatants would you say that you were when this so called, person shot Mr. Lafleur," Attorney Duntroon questioned?

"I'd say probably about a hundred and ten meters away," Officer Challor stated.

"How high off the ground were you flying at the time of the shooting,"

Informer 3

Attorney Duntroon enquired?

"Two hundred and thirty meters," Officer Challor said.

"Wow, you must have incredible vision to distinctively be able to tell it was Mr. Henry from that high and that far away. Do you wear glasses sir, any kind reading or whatever," Attorney Duntroon drilled?

"Yes, I do wear reading glasses from time to time," Officer Challor declared.

"Were you wearing your glasses when you observed Mr. Henry shoot Mr. Lafleur," Attorney Duntroon continued?

"No, I wasn't! But I don't need glasses to identify a killer," Officer Challor responded with a frustrating sigh!

Attorney Duntroon went over to their desk and picked up a paper that contained Officer Challor's vision level and eye prescription. "According to your eye specialist you should be wearing glasses not only for reading, but you might trip over something if you're not too careful"!

"Objection your honor, council is badgering the witness," Emma shouted while angrily rising to her feet!

"Objection sustained, Mr. Duntroon no more of that will be permitted inside my courtroom, you understand," Judge Steinberg warned!

"My apologies your honor. But I would like to enter into evidence Officer Challor's vision records, that prove there was no way he could correctly identify Mr. Henry from that distance," Attorney Duntroon responded!

Logan then walked over to the prosecution's main evidence and pressed play again on the DVD video. As they watched the video it became clear that nobody could absolutely determine who the shooter was, considering the Alliance fighters were all filthy with their clothes and skin drenched in the blood of their enemies. There were four men on the video who had long hair, three of which were dread locks and all with the approximate same built. The arresting officers initially believed that all the survivors were of dark complexion, until they were cleaned up and their proper identities revealed.

"Your honor I would also like to enter into evidence the photographs taken immediately after Mr. Henry and his associates were arrested at the park, plus their mug shots taken at the jailhouse," Attorney Duntroon lamented as he passed a set of the pictures to the court officer, who gave them to the judge. The defense attorney then gave the prosecution team a set of the same photos, before bringing his set of the pictures over to the witness on the stand. Logan passed some of the pictures to Officer Challor, which showed Kevin and his companions were bloody and difficult to identify.

"When you landed the helicopter did you still have eyes on Mr. Henry," Attorney Duntroon asked?

"No, I had to find a clearing to land which was a few meters away from the altercation, so I lost sight of him for a short time," Officer Challor exclaimed.

"Was Mr. Henry brought to the detention center in your helicopter," Attorney Duntroon demanded?

"No! The ground forces brought him in," Officer Challor stated.

"How many survivors were there amongst Mr. Henry's crew," Attorney Duntroon asked?

"I believe there was seven of them," Officer Challor said.

"Seven, so why is my client the only person sitting here!? No further questions your honor," Attorney Duntroon lamented!

"Thank you Officer Challor that will be all, you are free to go," Judge Steinberg declared!

There was an unease inside the courtroom as everyone distinctively sensed the first victory snatched by the defense team. Emma Larake was furious with the discredit of her star witness and prized evidence, after less than a session in court. None of her other witness were as compelling as Officer Challor, but there was still the chance she could salvage a victory. The next witness was an officer who handled Nicholas Henry during his transfer to the central jail. Constable James Decharmeau was an eleven-year veteran of the Montreal Police Department, who could offer important testimony about the defendant's status and possibly why the murders were committed.

"You may call your next witness Madam Larake," Judge Steinberg exclaimed.

"The prosecution calls Constable James Decharmeau to the stand," Emma called out from her seat?

The constable walked down to the stand and was sworn in by the court officer, before he took the seat in the witness box.

"Constable Decharmeau can you please tell us what you encountered when you came on the crime scene," Emma asked?

"It was a massacre! There were mutilated bodies covering approximately a seventy feet radius. Just bodies everywhere, hacked, shot, stabbed, beaten, severed body parts like some sort of meat house. Believe me nothing I've ever seen before," began Constable Decharmeau!

"Was there any weapon recovered beside Mr. Henry," Emma enquired?

Informer 3

"No, if he had one, he tossed it by the time they got to him," Constable Decharmeau answered.

"Did you see Mr. Henry shoot Martain Lafleur," Emma asked?

"No, my cruiser was the first on the scene and by the time I took up position with my weapon drawn, Mr. Henry and his armed friends were dropping their weapons. I kept my firearm pointed at them until other officers moved in and handcuffed everyone," Constable Decharmeau said.

"While transporting Mr. Henry to the jailhouse, did he mention anything such as why he killed Martain Lafleur," Emma enquired?

"I think he said something to the likes of, finally I got that fucking biker! But either way he didn't have any remorse about it," Constable Decharmeau implied.

"Objection your honor, cause to speculate," Attorney Duntroon yelled out!

"Objection sustained, the witness' last statement will be removed," Judge Steinberg indicated.

"Thank you, your honor, I'm through with the witness," Emma declared.

"Mr. Duntroon you may cross examine the witness," Judge Steinberg instructed.

"Constable Decharmeau did you find any identification on Mr. Henry's person when you searched him at the scene," Attorney Duntroon asked?

"No, he did not have any I.D on him," Constable Decharmeau answered.

"So how did you guys know who he was," Attorney Duntroon questioned?

"We were at the time looking into both Mr. Lafleur and Mr. Henry's business deals, so we had a good idea who they were," Constable Decharmeau stated.

"Did you ask Mr. Henry for his name," Attorney Duntroon enquired?

"He refused to say anything after he asked for his lawyer," Constable Decharmeau indicated.

"But you just made it appear as if he was extremely talkative during the transfer," Attorney Duntroon declared.

"Well… that's what I thought I heard hi…," began Constable Decharmeau, before the defense lawyer interrupted.

"No further questions your honor," Attorney Duntroon stated and sat down.

"Thank you Constable Decharmeau, you may go," said Judge Steinberg! "Madam Larake you may call your final witness before we take a break."

"The prosecution would like to call Kelsey Lee to the stand," Prosecutor Larake declared!

The court officer again brought the bible over to the witness and had her swear to tell, "the truth, the whole truth and nothing but the truth," with her right hand rested on it.

"I swear," implied the female!

"Mrs. Lee can you please give us your job title and explain to us what is it that you do," Prosecutor Larake asked?

"I am the Chief Forensic Officer at the Montreal Forensic Lab where weapons are checked for fingerprints or diagnosed to determine if it was used in certain shootings," Mrs. Lee declared.

"Mrs. Lee, were you sent to investigate the crime scene in Jean Drapeau Park," Prosecutor Larake enquired?

"Yes, with such a large crime scene they needed as much help as possible, so I went to help my technicians collect the evidence," Mrs. Lee responded.

"Can you describe the crime scene when you got there," Prosecutor Larake enquired?

"Wow, it was a mess with dead bodies everywhere! There were weapons of all sorts all over the place, from guns to knives to machetes to axes, pipe irons you name it! Unlike anything I've ever seen," Mrs. Lee stated.

"How many pieces of weapons did your team collect from the crime scene," Prosecutor Larake asked?

"I forgot the exact amount but there were hundreds," Mrs. Lee said.

"What became of all these weapons," Prosecutor Larake questioned?

"Objection your honor, cause for speculation," Attorney Duntroon argued!

"Mr. Duntroon they're along the same line of questioning. Objection overruled! You may answer the question Mrs. Lee," Judge Steinberg lamented.

"Well, we had to sort them all, collect fingerprints from everyone involved and determine who used what to kill who. But a few weeks into our investigation someone broke into our lab and used explosives to destroy all the evidence." Mrs. Lee explained.

"How did anybody mange to break into such a secured facility," Prosecutor

Informer 3

Larake enquired?

"The female who did all this was a professional. She hijacked our cleaning service and snuck in with them, where she freely planted the devices needed to destroy the evidence. After they had gotten away, she detonated the charges, assassinated those who could probably identify her and blows up their business to fully cover her tracks. Even after scanning her face through every facial imagery we have, we still can't identify who she is," Mrs. Lee explained, at which Emma introduced photos of the destruction into evidence.

"Who would you suppose might gain from all this," Prosecutor Larake asked?

"The defendant," indicated Mrs. Lee!

"Thank you, Mrs. Lee. That will be all you honor," Prosecutor Larake stated!

"You may cross examine the witness Mr. Duntroon," Judge Steinberg declared.

"Since you stipulated that my client stood to gain from all this, were their anyone else who could gain from destroying the evidence," Attorney Duntroon fired?

"There were others who survived that bloody carnage," Mrs. Lee calmly answered.

"So, any of these other survivors would have had the same motivation as my client, correct," Attorney Duntroon interrogated!?

"I guess you could say so," Mrs. Lee responded.

"Mrs. Lee did you at any time see my client holding any of these weapons," Attorney Duntroon asked as he walked over towards the bench?

"No, I did not," Mrs. Lee responded!

"To the best of your knowledge, was my client fingerprints found on any of these weapons," Attorney Duntroon enquired?

"At the time of the explosion we had not directly matched your client to any specific weapon, but you must understand we...," Mrs. Lee began before she was cut off.

"Was this intruder who broke into your forensic lab a male or female," Attorney Duntroon continued?

"A female," modestly answered Mrs. Lee.

"Have your lab found any evidence that linked this female intruder to my client," Attorney Duntroon questioned?

"No, we have not," declared Mrs. Lee.

"Thank you, Mrs. Lee. That will be all your honor," Attorney Duntroon said!

"Court will be in recess until 12:30," instructed Judge Steinberg who began gathering his documents to leave!

"All Rise," commanded the court clerk as the judge exited the courtroom!

When they returned from lunchbreak Emma Larake called up five different witnesses, three of whom were present in the park and watched the massacre unfold from a distance. The two male and female witnesses all reported that when the initial shooting began, they found cover away from the violence and watched from their hiding positions. None of the witnesses were close enough to definitively identify Nicholas as the person who shot Martain, and after sitting through such a debacle of a trial, none of them were willing to perjure themselves. It was evident to everyone inside the courtroom that Nicholas was well connected and going after him meant endangering one's life. Regardless of who the prosecutor called to testify, the defense team bored holes into their statement and provided the inconsistencies necessary to liberate their client. The case was wrapped up in one day, during which Emma Larake presented forensic scientists and other specialists to help make her case. Logan Duntroon believed he had done enough to sway the jury's decision, however during his closing arguments he included Kevin Junior's abduction to overemphasize the need to fully liberate his client.

After court ended it was another huge spectacle with reporters and paparazzi seeking pictures and reports on what transpired in court. Kevin and his entire entourage walked out to the front of the justice building, where he climbed aboard his limousine with his guards and left Attorney Duntroon to deal with the media. The defense team felt quite positive about their performance in court and would have been surprised at a guilty verdict, therefore the lead attorney spoke quite confidently about their chances of victory. The jury did not need much time to deliberate after the thrashing put on by the defense team, and made it known that they had reached a verdict within twenty minutes of the debate. Court was again scheduled for 9:30 AM the following morning to release the verdict reached by the jury, which found Nicholas Henry innocent of the charges laid against him.

Part 24

The main page of nearly every newspaper across Canada read, "Prime Minister Liberated by Ethics Commission Probe." Following the enquiry into the meddling allegations by Prime Minister Mathew Layton, Teressa Lablonde and the Ethics Bureau got scrutinized for siding with the incumbent government. In her report to the House Committee, Teressa wrote that her office found Prime Minister Layton acted with the country's best interest in mind. The report also stated that the Prime Minister was not guilty of meddling, because he acted on behalf of the country yet refrained from going into details for what they sighted as, 'National Security Concerns'. While she did reprimand the Prime Minister for a second unscheduled meeting, critics were extremely objective and thought the government and the Ethics Bureau were withholding valid information. Opposition leaders were enraged at the report as they all sought political punch lines for their ongoing election campaigns.

Two days after the report's release, Mme. Teressa Lablonde executed her resignation as Ethics Commissioner. Once words circulated that Teressa had stepped down from her position, the negative comments ramped higher with most politicians suggesting that 'she should have been fired for not effectively doing her job'. Through all the negative comments Teressa remained silent after learning her cancer had returned and that she was again in stored for another grueling fight. For the next month and a half Teressa went into hiding and listened to the negative press until she had had enough, therein she agreed to do an interview to clear away all the misconceptions. When she appeared on the Rogers Daytime Program it was obvious that the Ex-Ethics Commissioner was indeed sick as she looked physically drained and had already lost a few pounds.

Before she became too weak to conduct such an interview on live television, Mme. Lablonde appeared in public for the first time since her retirement, to disclose being diagnosed with Cancer for a second time and added that was her only reason for departing from her position. The diagnosis of her cancer was not something she had made known to her colleagues, therefore it came as a shock since many believed she was in training to compete in the Ottawa Marathon. When past critics saw the show most of them retracted or erased rude social media comments, they had made about Teressa, and instead replaced those with much more sensitive sentiments. The Daytime Program would be the last time anyone saw Teressa in public, as she checked into a cancer institution three days later and battled the best she could; but died six months later from the deadly dosage given to her.

***

The thought that thieves were able to remove documents from inside the confines of parliament's walls enraged Prime Minister Layton, who invited the new commander of the Royal Canadian Mounted Police to a meeting. Commander Charles Lenier had only been the top man at RCMP headquarters for only a month, but he was a thirty-one years veteran of the force who loved his job. When Commander Lenier met with the Prime Minister inside his office in Ottawa, he had no clue what the P.M wanted of him nor had he ever heard of the secret organization he was being asked to investigate. Prime Minister Layton had no physical evidence with which to commence an investigation after losing the information he had on the Quebec Secret Cult, but he pointed to Kevin as a point of interest and suggested the commander began there. Lenier felt confident that his department would uncovering such an organization, as long as they operated on Canadian soil. To unmask this secret cult, the RCMP commander promised to launch an investigation into the matter and only report his findings to the Prime Minister.

Once back at his RCMP command post, Commander Lenier instructed his secretary to summon three agents to his office, for what he referred to as a private briefing. The agents summoned were men who the commander wholeheartedly trusted, first of which was the department's Chief Research Officer Joel Sanduski, who primarily worked indoors from his computer and was an expert at searching the dark web for uncanny or historic sites. The next two agents were two of the best undercover officers on the force, Thomas Tups and Ty Golding who were both personally trained by Charles Lenier. Thomas and Joel were Caucasian men from separate regions of Canada; and Ty was a Vietnamese who moved to Montreal with his family when he was a baby.

Prime Minister Layton had requested that Commander Lenier keep the matter extremely confidential, therefore the only other persons who knew of their meeting were both men's secretaries. The P.M had a prearranged overseas trip to Europe the morning following his meeting with Commander Charles Lenier. On such trips the Prime Minister would always travel with a large delegation of people from news reporters to other politicians and members of government. When his secretary Joseline De'Lapine got home that evening she had several errands to run before leaving with the P. M's delegates the following morning. Joseline had been the Prime Minister's personal secretary for five months, after his regular assistant took maternity leave to have her baby. One of the places Joseline had to visit was her cleaners for a few suits she had brought in for cleaning. There was a pay phone posted against the wall along the plaza a few businesses down from the cleaners, and before reaching her actual destination, Joseline telephoned the center's private information line.

The secretary picked up the receiver and dialed seven consecutive zeros without depositing any money, waited for the double beeps then left her message. "A covert investigation into the organization was given to the RCMP."

***

Deborah Darfuse was selected as Commander Lenier's personal secretary when he took over the commanding position at the RCMP. When Charles selected Deborah, it was by no mere chance, but rather her qualifications were way beyond the other male and female candidates. The secretary was not with her superior when he visited Prime Minister Layton in Ottawa, but she was the person to arrange his transport and had to summon the officers selected for the covert mission. Whenever Commander Lenier spoke to his officers inside his office he always talked loud with clarity, therefore Deborah did not need to plant any sort of device or eavesdrop at the door to clearly hear the conversation. Both Deborah and Joseline were highly qualified for the positions they held, but both females were also graduates of the elaborate Secret Cult's educational system.

On her way home the evening following the meeting between Commander Lenier and his undercover detectives, Deborah stopped at the IGA Grocery Store three blocks from her apartment building. There were two public pay phones just inside the store's front entrance and before proceeding inside she made a quick phone call. Even though the secretary was not being watched, she looked around to ensure there were no eyes on her as she covered the dial pad and hid each button she pressed. Like Joseline Deborah dialed seven consecutive zeros, listened for the beeps, then proceeded to leave her message.

"Research Specialist Joel Sanduski, Thomas Tups and Ty Golding are assigned to investigate."

***

Back at the Royal Canadian Mounted Police command center, Joel Sanduski had begun his assigned duties by checking which unregistered cults across the country Kevin was a member of. Whenever certain keywords were entered into the search bar of any computer, the technicians at the Nest were immediately notified, thus even without the secretaries' information the investigation would have been uncovered. One of the newest tools used to recruit special talents to the Secret Cult's Foundation was the computer, thus finding their website was easy once the searcher knew what to look for. There were no public mentions of the cult's primary members outside the of the club, therefore Joel could not find any mention of the Jamaican's fellowship to any organization. The worldwide web provided several mentions of specific exploits involving Kevin Henry throughout the years; and as the detective read through each incident his interest in their prime suspect grew, but still found himself nowhere closer to uncovering the cult.

Joel was a member of the investigative team assembled to uncover what happened to the billionaires mysteriously killed, and after hours of searching without success he paused and started looking at a chart on his wall, on which he had stickers and notes of the crime. The thought that there could have been a connection with Kevin's sudden rise to wealth and power crossed his mind, so he then looked at Francois Trudeau and wondered how their relationship came about. That day ended with more questions than answers, but after hours of checking Kevin's and Francois' profiles Joel felt confident that the trail would eventually lead him to the exclusive organization.

When Joel looked up at the clock it was 7:00 PM, which meant that he would be at least two and a half hours late getting home. He telephoned his wife Gloria to advise her that he would be heading home when leaving the building, then jumped in his Ford Mustang and drove off the facility. Along his way home Gloria phoned back and told him 'to pick up cough medication for their son', so Joel headed to the pharmacy closest to his home. As Joel exited his vehicle and closed the door his cellular began ringing, but the phone was inside the car, so he decided to phone back whoever the caller was when he returned. A black tinted Marauder pulled into the parking lot as Joel ran across into the Jean-Coutu, with three Rough Rider bikers who all remained inside the vehicle with the engine running. While Joel was inside the store the bikers loaded and prepared their automatic handguns, then waited until he was walking to his vehicle, sped out from their parking slot and shot him eight times through the windows. With bystanders running for safety the driver of the Marauder sped off after his associates shot and killed Joel, whose items spilt from the bag onto the road.

***

Fifteen minutes before the Chief Research Officer was shot and killed, his partners who had finished working earlier went out for a few beers before heading home. Bar McGuire was a favorite drinking hole for many RCMP officers, who would gather there for a bit of entertainment after their long work shifts. Earlier that day after they received their new orders Inspector Thomas Tups and Inspector Ty Golding went out into the field to find anyone with knowledge of this secret cult. The RCMP inspectors first visited and spoke with the eldest world war veteran they could find, who was a sweet old man named Franklin Phillimore. Mr. Phillimore lived in an old age home on Avenue Centennial in the Quartier Cavendish area of Montreal, and was always open to visitors, therefore he agreed to speak with both officers.

The war veteran met with the detectives inside his personal suite, as he had been under the weather nursing a cold. When the inspectors entered the suite, they found Franklin seated on his sofa inside his greeting room, covered with a warm blanket and a mug of herbal tea on a nearby coffee table. Mr. Phillimore prided himself as a Canadian historian and had appeared on several television programs where he discussed great moments in the country's history, however proclaimed he had never heard anything of this private cult. The only assistance Franklin offered was the referral to a Jewish businessman uptown on Plamondon Avenue, named Caleb Adelman.

Mr. Adelman ran a jewelry and antique store and was the first cousin to Joshua Yurkovich, who was Natalie Royal's husband. Natalie was born to one of the wealthiest families in Montreal, which had also been a valued participant of the Secret Cult's Council since its inauguration. There was very little information available about Caleb on the RCMP Database, but the inspectors were able to uncover that he specialized in ancient artifacts from other sources. When Inspectors Tups and Golding entered Caleb's antique and jewelry store, they assumed Mr. Phillimore sent them to the right person because of the rare and exquisite items up for sale. After looking around the busy store the detectives spoke with one of the workers behind the jewelry counter and asked to have a word with the owner. When Caleb came out and spoke with the inspectors, they first showed their badges and identified themselves, before informing the owner that they were recommended to him by Mr. Phillimore. At the mention of the war veteran Mr. Adelman showed the inspectors into his private office, where they spoke for several minutes about their visit.

Celeb Adelman disclosed nothing about what he knew of the secret organization; but advised the inspectors that he would enquire into the matter and took their business card. When the detectives left his office, Celeb used his video surveillance system to zoom in on their license plate number, then captured still photos of both men from the same system. With his information collected Caleb telephoned a fax number and sent the photos, business card and license plate number in the message, following which he burnt the documents and erased all the video footage of the officers' visit from his security system. Inspector Thomas Tups and Inspector Ty Golding spoke with several other businessmen, clergy members and even retired civil employees, but were unable to advance their case on the first day.

***

Gilbert Stephano had to postpone his trip for France after he was summoned to the Nest moments before his scheduled flight was supposed to leave. Instead of a vacation Gilbert was sent to the Rough Riders' Blues Club in Verdun, with an envelope that contained instruction that needed immediate attention. Jim Bartello was downstairs inside his office and had no idea the cult's moderator was coming by. When Gilbert walked into the Rough Rider leader's office, Jim frightfully sprung to his feet and offered him a seat or a beverage, but his visitor slowly looked around then declined. The ex-waitress Carolin who once serviced him at the restaurant was snorting cocaine off a small mirror, however a feeling of humiliation forced the female to flee the room. There were certain traits of business within the organization that were always handled formally, and even though Monsieur Stephano would rather be elsewhere, delivering instructional packages was his duty. The cult's moderator watched as Jim opened the envelope and looked through the documents. Once Jim acknowledged what must be handled and responded with a nod, Mr. Stephano turned around and walked out with only a, "Good day to you sir!"

The instant his unexpected guest departed Jim began making the necessary preparations to fulfill his obligations.

"Wasp get in here," Jim shouted!

"Yeah, what's up," Lil Wasp answered?

"Get Rodney and the boys over here now, I got a job for them," instructed Jim!

Thirteen minutes later the Rough Rider bikers summoned by Jim were inside his office. Even though the six men were being sent out on an extremely serious errand, one might never tell as they joked about inside the office and got intoxicated while Jim issued the instructions. The biker leader first passed around the three RCMP inspectors' photos along with their addresses, then debrief the assassins on the men's hobbies and favorite places of leisure. The package brought by Gilbert Stephano contained every viable information on each of their targets, hence it became only a matter of locating them. Rodney and his associates were excited for the job opportunity, however being offered $5000 each instead of their regular fee provided added motivation.

***

When the RCMP inspectors departed from their fourth voluntary questioning candidate Reverend Mark Norquest, they drove to the Harvey's Restaurant on Decarie Boulevard for lunch. Both men purchased their meals and returned to their vehicle where they ate and debated how best to proceed. Neither Ty Golding nor Thomas Tups had any notion they had been under surveillance since they left the Cathedral, as they drove around doing their investigative duties. Throughout the remainder of the day the inspectors visited three others business professionals, who they asked the same questions they had been demanding answers to. At 5 PM the detectives decided to retire for the day and drove to Bar McGuire to unwind before they headed home.

After more than two hours waiting for the inspectors to leave the bar, the three assassins were tired and frustrated. They had the option to ambush the inspectors at their houses, but that would have been a much bigger challenge due to the area in which they lived. Any stranger to the officers' neighborhood could easily get lost in the maze, where four out of every five residents were law enforcement personnel. The drugs they brought along was nearly depleted and without some sort of emotion altering chemical to calm Headrush and Spinks, they were literally ready to explode. Rodney was the most charismatic and intelligent biker in their crew, but he was not amongst the group sent to eliminate Inspectors Tups and Golding. Through regular communications with Rodney's assassin team, the second crew were updated on their comrades' progress, hence they were aware that neither team had accomplished their task.

Twenty minutes after the assassins' final check-in, Inspector Tups, his partner and two other officers exited the establishment. The group of officers were joking amongst themselves as they made their way to their vehicles in the parking lot. Bar McGuire was the last business at the end of a small shopping plaza, from which several other stores operated. Most of the stores along the plaza were still open, therefore there were customers all throughout the property. Each of the assassins took one final toke from their mixed joint, as they pumped themselves up to earn their pay. The assassins had strategically parked their vehicle two rows over from the inspectors and planned to simply walk up to the unsuspecting officers and shoot them, but they were initially uncertain if the other two officers would accompany their targets. When the inspectors reached their vehicle the other two officers continued to their cruiser, which provided the assassins the opportunity they sought.

"Keep the engine running Lyle! Come on Spinks lets go," Headrush instructed!

The pair of assassins exited their vehicle and crouched between the parked cars as they quickly made their way towards the RCMP inspectors. Ty and Thomas had just entered their unmarked cruiser, put on their seatbelts and were about to start the engine when the shooters appeared from nowhere and opened fire through the side windows. Neither of the officers stood any chance of even arming themselves, as the assassins executed them then looked to escape. The officers who exited the bar with Ty and Thomas withdrew their weapons and opened fire at the fleeing assassins. Four other officers in the parking lot joined the response and pinned the shooters between three cars, which protruded them from making it back to their escape vehicle. Before long other officers joined the intense shootout with the bikers, who had no fear of retaliation regardless of the escalating number of cops. After realizing that his companions had no chance of escaping, Lyle got scared and drove away to save himself. The officers continued pressing and moved closer until they got into position, from which they shot and killed both assassins.

When Commander Charles Lenier learnt of the killings, he tried to warn his Chief Research Officer, who missed the phone call when he left his cellular inside his Ford Mustang. In less than twelve hours the men who the commander secretly assigned to solve the cult mystery had gotten killed, thus Lenier found Prime Minister Layton's private number and began dialing. Before he could press send his phone rang with a private number, thereby he answered to find out who the caller was.

"Hello, this is Commander Lenier," responded the RCMP Chief!

"This will be your only warning," said a male's voice!

"What," Commander Lenier argued!

Informer 3

"Kaboom," sounded an explosion outside the commander's window!

The Mounty Chief got up from his seat with the cordless receiver to his right ear and walked to his window, where he was shocked to see his personal transport in flames after it had exploded. Lenier's wife came rushing into the room terrified after seeing their family car blow up.

"Charles what's going on? Why did our car just explode," asked his wife?

"Just phone the fire department," instructed Commander Lenier, as he looked through the window at the security personnel canvasing the area!

"Instead of eliminating your inspectors, the next time you will be our first target! I suggest you terminate this inquiry given by the Prime Minister," threatened a male voice on the other end of the line!

"Who the hell is this; and how did you get this number," Commander Lenier demanded?

"Before you make a decision out of anger, think about your wife Ellie, Sue and Margret your daughters, your sons Benjamin, Steven and Calvin. If that doesn't do it for you, how about your grandkids Timothy, Kelly and Reece? There is absolutely nothing you can do to stop us from getting to you or anybody else we chose to, and that includes Prime Minister Layton! Just something to think about before you go and do something stupid," said the voice before the line went dead!

Commander Lenier sat and thought about everything that was said to him and contemplated what next to do. It was evident that the organization they were investigating had spies within the Canadian Government, people willing to die for their cause and no compassion regarding who they killed. The commander pulled out a piece of paper and began writing his resignation, but half way through the letter he decided to inform the Prime Minister of his decision. Charles knew the Prime Minister would be heading overseas in the morning and contacting him during such trips was difficult, therefore he found his private number and called.

"Good evening Commander Lenier, I trust this is not a social call," Prime Minister Layton answered.

"Good evening Mr. Prime Minister you're indeed correct! I am presently completing my resignation letter and will have it on your desk whenever you get back from your trip," Commander Lenier responded.

"Obviously such a quick decision must be due to our secret project," Prime Minister Layton argued?

"Sir the organization we are looking into is deeply rooted into our government! How far I'll never know, but they have no plans of getting uprooted and will kill anybody who tries to expose them! The inspectors I placed on the case earlier this morning were all killed; and this operation was top secret. Someone also just sent me a personal message by blowing up my vehicle in front of my house. Two of the shooters who killed my inspectors were shot and killed by fellow officers and have since been identified as Rough Rider hitmen. The local police department has taken the lead in the investigation to find the other shooters involved, so we have conceded the case and won't be investing any manpower. One of my reasons for this decision is because I personally know several officers who frequent the Blues Bar over in Verdun. Now, you can open another probe if you wish, but I won't be the person handling it, because I won't be gambling my family's lives for anything," Commander Lenier stated!

"Commander Lenier I won't be gambling my family either! Some anonymous caller just phoned my cell and threatened to kill me! While I was on the phone with this man someone else called my wife and threatened to kill her entire family, if I don't drop this enquiry! As Prime Minister I have never been rattled or afraid of anything said by any politician, but I believed every word that man said! So, you can shred that resignation unless you have some other important reason why you want to resign," Prime Minister Layton reasoned!?

"No sir I don't! Thank you, Mr. Prime Minister," Commander Lenier exclaimed!

Part 25

Chops and his three friends suffered the effects of deep frost bite, which restricted the flow of blood and oxygen through their bodies and left them horribly ill. Each biker's limbs from their fingers, toes, penises, noses and ears had gotten badly discolored to the extent that Valorie suggested they all seek medical treatment at the hospital. Instead of obeying the stubborn bikers chose to rely on Tylenol, Hot Chocolate, warm blankets and a Space Heater, expecting everything to return to normal once their body temperatures climbed. Kenny was a diabetic but never once mentioned it to any of his associates, hence as the hours ticked by, he developed a mild cough that gradually increased, until he sounded like a bulldozer demolishing a building. Each of the bikers' hands and feet had gotten swollen, but when Valorie went over and checked on Kenny his feet were humongous and black.

Although the bikers firmly objected to the hospital or doctors, Valorie became scared Kenny might die in her home and secretly phoned for an ambulance. When the ambulance arrived, and the technicians walked in and saw the men's condition, they quickly attended to Kenny and summoned additional

EMS workers to help the others. Kenny was rushed to the hospital and had to undergo an emergency operation to save his life or he would have died from blockage to his arteries and a host of other problems. Doctors at the new Children's Hospital in NDG had to amputate both of Kenny's legs and nine of his fingers, because of the bikers' ignorance and fear of what might had happened should the cops get involved.

When asked by nurses how they managed to get such terrible frost bite, Chops and the bikers who were last to arrive at the hospital stated they were all playing football outside in the snow. Canadians were renowned for doing weird fun chasing things during winter, so doctors were accustomed to treating patients with all sorts of ailments. The hospital administration did not suspect there was foul play involved in any of the men's injuries, thus they did not notify the police, but once the CBC News office learnt of the incident, they sent a reporter to capture the story. Chops and the two bikers who would recover without any form of amputation had planned what to say when questioned, however Kenny was not amongst them at the time, therefore he was clueless what to say if asked how the injury occurred.

The request for an interview with Kenny and any of the others was made to the Main Administration Office, which gave their approval as long as the patients agreed. The CBC reporter sent to interview the recovering bikers was Asha Cowhart and her cameraman was Brian Bondeau. The reporter was especially interested in speaking with Kenny, but when she got to the hospital he was unconscious, so she tried to interview the other bikers instead. Doctors had already advised the others they could return home within twenty-four hours, after they had kept them long enough for observation purposes. Chops shared a room with an old man suffering from Pancreatic Cancer, while his comrades partnered up across the hall where it was easier for them to transfer messages. Kenny was housed on a completely different floor in the Recovery Unit, after his successful surgery that left him in a mild coma. Chops and another biker refused the interview, but it was important they prolonged the façade, thus one of the bikers agreed to speak with Asha. Throughout the interview the biker emotionally translated the story they had falsified, which even brought the reporter to tears hearing how they went from playing in the snow to a friend's amputations. At the end of their interview Asha told the biker that she could not provide any guarantees, but the piece might get aired during the evening news.

Before Asha left the hospital, she went back to check on Kenny's status and learnt he had remarkably awakened. Kenny was high on the medication and unaware that he could deny the interview when asked to participate by his nurse. The Rough Rider biker was emotionally shattered trying to come to terms with his new reality, which was crushing for someone who only hours prior had the use of all his limbs. Instead of rejecting the interview, Kenny who was all bandaged up and connected to three different IV drips, told his nurse to show the news crew in. Asha and her cameraman entered the room and arranged everything before the started the interview.

"Kenny I would like to thank you for taking this interview with us today. Tell me, how do you feel following such a horrific accident," Asha asked?

"It is, it is really hard to believe I have no feet, most of my fingers are gone! I am, I am devastated," Kenny responded!

"Why did such a terrible thing happen to you specifically," Asha enquired?

Kenny misunderstood the question and broke down crying instantly, then started telling his version of what caused him to lose his feet and fingers. "I never wanted to be a bad guy, I mean I love being a Rough Rider, but I just wanted to have money and nice things like rich people. See me and my friends went to set up a meeting for our boss with this guy who none of us has ever met. Things got ugly fast and they ended up taking all our clothes and kicked us out in the cold! We had to walk about four blocks outside, that felt like ten miles in the freezing cold…"

Asha and her cameraman both developed a baffled look on their faces. "But according to your friend you guys were playing football outside in the cold?"

"Uh," Kenny shockingly responded!

When the 6:00 PM news aired Chops and both his peers on the same floor watched with high expectation to hear their deception strategy. None of them could believe their story actually aired and even cheered loudly as Asha introduced her assignment prior to broadcasting the news special. Chops and his friends had no idea the reporter had also spoken with Kenny, so while the first biker painted his deceptive portrait they cheered until Asha mentioned her contradicting interview. The moment Kenny's interview began, Chops and the other bikers stopped cheering and began removing the IVs from their arms, as they tried to vacate the premises before the cops began showing interest. With their feet still swollen, the nurses on the floor were surprised to see the bikers trying to check out, however neither them nor security could discourage the bikers and thus allowed them to freely leave.

For precautionary reasons Chops and his two hospital companions went and spent some of their recovery time in Vaudreuil-sur-le-Lac, just west of the island of Montreal. The bikers had an associate name Greg Maloney who owned a small house close to the lake, where they could hide out if the cop were enquiring about them in Ville-Saint-Pierre. Contrary to his disastrous experience at the hospital, Chops wanted revenge from the Jamaicans for more than what happened to his driver Kenny. Jim Bartello had appointed him a task and instead of reporting in on his progress, Chops began strategizing ways of evening up the score. The doctors had advised him that it would take weeks before he would be physically capable to do anything, nevertheless nothing was going to stop him from getting his revenge.

***

Tuesdays were relatively quiet nights at the Rough Rider's Blues Bar; however, the addition of bad weather outdoors had the hall nearly empty. The only patrons present were three regular customers who lived nearby, Cyndi the waitress, four bikers and Jim's girlfriend Carolin. Around 8:44 PM a well-dressed client walked into the establishment and went to the bar, where he ordered a shot of Whiskey and drank it in one shot. As he gazed around the bar he could barely manage to not get distracted by Carolin, who was dancing alone in the middle of the floor to music from the Jukebox. The man tapped the counter signaling he desired another shot, which he treat like the first then slammed the glass down. The client then asked Cyndi if her boss was downstairs, before tossing a $50 bill on the counter and heading down. All the thugs around the bar saluted the visitor as if he was some superstar and allowed him to freely descend to the basement without frisking him for weapons.

Jim Bartello was inside his office, when he received an unexpected visit from Logan Duntroon, who had been appointed as Chops' attorney in his case versus the police department and the government. Four weeks after getting the biker representative out of jail following his latest arrest, the lawyer received the Investigator's Discovery Report on the case and visited the bar to inform Jim of the circumstances behind Chops' arrest. As a security mechanism to ensure that no arrested biker aided law officials in any way, the club provided lawyers for all their endangered members.

Logan did not wish for their conversation to get overheard by the wrong people, therefore, instead of telephoning to transfer the message, he chose to deliver it in person. Chops had given his superiors the impression that his arrest and Quail's killing were circumstantial, hence the blame rested purely on his delivery boy and a known crackhead. With several main club rules broken, the offenders implicated by Chops were found and brutally killed as a result. The private attorney made it known that Chops had been secretly purchasing cosmetic drugs from an undercover officer. The lawyer also advised Jim that the prosecution team was trying to capture Quail; and used Chops as a pawn to find him, moreover they only decided to drop their case against the biker because they failed to recover the drugs they had sold him.

While conversing with the attorney, Lil Wasp knocked and entered to advise Jim of some circulating rumors. The rumors were of Chops and his companions, who were said to be in bad health after being robbed and exposed to the frigid outdoors without clothing. Lil Wasp also told Jim of Kenny's news interview, where he stupidly blurted out club's business on national television.

"It seems as if you need to do some spring cleaning to get your house in order," Logan stated before leaving the office.

Jim telephoned his biker associate who had neglected to inform him of the developments. The telephone rang without answer which led him to wonder what was going on? Having Attorney Duntroon deliver news of treason from one of his area leaders would be considered a blemish on Jim's performance profile, therefore he had no choice but to erase Chops. Their organization considered any form of voluntary interaction between certain members and law enforcement officials as reason of guilt for treason, which was only punishable by expulsion from the ranks and death.

"Take some of the mans and swing by Ville-Saint-Pierre, see if you can find out what's going down with Chops! If you see him, I don't want you to get him nervous, just tell him that I decided to deal with this NDG matter myself," Jim ordered.

"There is only four of us up there, how many mans you want me to take," Lil Wasp asked?

"Just leave me a driver. I'm heading home after this anyways, so I'll be alright," Jim said.

Lil Wasp left with two of the bikers and drove to Ville-Saint-Pierre to do as instructed. Five minutes after they departed Jim came upstairs and crept up behind Carolin on the dancefloor, who was enjoying herself despite being alone. It was evident that she was intoxicated as she stumbled to the beat of the song, so Jim placed her jacket on her shoulders and guided her to the rear exit. Their driver who was by the bar speaking with the waitress, noticed his boss was ready to leave and took off behind them. Jim and Carolin were slightly ahead of the driver when they exited the bar on route to their parked Range Rover. As they got close to the rear door, a black BMW X5 pulled up at the mouth of the alleyway, with an armed rear passenger who opened fire at the couple. The driver withdrew his hand pistol and returned fire at the BMW, which sped off after they struck both Jim and Carolin. An ambulance was called, and both patients were rushed to the hospital with life-threatening injuries, but Carolin was pronounced deceased when she reached the Emergency Ward.

***

Nine days after his injury Chops could barely grip a 357 Magnum handgun or hang onto the handle of an assault rifle; but he was intent on getting his revenge. Both his co-conspirators had injuries to their pelvic areas, but none of them were as severe or irresponsive to medication as Chops'. When they got ambushed by the Jamaicans, the thought of being killed sent unimaginable fear through their systems and weakened Chops' bowels, wherein he developed the urge to use the toilet. Their walk in the snowstorm thereafter was brutal, especially for Chops who was forced to clamp his buttocks and hold in his urine. The chance to relieve himself never presented itself until Chops returned home, which was devastating for his overall health and worsened his prognosis.

The doctors at the hospital had warned Chops that he might regain partial or zero sensation to his reproductive organ, which they initially wanted to amputate but he adamantly refused. The medical experts had to then wait until the swelling and discoloration retracted before they moved onto the next step, therefore Chops had to be fitted with a Urine Sac. Instead of divulging his prognosis to his Old Lady Valorie or any of his associates, Chops hid the news hoping that medication would cure him, but he stupidly left the hospital without getting a prescription. Even though the area leader wanted to give the impression that his only motivation was avenging Kenny, Chops had his personal vendetta to settle versus Lass and his comrades.

Following the irreversible damage done to the biker's manhood no form of apology could suffice, thus the only acceptable settlement on the table for Chops was bloodshed. The only person he told a gist of his condition was Greg, due to the fact he was the person who picked up their medical supplies at the pharmacy. Valorie kept him regularly informed of recent events in town and advised him that Lil Wasp had been by their residence, although she was unaware of the reason for his visit. With Jim in the hospital in critical condition, Chops knew the best time to get his revenge was then, so he contacted two bikers who were his personal cousins and arranged for them to swing by. To insight a gang war versus the Jamaicans, Chops then began circulating a rumor that Lass and the members of his organization were the shooters behind Jim's attempted murder.

Brock and Miles were members of the infamous Rough Rider's East Side Operations, who were brought into the organization by Chops. Even though none of the cousins were blood brothers, they all grew extremely close with their single mothers who were a bunch of tightknit sisters, hence the confidence they would support his cause. The two bikers made their money working for the organization by delivering products to the club's customers within their territory, nevertheless they could wholeheartedly be trusted. Even though Chops trusted his cousins, divulging his medical status was not an option he would consider, thus he kept using Kenny and Jim's injuries as the focal point for their retaliation.

With his cousins onboard Chops did not have to wait until he had fully recovered before carrying out his revenge mission. They all drove back into the city where they made a few enquiries around the NDG area for information on any of Lass' associates. The bikers were extremely cautious with whom they spoke, not wanting to notify either the people for whom they searched or members of their own camp. Chops' limited mobility meant his cousins would have to do all the physical work necessary, but they were quite up to the task. As drug traffickers the bikers knew the types of people throughout the neighborhood who would have encountered the Jamaicans on a regular basis. Knowing this they first went to the nearby corner stores and gas stations, where the Jamaicans would have most likely done some sort of transaction.

Brock entered every business they visited and pretended he was a crack addict looking for a trap house that belonged to some Jamaicans. An Indian cashier at the convenience store knew who Brock was searching for, but he advised the customer that they had relocated elsewhere. After checking all the businesses around the area, the bikers went back to the old drug base address where Brock walked up to the building's registry and rang the buzzer. Following several rings, a baldheaded Caucasian male came to the main door and asked what Brock wanted. Again, he pretended as if he was an addict who had been to that location before and wanted to know where the dealers had relocated to.

There was a nametag on the man's overalls that read Janitor Al and an equipped toolbelt around his waist. Because of Brock's expensive attire Al was not convinced he was an addict and began closing the door. If anybody in the building knew of the traffickers Brock knew that person would be the janitor, therefore with Al acting reluctant to surrender the information, he withdrew his 9mm handgun and barged his way in. Al was shoved inside a door that led to the staircase, where Brock pistol whipped him across the side of the face and threatened to kill him unless he surrendered the information. Out of fear for his life the janitor told Brock where Lass had moved to, but the biker angrily assaulted him thereafter and left him bloodied and unconscious.

As the bikers pulled up to the building located at the address given to them on Park Row East Street, Sammy exited the four-story edifice and began walking towards his vehicle parked along the side of the road. Chops could not believe their luck and instructed Miles to pull up beside the young helper, who was on his way to make a delivery. Sammy had his cellular phone to his ears chatting away and was not paying attention to his surroundings, when the bikers pulled up alongside him and ordered him to get inside the car at gun point.

While Brock and Chops held their weapons on Sammy, Miles exited the driver's side and went around to shove their hostage into the vehicle. Once Sammy realized who the partially inflated biker was in the front seat and noticed Miles coming towards him, he knew he was in terrible danger. There was nothing he could bargain with to save his life and no guarantees he would make it out the vehicle alive, so the helper thought of the next best thing and took off running and screaming, "Bikers help"! Sammy hoped the bikers would get rattled and speed away, but he barely took three steps before they shot him in the back four times. The bikers sped away from the scene leaving their victim spread out across the bonnet of a parked Nissan Altima.

Part 26

Kane drove back to the Nation's Capital, Ottawa Ontario, where he rented a cheap motel room on Montreal Road. As a Native Indian whose people were the first on these lands, Kane did not feel as if he belonged and fought against the thoughts of ending his life after he did something drastic. There were news of mass school shootings and violence on the news, which provoked the Mohawk to consider ending it all like others suffering with depression. The only thing that soothed his soul since the events in Shamattawa was alcohol, which he drank until he passed out and continued repeating the process.

One day after leaving the LCBO, which was the province's main source for alcohol distribution, Kane saw a blond prostitute and hired her for some pleasure. They drove back to his motel where they both began drinking, before the prostitute proceeded to perform fellatio and other sexual acts. The female was a crack addict and convinced Kane to purchase $100 piece of crack to smoke, which would then influence her to spend more time with him. To prevent the female from running off with his money, Kane gave her permission to invite her dealer to the room to complete the transaction. The Somalian dealer was at the motel within twenty minutes, where he made his money and left as fast as he came. Kane continued drinking and allowed the prostitute to smoke her drugs, until he felt the urge to rid himself of the thoughts he had been imagining and thus requested a hit. A single toke led to them calling back the dealer twice, thereafter, as they got high and drunk until Kane passed out on the bed.

There was a banging at the door that awoke Kane, who needed a few more hours of sleep after partying through most of the night. The television was on providing light and the room looked as if it had been trashed, when Kane rolled out of bed and wobbled to the door. The Mohawk Indian barely cracked the door to stop whoever the visitor was from seeing the customized pipes and the filthy room condition. The owner of the fine establishment was at the door seeking to find out whether the Indian would be paying for another week or else he had overstayed the time paid for. Kane told the owner that he would come along soon and pay for the room, once he showered and got dressed. Before leaving the man offered to send over the maid, but Kane declined and said, "that would not be necessary."

After closing the door and checking the bathroom Kane realized that the prostitute had left, however, she had searched through all his belongings and stole all his money from his wallet. The loud door banging had given him a slight headache; but realizing he had been robbed increased the throbbing instantly. The rude boy Indian felt like banging his head against the wall for being so stupid, if only he wasn't already suffering from a terrible migraine. Without money he would have to vacate the motel and sleep in his truck, sober up and constantly recount the things he had learnt, then come face to face with his own demons. While meddling in his sorrow Kane thought of his gun and some other items inside his truck, thereby he threw on his jacket and boots and ran out to his Ford Bronco.

Despite losing all his money Kane was happy that the prostitute did not raid his truck, where he had left his weapon, cellular phone and some personal memorabilia from Shamattawa. His friend Eshanwai loved carving small animals and birds out of wood and had given him a small eagle, however the sight of the carving was too difficult for him to look at, so he tossed it back into his glove compartment and slammed it shut. There was only one way he could continue his binge drinking to forget those he did not wish to think about, thus he dialed Kevin's number and spoke with his Jamaican friend. Kevin was in the middle of something and could not speak for long, but he took Kane's location and instructed him to visit the nearest Western Union within a half hour.

Kane went back into his room and freshened up by taking a shower and changing the clothes he had worn for the past few days. He gathered up all the liquor bottles and the self-made pipes and tossed them into a plastic bag, which he brought along to dispose of elsewhere. There was a Western Union store a few blocks down the road, where he threw the garbage in a container behind the building. The half hour window Kevin requested had passed, so Kane shoved his firearm in his jacket pocket, his Driver's License and Indian Card in the opposite pocket and walked into the store. To avoid being identified by anyone the Mohawk pulled his hoodie over his head and kept his amputated hand inside his pocket. The Vanier area was considered one of the most dangerous sections in Ottawa, and after getting robbed only hours prior the Indian was not about to risk losing the large amount he expected to collect.

There were not very many people inside the store when Kane entered, except for a female at the wicket with her daughter attempting to collect a money transfer. The Mohawk walked over to the service counter and filled out the correct document, then proceeded to the front of the line. A few minutes before the female wrapped up her transaction two colored men and a white female entered and stood in line behind the Indian. From eavesdropping on the new customers' conversation Kane uncovered that they came in to attempt getting a Pay Day Loan, even though the borrower already owed on a previous loan. After the lady and her daughter collected their funds and moved away, Kane stepped to the wicket and slid the document and his identifications through the available slot. The female clerk took one look at the paper and told Kane "to wait a minute while she got her manger", then went to the back and returned seconds later with another female.

The manager asked Kane to step to another window and instructed the clerk to deal with the new customers, while she dealt with the Native Indian. After asking several questions the manager returned to the back of the store then came back with a stack of currencies. The customers being served by the female clerk were denied their request, at which one of the men became cursing the woman they entered with. Kane pretended as if he was focused on the manager counting his funds, but the clerks' thick protective glass provided the reflections of other customers, hence he caught a glimpse of both males enviously watching the manager prepare his payout.

"Here is your Driver's License and Native ID Mister Esquada; and I'll put your $3000 in an envelope for you," commented the manager!

By the time Kane finished his business the three customers were gone, although there were new clients for the workers to serve. For precautionary reasons he placed the envelope inside his inner breast jacket pocket and gripped the handle of his 9 MM inside his pocket. If he still had the use of both hands Kane knew people would have thought twice before trying him, but as a one-handed cripple with money in had already learnt that anyone would try to take advantage of him.

Once Kane stepped out onto the sidewalk, he noticed the female walking down Montreal Road, but none of the men were with her. It was early in the evening and even though the day was cool and clear, criminals had no preference when they went about committing their crimes. As he walked behind the building and approached his truck, the two men came running at him from beside a parked car. Kane turned and faced the thieves who were armed with knives, then cowardly backed up against his truck. The young man who was raising his voice inside the Western Union moved in with the intention of placing his weapon to the Indian's throat. The rude boy Mohawk bated the thief in and waited until he was within arms length, then withdrew his firearm and jammed it underneath the man's chin.

The second male turned around and took off running down the road as if he was being chased by lions, without even looking back to check on his friend's status. Kane thought of shooting at the fleeing robber, kidnap them both, then teach them a lesson they would never forget, but one out of two wasn't bad. The brave-hearted thief froze like a soldier after he had stepped on a landmine and realized he just fucked up. "Ping!" sounded his knife as he dropped it on the ground instantly and stood at attention.

"Do I look like someone to fuck with," Kane asked?

The man could barely swallow not to mention speak, therefore, he simply shook his head with his eyes tightly shut as if he was praying.

"Empty you blood-clatt pockets," instructed Kane!

Jamaican dialect from an Indian was something the man had never heard before; therefore, he slowly opened his eyes to ensure it was a real native. Regardless of the Indian's status the thief knew he had violated and could easily be killed, so he began removing the items from his pockets. With every pocket turnt inside out and specs of perspiration forming on the thief's forehead, Kane stared at him with blood fury in his eyes and said, "Never disrespect your red skinned brother; and never try to steal from a disabled person! Get the fuck out of here!" Once the thief ran away Kane bent down to the ground and picked up $22.50 in paper and loose change, a pack of Zig-Zags, a plastic bag containing five grams of Marijuana, a lighter, his knife and half pack of cigarettes.

Following his ordeal at the Western Union Kane drove directly to the liquor store, where he purchased four bottles of Johnny Walker Whisky and two twelve cases of Miller Lite Beers in the can. The instant he got into his truck he opened a bottle of whisky and took a sizable drink, before lighting one of the cigarettes he stole. There was a diner down the road closer to Vanier Parkway where he had eaten previously, so he stopped there before returning to the motel and bought himself a decent meal. The assassination plot to kill the Columbian Presidential Candidate on Canadian soil had drawn international attention, nevertheless Kane had never heard of the incident.

Informer 3

The Mohawk Indian's interest in the story grew when the reporter showed pictures of all the men involved in the crime that included a photo of Kadeem, who was caught on security cameras downstairs and outside of the hall. Kane thought his friend was back in the islands after escaping death at the hands of the bikers and was shocked that he would return to Montreal. The reporter stated that the case had been wrapped up and the police had most of the assassins accounted for, except for Kadeem who mysteriously was not arrested nor was he being sought after by law enforcement. When asked by reporters why Kadeem was not arrested for his part in the assassination, Federal Agent Darcy who was assigned to the case stated that the matter was confidential and would not elaborate any further.

Although the agent stipulated that Kadeem was not being sought after for the assassination case, they did however wish to speak with him regarding a separate matter. Should Kadeem be watching the broadcast, Agent Darcy also provided his name and an address where he could be contacted. To explain to their viewers the reason why under any circumstance an individual would not get charged, the reporter separately interviewed a retired decorated federal agent who stated, "that the person involved would have to be an informant for law enforcement to be exempt from prosecution, period!"

Before leaving the diner, Kane bought himself a Grilled Chicken Poutine to carry back to the motel for his late-night appetizer, if he wasn't staggering drunk and passed out on his face by then. The first thing he did when he returned was to rent the room for another week, before he went back to his depressed state with his replenished supply of grocery. The Mohawk rolled himself a small Marijuana joint and smoked while he drank, as he sunk further in his sorrows and continued abusing the alcohol as the remedy to his ailments.

Part 27

One of the first resounding pieces of evidence the forensic team members noticed when they arrived on the crime scene where Jim and Carolin were shot, were the security cameras mounted around the Blues Bar building. There was also a camera connected to the store over on the next block that might have caught added information. A drive by shooting meant a wider crime scene, so to not miss anything the inspectors decided to wait until daylight to search the entire area. The investigators first blocked off three complete blocks to stop all motorists from passing through their crime scene. Detectives Kacey Carousel, his partner Bert Backstrom were extremely interested in finding out what footage the biker's security video caught, but there was nobody available to offer them entry into Jim's office where the recording device was kept.

The detectives working the case made a request to view the bar's security system, which if functional would have captured the shooters' vehicle information and possibly pictures of the shooters. With his boss laid up in the hospital battling for his life, Lil Wasp who was the only other person with access to the office, allowed the detectives to view their security recording. Lil Wasp rewound the video that was extremely clear regardless of the late hour and showed it from where the shooters' vehicle appeared on the scene. In the video everyone clearly saw the nationality of all the men inside the drive-by vehicle, but Lil Wasp was surprised to note they were Asians. The cops had Lil Wasp email a copy of the video to one of their email addresses and stipulated they would get positive identification matches once they ran the pictures through their photo identity scanner. Jim Bartello's do-boy was on his way back to the hospital when a colleague phoned him for clarification on the false rumors being spread by Chops. Seconds after Lil Wasp clarified what he had learnt to that caller, another biker colleague phoned to inform him that Chops and his comrades had killed a Jamaican. There was nothing Lil Wasp could do about the situation with Jim still in critical condition, nevertheless they had unnecessarily begun a war at one of the most sensitive times in biker's history. Without the guidance of their leader and a notable biker gone rogue, the entire Rough Rider clan was wide open to deception.

Things went from bad to worst when Lil Wasp returned to the hospital to hear that Jim Bartello had been placed under arrest by the Federal Justice Department. Jim was in a coma and connected to three separate IVs, yet they handcuffed him to the bed and advised his family he would be transferred to another medical facility once pronounced stable. The agents who went to arrest Jim refused to provide all the reasons why he was placed under arrest, but they posted an officer by the door and placed restrictions on who could enter the room. The only information the agents revealed was that Jim was being charged for multiple murders, though they would not stipulate the precise number of victims or mention their names. Lil Wasp quickly contacted the law firm where Attorney Logan Duntroon was employed and transferred all they knew of the situation to the receptionist. The bikers at the hospital were infused about the developments, however the female receptionist relieved their tension by advising them the officers were following protocol, nevertheless she would transfer the message immediately.

***

Alex and Adrian Hickston stepped off their chartered bus from Vancouver at La Petite Bourgeoise Motel in Verdun with eleven other bikers. La Petite Bourgeoise was a small bed and breakfast motel located a few miles from their club's Blues Bar. They were all booked at the motel during their business trip, which was dedicated to the late memory of their deceased brother Antoine. Like Kane, the bikers from Kelowna, British Columbia caught sight of someone they never expected to see back on Canadian soil, when they saw Kadeem's photo on the assassination news feature. Within the hour the Hickston brothers that were degraded from triplets to twins, boarded their bus with some of their most proficient killers from the west and an arsenal of weapons.

With everything happening with the Rough Rider's Montreal syndicate, the B.C bikers wanted to operate low key without drawing much attention to themselves. The motel they selected was on a basic residential street and resembled any old building throughout the area, so without their humongous Vancouver plated bus not many people in the neighborhood would know they were from out of town. To blend into the daily Montreal's, commute the bikers rented two black Chevy Yukon SUVs from Budget Car Rental and kept their bus parked along Manning Street in front of the hotel. There were six bedrooms rented amongst the bikers, with Alex and Adrian being the only pair selected to one room. Once comfortably in their room one of the first people the brothers called was Kevin, whom they had expected to hear from with the news they had learnt about Kadeem. Kevin was in a very frustrated mood having not recovered his son from the maniacs' intent on getting their revenge, thus they caught him smoking and drinking heavily which was all he had done since the trial, even though he informed friends that he was rather busy.

"Yow," responded Kevin with a slurred speed!

"Mr. Trudeau Sir this is Adrian Hickston; the last time we spoke you agreed to help us locate your former colleague Killa," Adrian stated?

"If I said that I was going to do something, then I'm looking into it," Kevin decreed!

"But we recently got word that he is here in Quebec. Did you not know this or were you not going to tell us," Adrian enquired?

"Do you think you fellas are the only ones with fucking problems? You think the world stop turning because you fuckers lost one brother? Thank the lord you still have one left," lamented Kevin before he disconnected the call!

The brothers looked bewildered at each other not knowing what to make of Kevin's last comment, whether it was just defensive chatter or an actual threat. Neither of the Hickstons were aware that Kevin's comments were made under the pressures of pure rage, not knowing where his son was or what condition the boy was in. Adrian then telephoned the Blues Bar to speak with whoever was handling the business until they found out more about Jim Bartello's future. The biker boss was said to be in serious condition and had been in a coma since his operation. Doctors had informed the family that he might never wake up or still experience complications due to his extensive injuries and died.

Even though the B.C bikers were family to Rough Rider gangs across the nation, for them to operate on anyone's turf they must first notify the main leader and get approval. The Blues Bar had been closed since Jim's shooting thus nobody responded to the telephone, so Adrian phoned another comrade and got Lil Wasp's cell number. Lil Wasp was part of Jim's protection unit plus one of his closest confidantes, therefore he was one of the bikers who felt mainly responsible for their leader getting shot. The Montrealer was in the middle of his argument with the arresting agents inside the hospital, so he took Adrian's location and vowed to pay them a visit.

When Lil Wasp arrived at the motel later that night with two of his biker associates, his companions joined some of their western comrades inside their suite and allowed him to meet with the Hickston brothers privately. The Kelowna bikers were remarkably disciplined and avoided causing unwarranted attention by staying inside their rooms and obeying most of the rules of the motel. Lil Wasp was surprised to find the motel still in tact without a hundred naked females racing about the corridors and the bikers behaving like rock stars. Alex and Adrian were drinking a bottle of Chivas Regal, Scotch Whiskey chased with Coke Cola and had approximately eight ounces of Cocaine on the table. The Hickstons were also smoking Marijuana and Cigarettes, with the room cloudy as if it was about to rain. Adrian was cleaning his firearms and loading his extra cartridges with bullets, as if he was expecting an attack shortly. Before they began any business talks, Lil Wasp prepared himself a couple lines of cocaine and snorted it through a rolled up $50 bill. There were extra plastic cups beside the liquor bottle and ice cubes inside their ice bucket, hence Lil Wasp fixed himself his own drink then sparked up a cigarette.

"How you holding up brother," Alex asked?

"I've seen better days man! What's up B.C," Lil Wasp stated as he fists bumped both men?

"Sorry to hear about Jim man. Any changes with his condition," Adrian exclaimed?

"Nothing man he is still battling, and all this couldn't come at a worst time right now! Even if he pulls through the feds now have him indicted up on multiple murder charges, so he could be facing a long time in the pen! One of our Saint Pierre overseer has been spreading rumors about who shot him; and somehow all this led to one of these other guys getting killed in retaliation! I'm going to have to get the word out about who really shot Jim, this is why I'm happy you guys are in town," Lil Wasp declared!

"Shit, sounds like you got some work to do with Jim's situation! Sorry but we only in town to hunt and bury this guy," said Alex as he passed Lil Wasp a photo of Kadeem!

"This guy looks familiar, who is he," Lil Wasp asked!

"The Jamaican coward who killed our brother, and he is back in Montreal again," Adrian stated!

"Jamaican! Fuck we might just be at war right now with those people! But if you guys can't help me, why am I here," Lil Wasp exclaimed?

"It's club policy to let our people know when we're in their city! Plus, we were hoping you could help us find him," Adrian responded?

"I could probably put out a citywide alert to all bikers! Maybe someone sees him, maybe not," Lil Wasp reasoned!

"This city ain't nothing small like Kelowna. Just let whoever sees him know to just watch him and phone right away," Adrian instructed!

***

Following Sammy's assassination Chops returned to his hideout where they joked about the incident and celebrated the killing. Many bikers had phoned and continued calling to speak with Chops regarding the rumors he had concocted. The fabricated story constructed through embarrassment threatened to reignite a dangerous moment in Montreal's history, where Martain Lafleur's regime looked to wipe out Kevin's Alliance crew. Chops did not give a fuck how many people died as a result of his lies, nor did he ever consider retracting his version of the story. Their membership numbers had grown to produce more bikers than the previous administration, so he was quite certain they could easily defeat the meager amounts of thugs in Lass' entourage.

The investigative team that collected the evidence at Sammy's crime scene, spoke with two very credible witnesses who helped them to acquire a lead in the case. The first person was an old woman named Isabelle Montcrete, who was out walking her dog and came around the corner off Boulevard-de-Maisonneuve right before the bikers shot Sammy. The second witness was Donald Smithers, who lived further up the road and heard the gunshots, then watched the shooters' getaway vehicle speed by him. Isabelle overheard when Sammy yelled "bikers" something; and saw the two main shooters one of which fired his weapon through the car window. "A fat doughboy" was how Donald described Chops, as one of the three shooters he observed inside the fleeing vehicle. With both witnesses' eye testimonies, the detectives determined they were searching for three bikers, one of which should be considered over weight according to Donald. The male witness also told police which direction the getaway car went after it passed him and reached the busy intersection. None of the witnesses could give a positive identification of any of the shooters, so it was up to the detectives to use what they have learnt to find their killers.

Informer 3

When Chops and his two other accomplices fled the hospital hours before they were scheduled due to the conflicting testimonies, that feature became a classical comedy skit inside many police stations across the country. Officers inside Precinct 15 laughed heavily when they watched the conflicting details on how Kenny lost his fingers and feet, knowing the tactic used was their most efficient maneuver to determine if a group of individuals were telling the truth. Even though law enforcement never investigated Kenny's amputation accident, his truthful revelation of what happened helped to provide the detectives with their main suspect.

To gain more information the investigators went back to the hospital where Chops and his soldiers were treated and spoke with the nurses who cared for them. Reflections on the incident brought out huge laughter from the nurses, who vividly remembered their frustrations trying to deal with the frostbitten bikers. The nurses advised the detectives that due to the bikers' condition their capabilities were limited, therefore firing weapons and such actions would not be possible until their swelling had resided. Knowing Chops' original partners were still incapacitated the investigators had to find out who his new accomplices were, so they uncovered the model and color of the car used by the shooters. With the vehicle's information at hand, detectives went to the city's Central Observation Office, which was a new traffic division that controlled video cameras at certain major intersection and roadways throughout the city.

On the day when Chops and his cousins murdered Sammy, their vehicle was caught passing through the intersection at Sherbrooke Street and Cavendish Boulevard a minute and fifty-nine seconds after the shooting. The video technicians caught pictures of Chops and Brock in the front seats of the car, but when they checked the tags they found out the vehicle belonged to their cousin Miles. With a mountain of data and high witnesses who can corroborate the likeliness of guilt, the detectives brought their findings to the District Attorney's Office and turned it over to a prosecutor. Within two hours the detectives received three warrants for the arrests of Chops, Miles, and Brock on murder charges.

Part 28

Kevin Junior was in his father's every waking thought and even haunted his dreams, forcing him to awake frightfully each night. The Jamaican rude-boy was frustrated to the point where he drank liquor and smoked Marijuana all day and kept his gun on him always. Yves and White Widow knew how agonizing it must have been for Kevin not knowing where his son was, therefore, they were in no rush to return the kid. The kidnappers had no fear of being found, after being loaned a private cottage on a ten acres property on the banks of the Ottawa River in Montebello, Quebec. The cottage was loaned to the pair by Marolina Veronovichi, who sometimes used the residence as a summer getaway.

Contrary to the humane treatment Kevin Junior received under the roof of Francois Trudeau, his new captors kept him tied to a chair and locked inside an empty room. The only freedom from his confines came when he ate or went to the bathroom, then it was right back into the very uncomfortable position. The kidnapped boy would have to sleep on the upright chair without a blanket in a chilly room, where the temperature along the river would drop each night.

During every interaction with his captors Kevin Junior would be get hit and abused, therefore, to avoid being beaten he would hold his need to use the toilet until he was close to soiling himself. Even though Yves was always harsh, White Widow would sometimes ease the pressures by not tying the ropes too tight or adding a few decimals on the thermostat on frigid nights.

With everybody from law enforcement to criminals searching for them, White Widow and Yves remained indoors and ordered everything they needed either from local restaurants or the grocery store. They abstained from even taking intimate walks and would respond to the door wearing some sort of disguise. There weren't many stores in the small town of Montebello, therefore they ate a lot of pizzas and homemade food from the local diner. Contrary to the larger cities with more delivery employees per franchise, whenever anyone ordered from Amazaro Restaurant the sole delivery person was Old Man Fredric, Indian Joel delivered pizzas for Pomally Pizza and Lloyd delivered supplies for the grocery store. Every citizen in town knew that the Veronovichi property was mainly a summer retreat for the wealthy owners, so when deliveries began going to the address in winter locals were curious. The security system at the cottage was never reported breached so there was no cause for concern, but everybody around town wanted the gossip behind the unseasoned visit.

After two weeks in captivity Kevin Junior knew he had to do something to try to help his situation or he feared Yves would certainly kill him to torment his father. From attentively listening through the walls each day, the kidnapped youth determined that they ordered takeout at least twice daily and never allowed the deliveryman to enter the cottage. One afternoon following a bathroom break, Kevin Junior complained to White Widow that his fingers felt numb, thus she loosely tied the ropes and exited the room. As soon as the female left the youth started fondling with the ropes in an attempt to free himself from the confines. Moments later when Kevin Junior realized that he had freed himself for the first time, he knew he had to do something effective without alerting Yves, who would certainly beat his ass to death.

The kidnapped youth knew that his captors had ordered lunch and wanted to get a message to the delivery person, but he also did not wish to get the worker killed. As he looked around the empty room for anything that might attract someone's attention, he overheard the old jalopy driven by Indian Joel approaching the cottage. Kevin Junior rushed to the window where only a pale blue curtain blocked out the outside light and began timidly waving it back and forth. When Indian Joel exited his old Nissan Stanza and approached the cottage, he looked up to the second level and noticed the curtains moving. Once Kevin Junior realized that he had caught the deliveryman's attention, he thought of ways to convey his situation and thus raised both his hands above his head and crossed them with a tight fist. Indian Joel thought the youth was playing around and simply smiled at him, before proceeding to drop off his delivery. While walking back to his vehicle Indian Joel looked up at the window, but Kevin Junior had moved away by then. To avoid being found out the kidnapped youth quickly wrapped the rope around his legs and wrists, then pretended as if he had dozed off and was asleep. Yves customarily watched the deliverymen who came on the property and noticed when Indian Joel looked up towards their captive's room while leaving, so he quickly ran upstairs to check Kevin Junior's status.

The male kidnapper angrily charged into the room and moved to slap Kevin Junior across the face, as a way of punishing the boy if he had done anything heroic. Yves used every opportunity he got to harm their captive and maintained the intimidation factor to constantly scare the kid. As he came close to Kevin Junior the cellular phone he held in his hand rang, to which he checked the number then instantly disregarded his intention. Yves responded to the call as he walked from the room, but Kevin Junior clearly overheard a female chastising him through the receiver. In his haste to include his female partner in the conversation, the vengeful kidnapper left the door slightly open and switched the phone to speaker access. It was evident that Yves did not wish for Kevin Junior to hear the conversation, moreover the caller must had been important for him to also involve White Widow, who was in the kitchen assorting the food.

"You assured me that my brothers were dead and made me make a fucking fool out of myself," Marolina blurted!

"But there was no reason to believe otherwise," White Widow responded.

"How the fuck do you screw up something that fucking easy? You assured me that you could kill two fucking people; and neither of them is in a fucking morgue," Marolina lamented!

"I personally put four bullets in your brother's chest, don't tell me he is still alive," Yves argued!?

"Well, they are both still fucking ticking! God damn it fuck," Marolina cried!

"We can still do the job at the hospital," White Widow suggested!

"At this point nobody will be able to get anywhere close to him with all the guards around! Even the nurses and doctors now have to show their ID's before being allowed in. With all these unexpected changes I must cancel our other arrangement, before any of this comes back to haunt me! I have wired your money to the account specified, but I want you off my property within three days," Marolina exclaimed then disconnected the call!

The eviction notice was disheartening and threatened to ruin the kidnappers' plans. As a result, White Widow sat with her partner and discussed their best possible option, which was to ransom Kevin Junior for money. Both kidnappers had accumulated a fair amount of wealth over their careers and stood to gain enough money to retire, yet all that was not enough for Yves. The former Rough Rider was convinced that becoming a member of the elaborate cult would allow them to get whatever guilty offenses against them expunged, contrary to fleeing the country and living abroad in exile. Thoughts of what may become of Kevin Junior crossed the female's mind, but she was far more interested in getting most of the father's wealth. Yves telephoned Kevin with a preposterous request wherein he demanded half his stocks in Trudeau Media Entertainment Corporation plus twenty million dollars in cash, prior to them arranging the date, time and place to conduct the trade.

When Kevin received the call from Yves he was as intoxicated as he had maintained for the past few weeks. Following their conversation, he immediately summoned Miss Cutthroat and ordered her to arrange twenty-five million dollars in Canadian currency. The Jamaican rude-boy scraped himself off the sofa and staggered to his bathroom, where he climbed into the shower and stood beneath the warm dripping water. It was almost three weeks since his son had been kidnapped and over that time the detectives had failed to produce any leads, therefore the kidnappers' contact was not something Kevin would relinquish to the cops or take for granted. Instead of his regular expensive attire the adopted Monsieur Trudeau opted for a comfortable Adidas tracksuit and a pair of Jordan sneakers, as he sobered up quickly knowing he had a long way to go. Yves had stipulated that they meet somewhere he had never been before, which was hundreds of miles away and only accessible by car. Other stipulations were for him to come alone and drive an un-tinted car, to allow for clear visibility through the vehicle.

With the ransom dollars prepared, Kevin got a thermos filled with hot coffee for the road and instructed his workers "not to follow him." Monsieur Trudeau then climbed into a Benz E500 coupe and began driving to the location he programed in his GPS, without any Marijuana or alcohol for the journey. The phone call and shower had begun sobering him up, thus without any hallucinate substances he looked to regain his focus during the long drive. Miss Cutthroat had watched her boss suffer from the lack of knowledge regarding his son and feared that something might go wrong, therefore she placed a tracking device inside Kevin's car before he left. Regardless of the instructions given, the concerned protector followed her boss and kept her distance to avoid alerting him. Kevin fought to maintain an appropriate speed to avoid getting ticketed or worst having the vehicle impounded, but nowhere along his journey did he operate beneath the posted speed. The thought that he might be driving into a trap was the furthest thing to mind, considering he felt assured that the kidnappers mainly wanted money.

There was no reason for Kevin to purchase gas with enough petrol for the roundtrip already aboard, but he made a pit stop at a gas station along the Trans-Canada Highway in Hudson, Quebec to use the bathroom and buy himself something to eat. The kidnappers had stipulated that they meet somewhere in Hawkesbury, Ontario to trick Kevin into believing they could have been hiding out in another province. A large section of south Quebec was connected to the northern regions of Ontario and one of the bridge crossings over the Ontario River between both provinces was the John Street overpass. There was a small island in the middle of the river to which the overpass was linked, and on that island were two observation parks where people could picknick during summers or just take a break from driving. Yves had instructed Kevin to pull into the park along the east side of the island, where he planned on making the exchange.

It had gotten dark by the time Kevin arrived at the location where only one other vehicle was parked in the open lot. As he pulled close to the parked vehicle Kevin placed his firearm on his lap and looked to see if anyone was aboard. The car was empty; therefore, he focused his attention on a large gazebo and a small building structure, but still no one around. While tampering with the GPS to determine if he was at fault, Kevin noticed a white Chevrolet box truck driving onto the property. The Chevrolet pulled in a parking slot directly across from him and as the driver reversed in Kevin saw that it was Yves.

Once Yves came to a complete stop he hopped out of the vehicle and slid open the side door, then dragged Kevin Junior from the vehicle and held him for his father to see. The first thing Kevin noticed was that White Widow was nowhere in sight, but once he saw his son he grabbed the money bags and exited the car with his weapon in the other hand. Kevin Junior painfully cried out "Dad" when he saw his father, expecting to finally return home and be reunited. Yves held his 360 Ruger to Kevin Junior's head and ordered Kevin to throw the bags closer to him for him to check the contents. Both bags were very heavy and difficult to throw at once, therefore the Jamaican dropped one and threw them separately. As Yves looked inside the bags Kevin attempted to calm his son's nerves, by advising him that "everything will be alright."

"What the hell is all this, where is the business papers I asked for," Yves snapped?

"There is twenty-five million dollars in those bags, the extra five is for your bitch severance pay! I don't intend to give you a penny more," Kevin countered!

"You think this is a fucking game? You think I won't put a bullet in this fucking kid's head," Yves threatened?

"Well then we all die out here tonight! Because I'm definitely going to put at least five bullets in your blood-clatt; and I suppose White Widow will kill me then and leave with the money," Kevin stated!

While both men stood staring at each other, what could only be described as a cannon blast echoed through the valley. When Miss Cutthroat arrived on the scene, she parked across the road in the opposite observation park and snuck her way towards Kevin's location. The vehicle alongside which Kevin parked was used by White Widow, who arrived there some half hour prior and hide behind the small building. The former Pigeon of The Secret Cult assembled a McMillian Tac-50 Calibre Sniper Rifle, with a mounted scope and waited for the other players to arrive. Once White Widow spotted Miss Cutthroat approaching, she open fire and struck her with one bullet that nearly tore her body in half. The eruption frightened Yves and Kevin, who both held their weapons at each other unsure of what had happened.

"That was that bitch Cutthroat for your information, and if you don't want to end up like her I suggest you drop the fucking gun," White Widow instructed, as she materialized from her hiding place!

Kevin thought long and hard about his son and in the end decided to lower his weapon and hopefully live to fight another day. Yves bounded his hands and placed both he and his son back into the van, then joined them while White Widow drove back to their hideout. As they got close to the entrance Kevin looked through the window and saw Miss Cutthroat's deceased body laying in the snow. The dreadlocks Jamaican knew that his bodyguard was dead because she genuinely cared for him, hence tears of sorrow ran from his eyes.

Part 29

Kadeem allowed a week to go by during which the chatter concerning the Columbian assassination calmed down, thereby he telephoned Enterprise Car Rental and got them to drop off a car for him to get around. Kevin's trusted old maid Miss Emma's residence had been his place of refuge since he left Montreal; and had it not been for some minor obligations he would have already departed from the country. Being the most wanted man on Montreal's biggest gang's hitlist brought its own level of stress, thus Kadeem wore a jacket with big pockets that permitted him to carry two handguns. Everybody became a suspect and anybody who looked at him remotely funny could potential get shot, thus he always kept one hand on a pistol.

The first place he drove to, was a travel agency in Chateauguay, where he gave the female travel agent seven names on a piece of paper and purchased seven first class plane tickets for them all. Kadeem made sure he bought himself an open ticket to Jamaica that gave him the ability to leave whenever he chose to. Once he acquired the tickets, Kadeem found the local post office and sent the package of seven by Priority Mail to Columbia. He had been communicating with Marquez' wife Esmenina over the phone since he parted company with Manuel's former employee turned snitch, thus he phoned her and told her when to expect the mail. To keep Marquez' family safe from Manuel's wrath, Kadeem sent enough money for them to flee to another part of the country, where he kept them indoors at a fabulous tourist hotel until all their travelling documents were issued.

Being a man of his word, Kadeem walked into a Royal Bank carrying a backpack filled with money and obtained a Safety Deposit Box, then placed the money he promised Marquez inside. Instead of leaving with the key he gave it to the bank manager for safekeeping, with instructions on exactly who to give it to. Kadeem then drove to a real estate office on St. Jean Boulevard in West Island and got an agent to show him the newest homes around the community. After two hours of searching he decided on a five-bedrooms, three story homes in Kirkland, then returned to the real estate office where they filled out the application form for the purchase. To ensure there was no competition over who the house was awarded to, Kadeem as the third-party representative offered the full payment in cash once the papers were drawn up. The offer was unlike any the agent had ever received, thus he practically guaranteed Kadeem the property before he left.

There was one person who Kadeem could not wait to see and meet for the first time and that was Marlene McDonald. Without Marlene's bravery and sacrifice it was assured that he would be dead or in jail, so he had much to thank the female for. Like Marquez' wife he also spoke a lot on the phone with his savior, who understood that he needed some time to elapse before he went anywhere outdoors. Marlene worked at Lasalle General Hospital as a registered nurse, therefore her schedule was also hectic, so he would have to wait until she was off duty.

While waiting for the designated time to pick up the female at work Kadeem drove to Verdun to see Foh Nuey, who had helped him in the past and was one of the only people he would do business with at that junction. Because Foh Nuey dealt arms on the Black Market it would be much easier to have him furbish and redistribute the weapons, without the concerns that came with trafficking illegal goods. With the Rough Rider's Blues Bar located in Verdun a lot of their members relocated throughout the area and some even did business with Foh Nuey, but none of such information was beknown to Kadeem. When he arrived at the location and found parking on the adjacent street, Kadeem stayed inside the rental and looked around for an additional four minutes before he contemplated exiting. Once he felt assured the coast was clear and there were no visible signs of danger, the Jamaican bad-man exited the car and threw the duffle bag containing the weapons over his shoulder.

It was a short walk through a back alley to Foh Nuey's establishment, but Kadeem preferred that to parking in front the business on the main street. Unlike walking about in Chateauguay, Montreal was a different place completely, so the wanted Jamaican threw his hoodie over his head for disguise. Foh Nuey was extremely happy to see him, although he had cause for concern knowing he seldom dealt with the bikers.

"Killa my friend, how are you? Long time no see," Foh Nuey stated as they hugged each other!

"You know me Foh, always in some shit," Kadeem joked!

"I see you on the news, so I know you back in town. But you must be careful, especially around this neighborhood now a days! Too many bikers," Foh Nuey whispered!

"After all the love you showed me, I had to bring you this business," Kadeem exclaimed, before he began removing the weapons from the bag!

"Any bodies on theses guns," Foh Nuey asked?

"Yeah, one or two a them," Kadeem responded!

"Perfect! I have a few biker clienteles who will be interested in these! I don't want you back around here my friend, so just write down where you want me send the money!" Foh emphasised, to which Kadeem wrote down his overseas information.

"How is the family," Kadeem enquired?

"Family everybody OK, thanks for asking. You look good my friend; and I thank you for coming to see me," Foh began! "One more thing my friend; I heard that some British Columbia bikers made the trip here for you, so be careful!"

"Thanks for the information Foh! Long life and good health my friend," Kadeem stated, to which they both hugged each other again before he threw his hoodie back over his head and departed!

After looking around to ensure that the streets were safe, Kadeem walked from the building and started back down the alleyway from which he came. There was no way to settle his uneased nerves, as he looked behind himself constantly to check if he was being followed. Foh Nuey's precautionary advice about the bikers managed to trigger his defensive mechanism and placed him on edge. As he approached the street on which his vehicle was parked, two Caucasian males came around the corner and started walking towards him. The thought that they were bikers didn't appeal to Kadeem, until one of them noticed that he was black and started causing a cuss.

"Who the fuck is this passing through our alleyway," argued the biker?

Kadeem gripped tightly onto both gun handles and tried ignoring the men by going around them, but they hurried across and blocked his path. The mouthy biker ripped off his hoodie to see who he was and violated the badman. Without uttering a word Kadeem withdrew both weapons and angrily shot the troublemaker in the chest. Before the chatty biker's body struck the ground, his partner threw both his hands in the air and started begging for his life, fearing Kadeem was going to shoot him also.

"Please, please, please sorry man don't kill me!"

"Get the fuck out of here," angrily stated Kadeem, to which the biker turned and ran away!

The Jamaican looked around to see if anyone else saw the incident, then threw his hoodie back over his head and ran to his car. Kadeem drove directly to Lasalle Hospital where he was supposed to pick up Marlene in an hour by the Emergency entrance and waited. While sitting and waiting he thought about the incident and tried to rationalize shooting the biker, but he knew that he could have simply scared them and fled. A few minutes after he reached the hospital an ambulance pulled up with the biker he had shot and rushed him inside. Even though Kadeem regretted shooting the biker and hoped he pulled through, he knew that should the bikers' friends find him there won't be any hospital, so it was strictly kill or be killed.

Since he separated from Marquez, Kadeem watched daily news broadcasts and read Montreal's Gazette Newspaper more than any other point during his life, to uncover want was happening around the incidents with which he was involved. Marlene helped to ease his worries by translating what she had learnt and served as the negotiator between he and the Columbians. Kadeem was aware that the Feds wanted to speak with him regarding a separate matter from the assassination and intended on talking with them, but first had some other obligations to handle. Moments before she exited the hospital, Marlene phoned to ensure that he was outside. To ensure that the nurse didn't feel nervous about driving with him, Kadeem placed the guns inside the glove compartment to stop her from seeing or feeling them. When they finally encountered each other for the first time it was as if they were long lost siblings, as they hugged tightly for seconds during which Marlene began crying. The Ruffneck Jamaican took the female's bags and opened the car door for her like a gentleman, before placing the bags on the back seat and sitting around the steering.

"I am so happy I was able to help you get away from those people," Marlene exclaimed!

"Without you I would not be here right now, so I really need to thank you," Kadeem said!

"So how you holding up," Marlene asked?

"I'm good, believe me! First of all, this is for you personally," Kadeem emphasised as he passed her an envelope! "And the bag by your leg is for my good friend Tank."

The bag that contained Tank's share felt much heavier than the envelope, but the female was so thankful for the ten thousand dollars. Even though the Jamaican bad-man tried to act relaxed, he would check all the mirrors regularly to ensure they were not being followed. When Kadeem arrived at Marlene's duplex building, they hugged and bid each other a fare well, knowing that they may not see each other thereafter.

Kadeem appreciated Miss Emma's Indian dishes, but he felt the urge for something with a bit more substance, so he drove to Little Bigman's Jamaican restaurant a few blocks away on Newman Boulevard. To have his vehicle close at hand he decided to park in the establishment's parking lot instead of going elsewhere, should anything unforeseen occurred. Before exiting the rental Kadeem ensured there was a bullet in the chamber of each weapon and placed them inside his pockets. It felt a little disappointing to see five other customers ahead of him in line, but the aroma smelt great and he could just anticipate the deliciousness of the Red Snapper Stew Fish Meal.

By the time Kadeem reached the cashier he was inside the restaurant for nearly twenty minutes and another seven people lineups had formed behind him. While the Jamaican gunman waited for his food, the biker who he allowed to run away in Verdun slowly cruised by the restaurant in a Chevy Malibu with three of his biker friends. There was another Rastaman in line and Kadeem stood behind a post that blocked him from the view of motorists on Newman, so the biker was not exactly sure but wanted to get a closer look. Once Kadeem received his food and started walking to his car, the Malibu went around the block and was turning into the restaurant's parking lot. The dreadlocks who the bikers originally saw was still in line and they were all focused on him. The instant Kadeem spotted the scruffy looking Caucasian males in the front seat of the Chevy, he popped off one of his 9mm and hammered three shots through the windshield. The driver of the Malibu instantly threw the gear shifter into reverse and backed out onto Newman faster than he went in, before taking off up the street instead of waiting to give pursuit. One of the bullets fired by Kadeem managed to strike the driver's left collarbone and decreased his interest in the target, whereby he drove himself straight to the hospital for medical attention instead.

Kadeem burst onto Newman Boulevard seconds after and startled an old man driving eastbound, who defensively swerved across the adjacent two lanes and nearly struck the center median. "Sorry pops," yelled the fleeing Jamaican who thought it weird that the bikers were surrendering so easily. When he got to the intersection at Thierry Street, Kadeem was forced to wait until some oncoming traffic passed by before he turned left; and as he looked at the approaching traffic behind him, he noticeably saw a black Hummer barreling towards him. With the Hummer approaching as if the driver intended on ramming the rental from behind, Kadeem changed his plans and instead continued straight on Newman.

There was an opportunity to turn left onto Lapierre Street when Kadeem got closer, so he safely turned ahead of some oncoming traffic and watched to see the Hummer be forced to stop. Instead of yielding to the oncoming traffic travelling westbound, the fierce Hummer driver swerved across three traffic lanes and forced the westbound drivers to brake. The Hummer clipped the rear bumper of a Ford Ranger in the third lane, which spun the vehicle one hundred and eighty degrees facing the opposite direction. As surprised as the motorists were, none of them were more startled than Kadeem, who pressed the gas pedal harder from that moment on. It was obvious that whoever was aboard the Hummer intended on getting him and was willing to go to great lengths to achieve their goal.

There was nothing but stop signs at each intersection from there until they got down to Sainte-Patrick Street, and while Kadeem slightly yielded to make sure he did not get into any collisions, the Hummer continued barging through each road sign without respect for the law. Along that stretch of Lapierre were factories and industrial buildings, thus the Jamaican contemplated how and where he could go to rid himself of the nuisances following him. The Hummer crept close enough to the rental for the bikers aboard to stick portions of themselves through the windows and shoot at Kadeem, who could do absolutely nothing to ward off the bikers.

As they drove closer to Sainte-Patrick Street the options were either to turn east or west at the T-intersection, thereby to avoid commuting through areas with which he was not aware, he swung left at the light. It was much easier for Kadeem's smaller car to maneuver around the corner, so he regained a slight separation between himself and the Hummer. While heading west on Sainte-Patrick Street, Kadeem noticed the railway indicator lights flashing up ahead for an industrial railcar being towed across the road. There were two other vehicles ahead of him preparing to stop and the oncoming traffic in the eastern lanes prevented a swift U-turn, so Kadeem stepped harder on the gas pedal and timed his maneuver just right.

A city transit bus and a Bell Canada service van rolled to a stop at the railway crossing heading eastbound and the two vehicles ahead of Kadeem had both lanes blocked, hence with the rail-arms blocking the traffic the rude-boy swung around the cars and flew across the train tracks narrowly missing the train. The speeding Hummer was forced to brake heavily to avoid a collision with either the vehicles ahead or the passing train. Kadeem knew luck was on his side and thus drove directly to the reservation, where he parked the rental behind Miss Emma's house to hide it from passing motorists.

Part 30

With Jim Bartello still in custody the Blues Bar remained closed until the boss' fate had been decided. Ranger and Slim assumed the establishment would open regardless and staked out the building for more than an hour one evening, waiting to spot and assassinate any Rough Rider Biker who showed up. The Jamaicans had two other countrymen inside the vehicle with them, who were extra shooters brought along to ensure added damage. Dull Boy and Rugid were pilot and copilot of their black tinted Chevy Tahoe, while Ranger and Slim sat back in the rear. Everyone inside the vehicle was heavily armed with assault rifles and handguns, which were all locked and ready to fire. A cloud of white smoke had engulfed the interior of the vehicle, caused by the amount of Marijuana being smoked.

Since the killing began Lass changed his movements and rarely went out in public, while he vamped up his personal security and increased his shooters. At 10:35 PM Ranger and his companions finally decided to leave the premises and seek out other victims in retaliation for what the bikers did to Sammy. Before departing however, Ranger sent their associates to set the establishment ablaze for his disappointment. Both Rugid and Dull Boy camouflaged their faces then walked casually behind the building and broke in through a small window, where they started a fire and exited the building. As they drove away from the premises the fire could be seen engulfing the interior and smoke alarms were sounding loudly, nevertheless they were far from content.

They drove from Verdun to the downtown core, where they parked half a block up the street from the Rough Rider's gentlemen's night club on Sainte-Catherine-Street. The temperature was far less frigid than it had been, so the streets were much busier with a lot of people walking about. Not even three minutes after they parked, two deliverymen exited the establishment and began walking to their vehicle off St. Alexander Street. The Jamaicans determined the men were Rough Rider members by their bandanas, which bikers always carried in their right back pockets. Neither of the bikers were known to the Jamaicans, nevertheless they followed them to their vehicles which was parked inside an open paid lot. There wasn't anybody on duty to collect the parking fee and access to the lot was open to the public after certain hours, thus the Jamaicans pulled in as if they were simply seeking parking.

As the Tahoe drove by the bikers' car it suddenly stopped and the armed shooters jumped out at their victims. The Jamaicans looked like Muslim females with their entire heads covered to help protect their identities in case any cameras were mounted about the parking lot. Even though both bikers were armed, the unexpected attack caught them off guard, therefore they quickly threw up their hands and surrendered. While Slim, Rugid and Ranger held their weapons at the nervous bikers, Dull Boy searched them and confiscated their money and weapons. He then went through their vehicle and removed a small bag that contained several types of drugs and profits already made. Even though the Jamaicans chose to rob their victims, once Dull Boy stepped away from the bikers his companions opened fire and killed them both. The shooters then climbed into their Chevrolet and sped out of the parking lot, then quickly vacated the area.

***

Drex worked for the Rough Rider Biker Club as a deliveryman and was close friends to the slain bikers, therefore news of their death infuriated him. Unlike his comrades Drex was a bit Dyslexic and took a short time to decipher certain things, thus he was extremely short tempered due to his condition. Even though local law enforcement had reported that they were investigating to find out who the unknown assailants were, some bikers believed they knew exactly who did the shooting. When the two bikers got killed, they were at the strip club with fellow gang members celebrating Drex's birthday, and only left temporarily to traffic their illegal products to some waiting customers. The thought that his friends were killed after attending his event ate away at Drex, thus he decided to retaliate instead of waiting for confirmation on exactly who did the killings.

Lil Wasp had circulated the news about Jim's true assassins, but to justify his actions Drex argued that both the Chinese and Jamaicans may had been working together. Days later Drex heard of a scheduled soccer exhibition match being held in a week at the Soccerplexe Catalogna facility in Lachine, between a local Jamaican soccer team called Earth Love United versus Canada's National Team. With such a match being held at the indoor soccer complex there was no doubt countless Jamaicans would be on hand, therefore Drex thought he had found the perfect event to conduct his revenge plot.

For assistance carrying out his murderous plan Drex found someone who shared his beliefs and was readily available for whatever cockamamie schemes his friends conjured up. The biker was known as Kujo and had the intelligence of a teenager, after dropping out of school at the age of thirteen. Neither Drex nor Kujo spoke much English and both men despised men of colour. To recruit Kujo, Drex hooked up with him three days before the scheduled match and spent their first twenty-eight hours smoking Crystal Meth while drinking Molson Beer and Grey Goose Vodka, with two hookers who danced around naked and performed various sexual acts. After they disposed of the hookers and Kujo had been properly intoxicated Drex sprung his idea on him and received a resounding agreement. By the thirtieth hour they were both fully charged and eager to carry out their attack, as they loaded bullets into their extra magazine clips and ensured their automatic guns were prepared to fire. The closer the time got to their appointment the less alcohol they consumed, but the Meth smoking remained a constant right through until they were on route to the stadium.

Drex did not have a definitive plan except to get within the midst of the crowd and begin assassinating everyone in sight. None of them were soccer fans or have ever been to the Soccerplexe Catalogna Facility, thus they were blown away by the size of the crowds as they slowly drove towards the parking area. It took over twenty agonizing minutes to get onto the complex grounds due to the number of vehicles seeking parking, but once the bikers were through security, they felt more relieved. With their vehicle parked on the grounds, both bikers sparked up their last pieces of Meth to settle their nerves before they exited the car. They had packed their rifles inside the trunk underneath the spare tire in case security searched them and thus walked directly to the rear, where they removed an APS-95 Assault Rifle and a Beretta Rx4 Storm Automatic Rifle then finally fist bumped each other.

"Montreal is the province of Rough Riders only," Drex shouted in French!

A black woman who was parked two cars over noticed both Frenchmen brandishing their rifles and screamed, "them have gun," before she ducked between the cars to hide.

The sounds of assault weapons being disbursed rang out across the parking lot, as the bikers took aim at anyone they saw walking. Soccer enthusiasts were forced to scamper for cover or hide behind parked cars as the bikers walked about firing callously. After approximately forty seconds of assault rifle firing, the first sound of a none combatant was heard, as a Jamaican in the parking area returned fire from his M9 hand pistol to ward off one of the shooters. That one gunshot soon multiplied to two and continued multiplying, as soccer patrons illustrated that they also carried arms. Kujo was the first biker shot and killed, after he paused to reload his rifle and got shot in the head by a licensed weapon's holder.

When Kujo's weapon went silent Drex turned around to check his status and got shot in the abdomen. Drex ducked his head and ran back to their vehicle, which he started up and sped out trying to escape. As he turned and drove towards the entrance that was packed with cars, three responding officers saw him and fired at him through the windshield. The officers managed to hit him twice and killed him instantly, thus he swerved into a parked 4x4 and crashed. The incident was bloody and caused the deaths of twenty-one soccer lovers, therefore the exhibition was cancelled as a result.

***

Lil Wasp and three of his biker associates went to the IGA Grocery Store on Côte-Saint-Luc-Road, to purchase some groceries and beer. The grocery store was attached to the Côte-Saint-Luc plaza, which also had several other stores that served the community. Rugid had accompanied Ranger and his girlfriend Pauline to the same grocery store, but while they shopped inside, he decided to wait in the Lexus 4x4 until they returned. While chatting on the phone with his lady friend, Rugid noticed a Ford Explorer pulled into a slot and four Rough Rider bikers dismounted and entered the store. After abruptly ending the call Rugid phoned Ranger to inform him of the bikers inside the facility, but the phone rang inside the vehicle instead. Knowing he was obligated to tell his companion, Rugid walked towards the store but passed by the Explorer and jammed his knife into two of their tires.

Inside the store Ranger had his girlfriend were at the cash register having their items calculated when a huge commotion started in one of the isles. It was quite easy for Rugid to decipher where inside the store the bikers were, considering they were the ones amid the commotion. When the bikers entered the store, they came across an old colored lady in the fruit section who was picking out apples from a pile. One of Lil Wasp's companions grabbed the lady's bag of fruits and placed them inside their grocery cart, then shoved the woman aside. The store employee who attended to the fruits ran to help the woman, who began giving the bikers a serious tongue lashing.

"It is obvious that your mother never taught you any manners! But kindly give me back my fruits before I fuck you up in here," argued the old lady!

"Old lady you and your black people all need to go back to your fucking country," stated the same biker!

"Since you name Mr. Canada then come and put me on the plane," fired back the old woman!?

By the time Rugid met Ranger and Pauline by the exit the racist conversation between the bikers and the old woman had escalated to where they were referring to her in derogatory terms. The store manager and other employees could be heard attempting to settle the dispute, however Ranger was infused by then at the bikers' audacity. Rugid had left the car doors open with the key inside the ignition, therefore Ranger told the female "to toss the groceries inside the trunk and wait behind the steering wheel with the engine running!"

Both Jamaicans then re-entered the store with their handguns at hand and went directly for the obnoxious bikers, who were by then picking up beer in the alcohol isle. Lil Wasp was holding the grocery cart and had his back to the Jamaicans, who turned into the isle and raised their weapons to fire once they saw their targets. The biker who primarily disrespected the old black woman had just picked up a twenty-four case of Coors Light from the shelf and was about to place it inside the cart when he spotted the armed Jamaicans coming towards them. Another biker who was taking bags of chips off a different shelf also noticed the two shooters and grabbed for his weapon.

"Pussy-holes you only have strength for old ladies," shouted Ranger!?

"Bam-bam-bam," erupted Ranger's TP9SF Semi-Auto 9mm pistol, which struck Lil Wasp in his upper right shoulder and blasted off a second biker's left ear, hence the injured bikers took off running down the isle.

Before the biker who quickly armed himself could get off a round, Rugid fired his Luger P320 Nitron RX 9mm at the man, who ducked and took off down the isle with his friends. The bikers abandoned their grocery cart with supplies and tried running away with their heads lowered, while the Jamaicans gave chase. As they scampered away two of the bikers callously fired behind themselves to keep their attackers at a distance, thus the Jamaicans had to approach with caution. Shoppers and store employees were forced to seek shelter or run for their lives as both parties shot at each other as if they were playing a video game. The combat spilt out into the parking lot where the bikers tried to protect Lil Wasp, who was right handed and couldn't shoot straight with his left.

Within thirty seconds the loud sounds of sirens could be heard coming towards them, therefore both parties veered towards their vehicles yet continued shooting at each other. Before either Ranger or Rugid could close their doors, Pauline took off through the parking lot and sped out onto Côte-Saint-Luc Road, where she drove away from the scene and passed several police cruisers heading towards the location. When Lil Wasp and his companions went to drive away, they noticed the flat tires and thought of hijacking someone's car, but that would not be possible with the number of cruisers bearing down on them from every direction. The bikers decided to run for their freedom and began racing in different directions, but officers had received information they were involved in the shootings and went after them. Instead of surrendering two of the bikers tried shooting at police and were shot and killed, but Lil Wasp and the other injured biker were taken into custody.

***

Chops sent his cousin Brock to collect some items from his girlfriend in Ville-Sainte-Pierre. Should ever the area overseer get arrested or find himself indisposed, Chops taught Valorie exactly how to handle his miscellaneous tasks, hence his mechanic shop and trafficking businesses were always operational. Brock was supposed to pick up a parcel with money for Chops to pay the biker club for his resupply order, along with some new clothes and other accessories. When Brock arrived at Chops' shop, he hailed all the mechanics and asked one of them to install a new set of wiper blades on his car. As payment for the job instead of offering cash, Brock gave the worker a dime bag of Marijuana for which he was extremely thankful.

Valorie was inside the business office speaking with a customer over the phone, when the young thug walked in and greeted her with a smooch on both cheeks. There was a huge transparent glass through which they could see inside the garage, thus Brock watched the mechanics while he waited to speak with the female. As he lit up a cigarette and took his first drag his cell phone rang with Chops on the line. Their conversation was short and Brock was off the phone in ten seconds, considering his cousin only called to ask him to pick up beer at the store. When Valorie finally got off the phone she first lit herself a cigarette, then transferred a bag she kept underneath the desk to Brock. It was evident that she was tired and stressed as she withdrew a bottle of Crown Royal from the top drawer, took a solid drink, reclosed the bottle and returned it to the drawer.

"Be careful driving around here, almost every day there has been some shooting between the Jamaicans and our Double R brothers! Just last night Geoff and his people killed some black kid up on Sainte-Jacques Street, and two nights before some black guy stabbed one of our delivery boys over on Eighteenth Avenue! It`s become a war zone out there," Valorie said!

"Did they ever find out who killed Mac and Bizz downtown?"

"Nope, cops say they are investigating. But word is the cops found out about the new turf war, so they released pictures of the people who they claimed shot Jim to end the dispute! The thing is they should have done that weeks ago. May not have changed anything, but now it`s crazy," Valorie stated!

"Nobody is gonna believe them lying cops," Brock argued!

"Lil Wasp was spreading the same story! But I bet he will change his mind after what happened to him," Valorie declared!

"I heard that Jim has bail hearing next week, he probably gets out," Brock stated.

"Hope he gets out, God knows Rough Riders need guidance right now! Anyhow, here is the bag with the stuff for your cousin," Valorie said and passed Brock the items he came for!

Brock took the bag, gave Valorie a hug and walked out to his car that had been repaired. As he pressed the remote door opener and moved to open the car door, a black Ford Transit 150 drove onto the property and stopped by the huge hanger doors. Within the blink of an eye six heavily armed black men carrying assault weapons jumped from the vehicle and simply opened fire at everything inside the garage. None of the mechanics stood a chance as bullets ripped through every area of the shop, forcing Valorie to hide beneath her office desk and screamed her head off. The driver of the Ford Transit was ordered to stay behind the steering wheel and prepare to drive, but while watching the overall scenery he noticed Brock withdrawing his firearm and disburse his Glock 9mm through the windshield. When Brock crashed to the ground from his bullet wounds the bag given to him fell and opened, exposing the contents, thereby the driver quickly ran out and picked it up. Valorie was the only person left alive and suffered a terrible shock from seeing her dead comrades, so paramedics brought her to the hospital for an assessment and PTSD treatment.

Part 31

Indian Joel was watching the local newscast at his house when the reporter spoke about a deceased female from Montreal, who police refused to name before they advised her family. The reporter also said that investigators wanted to know if the dead female had anything to do with an abandoned Mercedes that belonged to Kevin Lafleur, whose son had been kidnapped for weeks. The investigators told the reporter that they would very much like to speak with Kevin who very well could be an eyewitness, but nobody knew where he had disappeared to. A few commuters from across the adjacent park told the reporter that they saw Kevin and someone else get thrown into a van, but the police could not corroborate their story.

Thoughts of the little black boy in the window at the Veronovichi cottage came back to mind, thus Indian Joel picked up his phone and called a mutual friend of his and Kane. Indian Joel was knowledgeable of the tremendous friendship between Kane's family and Kevin, so he called Miss Emma and told her what he suspected. The little black boy was completely out of character and the deliveryman had not seen him since, thereby there was too much coincidences for Indian Joel not to consider warning his native people. Miss Emma took the location and every information the informant had, then began telephoning Kane from 11:17 PM on a Tuesday.

The following Thursday at 5:19 PM, Kane who was passed out on the bathroom floor inside his motel room began hearing the continuous ringing of his cellular phone. There was vomit all over the toilet seat and floor as if he had tried to throw-up in the toilet and missed. As he peeled himself off the floor, Kane grabbed for a towel and wiped the filth off his face, then took a long stare at himself in the mirror. The more Kane stared at himself the more he hated what he saw, therefore he punched the glass and broke it. When his phone began ringing again Kane knew that the call must had been important, thus he staggered out of the bathroom and answered it. The news of his Jamaican brother's abduction was all that was required to get Kane motivated, as he jumped in the shower and freshened up before he vacated the motel and headed home.

Within two hours Kane was at Miss Emma's door for the information she refused to divulge over the phone. Instead of surrendering the location she had received from Indian Joel, Miss Emma thought Kane could use Kadeem's assistance. The retired maid would also like to see the friends back together again, knowing they would always need each other in the white man's country. When Kane and Kadeem saw each other both men hugged tightly knowing the friendship they had forged from the battles they had fought together.

They all gathered around the dinner table inside Miss Emma's kitchen over mugs of hot chocolate, which was all their favourite warm beverage. Kadeem had no idea what had happened to Kevin and his son, nor did he cared to rescue the man who had sold him out like they did Jesus. Kane understood why Miss Emma had him drive to Montreal, but he thought that her trust was displaced in the notion that Kadeem would ever help Kevin again. To save her former boss Miss Emma was willing to go to any means necessary and used everything at her disposal, yet still Kadeem refused to lift a finger to help.

For her final attempt, Miss Emma told Kadeem that, "In life you have to conquer wrongs by doing what is right. You spent these years with Kevin because you trusted him, but sometimes our friends go astray. Kevin gave you both the platform to do great things… you help to show Canadians that the first people here are still here and need listening to; and you helped to involuntarily put away a tyrant who has killed many families. Getting old has a way of reminding those who are true to themselves, of the people who helped them along the way. One day Kevin will realize who his greatest friends were… you will see. But this isn't all about your ex friend! I know you spent most of your time searching for Junior, but I don't want anything to happen to that little boy I helped raise!"

"I hear you Miss Emma! Kane let's role," Kadeem stated!

***

The tight rope used to secure Kevin to a wooden chair was all that held him from tumbling forward, as he slumped over unconscious from the intense beating given to him by Yves and White Widow. Kevin's entire face was bloodied from several lacerations, his jaw had been broken, cheek bones fractured, nose broken and had been knocked unconscious several times already. Apart from the visible injuries Kevin also had many interior fractures from being beaten with a baseball bat, kicks and punches. Through all the beatings his captors kept his son tied up on a chair across from him, as an incentive to give them what they wanted, nevertheless Kevin refused to give in.

Yves and his accomplice whooped Kevin until he passed out, at which they took a break until they were prepared to go another round. After punching Kevin with both fists for hours Yves' knuckles were blistery and swollen, thus he laid back on their bed watching television with his hands soaked in ice. While the Caucasian male relaxed his partner spoke on the phone with Marolina, who continued expressing her desire for them to leave her property. White Widow came off the phone agitated and slammed the handset against the base, then picked up her half full glass of liquor and chugged the contents.

"That bitch still wants us out of here by tomorrow evening," White Widow stated!

"Don't worry baby, in the morning I start working on the kid: we will get what we want before 10 AM," Yves calmly answered.

"We have been beating that bastard for days now, and he still did not give us what we want! What makes you so sure he will," White Widow asked?

"Tonight, I will dream whether I start by cutting off the kid's toes, his fingers, his ears or maybe even his little Peepee," Yves declared!

White Widow ran and jumped on top of her partner and began kissing him. "I love it when you talk dirty like that, it gets me really horny!"

Yves removed his hands from the ice and grabbed his mate, who began ripping off his clothes while he undid hers. The Frenchman then shoved the ice containers off the bed and flipped White Widow over onto the bed and began kissing her earlobes then neck, and slowly down to her breasts. After squeezing and succulently licking both breasts for a few minutes, Yves continued kissing Fiona's stomach and moved down to her crotch, where he hiked both her legs high in the air and performed oral sex. The stimulation caused the female to moan loudly, to the extent where Kevin Junior heard their passionate outcry down the hall.

"Dad, dad, dad you must wake up! Get up dad we have to get out of here or they are going to kill us," whispered Kevin Junior, but his father remained unresponsive! Throughout most of their captors' lovemaking sequence the young lad tried to wake his father, until Kevin's growling signalled that he was somewhat alert. With tears flowing down his face not knowing if his father's eyes were closed or open due to the amount of blood dripping from him, Junior pled for his superman to get up and save them.

"Sorry son, but I don't know, if I can even walk," Kevin slurred.

"It's OK dad, this is all my fault," Junior cried!

"Don't ever blame yourself son, lots of bad people, in this world," Kevin again slurred.

"A lot of people from my school thinks that you are a bad man," Junior argued.

"They are all wrong son... In this world, you have to stand up for yourself, or else some people, will take advantage of you. I just refused, to be taken advantage of, by anyone," Kevin exclaimed!

***

When Kadeem and Kane arrived at the address reported to Miss Emma, they parked the rental car half a block away from the location and went in on foot. It was a dark night and the town of Montebello became a ghost town with nobody on the streets after certain hours. Both men were initially worried about video cameras and other means of surveillances prior to their arrival, but once they saw the type of ancient town Montebello was their fears vanished. The estate was also located on a private street, therefore in case shots were fired they believed they would have enough time to escape before law enforcement arrived.

As they snuck towards the cottage Kane suggested they separated and entered through different means, however, Kadeem knew how dangerous both kidnappers were and insisted they stayed together. The intel they received suggested they entered through the rear French Doors, thus they crept around to the back and tried opening it, but the doors were locked. As they inspected the lock Kane noticed that it had been tampered with previously and began looking around on the ground. There was a loose brick in the garden wall that Kane went over to and pulled out, then returned to the door and used it to hit the lock.

"What the hell you doing they go hear us," Kadeem lamented?

Inside the cottage on the second floor where the bedrooms were built, Yves and Fiona were engaged in wild and passionate coitus, when the former biker paused his motion believing he heard something strange. After pausing for a few seconds Yves assumed it might had been Kevin or his son, hence he went back to pounding his lover from behind. Kane ignored his companion and stuck the lock again, but on his second attempt the lock broke off. The Indian then used his knife to retract the deadbolt and the door slid wide open. Yves had no doubt something wasn't right and extracted himself from Fiona, who also heard the eruption and reached for her firearm.

The last thing any of the kidnappers thought of was clothing, as they looked out down the hallway and began making their way from their bedroom. The lights that were previously illuminated downstairs had been shut off and the entire cottage was dark as night. Neither White Widow nor Yves had any idea if one or both their captives escaped, thus they slowly made their way to the bedroom where they housed them. Yves snuck a peek into the bedroom and realized that both Kevin and his son were still tied up, thereby they had to check the rest of the cottage to uncover the cause of the disruption.

Before descending downstairs both kidnappers stopped at the top of the stairs and looked at each other, to which Yves grabbed Fiona by the crotch and gave her a passionate French kiss. They slowly began making their way to the main floor and reached half way down the stairs, when Kane and Kadeem ambushed them with a barrage of gunfire. Both Fiona and Yves managed to return fire at their ambushers but lost the gunfight, wherein Yves was shot four times and rolled down to the floor, while White Widow died on the steps from her wounds. Yves was shot twice in the stomach, once in the upper chest area and once in the leg yet was still breathing despite the serious wounds.

Kane turned back on the lights and began running upstairs towards the bedrooms but took time to kick the dislodged handgun further away from Yves. There was no need to check White Widow's vital signs by the sight of her wounds, so Kane went pass her and continued up to the bedrooms. Kadeem remained downstairs and kept watch over Yves, whose death he knew would finally close a major chapter in Kevin's life. Shortly thereafter Kevin Junior came running down the stairs and ran directly into Kadeem's arms and hugged him dearly.

"Thank you Uncle Killa I knew you guys would come; I really missed you," Junior said!

"Missed you too champ! But it's Uncle Kadeem from now on, cool," Kadeem responded as they both embraced!

Informer 3

"Cool Uncle, I always preferred that name anyways," Junior lamented!

Kane had to help Kevin down the stairs as he walked with an awful limp. When Kane released Kevin at the bottom of the stairs, the first thing he did was to walk over to the fire mantle and removed a photo off the wall. Kevin then hobbled over to Kane and took his firearm from his grasp and stood over Yves staring at him with a despicable look.

"Killa can you please bring Junior outside to the car," Kevin asked?

Without any disputes Kadeem found Junior's winter jacket and boots and made him dress for the chilly outdoor weather before they left to get the car. Kevin restrained himself until they were well away from the cottage, before he fired the first shot into Yves' right knee and followed that with a second bullet to the opposite knee.

"Ahhh! Go ahead and kill me you son of a bitch! Do it you Bastard! You fucking robbed all my dreams! It was me who stole your precious payment to that motherfucker in Florida; and after giving Martain that money I abandoned my long-time friend to be with that Old Man! And then you came and fucked everything up! I loved that Old Man, but he turned against me for a fucking nigger," Yves said!

"Bam," sounded Kevin's Glock 9mm which discharged and shot Yves in the groin!

"Ahhh," screamed the Frenchman!

"Kane can you please run upstairs to the room these two fuckers used to sleep in and grab the two black Duffle Bags with the money," Kevin politely asked?

"No problem Brother," Kane stated, then run upstairs and recovered the money!

In Kane's absence, Kevin picked up a candle from a shelf and went to the kitchen, where he turned on the gas, lit the candle and placed it close to the stove. By the time Kevin returned from the kitchen, Kane was back with both bags and eager to leave, knowing that close neighbors might have heard the gunshots. To ensure that he had seen the last of Yves, Kevin shot him directly through the forehead then callously tossed the gun to the floor. The Mohawk Indian held both bags in his left hand and threw Kevin's right hand over his shoulder to help him along, as they scurried to exit the cottage. Kevin Junior and Kadeem pulled up out front in the rental just as they came through the door, therein Killa popped the trunk to allow Kane somewhere to place the bags. Kadeem compassionately came around to help Kevin into the vehicle, before he and Kane climbed aboard and drove away. While driving down the driveway a loud explosion sound behind them, at which the cottage went up in flames and burnt.

"Thanks for coming to get us uncles," Kevin Junior stated!

"If you guys didn't rescue us, they would kill us for sure. Thank you both man," Kevin exclaimed and broke out into tears!

"You alright brother," Kane asked?

"Now I am brothers! Now I am," Kevin declared!

"Where to Big Man," Kadeem questioned?

"Right here for me and Junior my brothers! I have to make up a story to tell the police and that can't happen with you boys around! So, go ahead and I'll meet you guys at Miss Emma," Kevin exclaimed, to which Kadeem stopped the vehicle and allowed them to exit just before they reached the main road.

The police arrived at the location within eight minutes, but it took nearly twenty-four minutes for the firetrucks from the neighboring community to reach the cottage. By the time the fire engines reached the cottage the residence was badly damaged and had begun failing, thus within seven minutes under heavy water pressure the entire structure collapsed. Watching the fire destroy the cottage brought a huge smile to Kevin's face, knowing that once evidence was tampered with it became much difficult for investigators to piece things together.

From the instant Kevin saw the first officer he frantically flogged him down and began playing the victim card; thereby he got treated as such especially due to his son. While the officer did his duties and assisted wherever necessary once the fire brigade arrived, he allowed both victims to sit inside his warm cruiser until a decision was made how to proceed. When the senior officer arrived on scene and got the details of what transpired, he ordered the officer to transport both victims to the hospital for checkups, and document Kevin's recollection on what happened inside the cottage.

By the time they reached Hawkesbury-And-The-District-Public-Hospital, local news reporters had gotten a whiff of the story and gathered to get the highlights from the victims. At the hospital, Kevin acted as if he was concerned for Junior's mental health and did not want him to recollect what happened, therefore he declined to have his son questioned by the police. The Mounty however had to wait to interrogate Kevin, who had to undergo X-Rays and several other examinations. With Junior being attended to by a female nurse, once Kevin became available he told his interviewer what happened to Miss Cutthroat and how he was kidnapped and beaten for a ransom he initially refused to pay. When the kidnappers started beating Junior, Kevin stated that he agreed to pay twenty million dollars to save both his and his son's lives, which was the only thing that saved them.

To cast an illusion over the sequences of events, Kevin lied that both kidnappers were fighting internally over who should get the greater share of the ransom. The Jamaican claimed that an argument developed between the partners, at which Yves plotted to keep all the money for himself and terminate everyone else. With the kidnappers' disagreement escalating, Kevin stated that he managed to free his hands from his bondages and snuck from the room down to their bedroom, where he found a 9mm handgun and started back to rescue Junior. As he reached the room door Kevin claimed that he heard White Widow arguing while climbing the stairs, when Yves frustratingly opened fire from downstairs at her. Both kidnappers were said to exchange gunfire, during which Fiona was killed and Yves received a flesh wound injured.

With Yves attending to his minor gunshot wound inside the kitchen, Kevin stated that he started sneaking downstairs with Junior. Yves believed they were still securely tied up and began getting cleaning supplies and other items to dispose of the body. Just before he and Junior came down the stairs, Kevin sighted that Yves unexpectedly walked from the kitchen, therefore he had no choice but to kill him. The explanation was documented, and the mounty collected Kevin's basic information before they shook hands and he departed. The doctors asked Kevin if he would like to appear live with them before the reporters to answer questions about his and Junior's wellbeing, but he declined and told them to handle it. Instead of a long car ride back home, Kevin had his handlers send a helicopter to the nearest landing pad, where he and Junior caught their flight.

Part 32

At Jim Bartello's bail hearing, the defendant was scheduled to participate from his hospital confinement via satellite, however Logan Duntroon his lawyer had him transported into court to show the judge his client's present predicament. Jim was rolled in sitting in a wheel chair connected to an IV and placed at the defense table next to his team of lawyers. Regardless of his predicament the prosecution team led by Elizabeth Marcion wanted Jim back behind bars and presented a solid case why he should be remanded. With conspiracy murder charges against Federal Agents and murder charges against an elderly hotel owner, prosecutors did not see any way the judge would allow Jim back onto the streets.

Nevertheless, Attorney Duntroon argued that his client was pleading not guilty and may never walk again, hence he was no flight risk and should be allowed to reconvene his life. The defense attorney pointed out that Jim was an upscale businessman in the community, whose businesses were suffering because he was not available to mange them. Logan pointed out that the prosecution's entire case was circumstantial, and his team was eager to debate their

Informer 3

findings under the law. After hearing both sides' arguments, Judge Poitier took a short recess to consider the terms of the case and decided if he should award the defendant bail. While back in his personal quarters Police Chief Arnold Dubois, a professional friend, phoned the judge and spoke to him off the record concerning Jim Bartello. The Rough Rider Bikers were on the verge of escalating a small disagreement into a humongous street war that had already cost the lives of innocent citizens, so the Police Chief requested that Jim Bartello be granted bail to help rectify the situation.

Judge Poitier reconvened his courtroom following a twenty minutes break, which excited the prosecution team that assumed he would side with them. To justify his decision the judge began by pointing out the defendant's crippled state and implied that they had noting to fear from Mr. Bartello. The judge then demanded the defendant surrender his passport to the courthouse to commence his long list of conditions. In his judgement Judge Poitier pointed out that it was inhumane to stop a person's livelihood and the defendant had every right to be considered innocent until proven guilty. Following all the explanations Judge Poitier offered Jim a two million dollars bond, which he knew would upset and slightly appease the prosecution team. Within four hours Jim was back on the street with a host of Court Restrictions which he had to abide by if he wanted to stay out of jail until the termination of his trial. When Jim's biker entourage picked him up from the courthouse the instant he entered the Handicap Transport a colleague handed him a cellular phone with one his fellow bikers on the line.

"Make sure you boys bring them in alive," Jim exclaimed and disconnected the call!

***

That same evening was a busy supper period at Cheng Lo's restaurant, thereby he had to help his employees who were swamp with customers. At 8:09 PM during the busy dinner rush, a GMC Savanna Cargo Van reversed up to the rear door as if the driver intended on making a delivery. The Caucasian male banged on the rear door to gain entry, hence the kitchen helper Din Suh opened the door.

"Can I help you," asked Denny Suh?

"I have a delivery for your boss," said the Savanna driver.

"Isn't it too late for deliveries," asked Denny Suh?

"Man, I don't know I just deliver the stuff," responded the Savanna driver!

"What type of product do you have to deliver," questioned Denny Suh?

"I believe it's vegetables, but I'm going to need your boss' signature," stated the Savanna driver?

"OK you can bring the stuff in and I'll get my boss," said Denny Suh.

The Savanna driver stood by the vehicle's rear doors instead of unloading the items he had described. When Cheng Lo came to the back door he immediately began disputing the order, knowing neither he nor any of his employees did as such. As Cheng began his dispute, the driver of the cargo van opened the vehicle's rear doors to the surprising display of two assault rifle carrying bikers. Cheng Lo was tossed into the back of the GMC Savanna and the driver slammed the door, before he hopped in the driver's seat and departed.

***

Zue Ki Chi was a Chinese national who got hired by the Chinese Drug Syndicate to assassinate Jim Bartello. Mr. Chi learnt he was being sought after by the Montreal police, so he booked a flight back to China that was slated to depart from Vancouver the next day. To catch that flight Zue booked an early morning flight from the Pierre Elliot Trudeau International Airport that would arrive three hours before his Chinese flight. While the cops relied on their basic investigative tactics to locate wanted criminals, the bikers had their more sophisticated national network do the tracking. According to their preliminary report from the network, Zue was hiding out in the Park-Extension area of the city, on a street and building that were predominately occupied by Chinese. The report pointed out that Zue was with one of the men he did the shooting with plus the man's girlfriend, who was said to be considered dangerous. The accomplice's name was Hang Fow and unlike Zue who mainly resided abroad, he had no plans to leave the country.

There was absolutely no way that a raid on an apartment building versus armed and dangerous individuals would turn out profitable for the bikers, so they had to find alternative means of capturing without violence. On the morning of Zue's departure the same bikers who captured Cheng Lo followed the Toyota Avalon that transported him to the airport. It was no secret that the Chinese aboard the Avalon were heavily armed, therefore the bikers pursued without altercations.

When they reached the airport, the bikers parked three cars length behind the Toyota and watched as the Chinese associates said their goodbyes and separated. Once Hang and his girlfriend departed, two of the bikers exited the cargo van and followed Zue into the airport. The bikers watched as the want-

Informer 3

ed Chinese checked his suitcase and himself in, then approached him as he walked towards the Security Checkpoint. Both bikers came up on either side of the Chinese National and stopped him by quickly flashing a black Exclusive Member's, Costco Card from one of their wallets. Zoe did not clearly see the ID and knowing he was a wanted man deterred him from asking any questions.

"Mr. Chi we are with the local police department and we would like to question you about a shooting? If you could peacefully come with us that would be greatly appreciated," said one of the bikers as they calmly held onto the Chinese man's hands?

"But they just put my luggage on the plane," Zue argued.

"We know that sir don't worry about it, your bag will be taken off the plane," said the other biker.

Zue assumed he was caught and freely surrendered, to which they all walked directly from the airport terminal, climbed into the cargo van and drove away.

***

Kim Lang was the driver of the drive-by vehicle used in Jim Bartello's attempted murder incident. Kim's father Dim Ho Lang who resided in Hong Kong was one of the head syndicate members of the Chinese drug trafficking. In retaliation for disrupting their distribution connection in Canada, Dim Ho and his associates decided to strike back against the Rough Riders and sent Zue Ki Chi to assassinate Jim. When Zue got to Montreal he realized he would need additional help to get to the Rough Rider leader and thus brought in Kim Lang, who in turn involved his best friends Hang Fow and Li Mai.

Kim had a girlfriend who resided in Laval just off Montreal Island, who he spent a fare amount of time with weekly. A few hours after Cheng Lo was abducted Kim left his girlfriend`s apartment at 1:47 AM for home. The Chinese Canadian male drove a brand-new BMW X6 with an automatic starter, so before leaving the building he pre-started the vehicle to warm the interior. As Kim descended the steps that led up to the apartment building, a GMC Savanna pulled up ahead of him and the passenger's siding door slid open. Two armed Caucasian bikers leapt from the cargo van and caught Kim off guard, to which they then tossed him into the van and drove away.

***

Hang Fow finished his shift at work and ran into the Atwater Metro Station to catch a train home. Atwater was a very busy station considering it was attached to Dawson College and had a shopping center area with a movie theatre. The space was usually busy so Hang payed no extra attention to five Caucasian men who began following him once he came out of work. When sliding his monthly transit pass for access, Hang heard his train entering the station below and began rushing to get aboard. The five Caucasian men had tickets and quickly slid them into the machine, as they also hurried to catch the arriving train. There were other commuters rushing to get aboard the metro, therefore Hang again had no reason to specifically suspect the five men.

The metro car they rode on heading towards Angrignon Station was packed from Atwater to Lionel Giroux Station, but most of the passengers de-boarded at Lionel Giroux. There were way more seats available, so Hang took a window seat and stared through the window as they departed from the station. One of the bikers sat to the right of Hang and another on the seat ahead of him. The other three bikers stood around them and stared down at the Chinese male, who continued mining his own business and looking through the window. The biker next to Hang poked him in the ribs with the mouth of a firearm and pulled his earphone from his ears. When Hang spun around to protest the first thing he noticed was the 9mm Glock pointed at his ribs, before the intimidating biker faces forced him to reconsider.

"At the next station we will all get off this train. If you do or say anything we will kill you," said the Frenchman!

When they reached Charlevoix Station, Hang calmly got up and looked around inside the metro car, but the four ladies and three men aboard were not enough re-enforcements to yell for assistance. The bikers surrounded Hang and walked him out onto Charlevoix Street where their GMC Savanna awaited them, thus they all climbed aboard and drove away.

***

Li Mai shared a two-bedroom apartment with two friends on Langelier Boulevard in the east end of the city. An abduction report filed by one of his roommates stipulated that at 11:23 PM, four Caucasian assailants gained entry into the building by unknown means. The men rode the elevator up to their apartment on the sixteenth floor and knocked the door, to which said roommate opened the door. When asked by police, "why he opened the door to strangers", the roommate responded that "they live in a very safe building, so he never expected anything crazy to happen"!

Informer 3

The four pistol carrying bikers broke in and while one of them held the roommate at gunpoint, his three companions searched quickly through the apartment. They found Li Mai sleeping inside his bedroom and dragged him out in his boxers only, before they tied up their helper and left the apartment. It wasn't until the third roommate returned home some forty-six minutes later that they called the police and filed the abduction person's report.

***

Jim Bartello was brought to a warehouse in the northwest Roxboro sector of town. Inside the warehouse were several bikers with the five abducted Chinese nationals who were all beaten. Due to Jim's limited motion he could not get the personal satisfaction of inflicting his judgement, but he took pleasure in watching the shooters get electrocuted and beaten with baseball bats. Cheng Lo was the only person against whom Jim instructed his enforcers not to harm, until he had gotten the opportunity to thoroughly interrogate him.

By the time Jim arrived at the warehouse the shooters had already been getting tortured for hours, yet he sat and watched them get additional punishments for more than an hour. Cheng watched Jim's facial expression throughout the torture sequence and saw that the biker leader did not care what became of their abductees; nevertheless, he would do anything to avoid the same fate. The Chinese shooters had been electrocuted and beaten to unconsciousness several times, but each time they were awakened with a bucket of water to the face, for the process to painfully continue. Throughout the torture session Jim only reminisce on his deceased girlfriend, whom he knew took several bullets that were intended for him. Once Jim grew tired of the constant screaming, he took a temporary break, by ordering his executioners to take a minute while he questioned Cheng Lo.

"You and your friends in China tried to kill me," Jim declared!?

"I, I, I would never betray you Mr. Bartello! They tried to get me to help them; and send that guy Mr. Chi to scare me, but I say I won't help them! Please, Mr. Bartello we do good business, you must believe that I would never," Cheng pled!

"I might never walk again because of you all! For that your lives end right now," Jim threatened and nodded his head for the executioners to continue!

"Please Mr. Bartello, I swear I would never betray you! Please sir don't do this, I had nothing to do with them! Please sir, please, please," Cheng begged!

Instead of hurting Cheng an enforcer chopped his confines and set him free. Cheng felt so relieved to be released that he ran over to Jim and hugged him, while praising and thanking him for his generosity. The enforcers then continued where they left off by electrocuting and beating the assassins until they seized breathing. Jim drove away on his electrical wheelchair before the killers died and was accompanied by Cheng when leaving.

The Chinese assassins were killed and later reported to emergency services by an unknown individual. Law enforcement officers and health technicians flocked to the location and eventually brought the victims to the Lakeshore General Hospital's Morgue in the West Island. A forensic team was also called in to begin an investigation into why this happened and who committed such a horrible crime. When the victims reached the hospital all four men were left in a corridor for the first few hours, until proper clearance was granted to perform the autopsies by the Chinese Councillor. Following several analyses such as the estimated time of death, date, visible wounds and body identification, the bodies were cut open and examined for the actual cause of death, tagged and finally placed in freezers.

The following night at 1:33 AM, a private ambulance pulled up at the emergency entrance, but instead of dropping off a sick patient both operators went directly to the morgue. A few minutes before the paramedics arrived, the morticians on duty coincidentally went on his break and left their department. The hospital hallways were nearly empty, and most departments were closed for the night, therefore there was nobody available to question or stop the technicians. The ambulance paramedics knew exactly who they wanted and thus removed Zue Ki Chi's body from the freezer and stole it.

Zue Ki Chi's body was taken to a private morgue in Baie D'Urfe, where a mortician reopened his incision to expose his interior organs. The mortician then placed a newly designed remote activated C-4 Plastic Explosive Device into the dead man's stomach, that was specially designed to surpass body scans at airports. To secure the device the mortician attached it to Chi's Liver and resealed the wound, before the body was brought back to the West Island Hospital. Mr. Chi's body was returned to the freezer from which it was taken by 4:49 AM, prior to the arrival of the doctors and other day shift employees.

It was initially believed that all those tortured and killed were Chinese Nationals, until the Immigration Department confirmed that Zue Ki Chi was the only visitor to the country. Being on foreign soil with none-residential status meant that the body would have to be flown back to China for burial, hence proper arrangements were made by the Chinese Council to return Zue's body to the Mainland. Two days after the killings a Chinese female named Lyn Chow turned up at the Chinese Council Facility, claiming she was Zue's cousin and would be honored to accompany the body to China. Instead of paying additional charges to have the body attended to when it reached its destination, the female was given authorization over the corpse after they landed. Once all

Informer 3

the paperwork was drawn up Zue got flown back to China on a commercial airline, within ten days after being killed.

When they reached Hong-Kong, transportation was already prepared for Lyn, who used the documents she obtained in Canada to collect the coffin. The driver of the hearse and Lyn brought the dead body to a warehouse location, which was the Chinese Syndicate's main drug operation headquarters. Both Lyn and her driver knew they were in dangerous territory and would be killed if found out, so the female armed the remote detonator and held onto it inside her jacket pocket. None of the Chinese gangsters who attended to the door were willing to accept the corpse delivery, until one of their bosses got summoned and came out to check the coffin and see who exactly was in it.

"Why was this body sent here," asked the drug syndicate boss in their Mandarin tongue?

"Mr. Chi was murdered with some other Chinese men in Canada, and he has no other reported family here in China," Lyn responded in their language.

"I am aware of what happened! There is a colleague of mine inside mourning the death of his son right now," stated the syndicate boss!

"I am truly sorry to hear that sir, but unless you accept Mr. Chi's corpse, he is scheduled for the furnace," Lyn declared.

Zue Ki Chi had served the Chinese drug syndicate for decades and died in their honor, thereby to show face to his other employees the drug boss accepted the corpse. The thought of foul play was the furthest to the boss' mind, knowing that the body had been through immigration screening and checkpoints. Lyn had the boss officially sign for the body to maintain the authenticity of the deal, before they watched the gangsters wheel the coffin into their warehouse. With all the official business handled, Lyn and her driver climbed aboard the hearse and slowly drove away. Approximately sixty yards away from the warehouse Lyn withdrew the remote detonator and pressed the button.

"Kaboom," sounded a huge explosion as the warehouse blew up and caught fire!

Lyn was driven directly to the airport where she waited the next five hours for her flight back to Canada and did not hesitate to leave China.

Part 33

Marolina Veronovichi went shopping in Italy for four days and was summoned for questioning by RCMP investigators during her absence. Upon her return to Canada, Marolina, Andrea her husband and their lawyer Fabian Survalley presented themselves at the RCMP inquiry, into why two wanted kidnappers' charred remains were found inside their private cottage. Instead of arresting the Veronovichi couple for possibly conspiring with the kidnappers, investigators wanted to hear how did the wanted criminals legally acquired the resident's keys. Constable Floyd Landroit, who was the Mounty who questioned Kevin at the hospital, headed the enquiry with two other inspectors, Jane McNabb and Miller Nacovork.

"Monsieur and Madam Veronovichi you have been summoned here today for an enquiry into the reason why two wanted kidnappers were found inside your destroyed cottage," Inspector McNabb a French born inspector began?

"What, we don't have any knowledge of any kidnappers," Andrea interrupted, to which Marolina reached over and grabbed his hand to disrupt him!

"Monsieur, monsieur please wait until I am finished, I am still highlighting the reason you are here today, so when I am finished you can say what you want to say then," said Inspector McNabb!

"OK," stated Andrea, as he looked over at his wife and realized that she might know something!

"Like I was saying, these two people that were found in your cottage, who were holding a man and a little boy hostage! I must advise you that this enquiry is being recorded, and that you are required to give the truthful answer to all the questions. If you have any questions you may ask them now, or if not my colleague Inspector Nacovork will proceed with the enquiry," Inspector McNabb declared!

"Allo, I have a few questions for you both. Now did either of you know Mister Yves Buchard or Miss Fiona Pierson," Inspector Nacovork asked?

"Yes, knew Fiona and her boyfriend Yves," Marolina firmly answered!

"In what capacity did you know Mister Buchard and Miss Pierson," Inspector Nacovork asked?

Attorney Survalley reached over and whispered in Marolina's ear, "Be very careful how you respond to this question!"

"Fiona was a friend of mine down on her luck and I simply gave her somewhere to stay until she got back on her feet," Marolina stated!

"Did you know Kevin Trudeau and his son Kevin Junior," Inspector Nacovork asked?

"No," Marolina declared!

"When did you loan your cottage to Fiona Pierson," Inspector Nacovork asked?

"I'm not exactly sure, it could be two months," Marolina asked?

"Mr. Veronovichi did you know any of the people I mentioned," Inspector Nacovork asked?

"No sir," responded Andrea, whose eyes were pasted on his beautiful wife!

"Were you aware that Mister Buchard and Miss Pierson were wanted for kidnapping," Inspector Nacovork asked?

Attorney Survalley again reached over and whispered in Marolina's ear, "you do not have to answer if you do not wish to!"

"No, I wasn't Inspector Nacovork," Marolina lamented!

"Did you conspire with the aforementioned kidnappers to solicit money through ransom," Inspector Nacovork asked?

"If these are the lines of questioning you are going to ask my clients then I'm afraid we will have to leave! We came here voluntarily not to be harassed...," Attorney Survalley fired back, as she stood up and began preparing to leave.

"Inspector Nacovork between my husband and I we are worth nearly three billion Euros, so I have no need for ransom money from anyone," Marolina exclaimed as she joined her husband and lawyer who were preparing to leave!

When they reached the parking lot, they all shook hands, before Attorney Survalley hopped into his F-Type Jaguar and they separated ways. Both Andrea and Marolina climbed into their Continental GT Speed Convertible Bentley and headed for lunch downtown Montreal. Andrea was generally a very reserved individual but hearing that his wife possibly conspired with criminals angered him. Throughout most of the journey they argued about the enquiry topic until Andrea grew tired of the conversation, thus while stopped at a red light he withdrew a small vile that contained his personal stash of cocaine; and did a hit up each nostril off his pinky finger. For the remainder of the trip, Andrea grew silent and seized his dispute knowing he would never win an argument versus Marolina.

As Andrea turned off René-Lévesque Boulevard onto Mansfield Street they came upon a tow truck that appeared to be searching for someone's vehicle. A city garbage truck pulled onto the street directly behind them and closely pursued for half a block. When they reached the middle of the block they came to a point where there were two large moving trucks on either side of the street. While Andrea thought of how perfect a camouflage the trucks were, the tow truck suddenly stopped, and the driver began remotely descending the Hydraulic Vehicle Lift. The garbage truck pulled up directly behind the Bentley's rear bumper and protruded the car from reversing. While Marolina and Andrea contemplated which vehicle the tow truck driver planned on towing, a Caucasian male wearing a black jogging suit with the hoodie over his head and an Expos Baseball Hat, threw a piece of Spark Plug at the female passenger's window that shattered it. Marolina screamed out in terror as glass splinters cut the side of her face. The man withdrew a firearm and pointed it at both passengers, reached inside and opened the car door, then climbed into the back seat and closed the door.

"Shut the fuck up bitch," said the carjacker as he gun-butted Andrea in the back of the head! "Turn off the engine and take off those fucking seatbelts! Now get the fuck down low so nobody can see y'all in the bitch! I wish one of you move so I can put two bullets in your fucking assess!"

The tow truck backed up to the Bentley and hoist the car, then drove casually down the street without anyone noticing the carjacking that took place in broad daylight.

***

Marceau Demerit spent nine weeks in critical condition, before his status finally got upgraded to serious. Doctors at the Royal Hospital had to place him in a coma for the duration of that time to allow his body to slowly recuperate. There was still a long road to full recovery and Marceau would probably have to learn to do a lot of things again, such as walking, speaking properly, even the use of his hands, but each day his prognosis slowly improved. It took a total of four separate surgeries to fully get Marceau on track to recovery, however there was a severe disparity to the amount of prayers made on his behalf. Following Marolina's visit she neglected to return to check on either of her brothers, although she sent each of them flowers daily. Elise Demerit always knew Marolina to be a very aristocratic and selfish individual, therefore she thought nothing of the neglect, but ironically, she spent every minute of her husband's stay by his side.

Maurice Demerit had been released from the hospital for more than six weeks and had slowly been getting back into the groove of things. The stab wounds could have killed him had he not received medical attention instantly, as a result both brothers were extremely lucky. The younger of the two brothers cared more about his sibling than their sister, hence Maurice went to the hospital to check on Marceau for an hour each day. Marceau's private room resembled a garden with flowers everywhere and each day more presents and cards were delivered. Their bodyguard Spencer stood guard at the door every day that the family was there and had a paid off-duty officer present whenever he went home to rest. Three days after the doctors speculated that Marceau might awaken, he was still unconscious and irresponsive, but his daughter and instant family were confident that he would awaken soon.

On the fourth day following the prediction, Elise and Adriana were passed out on the cots provided by the hospital at 5:57 AM, when Marceau opened his eyes and called his wife's name. It was somewhat of a struggle for Marceau to speak clearly, but he could be understood. The joy both mother and daughter felt that morning was unmeasurable, as they rushed to Marceau's side and gently squeezed his hands. After emphasizing how joyous she was that he was alive, Elise went and alerted the staff nurses who eventually showed up with the doctors to check Marceau's status. Once the patient got re-evaluated doctors became more optimistic that he could make a remarkable recovery, considering he could already do much of the things they believed he would not.

Spencer who began his all-day shift at 6:00 AM, was the most relieved employee on Marceau's payroll. Even though the bodyguard had safely protected his client for many years and had an exceptional work history, having such a blemish on one's record could have been futile for his career. Marceau was a delightful and generous boss and Spencer loved working for him, hence after everyone cleared out of the room later that morning he went in and expressed, "how sorry he was for failing to stop the attack and how happy he was the boss pulled through". The first question the boss wanted answers to was if they had caught the shooter, but his bodyguard told him that "the man was yet to be identified". The frail billionaire had no idea that Maurice was also injured following his assassination attempt, thus Spencer revealed all the information he had acquired to that point.

When Adriana and Elise returned from the cafeteria where they went to have breakfast, both Marceau and Spencer seized their conversation. Elise brought Spencer a cup of coffee and gave it to him before he exited and returned to his post. Maurice who often visited during the afternoons got message his brother had awakened and came by earlier than normal to visit with him. Although Elise also reached out to Marolina, she neglected to visit her recovering brother in person to verify his status for herself. Marceau spent the next three weeks in the hospital before he got transferred to a rehab center, where he continued his recovery process.

Part 34

Canadian Prime Minister Mathew Layton felt somewhat emboldened during his G-7 Summit in France, where he and the six world leaders involved met to discuss ways of keeping their countries safer. As leader of one of the world's largest countries, Mr. Layton believed there was nothing beyond his knowing and secretly plotted to expose this Quebec Secret Cult. The problem the Prime Minister had in doing so was the fact he did not know who to trust, nor did he want the people of interest to uncover his private investigation. Following his dealings with one of the country's largest policing firms the RCMP, Monsieur Layton's confidence in all his law departments was shaken, thus he seriously contemplated who to approach with his concerns.

It had been more than two weeks since he and his wife received those threatening phone calls, yet the chilling sensation still haunted them both. The Prime Minister thought that it could be possible his phones were illegally bugged, so to discuss his concerns with someone who might be able to help him, he used a payphone at the French hotel where he stayed. Monsieur Layton called the private line of Sr. Patrick Johnston, who served as the Head of The Canadian

Spy Agency.

The phone rang several times before it was finally answered by a harsh toned individual. "This is Sr. Patrick Johnston how may I help you?"

"Patrick this is Mathew Layton here in France!" answered the Prime Minister who spoke very softly to avoid being heard by anyone.

"Is everything alright Mr. Prime Minister? Why are you phoning me from an unsecured line," asked Monsieur Johnston?

"I'm afraid this is the only way I can talk to you without certain people listening in on our conversation," said the Prime Minister!

"This would be considered the lease safest method at the agency's standard, but if you believe so, go ahead and tell me what's bothering you Sir," Monsieur Johnston enquired!?

"Listen Patrick this stays between you and me, no one else you understand," exclaimed the Prime Minister!

"You will never hear of this again from anyone else Mr. Prime Minister," Monsieur Johnston declared!

"I better not or you best find another means of employment! Now, a couple of weeks ago some members of this Canadian Private Cult phoned me and my wife and threatened us both," explained the Prime Minister!

"What! That's automatic jail time for anyone who violently threatens you Sir! Haven't you notified the RCMP or the Federal Department," Monsieur Johnston stated?

"Yes, I spoke with the RCMP Chief, but this cult found out about our arrangements and killed the agents placed on the case. Before warning us all to stop meddling," Prime Minister Layton explained.

"Do you have any Insignia's or physical evidence I could start with," Monsieur Johnston asked?

"I have no idea how these people do the things they do, but somehow after I turned everything I had over to my lawyer, they stole it right from his briefcase," said the Prime Minister.

"That would all be very helpful to start, but I'll get the ball rolling on this and we will find out who these people are Sir," Monsieur Johnston emphasised!

"Good, I'll phone you from various places from time to time to hear about the investigation; and remember Patrick, not a word to anyone," stated the Prime Minister!

Informer 3

"Yes Sir," Monsieur Johnston lamented then disconnected the call!

Sr. Patrick Johnston came off the phone with the Prime Minister and looked over at his degree on the wall, which he had received after graduating from the Secret Cult's elaborate educational system. The Spy Agency's main man picked up his cigar from the ashtray and sparked it ablaze, then picked up his telephone and phoned the cult's alert line. Instead of opening an investigation as promised, Monsieur Johnston told the center of the Prime Minister's continuous aggression towards them and ignored the request made of him.

***

Bryce Layton was the Prime Minister's favourite cousin, whom he had spoken of on several occasions. A week following the Prime Minister's controversial decision, Bryce chartered a helicopter to travel to a friend's private island on 1000 Islands. The trip was one taken by Bryce several times before, where he and whomever his guest was would drive to the Billy Bishop Toronto City Airport Hanger. From there they would take the half hour helicopter flight to his friend's island, which was equipped with its own landing pad. Mr. Layton would typically spend from a weekend to however long he decided, fishing, jet skiing, etcetera during his summer visits; and simply relaxing during off season visits. Instead of his usual single companion Bryce decided to bring along his girlfriend Tara, who went along with his friend Melvin Hill. Their plan was to spend an entire week on the island, therefore they each had to pack a little extra for the longer stay.

Cooper McFarlin the helicopter pilot returned from a tour guide trip around the Greater Toronto Area, twenty-eight minutes before his scheduled flight with Bryce Layton and company. The couple who rented the tour claimed they were from Quebec City and had never been to Toronto, therefore they wanted the best view possible. The female tourist was Cyndi from the Rough Rider's Blues Bar in Lachine, with another Montreal biker known as Presley. When they returned from the tour Cyndi went into the business hanger to use the toilet, while her male partner waited by the helicopter. Cooper showed the female to the bathroom and had their engineer refill the helicopter, while he brought his flight log and documents into the office.

While the engineer refilled the helicopter's fuel and made sure the aircraft was prepared for its next flight, the curious spectator walked around and inspected the vessel. To set the engineer's mind at ease Presley asked several questions relating to the helicopter's repair. Following the forth question the man was clearly annoyed and only wanted to finish his job, so he ignored the fueling and attended to other issues. With the engineer attending to something inside the aircraft, Presley went by the gas compartment section and placed a spark device inside. When his female partner exited the office, they both casually left the facility without anybody noticing what he had done.

Moments after they departed Bruce and his two companions arrived for their scheduled flight to his friend's island. The engineer loaded their luggage on the helicopter while Bryce signed the contract and finalized the trip arrangements. Once everything was complete Bryce, Melvin and Tara boarded the helicopter with Pilot McFarlin, who started the engine and eventually received the clearance to depart. Within no time they were off the ground and in the air enjoying a loud yet comfortable ride to their destination in 1000 Islands.

Cooper flew out towards Lake Ontario and began flying up the river, while his clients looked out the windows at the beautiful scenery and took videos and pictures. The device that Presley placed inside the gas compartment began sparking and started a small flame, which quickly expanded and sat the entire helicopter on fire. One minute the aircraft was travelling without issues and within seconds it could be seen barrelling towards the river engulfed in flames. The chartered helicopter exploded before it crashed into the Ottawa River killing all four passengers aboard.

Monsieur Elan Melvick who was the owner of the private island to which Bryce and company were destined, phoned Prime Minister Layton and gave him the horrific news. Prime Minister Layton was at his office in a staff meeting when he got the call, thus he excused himself and went into his personal bathroom, where he cried to himself and questioned his decision to continue the Secret Cult's investigation. After promising he would abandon the inquiry to his wife and others, Prime Minister Layton could not tell anyone of what he had suspected and was forced to live with the guilt of his actions.

Part 35

Chops raced to the Children's Hospital to be with Valorie who was in shock, as if she had seen a ghost. The despicable sight of the dead mechanics and Brock unnerved the female, who had never physically seen people's intestines and brain morrow splashed across the pavement. The hospital had a division where psychiatrists and Mental Health personnel worked together, which was located on a separate wing from the Emergency Department. To help Valorie come to terms with what happened and recover without lingering effects, a trauma specialist spoke with her privately and allowed her to express her sentiments.

When an enraged and vengeful Chops entered the Emergency Department with three other bikers, he immediately walked into areas where the nurses advised him were off limits to patients and visitors. The security guard posted in the Emergency Department had stepped outside to help sort an incident in the parking area, thus there was nobody qualified to deal with the bikers. The troublemakers were all high off Laughing Gas, which made its users to do unethical things while joking about it. Chops had both his recuperated companions and his cousin Miles with him, hence he felt somewhat mighty as if he was above enquiring at the receptionist's desk like regular folks. Instead of obeying the rules of the hospital which included being courteous to others, Chops was extremely disrespectful and became less tolerable when he failed to find or hear Valorie's voice.

While Chops terrorized the nurses and patients, the female receptionist grew scared for their safety and telephoned the police for help. At the sight of police cruisers pulling up to the Emergency Entrance, the guard who was settling a fender bender incident between two old folks and a pregnant woman, excused himself and ran to his assigned post. Four officers formed a tactical group and entered the hospital with their weapons drawn. The security guard had no idea what had developed during his few minutes away from his post, but he knew that the sight of armed officers meant anything was possible. As the guard reached for his two-way radio to enquire if headquarters knew anything, shots began ringing out inside the hospital.

When the officers rushed into the Emergency Ward and Miles saw them, the biker immediately popped off his Berretta 9mm and fired several shots at them. The coppers returned fire and struck Miles in the back as he turned to run away down a hall. Had they not been under the effects of a controlled substance, the bikers might have been abled to put reasoning first, however they felt vengeful for what happened to their comrades and were eager for bloodshed. Once the shooting began both group of participants forgot where they were and completely ignored the screams and terrified reactions of already hurting patients and their care takers. There were several patients on gurneys and in wheelchairs who could not move themselves and had no choice but to remain within the line of fire.

The other two bikers also opened fire at the police from different sections of the Emergency Ward; and managed to shoot one officer in the shoulder and another in the leg. The bikers' aggression forced the tightknit group of officers to separate and find cover or risked dying. Lights and sounds of additional cruisers could be heard pulling up outside, yet still both bikers continued dumping bullets on the first responding team. Contrary to the bikers' violent stance, more officers poured into the Emergency Unit and added support to their pressured responders. The increased number of officers quickly transformed the battle spectrum and forced the bikers to rethink their strategy, hence they chose to surrender and tossed their weapons. Officers violently charged at the disruptive bikers and placed them all in handcuffs. Chops was not armed and could not have done anything to help his friends, nevertheless he was also arrested and taken into custody. Despite Miles' injury officers still placed him in handcuffs and had to be begged by emergency technicians to release him, so they could rush him into surgery. At the end of the bullet exchange, two separate male patients, a nurse and a female visitor were accidentally shot and had to be treated for their injuries.

***

The increased levels of violence throughout the city had citizens, politicians and bureaucrats calling on law enforcement to do something. Pauline Hibbert was at home getting ready to go to work one afternoon around 1:10 PM, when four police officers knocked her door. The officers were searching for Ranger and Rugid, however they also had an arrest warrant for Pauline's involvement in the grocery store shooting. The single mother of two cildren worked the evening shift and was expected at work for three o'clock. Tamara her youngest daughter who was four-year of age thought that the person at the door was her babysitter and opened it without asking "who was there?" As soon as Pauline stepped from her bedroom and the officers saw her, they all rushed inside whereby two of the officers threw her in handcuffs, while the others searched the apartment. Her daughter Tamara got overly emotional and thereby rushed in and grabbed onto her mother, as she plead for "the coppers to leave Pauline alone!"

Angela the babysitter arrived and took the little girl, who cried and tussled to get back to her mother. A female officer explained to the babysitter that, "a warrant had been issued for Pauline's arrest and Social Services would take the child if she was unable!" Pauline's eldest daughter went to Westmount High and would be home soon from school to help, therefore Angela agreed to care for the children until their mother returned. After ensuring none of their other suspects were present, the gang of officers left with Pauline who felt scared and ashamed.

The late hour arrest meant that Pauline had to spend the night in jail, before she could appear before a magistrate. While in lockup that evening Pauline was granted the opportunity to search through a list of lawyers to find herself legal representative for court in the morning. After looking through the list she decided on a female Legal Aide Attorney named Brenda Beaudeau and phoned the number posted, spoke with the assistant on duty and gave her information. Later that night while she paced about the cell, the guards brought in a drunk and mouthy Caucasian stripper and placed her in the same holding cell.

"Officer Sparks only arrested me because he is the only baldheaded motherfucker on the force I refuse to fuck! Every other week that bastard halls me down here for what!? I told the pervert that if he ain't paying for the pussy he can kiss my ass, and even that he must pay for too! Officer Sparks, come let me out you little dick motherfucker! Fuck you, your boyfriend and fuck you again!" After cursing out the guards and arresting officers throughout the first sixteen minutes of lockup, the stripper finally calmed down and became a regular person once her alcohol level decreased.

Both females were high on energy and disinterested in sleeping, therefore they spent the remainder of the night talking. The stripper whose real name was Cherry Sibbles had been through a lot with pimps and boyfriends in her life, hence she gave the nervous mother excellent good advice regarding her case. Cherry told Pauline that the only way she could walk away with only a slap on the wrist, was if she acted as if she was a victim forced to help during the incident. Having gone through numerous court appearances, Cherry knew how to play the system especially when it came to battered females. When Pauline departed for court the next morning was the last time she ever saw Cherry, however the lessons she learnt helped her throughout her court ordeal.

The first time in criminal court for anyone was innerving and the same stood true for Pauline, who felt as if her heart was jumping from her chest. There was nobody to support her in court, which made what the female had to do much easier, with thoughts of her children before all. The prosecution team was led by Madam Emma Larake who described her to the court as, "an expert getaway driver who couldn't be caught by police during a car chase." Even though Pauline did not physically participate in the shootout, the prosecutor made it appeared as if she was spraying an Uzi across the parking lot at any and everything. The mention of 'Public Endangerment' by Prosecutor Larake earned a stern look on the judge's face, which remained intact throughout their entire argument against allowing bail.

In court Pauline had her attorney Brenda Beaudeau presented her to Judge Simpson as an abused and battered woman, who was trapped in a violent relationship. Certain emphasis such as the fact she had no criminal record, was available to aide detectives on the case and worked to raise her children alone were made, however, they continuously made it appeared as if she lived a submissive and controlled life. To conjure up added sympathy, Attorney Beaudeau also casted the illusion that Pauline's children were also being abused by her boyfriend. Nevertheless, it wasn't until Brenda stated that Pauline was physically instructed to drive on the day of the shooting, that the stern look subsided and a more compassionate glare appeared on the judge's face.

Following the lawyers' statements, Judge Simpson decided to grant the defendant bail with several conditions, one of them being to stay away from Ranger and Rugid. Pauline was also instructed to speak with Social Services and seek help from Battered Women Shelters if necessary. Should Ranger or Rugid attempt to visit or call her, the female was ordered to phone the police immediately and inform them of the incident. The defendant fought to conceal her happiness following the judge's ruling, but once she reached the Bull Pen she jumped for joy. The judge had her returned to court twice over the coming months to evaluate her progress; and after eighteen grueling months at which she complied with all the requirements imposed, the case against Pauline was dismissed.

Informer 3

***

Donavan, Little Rex, Ninja-Kirk and Rugid were in the trap-house at the corner of Park Row East Street and Du-Maisonneuve Boulevard gambling at Poker. Local detectives had been searching for Ranger and Rugid for a few months and received a tip that they were at the location. Officers had received several false or unsubstantiated information about the wanted pair, wherein by the time they acquired the legal search warrant and reached the location they had already left. To ensure that the Jamaican gunmen were inside the apartment, a plain-clothes female detective named Annabelle Kaboiller agreed to impersonate a crack addict and purchase drugs from the trap-house.

Apartment 29 where the Jamaicans stayed was located towards the rear of the building, but according to the building report the detectives received, they knew the dealers had ample video surveillance of both entrances. If they were spotted before they reached the apartment on the second floor their targets could flee through an emergency exit or ambush them, so they needed to get inside the building without being spotted. There was an escape door that led to the roof of the building that became their focal point of entry, so they coordinated their effort wherein they were prepared to enter the building as soon as they received confirmation.

To get on the roof six officers went to the Police Air Surveillance Division where they boarded their company's Sikorsky MH-60 Jayhawk Helicopter and flew to the location, while Annabelle got dropped off by car a block away and walked to the building. The male officer who dropped Annabelle off then drove around the block and parked up the street from the building, where he sat and awaited further orders. Ninja Kirk attended to the buzzer and assumed Annabelle was one of their local prostitute customers, so he buzzed her into the building and watched to ensure no one else entered. The undercover female quickly ran up the stairs to the roof's access, where she unlocked the door and raced back down to the apartment. Even though Annabelle took longer than expected to reach the door yet was completely out of breath when she reached, Ninja Kirk thought nothing of it and still allowed her entry.

"How can I help you," Ninja Kirk asked?

"Charlene told me I could come by," Annabelle answered.

"OK what you want," Ninja Kirk asked?

"Can I get a $100 piece," Annabelle requested, so Ninja Kirk went into the bedroom to retrieve the product?

The drug base was managed in a small single bedroom apartment, so as soon as the undercover entered, she clearly noted everyone present. All the men of color inside the apartment were drinking Heineken Beers, with either Cigarettes or Marijuana Joints hanging from the lips, while the latest Dancehall Tunes played from a portable stereo. The undercover female noticed immediately that two of the men were armed, which made it a resounding possibility that they all were. With all the remaining dealers staring at her, Annabelle felt somewhat nervous but got a precise look at everyone. To avoid any complications during the mission Annabelle's peers refrained from making her wear a wire, which meant she had to confirm the sightings after she safely exited the apartment. Ninja Kirk eventually returned and sold her the $100 piece of Crack she paid for, before she graciously exited the apartment. As soon as the door closed behind her and she got a short distance from it, Annabelle took out the two-way communication device given to her and alerted her comrades on route that, "One of the two wanted men was present." Once everything had been confirmed and the mission was 'a go,' the female undercover got dispatched to the rear exit, while her male driver got assigned to cover the front entrance.

The Sikorsky MH-60 Jayhawk Helicopter soon arrived and hovered high above the building, as the officers onboard threw out a pair of ropes which reached the roof, then slid down. The loud music inside the drug dealers' apartment prevented them from hearing the helicopter's engine, which hovered over the building for less than twenty seconds before it was gone. The team of officers then quickly moved into the building and down to the second floor, where they attached a small explosive charge by the Deadbolt Lock at apartment 29. All the officers stood back to protect themselves from the blast, before the man holding the detonator exploded the device. As soon as the lock got blown to shreds all the officers charged into the apartment yelling, "Police raid, get the fuck on the ground!"

While the officers descended from the chopper, Ninja Kirk who sat closest to the balcony door thought he overheard the helicopter's engine, but he could not be sure over the loud music. When the officers reached the front door and gently attached the explosive charge, Ninja Kirk again thought he held something. However, when the lock shattered, he became positive he heard the noise, grabbed his jacket from the back of his chair and ran through the balcony door. Before any of his peers fully realized what was happening, Ninja Kirk had hopped over the balcony and climbed down to the first-floor balcony, where his 9mm Glock fell out as he readied himself to leap down to the ground. Annabelle who guarding the back exit heard when the weapon fell and looked around to see Ninja Kirk climbing down from the balcony. As soon as the fleeing dealer's feet touched the ground, the female kicked them out from under him and jammed her weapon against the back of his head while he laid face down.

"Going somewhere Buddy-Boy? You're under arrest, hands behind your back now before my finger slips on this trigger," Annabelle threatened, to which Ninja Kirk quickly obeyed!

The officers who charged into apartment 29 disarmed the stunned Jamaicans and arrested them all without further incident. Even though the investigators went to apprehend one individual, all the men were arrested and charged with possession of weapons and drugs. As a sign to the community that they were doing their best to tackle the guns and gangs' problem, officers called in the various news coverages to relay the story to the public.

***

Ranger had another girlfriend named Dawn who lived in St. Leonard on Louis Xiv Street, whom he dated privately and kept confidential. Angela who babysat for Pauline went to high school with Dawn and was good friends with her, therefore even when Ranger felt assured his secrets were safe others knew of them. With the streets heated and potential cops on the lookout for him, Ranger hid out by the female dental assistant's apartment instead of going to his own place. Dawn already had a seven-year-old son from a previous relationship who also lived with her and was at school while his mother worked.

The night following Rugid's arrest, Ranger was having sex with his girlfriend inside her bedroom when the front door got busted in by police. It was as if the officers knew exactly where to search as they went directly to Dawn's bedroom, where Ranger was trying to escape through the window. The intruding officers placed Ranger under arrest and allowed him to put on a pair of boxers, before they dragged him off to jail. Dawn's son was frightened by the loud disruption and ran into her room, but the officers left them both embraced on her bed, instead of dragging them down to the station also.

Part 36

Kevin, Kadeem, and Kane sat around Miss Emma's dining table drinking, while she spent time watching movies with Junior in her bedroom. There was a bottle of Cognac in the middle of the table that was well beyond the half level and all their glasses were filled with liquor. Kane initially did not want to drink and claimed, "he would abstain from indulging in the future", but sighting it was an important occasion he decided to make an exception. The time had come for them to part ways as they should have done initially, like comrades and great friends who had sacrificed everything for each other.

"Our bad deeds have given us the platform to do great things for others! My father for years has tried to get me to understand, that in this world you live for yourself, but you must put others first at times! Especially if you are in a position to help them. I am back to help my people, no more shall I live in the dark, because you both taught me that! Killa have shown me also that no matter what you must be wiling to forgive and forget," Kane stated!

"Kadeem from now on family, I think I kind of outgrew the name Killa," Kadeem commented!

"I must admit that I lost me way. I used to have big dreams for us all… but I reached a point where I look left and I look right, and it was only I alone. Then the fame and the money start fuck with my head, next thing I know my plans for us turn plans for I alone! Mi can never repay you guys for putting your lives on the line for my son and I! But mi started out to build an empire for us; so, from this moment the Trudeau estate is partly yours, as it should be," Kevin exclaimed!

"We always been family, sometimes it just takes a mother to bring her boys back together," Kadeem said as he stared at Miss Emma with Junior passed while resting on her!

"I love you my brothers," Kane cried!

"I love you guys man! But mi have one good advice for you bro; leave this country as fast as you can cause some dangerous people searching for you," Kevin declared!

"I love you guys, real talk! I plan to bro, real soon," Kadeem stated!

There was an authentic emotional camaraderie between the long-time friends who genuinely cared for each other, and knew they had a brotherhood closer than most families. Miss Emma looked on from her bedroom and smiled at seeing the old friends reunited. Not many people would understand the impact each man had had on the other, but the woman who had been there throughout their earlier years knew the severity of their reunion. Whether others saw the group of friends as tyrants was of no significance to Miss Emma, who believed they were truly soldiers of God sent to demolish the wicked. The friends drank until they all passed out from fatigue, at which Miss Emma brought around blankets and covered them all.

***

Kadeem went to the Pierre-Elliot-Trudeau-International-Airport the following afternoon to pick up Marquez' wife, children and parents. When he reached the airport and drove in to park in the Arrival's Parking Section, he narrowly passed a vehicle with two Rough Rider Bikers inside who were watching the Departure Entrance. Several bikers had gotten assigned to survey the departure terminal and ensured that he did not safely get on an airplane and flew out of the country. To offer some form of disguise Kadeem placed a Canadians Hockey hat on his head and drew it down just above his eyes. The

Jamaican seriously contemplated carrying both his weapons, but he feared unknowingly passing through some detector that might reveal his concealed arms and decided to leave them. As he walked towards the terminal building two other bikers saw him from behind and watched to see where he went, until he turned in the direction marked New Arrivals.

The Rude-Boy Jamaican had arranged for a stretched limousine with its own Spanish speaking chauffeur to transport the family to their new home. The limousine driver had suggested they meet by the Tim Hortons inside the arrival's lobby, and as Kadeem approached, he immediately noticed his company by his attire. Keith the limousine driver had already prepared a welcoming sign with Esmenina's name written on it, so the family knew exactly who was there for them. A sum of twelve bikers scattered throughout the departure area of the airport, yet stunningly the man for whom they searched waited on the lower level for another eighteen minutes before Marquez' people exited the Immigration doors.

Esmenina immediately saw their family's name on the sign and speculated that the guy standing next to the uniformed driver was Kadeem. As they walked through the winding passage metal barriers and exited, the thankful mother dropped the bags from her hands and ran directly into the Jamaican's arms. Kadeem felt overwhelmed as the remainder of the family members surrounded him and hugged him as if he was their long lost relative. None of the newcomers were fluent in English but Esmenina spoke just enough to carry certain conversations, thus Keith took hold of the situation and translated everything that was happening.

After a few minutes by the baggage carrier the seven family members received their luggage and exited the airport to an awaiting limousine, which drove them directly to their new house in their new country. On his way towards his vehicle inside the parking lot, Kadeem stopped to pay for the parking ticket at a pay station. While operating the machine with his back turned, three Caucasian men passed behind him in search of somewhere to smoke. As Kadeem turned around his eyes met with a biker's, but the biker did not recognize him and thought he was some nobody who was there to pick up someone. Even though their stare was brief the Jamaican observed something that truly innerved him thereafter, when he saw the Rough Rider's Biker Patch on the shoulder of the man's leather jacket. Kadeem casually hid his face and cautiously made his way to his vehicle, where he placed one of his weapons on his lap and sped from the parking lot.

When they reached the new house in Kirkland and Marquez' family members exited the limousine, everybody began crying and praising the Jamaican. The keys were left inside a Combination Lock fastened to the door, therefore Kadeem opened the entrance and showed them inside. The entire house had already been decorated with furniture and the refrigerator was half stacked with fruits, juice and food. Everybody including the limousine chauffeur were ecstatic at what Kadeem had done for total strangers, whose relative was once assigned to kill him. As they walked through the house for the first time the telephone that was already connected rang with the imprisoned Marquez on the line. Before speaking with Esmenina and the others, Marquez briefly chatted with Kadeem whom he thanked for everything he did to help both his family and him. While Marquez spoke with his children whom he had not spoken to in weeks, Kadeem brought Esmenina into her bedroom and showed her a digital safe filled with money and some other documents. After another fifteen minutes with the Columbian family Kadeem said his goodbyes and again got mobbed by the entire family before he departed. Keith the limousine driver was paid throughout the evening to show them around the city, therefore as soon as they got settled he brought them all for a tour of the beautiful city of Montreal.

With all his responsibilities handled Kadeem decided to visit the double grave funeral plot of his murdered son and girlfriend for the first and final time, knowing he would never again get the opportunity to do so. It was not until the Jamaican reached the cemetery on Cote-des-Neiges Road that he realized that Martain Lafleur was buried on the same grounds, although none of that could have hindered him from what he was there to do. When the rude-boy finally found the grave that had a very small head plaque to commemorate the people inside, it took some time before he could conjure up the strength to exit the rental. Kadeem sat and stared at the snow receding plot from inside the car with tears rolling down his face, before he finally got out and walked to the foot of the grave. Even though he could speak no words due to his levels of personal guilt, he vowed in his heart to change that disrespectful headstone and replace it with one more-worthy to describe the people within.

As bad luck would have it, there was a female Rough Rider Biker who used to sleep with Martain Lafleur that was in the cemetery visiting his grave. The biker female's name was Tammy and life had not been too kindly to her since the boss' killing. Following her visit where she spent the duration of her time complaining about her tough life conditions, Tammy was walking from the graveside when she noticed Kadeem on his knees in the melting snow. Convinced that Martain provided her with a solution to her problems, the biker female quickly phoned the members of the B.C Rough Riders, who had been searching the city to find Kadeem.

The Jamaican remained by the graveside for another seventeen minutes before he rose to his feet and turned away towards his car. Approximately five metres away from the rental Kadeem began casually looking about the grounds when he noticed Tammy on her phone, pointing and jumping as if her escaped dog was running at Kadeem. It was beginning to get dark yet still the rude-boy could identify the Rough Rider Insignia on her Bomber Jacket, so Kadeem withdrew one of his 9mm Glocks and fired three bullets at her.

Tammy ducked behind a tree before she rose to her feet and took off running towards the north-western section of the cemetery.

Kadeem fired up the rental's engine and sped along the right side of the cemetery's separated roadways, but as he got close to the entrance the Hummer from days prior turned onto the property. The Hummer started speeding up the opposite side of the street, until the bikers aboard saw Kadeem's rental and began cutting across the field by driving over the graves. Once Kadeem saw the Hummer's windows lowering, he knew the ruckus was about to begin, as the bikers opened fire with several high-powered weapons which struck sections of the rental. Instead of trying any heroics Kadeem levelled the gas pedal and sped from the graveyard onto Cote-des-Neiges Road, where he turned right onto the main road and was fortunate there was no vehicles coming. Seconds later the Hummer barreled onto the street and struck the frontend of a Toyota Camry and thus significantly damaged the car, yet barley dented the truck's bumper. Despite the accident the Hummer failed to stop and continued pursuing the rental, which was approximately three hundred metres ahead.

It was evident that the bikers meant business and were not about to let Kadeem slip through their fingers another time. Inside the Hummer were the rebranded Hickston twins sitting in the rear with two of their British Columbia bikers in the front compartment. The revenge seeking twins were heavily armed with a pair of Ares Defense Shrike 5.56 Assault Rifles, while their companions carried a Chinese made 250x141px Assault Rifle and a 38 Calibre Handgun. Kadeem knew he could not afford to allow them to get much closer, so as he approached Cote-Saint-Catherine-Road where the traffic light showed red, he noticed a slight window through the oncoming traffic and sped faster. When the fleeing Jamaican flew through the narrow passage a police cruiser that was two car lengths behind the moving traffic, threw on his flashers and siren and began chasing the rental.

There was a dump truck going through the intersection that forced the Hummer to yield briefly, but as soon as the truck passed the bikers continued through the intersection where all the other cars had stopped for the pursuing officer. The sight of the police chasing him slowly decreased Kadeem's racing heartrate, as he expected the bikers to become fearful and abandon their chase. With some heavy traffic up ahead, Kadeem decided to pull over and try his fear theory, but as he began slowing down he observed the Hummer ram the police's cruiser as if they weren't intimidated. The shocked officer inside the cruiser had his attention focused on stopping the manic inside the rented vehicle and did not notice the Hummer until it rammed his cruiser and nearly caused him to crash. As soon as the officer regained control of the cruiser the B.C bikers opened fire at him, which then forced him to crash into a vehicle parked along the side of the road. All throughout the area the sounds of police sirens could be heard converging on the location, as the crashed officer updated his dispatcher of the incident.

Informer 3

Kadeem's heartrate again began racing as he floored the gas pedal and swerved into the southbound lane to pass several cars stopped at a red light. As the rental approached Edouard-Montpetit-Boulevard the driver of a Smart Car that was originally travelling westbound, turned left onto Cote-des-Neiges-Road and forced Kadeem to narrowly avoid the collision by swerving left onto the same street. There was a police cruiser responding to the crashed constable's alert who was driving up the hill towards the incident on Côte-des-Neiges-Road. The constable had attracted the attention of commuters along the southbound lane, who had pulled to the side to provide him a clear path to the disturbance. The bikers' Hummer and the approaching cruiser were on pace to simultaneously enter the intersection, therefore, to clear their pathway the Hickston brothers and their shotgun rider all opened fire at the cruiser through the windows. The officer on board threw himself onto the passenger seat and slammed on the brakes to avoid getting shot, however his engine exploded and caught fire and forced him to abandon the car once bullets stopped colliding with it.

When the officer was finally abled to exit his cruiser he immediately went to the trunk and fetched the Fire Extinguisher, then quickly hurried around to extinguish some of the flames. While maneuvering to put out the flames, the officer contacted his dispatcher and said, "dispatcher, the gentlemen in the black Hummer just shot up my cruiser and are now heading westbound on Edouard-Montpetit-Boulevard, be advised these guys are heavily armed!"

Kadeem felt as if his options were extremely limited, knowing that any of the bikers would murder him directly in front of any law enforcement officer at that point. There was no way he would make it through the busy city to the Indian Reservation with all the interior traffic; and even though Kevin and he had patched up their relationship he could not bring his problems to his friend's doorstep, so he had to find another solution. To maintain or increase the distance between both vehicles, Kadeem drove to the next intersection and turned left onto Gatineau Avenue, raced up to Côte-Sainte-Catherine-Road and turned right, sped down to Decelles-Avenue made the same right turn and raced back to Edouard-Montpetit-Boulevard where he again turned left. The Hummer did not handle as quick as the rental car did onto the residential side streets, hence Kadeem gained a slight separation between himself and the bikers, yet they still maintained pursuit.

When Kadeem turned back onto Edouard-Montpetit-Boulevard he remembered the federal agents' contact information he had received from Miss Emma, who copied it from the television news report following the assassination debacle. The Jamaican had thought about chatting with the investigators but was never ordered to, so he had planned on trying to sneak from the country without undergoing the interview. With the federal agents being the sort of help he required at that moment, Kadeem retrieved the paper from his pants pocket and began examining the agent's name. While looking at the information the fleeing thug snuck a peek through the rear-view mirror and saw a Hyundai Sonata raced through the intersection without yielding. Even though there was almost four hundred metres between both cars, Kadeem watched perplexed as a passenger inside the Sonata fitted himself through the sunroof and opened fire at him with an AR-15 Assault Rifle. Despite the slight distance, bullets from the AR-15 collided with the rental and shot out the right brake lights. Having witnessed the Hyundai occupants' intentions, Kadeem kept his head lowered and stepped harder on the gas hoping to sneak a bit more speed from the rental. There were four other bikers inside the Sonata who joined the chase ahead of the Hummer, which also turned onto Edouard-Montpetit slightly thereafter.

The documented federal agents' address was less than ten minutes away in a small business district behind Decarie-Smart-Center on Jockeys-Street. Kadeem did not know where the address was, so he inserted the information into the vehicle's GPS System and followed the directory service. With the B.C maniacs behind him shooting callously, he barely slowed the vehicle to ensure his safety as he drove through the next two stop signs. To avoid the busy traffic on Decarie Boulevard, Kadeem drove down to Trans-Island-Avenue which travelled parallel to Decarie. There were no traffic lights at any of the busy intersections from there to Vezina Street, so as Kadeem approached each of the next five crossings, he yielded slightly to ensure there was no traffic coming before speeding across.

As the rental approached Vezina Street where the GPS indicated he should turn left, a police cruiser blocked the road and the two onboard officers positioned themselves behind their vehicle. With their weapons aimed at the approaching vehicles, the officers started shooting at the rental in hopes of stopping the ongoing violence. Kadeem was caught between Hell and Hell and had no options but to plow straight ahead, so he ducked his head below the steering console as bullets flew through the windshield. Approximately a hundred metres from the intersection Kadeem heard a loud car crash ahead, before the police onslaught suddenly seized, hence he looked up and saw the B.C bikers' cross-country bus wiped away the cruiser and its occupants.

There was an opening created behind the bus and Kadeem sped through onto Vezina Street and was extremely lucky thereafter to catch the green light at Decarie Boulevard. The Jamaican was thankful that the bus pulverized the cruiser and its pilots, but his concerns grew knowing that meant there were added bikers to the already stacked toll. After crossing both the northern and southern sections of Decarie Boulevard on solid yellow lights, Kadeem looked through his rear-view mirror and became frustrated at the sight of the damaged bus leading the other biker vehicles through the red lights. It was already evident that there would be no easy fix to his present biker issues, thereby the Jamaican Shotta proceeded to the address for which he searched.

Informer 3

When Kadeem reached the address on Jockeys-Street he drove up onto the property and stopped directly by the front door, where he ran from the rental into the building. To avoid any security issues the Jamaican abandoned his weapons inside the rental, even though he would prefer having his own protection at such a dreadful time. Seconds later all three biker vehicles pulled up in front the building and parked. All the bikers from the other vehicles convened inside the bus, where they made their final decision on how to proceed.

There was no mistaking the Federal Agent Building for anything else with the huge sign on the front lawn of the property. The British Columbia Bikers were brave enough to discard with the local police, but their wanted man believed they would think twice about fucking with the Feds. Inside the building Kadeem ran up to the receptionist and asked to speak with Federal Agent Darcy who he claimed was expecting him. While looking around the office Kadeem noticed a well tattooed Caucasian male who was sitting with his girlfriend, and thereby tried to hide his face. There was a security monitor showing four screens from around the building on a desk inside the receptionist's area, so instead of taking a seat as instructed Kadeem stood by the counter and kept his eyes on the bus. The male receptionist rang Agent Darcy, then told their visitor that he would be down to see him shortly, but the Jamaican grew more impatient by the second.

The Hickston brothers spoke briefly with their comrades inside their bus and got volunteers who would physically enter the building and assassinate Kadeem and whomever got in their way. The gang of western bikers were all cop haters and would go up against any police force regardless of their stature, so Kadeem was in for quite the rude awakening. Those who volunteered for the mission were then given a canister of Laughing Gas, to spike their aggression and entrust them with a sense of invisibility. The team of shooters and their club brothers knew there was no guarantee any of them would return from the mission, but instead of sorrow in parting the bikers boisterously encouraged and pumped up their comrades.

"For our brother Antoine," yelled all the volunteers once they had been fitted with their weapon's system and were ready to extract revenge!

After fidgeting while staring at the screen for nearly three minutes, Kadeem observed the bus door reopened and nine heavily armed bikers dismounted. Each biker had been fitted with a Bulletproof Vest and a Clutch Bag to provide added bullets for their assault rifles. As the bus drove away with the remaining bikers, the nine gunners began walking towards the building like a dark cloud that brought a raging thunder storm. The receptionist had evacuated his post and was inside the back room, which left Kadeem nervous without any options. Just before the bikers reached the building's entrance, a side door opened, and Agent Darcy walked out into the lobby.

"Mr. Kadeem Kite thank you for coming to see me, I'm Federal Agent Darwin Darcy! I've heard some pretty nice things about you from a Mr. Marquez," Agent Darcy introduced himself!

"Can we take this interview somewhere else? Oh, and by the way nine-armed Rough Rider Bikers are about to break in here and shoot up the place," Kadeem declared!

"What," Agent Darcy exclaimed as he grabbed for his sidearm!?

When the first B.C biker entered the reception area and spotted Kadeem he immediately opened fire in their direction until Agent Darcy shot him twice in the vest. Both bullets managed to knock the biker off balance and nearly threw him to his backside, until his associates grabbed and helped him to recover. To survive the onslaught the tattooed visitor and his girlfriend ran into the visitor's bathroom and hid inside a stall. The second biker through the door shot Agent Darcy in the right shoulder, as the first biker regained his balance and aimed his weapon at the agent. Kadeem grabbed Agent Darcy's left hand and pulled him through the door he exited prior to save them both from being slaughtered. The receptionist ran from the back room and fired off a few rounds at the invading bikers, but the heavily armed intruders shot and killed him. There were eighteen other employees working on the first floor of the six-story building, some of whom were office clerks and administrative staff, however twelve of them were armed agents. To protect themselves and their co-workers the armed agents secured others in closets and other safe places, then found defensive shields from which they could counter against the rifle brandishing bikers.

Agent Darcy realized he could no longer defend them and passed Kadeem his 9mm, which was against his department's policy. Four of Agent Darcy's fellow agents were moving towards the disturbance when they entered, so to clarify the situation the injured agent instructed them, "they were under attack!" Kadeem rushed Agent Darcy into one of the personal offices, with hopes of finding a window through which he might escape. The main office had an open floor concept with twenty personal work stations to the front and four personal offices for senior management staff in the rear. There was a female employee inside the office who was unarmed, therefore she hid beneath her desk and only exited when she heard her co-worker's voice.

The four co-workers to whom Agent Darcy gave the instructions changed their attack strategy and hid behind four desks to set an ambush instead. It was evident that their attackers were armed with more powerful weapons than they presently had, therefore, to survive they had to be intelligent with their response. There was no other means of exit from the office, thereby Kadeem could not escape and had to fight like everyone else to survive. While the female assisted Agent Darcy who was in terrible pain, Kadeem sat his own trap by waiting in the corner behind the opened office door with his weapon aimed through the crease. The biker who shot Agent Darcy and three of his associates walked in through the employee's entrance and immediately began shooting up the office. Without any room for failure, Kadeem controlled his breathing and aimed at the first intruder's head, before he disbursed a bullet that struck the biker directly in the forehead. The other three bikers were unsure from where the bullet came and began callously firing at the office and nearly shot Kadeem who had to dive onto the floor.

The sounds of assault rifles rang out from different sections of the first floor, as the bikers panned out in search of their assigned target. With bullet exchange in the adjacent receptionist area favoring the bikers, one of the agents who patiently hid behind a desk for their opportunity to return fire, got overzealous and jumped up before the opportune moment. The continuous spraying of bullets from the bikers' assault rifles annihilated the agent before he could get off a proper shot, and thus placed the remainder of his handgun carrying comrades at risk. Suspecting that there might be additional agents hidden amongst the twenty office desks, the bikers began swiping the area with bullets as they advanced towards the offices.

Shortly thereafter a second agent got shot and killed when bullets ripped through his office desk shield and struck him. Kadeem could see one of the two remaining survivors crawling towards the offices, while the fourth agent hunkered down and shivered with nervousness. With the murderous bikers moving towards him, Kadeem realized he needed to make a decision instantly or suffered the same fate as those already killed. The bikers were more focused at eliminating every aspect of danger from the hidden agents amongst the twenty desks, thus the concerned Jamaican unexpectedly ran from the office towards a hallway to the left, while shooting callously at the bikers. Even though Kadeem was only concerned about saving his own ass, he managed to shoot one of the bikers in the thigh and distracted the other two bikers long enough for the two remaining agents to assist. Once the under-sieged agents realized their intruders' assault had been diverted, they leapt from their hidden positions and shot all three bikers dead.

With five other bikers engaged in shootouts with other agents, there was still much work left before the building could be rendered safe. The two agents who received the assistance appreciated what Kadeem had done, but they quickly disarmed him to avoid some unforeseen accident. Seconds after the agents took Darcy's firearm from Kadeem, an elevator door open with six heavily armed agents from upstairs. The team of agents were also armed with assault rifles and got joined by the two handgun agents, before they quickly proceeded to the other points of conflict. While the gunfight raged on inside the building, local officers blocked off the road outside and positioned themselves tactically instead of charging inside.

Kadeem felt less threatened with the backup team of agents and hid inside the office as directed with the female and Agent Darcy. Although the building's windows could not be opened for security reasons, Kadeem and every other survivor could look outside and gained a sense of caring from the emergency response. Local police officers had the entire building surrounded and did not wish to complicate matters, therefore they stayed back and waited until the situation escalated before they would consider entering. There were agents throughout the building in constant communications with the officers outdoors and provided them with timely updates on the fluent situation.

The remaining five bikers were separated into two teams, both of which had agents stuck in areas where their survival rates were quickly dwindling. Two of the bikers were duelling three male agents who were trapped inside the officer's male room, while the other three tackled four male agents and a female colleague. The team of responding agents used the sound of the bikers' automatic weapons to plan their course of attack and first struck the group of three who were up against the five agents. All five agents were forced into the holding cell area where they used the cemented walls and metallic doors as shields, to protect themselves while they fought off the intruders. When the team of agents came up on the bikers who had their comrades pinned with their high-powered weapons, the only warning the intruders received were the barks of heavy automatic machinery that shot them in their backs.

From there the team of agents circled back through another hallway and came up on the last pair of bikers, who had their adversaries trapped inside an employee's bathroom. The bikers were aware that there were new players on the field, therefore it was more difficult to sneak up on them. As soon as one of the bikers caught a glimpse of the approaching agents, the man opened fire in their direction then touched his partner to signal their departure. Before moving out both bikers showed they came overly prepared as they withdrew extended magazine clips and reloaded their weapons. With their opponents inside the bathroom already supressed, both bikers turned their weapons on the approaching agents as they backed away from the conflict and moved towards the front door. Dozens of police officers were on hand when the two bikers backed out of the facility, along with ambulance technicians, fire trucks and spectators who were all kept at a distance. Neither of the bikers considered there might be officers outside until the reflections from emergency flashers against the facility caught their attention.

"Drop the guns and get down on the ground now," shouted an officer over his loudspeaker!

The bikers were startled by the loudspeaker and instead of releasing their triggers spun around shooting, thereby they were shot and killed on the front lawn of the Federal Agent Building. With the situation under control the wounded got treated then transported to the emergency ward, while the deceased re-

Informer 3

mained in place for investigative purposes before they were brought to the Children's Hospital Morgue. The tattooed visitor and his girlfriend were found crouched behind a toilet inside a bathroom and were extremely happy when they got detained. Agents immediately began looking through every piece of information to find the motive for the bikers' attack, including speaking with all witnesses. Before being dragged off to the hospital Agent Darcy gave his recollection of what happened to the Department's Chief Director Charvelli, who was none too happy to hear that his agent gave his weapon to a civilian.

Due to Agent Darcy's misconduct Director Charvelli took him off the case and assigned another agent to question Kadeem. Despite Charvelli's disappointment with the overall handling of the incident, he was forced to recognize Kadeem for saving his agents and as such thanked him. The agents who were saved by what they considered a selfless act praised Kadeem, although saving any of them was the last thought on the Jamaican's mind. Nearly two hours after the shooting incident ended Kadeem met with Agent Darcy's partner Agent Kenval Cortier and Lieutenant Paula Pritchet in an examining room.

"Quite the excitement huh! How are you doing Mr. Kite, I'm Agent Kenval Cortier and this is my Lieutenant Paula Pritchet," said Agent Cortier!

"I'm OK man, nice to meet you," Kadeem stated!

"Before we begin, I'd like to thank you for what you did for Agent Darcy and the rest of this department," Lieutenant Pritchet exclaimed, to which Kadeem simply nodded his head in acceptance!

Agent Cortier then removed a plastic bag that contained a single assault rifle bullet and placed it on the table before them. "Must have been a tough few weeks for you?"

"You have no idea," Kadeem answered!

"Please be advised that we will be recoding this conversation for evidence purposes strictly. Ahh, we were made aware of your Columbian abduction by Senior Manuel Lagarza. But there is still some unsubstantiated information we would like for you to clear up for us. Now this bullet was taken from the coat pocket of Ricardo Alvarez, who was one of your kidnappers. After we ran it through ballistics, we uncovered that this 5.56x45mm NATO Cartridge was used in a shootout where four bikers were killed. Could you give us your recollection of what happened at that rented condo," Agent Cortier asked?

"From the moment Lagarza said he was sending me back to Montreal I told him it wasn't a good idea! But nobody tells the boss what to do, so him send me here," Kadeem stated.

"Why did he go through the trouble to kidnap you from Jamaica then escort you here," Agent Cortier enquired?

"I'm afraid you have to ask Senior Lagarza that," Kadeem said.

"So, you weren't indebted to him in any capacity," Agent Cortier demanded?

"I'm afraid you have to ask Senior Lagarza that," Kadeem calmly responded.

"Explain to us how your deceased kidnapper came by this NATO Cartridge when we did not find any weapons at the location where the body was found," Agent Cortier asked?

"Some Spanish gun dealer named Pablo I believe, brought them the guns and ammunition they used," Kadeem responded.

"Ah, weapons dealer Pablo from where," Agent Cortier asked?

"I don't know, I heard them say Manuel arranged everything," Kadeem declared.

"So, tell us what happened when these bikers came to the condo," Agent Cortier demanded?

"I don't know, they had me tied up and locked inside the bedroom. But I could hear Ricardo, Marquez and Pablo telling each other what to do. About three minutes later them get me from the room and we escaped through the back entrance. By then Pablo was gone and I haven't seen him since," Kadeem exclaimed.

"Why is it that in this entire world you are the only person who the Rough Riders Biker Gang is willing pay a reward to have killed," Lieutenant Pritchet demanded?

"I'm afraid you will have to ask the Rough Riders Biker Gang that question Lieutenant! By the way for all my assistance, plus considering this great threat against my life, can I get a personal escort back to the sweet island of Jamaica mon," Kadeem jokingly demanded?

"Protecting the public is our duty Mr. Kite! I'm sure something can be arranged," Lieutenant Pritchet declared.

The Hickston brothers and two of their remaining comrades were well off the Island of Montreal by then, on route back to British Colombia's West Coast. There was a grave silence inside the bus as the club members sat with tears running from their eyes. Everyone except the driver watched the news footage of the shootout, which was described by reporters as a deliberate and vicious assault. The West Coast Bikers all had glasses of liquor raised to commemorate their fallen allies who were all killed during the attack. The gang of bikers listened intently for description of the six none combatants reportedly killed, but instead of mentioning names the reporter reported that, "five employees and a visitor to the facility were killed." Without confirmation

Informer 3

that Kadeem was said victim the bikers felt somewhat unsatisfied, knowing the escape artist the Jamaican had been thus far. Until absolute confirmation of Kadeem's death was received the bikers had no intentions of seizing their efforts, hence Alex Hickston made a phone call and gave the people on the other end several instructions.

The following day slightly before the afternoon hour, Kadeem got escorted to the Pierre-Elliot-Trudeau-Airport under tight guard by five heavily armed agents. When they reached the airport and hoped from their Cadillac Escalade SUVs, all five agents surrounded their detail and rushed him into the building. As they walked through the terminal Kadeem kept his head on a swivel as he constantly looked around, knowing the snake in the grass mentality of his biker opponents. The agents believed their impressive weaponry would scare off any would-be assassin, therefore they simply kept their heads straight and moved forward. Approximately thirty-two metres from the airport's security check station, two bikers dressed like businessmen wearing suits with ties walked from a jewellery store and stood by the display window staring at the merchandise. Directly ahead of the escort team in the middle of the hallway was another well-dressed biker who casually sat reading the day's newspaper, on one of the public seats assigned for tired and weary travellers walking through the huge terminal.

Instead of getting fascinated by the designer stores and merchandise along the corridors Kadeem kept watch for Rough Rider attackers. As the security detail drew close to the bikers, the alert Jamaican observed when one of the two standing bikers glared at them over his right shoulder, before the seated assassin nodded his head at the other biker.

"Bikers business suits to the right and straight ahead," Kadeem shouted, to which his guards quickly singled out the persons described!

All three bikers were armed with 9mm handguns that had been accessorized with the Bump-Stop Technology that enabled the weapons to fire like automatic rifles. The two bikers in front the jewellery display window spun around with their firearms aimed at the agents but got lit up before they could cause any damage. Passengers throughout the terminal began scattering for cover, as women and children could be heard screaming in terror. The spotter who was seated in the corridor began disbursing his weapon at the agents and shot the pack leader three times in his bulletproof vest and twice in the legs, before he too got killed by the other agents.

With all the ambushers eliminated, one of the agents stayed with their wounded teammate and tried to help him, while the others rushed Kadeem to his awaiting flight. Instead of patiently waiting in lines like other travellers, Kadeem was wisped through security checkpoints without having to undergo the intrusive searches. When they reached the Boarding Gate, the agents gave the gate attendant the ticket information then placed Kadeem in the custody of the Air Marshal, Errol Evans. The flight had already been boarded by the other passengers thereby Kadeem had no idea if any bikers were onboard, hence he felt nervous boarding without the team of agents who had brought him to that point.

The Jamaican had no idea what any of the agents' names were except for Agent Kenval Cortier, but he felt incredibly grateful and thanked them before they parted. The air marshal brought Kadeem onto the airplane and gave him the seat next to him, which was in the middle of the aircraft just at the edge of the left wing. As they walked to the seats Kadeem looked around at the passengers' faces to determine if anyone appeared out of place, but most of those with whom he made eye contact seemed like overly-exuberant vacationers. It was quite difficult nevertheless for the wanted Jamaican to settle into the flight, whereby he felt the urge to urinate but held onto it instead. It was a bit chilly on the aircraft, so Kadeem requested a blanket, although he did so for a separate reason than expected. Fifty minutes into the flight and a can of Canada Dry Gingerale later, the urge to urinate had gotten unbearable, so Kadeem got up from his window seat, patiently slid by the two closest passengers and headed to the rear bathroom. On his way to the restroom, again Kadeem tried to make eye contact with every passenger he passed, although he was not as successful then. To provide the illusion that he felt cold, Kadeem wore the blanket over his shoulders, but wrapped it around his left hand as he headed back to his seat.

The instant Kadeem opened the bathroom door two muscular Caucasian males rushed him and tackled him against the back siding. One of the men had a shank made from Plexiglass that he used to try stabbing the wanted Jamaican in the chest, but Kadeem barely grabbed a hold of his hand and stopped the blade from being inserted too deep. Kadeem kicked away the second male who was trying to hold him still while his associate stabbed him to death and clawed his fingers into the next biker's left eye. Despite being incredibly strong and muscular the biker was also strung out on Ecstasy Pills; and reacted to the eye gouging as if it was of no significance. The biker withdrew the blade and was about to stab Kadeem in the neck, but the Jamaican used the blanket around his arm to block the assault. With other passengers screaming at the unexpected attack, Air Marshal Evans jumped from his seat and withdrew his firearm; but had to announce himself continuously and shoved spectators trying to record the footage out of his way. When Errol reached the ruckus both bikers had managed to secure Kadeem's hands and was about to stab him for the second time. Air Marshal Evans had to shoot the Plexiglass Shank wielding maniac in the shoulder, which cause him to drop the blade and grabbed for the wound. Kadeem angrily threw a right hook at the other biker, who caught the punch on his chin and fell unconscious to the floor. Both bikers were arrested and placed in handcuffs, before they got buckled into their seats and detained for the remainder of the flight.

Nerves and adrenaline flow kept Kadeem alert throughout the remainder of the journey, therefore, he was unable to feel relaxed until they safely landed on Jamaican soil. Once they landed and reached the terminal, the air marshal made everyone else de-board the plane, at which police officials then came onto the aircraft and escorted them off. Kadeem had to give a formal statement on what happened during the flight and was initially skeptical, until he considered the amounts of bullets fired at him by the Rough Riders and filled the complaint. When the airport security got through with Kadeem and he thought he was free to go, two local police officers from the St. James Parish Police Department approached him and ordered him to accompany them to the local station for questioning regarding a past matter.

Kadeem felt certain that the Rough Riders Gang had employed the officers to assassinate him, therefore, he wished there was someone to whom he could appeal, but there was no help forthcoming. The officers brought Kadeem out to their cruiser where they all boarded and drove to the station a few minutes away. It wasn't until they reached the precinct that Kadeem felt less terrified, even though he was not subjected to wearing handcuffs during the commute. The officers led Kadeem into the station where a Detective McPierson questioned him regarding his murdered bodyguards. Following their forty-five minutes discussion, Kadeem was finally allowed to return to his normal life and got transported to the Holiday Inn Hotel by the same two officers, who initially brought him to the station.

Part 37

To defeat his enemies Lass understood that he needed to make certain strategic moves or else they stood no chance at the larger biker gang. Lass and his N.D.G crew members were also more interested in taking the bikers' inventory and money, than they were in shootouts and gang warfare. Therefore, when the Jamaican hustler got word of the bikers' 'Break and Entry Program' from a crackhead who spent his last three years in prison, he had to try hijacking their shipment. Toothless who was convicted of breaking into five pharmacies and stealing medication for trafficking, got housed in prison with a biker who was also convicted of theft. Over the period of such a lengthy coupling Toothless learnt a lot about the Rough Rider's operation, even though he would often pretend to be uninterested in his cellmate's discussions with fellow bikers.

With some of his main gunners behind bars Lass entrusted Slim, Dull Boy and Pickard with the task of confiscating the bikers' stolen inventory during transport. According to Toothless, the bikers stored all the stolen items collected throughout Quebec inside a huge warehouse in the Technoparc Montreal area, off Alfred-Nobel Boulevard. Once at the warehouse, a team of workers removed all serial numbers and identification tags from the items, before they were sorted and sent to one of their Pawn Shops across the island. To ensure that the information was correct, and his hijackers were not heading into some unexpected trap, Lass covertly held Toothless captive during the hijacking by giving him free crack to smoke.

Lass' team of hijackers parked down the street from the warehouse at 3:00 AM and watched for thirty-five minutes before a delivery truck exited the facility on route to restocking the West Island, Variety Pawn Shop located on Saint-Charles Boulevard. Toothless' timing may had been off by a few minutes, but his description of the decorated delivery truck and their scheduling was on point. The streets were deserted at such a late hour and the route chosen by the bikers went along private back roads, therefore following a few turns onto Marie-Curie Avenue the Jamaicans decided to proceed with the hijacking.

One of the most important factors that Toothless neglected to mention, was the automatic weaponry kept onboard each of the bikers' twenty-eight feet length delivery trucks. Another of such life saving information was the arrogant bikers associated with the Break and Entry crew, who had no fear of shooting at anyone at anytime. The team of bikers had an impeccable delivery record, wherein they were never stopped and always delivered the merchandise. The moment they turned off Alexander-Fleming Street onto Marie-Curie Avenue and noticed the approaching 4X4, everyone aboard the delivery truck prepared their Uzi Automatic Mini-Rifles for a confrontation. Pickard drove up alongside the delivery truck and honked the horn several times, at which Slim began waving his Glock 45 at the truck driver to direct him to pull over. At the sight of the weapon, the driver's window slowly descended, and the other two delivery passengers shoved their weapons through the window and opened fire.

"Stop the fucking van," Slim yelled, as he reached across and spun the Toyota 4X4 steering wheel towards the vacant parallel lanes! Bullets struck the left side and engine compartment of the van as it screeched to a halt, while the delivery truck continued undisturbed. Slim felt his head down to his knees to check if he had gotten shot anywhere; and was elated that he managed to escape what looked like certain death. None the hijackers were harmed in the brief onslaught, therefore having surrendered their element of surprise they canceled the ambush plot and disappointingly drove back to base.

***

Despite orders to seize all violent confrontations with Jamaicans island wide, three bikers were stopped at a red light on O'Brien Avenue and Tassé Street the following Friday night at 2:24 AM, when a Jamaican couple pulled up across from them. The couple was on their way home from a party and was having a decent discussion about their evening, not knowing they were about to be targeted. The bikers were listening to very loud heavy metal music as they passed around a joint lased with Crystal Meth, before one of them noticed a small Jamaican flag hanging from the rear-view mirror inside the couple's car. The biker tapped his friend in the front seat on the shoulder, then nodded his head in the direction of the colored couple. Without transferring a word both bikers rolled their windows down and aimed their 9mm handguns at the couple; then commenced firing. After dumping eleven bullets into the couple's car the bikers sped away from the scene and left the man and woman deceased.

When word of the latest victims reached Lass, the drug boss became increasingly concerned for his family's safety and thought of ways to help protecting them and himself. Should anything unforeseen befall him, Lass wanted people with the capability of resolving issues to know who the primary suspects were, so he abandoned his guards at their new trap-house on West-Hill Avenue and drove out alone. After driving around for nearly twenty-five minutes to ensure he was not being followed, the N.D.G drug boss headed to the Pierrefond Police Precinct on Sources Boulevard. The drug trafficker knew that he had been on the radar of undercover detectives for years, yet all that paled in comparison to his immediate threat. Once Lass entered the station, he approached the front desk with an officer's personal business card in hand and asked for Detective Devenir. The desk sergeant asked him to wait a few minutes as he contacted the desired officer, who was in the building at his work station.

When Detective Devenir got word that Lass was there to see him he was quite astonished. Both men had met years before during a shooting which left one a Jamaican man dead, at a night club in West Island that was owned by Lass. Following the shooting Lass was questioned by Detective Devenir who gave him the card for future references. The mental and physical toll that killing took from Lass led to him closing the club, hence he began donating more of his time to the hustling game. To discuss what brought Lass to the precinct Detective Devenir pulled him to the side and spoke privately.

"Hello, how have you been," Detective Devenir said as they shook hands?

"I've been better! Listen I have a business proposition for you guys, but I'm going to need confirmation from your superiors," Lass stated?

"What sort of proposition if you don't mind me asking? I'll need the information to pass on to the chief," Detective Devenir asked!

"I have some information about the Rough Rider Bikers that I'm sure he will find interesting, but before I give up my information, I'm going to need something in return," Lass whispered?

"If you don't mine chilling out here for a few minutes, I'll run up and pass on the information to my lieutenant who will then notify the chief," Detective Devenir said!

After several minutes two officers came and thoroughly searched Lass, before they led him in the officer only department and into a boardroom. Shortly after Lass got led into the room Detective Devenir entered with three higher ranked officers and closed the door behind them.

"Mr. Brown this is Chief Rainer, Lieutenant Fallow and Sergeant Plut, who are all here to listen to your story and determine if whatever you wish can be allowed," Detective Devenir stated.

"Hello Mr. Brown, what would you want for this information," Chief Rainer enquired?

"I want protection for my family," Lass declared!

"Who do you want protection from," Chief Rainer asked?

"The Rough Rider Bikers," Lass stated!

"Sir we are the police we don't offer personal security, so if you want officers following your family members around, we don't do that sort of work," Chief Rainer added.

"You people don't have to go that far, just maybe a police cruiser parked outside my house and a bit more regular patrol throughout my area? Plus, if I ever find myself in a jam and need some help, you guys will rush to my assistance," Lass suggested?

"Well, if that's the sort of protection you have in mind, that could be possible. But it all depends on what you have to offer us," Chief Rainer said!

"The bikers have some crew of thieves who break into people's houses across Quebec every day when they away at work and steal everything out their house. These bikers then either sell these products online or through one of their pawn shops here in Montreal," Lass informed.

"We have been trying to apprehend these people or find out what they do with these stolen items for years sir, this sounds like a major break in this case," Lieutenant Fallow declared!

"What problems do you have with the bikers," Chief Rainer asked?

"They want me dead," Lass lamented!

"Why," Chief Rainer asked?

"Because a black mustn't have anything according to some white people," Lass argued!

"What do you know of these thieves, because they seem to know everything about these places they rob ahead of time? Even if we mange to get to the location, they have taken what they went for and are always gone before we arrive," Sergeant Plut exclaimed!

"I don't know them individually, they are all mostly young men and teenagers, but I do know where they sell their stolen goods," Lass stated!

***

The Variety Pawn Shop where the Rough Rider Bikers sold everything from tools, to home appliances, to jewelry, etcetera; received their weekly resupply of merchandise each Wednesdays at 4:17 AM. Even though the proprietor of the Pawn Shop sold mostly stolen items, they had an ideal location on Saint-Charles Boulevard in the SAQ shopping plaza, at Kirkland intersection. Detectives had been watching the business for almost two weeks since they received information about their business practices; and were prepared to raid the establishment that very morning. Instead of restocking the store during daylight, the bikers chose the dark of night to sneak their inventory in; and after watching them bring in several unpackaged items the investigators understood why. The detectives and supporting officers waited and recorded the bikers for ten minutes, before the all threw on their sirens and corralled the facility.

The three bikers transferring the items into the store were all armed and had lengthy criminal records, therefore they opened fire at the approaching officers. The coppers were forced to stop a short distance away and exchanged gunfire with the bikers, who thought they could escape through the front entrance. While two of the bikers held the officers off at the rear of the building, one of them ran to check if the front entrance was usable. There was also a team of officers waiting should the bikers attempted to escape through the front, hence they were trapped with nowhere to go. Despite holding their own against the larger team of officers, the bikers eventually ran out of bullets and were forced to surrender. The ensuing investigation gave police an insight into a sector of the biker's organization they never knew existed, which brought in millions in revenue annually.

Part 38

Almost every newscaster around the world highlighted the kidnapping of the Veronovichi couple, which remarkable took place in broad daylight in the middle of downtown Montreal. The car hijacking was the most sophisticated and brilliant strategy the police had ever seen, as the hijackers used large sized trucks to disguise their actions from pedestrians and motorists along the roadway. Following the kidnapping the couple's Bentley Coup was placed on the Underground Black Market and sold to Russian businessman, who received the vehicle two weeks later with legal documents that proved ownership. With their vehicle sent thousands of miles away, the couple was brought to an old mansion in Saint-Eustache, Quebec where they were locked away inside the dungeon. Marolina and Andrea Veronovichi were securely tied to two chairs inside the dark and grungy dungeon with black sacs placed over their heads that protruded them from seeing anything. For three consecutive days they sat inside the damp room, where apart from the occasional sounds of pigeons that nested by the window, there was absolute silence. Their captors had neglected to provide any form of nourishment, fluids or added warmth, thus if the Spring temperatures had not begun it would have been brutal for them both.

Andrea was an honest businessman and had no idea why anyone would wish to do them harm, however after thirty-six hours of confinement fear drove Marolina to confess what she did. To try getting help, both husband and wife screamed out their lungs to no avail, as there was nobody within miles of their location. Neither Andrea nor Marolina had any concept of time, therefore they both went through a wide rage of emotions which often caused them to cry themselves to sleep. Even though they were candid and honest with each other, Marolina only went so far with the disclosures, as there were still secrets, she would never share with her husband.

On the third day of their abduction Marolina was awakened by a Caucasian and a colored man, who untied her, ripped her clothes off and strung her up with both of her hands tied to hooks on the ceiling. Marolina screamed and begged from the second they frightened her from her sleep, which also made Andrea began pleading for their lives. When the sacs got removed from over the captives' heads, they both struggled to see initially, until they drew accustomed to the glares of light. Once their visions cleared the Veronovichi couple saw Kevin comfortably seated on a chair across from them. Even though Andrea and Kevin had never crossed path, Mr. Veronovichi had watched and read enough local news to know who the adopted Monsieur Trudeau was.

Kevin was puffing on a huge Marijuana Joint and said absolutely nothing for the first three minutes, while Andrea expressed his sorrow, offered an insurmountable amount of money for their freedom and begged for their lives. Marolina on the other hand knew there was nothing she could say to alter the rude-boy decision, so she left her husband to reason on their behalf. Despite Andrea's business propositions Kevin remained silent and stared mindlessly at Marolina, who was unintimidated and stared right back at him.

"There is never enough wealth and power for you white motherfuckers is there? Do you have any clue the shit I passed through to get where I am today? I wasn't born with that gold spoon they used to feed both of you; so now that I took mine, you think mi go make some snot nose bitch come take this!? I also bet you thought I was going to forget about your involvement in all this shit? If it wasn't for certain business aspects, I'd kill both of you right here; but instead of that I decided to settle for punishments," Kevin warned!

"What do you mean by punishment monsieur," Andrea asked?

"I'm sure none of you have ever gotten a proper buss-ass; or else you especially would know there is consequences for every bad deed," Kevin lamented!

"One day I'll put your fucking black ass in the grave for killing my father! You son of a bitch," threatened Marolina who was stripped down to her French Cut Underwear!

"Twenty lashes for this bitch! Five for Junior and fifteen for me," Kevin ordered!

The colored man removed a long black whip from a paper bag and lashed Marolina across the ribcage as he attempted to correct his distance. Once the executioner got the appropriate length measured, he began whipping the frail skin matured woman without mercy or conscience. The tough talking female screamed to the heavens with each of the first seven connections, before she fell unconscious under the duress. Andrea could not stomach watching his wife get whipped like a slave and turned his head aside, to avoid looking at the cruelty. Twenty lashes later Marolina's back was scarred from just below her shoulders down to her buttocks, with long lacerations that would torment her for the remainder of her days. After the flogging both assistants unhooked Marolina who was unconscious, dressed her and secured her back on the chair.

The men then untied Andrea who was kicking and screaming and dragged him over to where they had his wife previously; and hooked him up as they did her. Because he had nothing to do with the kidnapping or killings, Andrea believed he should have been exempt from the punishments and tried reasoning with Kevin.

"Listen Mister Trudeau, Marolina acted on her own, and I swear I knew nothing of any of this, until a few hours ago! I am willing to do anything to stop this right now, I will pay whatever it takes, but please, you must listen to me," Andrea pled?

"You're married to the bitch, so half of what's hers is yours! Either way, ten lashes under him blood-clatt," Kevin ordered!

"Please don't do this Monsieur, I beg of you as a gentleman," Andrea shouted?

Kevin's Caucasian associate took over the whipping duties and began flogging Andrea Veronovichi, who yelled in pain as the whip ripped into his skin. While his companions flogged each of the married couple, Kevin sat back and used a camera to capture every second of the whooping. Unlike his wife Andrea stayed awake throughout the entire beating and was returned to his tied-up position thereafter. Once Kevin and his associates were finished, they left the couple as they were with the sacs over the heads and locked them away. Despite his weakened state Andrea called out to Kevin several times before he again shouted for help, yet most of his appeals went ignored or unheard.

"Before you go please, some food, water? Help, Help, somebody please help us! Help, help," yelled Andrea!

Marolina began slowly regaining consciousness and coughed several times, before she realized they were still in the same predicament. Even though she was in immense pain from the whipping, Marolina acted more concerned about Andrea's wellbeing and shouted for him.

"Mon Cher are you alright," Marolina whispered?

"Don't ever refer to me like that from today you bitch! Because if we manage to get out of this place, I want a divorce; and when my lawyers come calling Marolina? I suggest you sign every piece of document they present to you," Andrea exclaimed!

Moments later the door to the dungeon reopened and the captives could hear someone moving closer to them, although they were incapable of knowing who it was. Marolina and Andrea could be heard breathing heavily with fear, uncertain if they were in for more punishment. The black male who participated in the flogging returned with bottles of water and fed them to both captives using straws. After the kidnapper was through providing the refreshments, he turned around and exited the room and locked the door behind himself.

***

When Kevin departed from the mansion, he left his flogging executioners to guard the residence and climbed into his Range Rover Sport 4X4, which was being driven by his chauffeur Miss Nutcracker. The female guard drove him to his next appointment, who lived quite a distance away in Sainte-Anne-des-Plaines, Quebec. Even though the Veronovichi couple was held clueless about the time, date, outdoor temperature and their location, it was actually late morning just after 11 AM and the weather forecast for the day was expected to be cloudy with rain across Quebec. Miss Nutcracker brought Kevin to a private meeting between he and their cult's moderator, Monsieur Gilbert Stephano, who personally phoned and arranged the link.

Like every other cult member of the private club, Monsieur Stephano lived on his own property and had a large multi-million-dollar mansion. Instead of allowing his maid to show Kevin in, the spokesman met his Grand Chancellor by the front door and showed him into his entertaining room. Even though Kevin had no reason to feel threatened he brought Miss Nutcracker inside with him and carried a concealed 32mm handgun. Miss Nutcracker stood by the entrance to the entertainment room throughout their meeting and only allowed the maid inside once with the refreshments. Both men sat down over tea and cigars, then dived right into the business at hand, which had to do with the impending gang war between Lass and the Jamaicans versus the Rough Riders Biker Gang.

"I would like to thank you for coming here to see me today Grand Chancellor Trudeau," Monsieur Stephano stated!

"You have a beautiful home Mr. Stephano; the pleasure is all mine," Kevin answered!

"I am aware that you have been occupied with the recovery of your son and might not be up to date on current events. And I also knew the sacrifice you have made for independent hustlers especially of your Jamaicans to operate without the services of the Rough Riders, but the organization you have pledged your life to protecting and those who you fought for are about to clash once again," Monsieur Stephano informed.

"How did all this come about," Kevin enquired?

"With our expansion every territory across this country gets our services, and there will be no exceptions! You have made it possible for all these street side dealers to market other people's products, but they will now have to also provide our products from this point on! Whatever the ratio at which they move our products is unimportant, but unless they do, they will be placed out of business. As an organization that was created to govern covertly and create massive wealth for its members, we hope that you could find a way to settle this matter peacefully, or I'm afraid your countrymen might all perish," Monsieur Stephano exclaimed!

Kevin thought about all he and his friends had done to change the hustler's business landscape across Montreal. He had accomplished way more than he had sat out to and graciously shared his wealth with those who were in the trenches with him, so Kevin had no reason to place himself back in harms way.

"I'll deal with it right away," Kevin declared!

"Wonderful, a lot of ears will be happy to hear that news," Monsieur Stephano said!

With their meeting concluded both men rose to their feet and shook hands, before Gilbert showed his visitor to the door. As soon as Kevin climbed into his chauffeured driven transport, he telephoned an informant who knew everything he needed to about Lass and received valuable information on the drug dealer's business connections.

Part 39

Bail was denied to Chops and his accomplices by Magistrate Maxine Durue who was disgusted by the bikers' actions at the Children's Hospital. The Ville-Saint-Pierre overseer who had upcoming criminal trials got remanded to the Central Jail, which was a twenty-three hours lockdown facility downtown Montreal. Chops was facing a grand total of twenty-four years in prison if convicted of all the charges, thus he was projected to be at the facility for at least two years. The high-rise building was mainly used to house detainees who had ongoing court cases and were yet to be sentenced. Detainees were allowed an hour from their cells each day to walk around the concrete wall surrounded exercise yard and take showers. Meals were served to each detainee inside their cells by orderlies, who brought in the contraband items, cleaned the facility, distributed reading materials and were allowed the most freedom inside the detention center. The prisoner turnover rate at the facility was a continuous process, therefore there was never any guarantee who one's cellmate would be.

During Chops' fourth week at the detention center, he went to shower one afternoon and was under the warm flowing water, when some loudmouth Caucasian came into the bathroom. There were several other showers from which the man could have chosen, yet he distinctively wanted to bath under Chops' shower. The biker initially had his back turned to the loudmouth and spun around to find the man standing directly ahead of him with his penis at hand, as if he was jerking off while staring at him. Chops became irate after noticing that other detainees were laughing at him, thus he charged at the loudmouth inmate with a shoulder tackle and spiked him on the floor. With the remaining detainees yelling at the excitement, Chops proceeded to rain punches at the loudmouth and busted up his face before the guards rushed in and pulled him off. The Ville-Saint-Pierre biker got sent to the Segregation Unit, where he spent two weeks before they transferred him to Bordeaux Detention Center.

The detainee who Chops whooped was taken to the infirmary, where Nurse Treneger cleaned and dressed the wounds to his face and check the patient's ribs where he claimed to have gotten hit. The detainee was a sentenced prisoner who was already serving a seven-year sentence for Aggravated Assault and Kidnapping; and was back in court to answer to manslaughter charges after Quebec police found evidence of human remains in the woods behind his house. To soften up Nurse Treneger, the patient cried and complained about his frightful experience and was given pain killers for the pain.

"Oh my God that guy went crazy and almost killed me for no reason! I can't believe my wife has to come here and see me like this... I wish I could spare her the grief, she already has a bad heart and seeing me like this might give her another heart attack! Oh God, what can I do, life has been so tough, and she is the only one who believes in me! Oh please, somebody help me," sobbed the inmate?

"Listen Mr. Van-Dier, this is against the institution's policy, but I'll lend you my cell phone to quickly phone your wife and tell her what happened to you, so she won't be a nervous," Nurse Treneger offered!

"Oh my God Nurse Treneger, nobody has ever done anything nice for me! Thank you, thank you," Mr. Van-Dier stated!

After the nurse finished patching up the patient, she snuck him her cellular phone and left the examining room for a short time to offer some privacy. Had Nurse Treneger checked through the patient's dossier, she would have seen that his ex-wife was one of the people he was convicted of kidnaping and assaulting. The ex-wife was eventually who got him arrested and charged, therefore there was no way she would be coming by to pay him any visit. Mr. Van-Dier waited until the nurse was out of the room before he placed the call, but not to his wife as he made it seemed.

"Ring, ring, ring," sounded Lil Wasp's phone to which he responded! "Hello!"

"That job has been handled," Mr. Van-Dier whispered.

"Well thank you for working so fast," Lil Wasp said!

"Cut the crap Lil-Wasp, when will I get my money," Mr. Van-Dier asked?

"Check your commissary account, that five thousand should last you for the remainder of your sentence," Lil Wasp instructed before the line went dead!

***

Following their rampage throughout the city of Montreal, the Hickston twins safely made their way back to Canada's West Coast, and telephoned Mr. Bartello after they received word that he was recovering at home. News editors in Canada who wrote about their exploits in Montreal, all made it appeared as if the West Coast bikers were hired by Jim and company to perform an assassination on the East Coast. The brothers phoned to offer their sympathies for what happened to Jim and apologised for the entire Kadeem incident. Lil Wasp had briefed Jim on the specifics of the Hickstons' visit following his release from lockup, yet Jim pretended as if he had not been informed. As means of an apology, the Hickstons offered to send the Montreal biker boss a case of Irish Scotch, and their assistance, if there was anything they could do to help find the shooters. All three men had a lengthy conversation which led to the Montreal biker boss agreeing to keep the manhunt for Kadeem a priority. The Hickstons negotiated a deal where should Kadeem get spotted anywhere in Canada by a Rough Rider, he would undoubtedly to get killed on the spot. Jim had to wrap up their conversation with several of his biker associates coming by for a meeting, but the Hickstons made him vow to visit Kelowna, British Colombia, whenever he had fully healed.

"Why didn't you tell them that we already answered those Chinese mobsters who tried to kill you," Lil Wasp asked, as he walked over and placed a newspaper page on Jim's lap?

The newspaper page was from a recent article in the Montreal Gazette, which showed a photo of the destroyed Chinese mobster's factory with the headline, "Canadian Bomb Kills Chinese Mobsters."

"Just maybe other players were involved, and if so, I plan to find out who they are and tie off all loose ends," Jim stated, as he read some of the article!

"So, what about this loose end," Lil Wasp asked, before revealing another

Informer 3

newspaper page of the female used to transport the coffin back to China?

"I guess it's time to permanently silence that one," Jim instructed!

"I will see to it that she gets taken care of," Lil Wasp declared!

Jim Bartello had arranged a secret meeting for the biker club's area overseers only and held the proceedings in the privacy of his home. The nurse who took care of Jim came in and checked to ensure her patient was comfortabe in his living room sofa and arranged everything to his liking, before she left him to entertain his guests. The biker club leader had made drastic improvements since his shooting, wherein he pushed himself daily to manage the hardships of rehab. Although Jim couldn't quite walk, he could use his arms sparingly and had improved his vocabulary, but moreover he was determined to return to his former self. Everyone who attended was genuinely happy to see Jim out of jail and the hospital, and some even brought gifts to show their support. A Rough Rider gathering would not be complete without gratuity drugs for the guests, as a result Jim had a table stocked with a variety of choices. There were two main topics on the agenda and one had to do with the handling of a fellow area overseer, who was believed to be conspiring to turn evidence against the biker club.

Once all his invited guests had arrived, Jim made Lil Wasp serve as his spokesman and informed them of everything they had learnt thus far about Chops' dealings with undercover officers. The Rough Rider Gang allowed for their members to financially strive and expected loyalty in return, therefore dealing anyone else's products rather than the club's was against policy. Lil Wasp detailed everything including Chops' mission to spark an all-out war between them and the Jamaicans, to illustrate that their former colleague plotted to betray them and destroy their brotherhood. When the final vote got tallied there wasn't a single biker in support of Chops' dealing with the police, therefore the motion to expel him from the club was unanimous. Regardless of being incarcerated, Chops was tried and convicted without representation; resulting in the most severe punishment handed out by the biker club in years.

To get the sanctioned assassination message secretly to the correct ear, the bikers assigned the task to one of their soldiers who checked into the Bordeaux Correctional Facility every Friday evening and spent the weekend. Guychard Larond was an accountant who got sentenced to eight months for swindling money from the government for his clients, which his lawyer negotiated to weekend due of his obligations during tax season. The entire governing sector of the Rough Riders kept their decision quite until Lil Wasp met with Guychard half an hour before he checked in for the weekend and gave him the message. Lil Wasp then drove Guychard directly to the prison and watched him check in, to ensure there wasn't any chance of lip slippage.

For weekenders who the guards were accustomed to seeing, re-entering the institution went much quicker than other inmates. Once Guychard passed through the processing department Rene Wamblay who worked in the clothing assignment department was the first biker he came across. Lil Wasp had instructed him to pass the message to Rene, therefore during the clothes handout he leaned close to his biker brethren and whispered, "Lil Wasp says call Bartello for confirmation, they want you Patrice and Joseph to do Chops in!"

High-profiled biker executives were a rarity in detention centers across the island, therefore Chops ruled Bordeaux facility from the instant he got transferred there. From the moment the biker overseer reached Bordeaux and his arrival got announced, royalty treatment got rolled out as if he was a king. The Administration Department assigned him to B Wing, which was loaded with Rough Rider Bikers from across the province. Bordeaux offered way more freedom than the central jail and had living pods that were watched by guards inside a round central observation station. Instead of all-day lockup inmates could move freely about their pods during open cell hours, went to the dining hall for meals, assembly hall for church and had several classes at different areas of the jail.

Rene and the two inmates mentioned by Guychard were all assigned to the same living quarters as Chops, who felt safe and secure in the company of his fellow bikers. Wherever the Ville-Saint-Pierre overseer went around B Pod, he was constantly followed by at least three bikers to ensure he was always protected. The guards were elated to have someone of rank within the biker club, who could help defuse dangerous situations that arise occasionally. There have been many gang wars inside the correctional facility between members of the Diablo Biker Gang, Chiney K members and even racial wars against men of color.

That same evening following lockdown, which allowed for the guards to change work shifts, Rene corralled the two men mentioned and gave them the news. For clarification as ordered, all three men telephoned Jim Bartello and got the green light to proceed with the hit against their own biker brethren. As pastime for most of the inmates during open cell hours, the basement was an option with games, weights for workout and a television room. During such free time inmates took showers, called loved ones or even hung out inside their cells. With the assassination order confirmed the three bikers went about their individual ways to obtain shanks, then regrouped and went to the basement where Chops was inside the television room watching a movie. There was a timid Jewish inmate named Nathaniel Rosenburg who Patrice would often assault, in addition to stealing his commissary items and hygiene products. When the three assassins reached the basement, Patrice and his companions pulled the Jewish inmate off camera and gave him a Cosmopolitan Magazine with added instructions.

Nathaniel was terrified for his own life having watched Patrice and Joseph knocked people out in the past, but he had no choice but to do what was ordered. Seconds later the Jewish inmate walked into the television room, where he sat in the front row beside the camera that was installed to capture everything inside the room. Patrice had instructed him to countdown from sixty after he took a seat, therefore once he got down to one, he stood up by the camera and used the magazine to disrupt the guard's view. Rene, Joseph and Patrice all rushed into the dark tv room and moved directly towards Chops, who never thought they were attacking him until they were within striking distance. All the other bikers scattered and moved away from Chops as if they knew what was to come, thus the assassins stabbed their target sixteen times before they all ran from the room and left the Ville-Saint-Pierre overseer in a pool of his own blood.

The observers inside the monitoring room rang the alarm and almost immediately a gang of guards rushed into B-Block. The entire B-Wing got locked down instantly and every man sent to his cell, as guards fought to save Chops' life and bring order back to the pod. The warden was called to the scene and came in to look at the situation, that quickly escalated to a murder scenario once Chops stopped breathing. Nathaniel Rosenburg was the first inmate dragged away by the guards for questioning, and it wasn't long before they returned and hauled off the three main assassins. Word reached Jim Bartello relatively quickly as inmates from other pods watched as the guards brought away the four men involved in handcuffs, then rolled out Chops' bloodied corpse on a stretcher.

Part 40

Kane was back on his home soil which belonged to the generations of his people who came before him, and he had no intentions of abandoning his territory again. Miss Emma advised him to put his life's experiences to good use and help lead the Mohawk into a new era, but Kane had no interest in joining politics. Even though he had heard otherwise the renegade Indian's main concern was whether an arrest warrant had been issued for him, therefore when he left Miss Emma's house he drove directly towards the police station. A few miles down the road he came across an Indian whose dog had produced a new litter of wolf descendants and thus had a pair of dogs for sale, so not wanting to be alone at home with something to care for, Kane pulled over and bought both pups. From that initial purchase rumors began circling that he was back in town, but confirmation was made by an elderly Mohawk female who watched him walk into the local precinct. The elderly woman could barely see five feet ahead of herself, yet she claimed she clearly watched Kane from across the street and his shadow was that of an

Informer 3

Indian Chief wearing his Tribal Porcupine Headdress.

When Kane entered the Mohawk Reservation Police Precinct the front desk post was vacant, so he rang the bell provided and waited to be attended to. Officer Tamoalee who helped with the search and rescue procedure following Kane's Mercier Bridge incident, walked in and froze as if he saw a ghost. With the officer's associate John Jarrett serving time for presumably killing the lone Esquada survivor, Officer Tamoalee instantly turned aggressive and circled around to the visitor's side of his desk. Kane stood his ground and watched the officer charged towards him, but as Officer Tamoalee drew within eight feet the two pups stepped ahead of their new master and barked at the officer. Instead of acting on his impulses, Officer Tamoalee stopped short and began cursing with his index finger pointed directly at the rude-boy Indian's face.

"You son of a bitch, I wish we had probable cause to lock you up right now for making a good man have to go to prison for your worthless life! What the hell do you want anyways? You are not welcome in here, so get the fuck out before we throw you out," Officer Tamoalee threatened!

The desk sergeant and two other constables overheard the shouting and came out to see who the deputy was referring to. Once the sergeant realized that it was Kane, he also became defensive and supported the officer instead of reprimanding the constable. With Kane's concern addressed the bad-boy Indian turned to walk out of the precinct, when he distinctively heard Officer Tamoalee said, "It won't be too long before we come pay you a visit"! Having such a threat issued at him told Kane that his problems with the local police department had just begun, therefore his only means to combat such hostility was to follow Miss Emma's advise.

"It has been many years since anyone challenged our council chief for his position; I take it I have you officers support during the upcoming election," Kane lamented!

"What upcoming election, there was no mention of an election," Officer Tamoalee frightfully stated?

"Well, I just came in here to let my police force be the first to know," Kane declared before he exited the station!

"Don't get your hopes up, the Mohawk people will never vote for a criminal like you over the Tribal Chief," said the sergeant, whose mouth fell open when Kane exited to a loud uproar from a large crowd of supporters!

"Yeh, yeh, yeh… Kane, Kane, Kane…," cheered the crowd, which gathered to ensure their young motivator was not detained!

One of the officers who watched the exchange between his comrades and Kane was Officer Tamow Maknahawi; who slid into the male bathroom thereafter and made a private phone call. When the receiver answered the phone Constable Maknahawi simply said, "you were right he is alive", before he disconnected the call. Constable Maknahawi then joined his fellow officers and watched the young Esquada warrior mesmerize the crowd, which appeared to wholeheartedly believe in him. Kane allowed them to continue cheering his name before he raised his hands and got the crowd to simmer down. The gathering was inspirational for the last of the Esquada's, who knew he could do much more for his people. There were still people coming from all directions to lend their support, therefore with his movement growing Kane addressed his people from the heart.

"As owners of these lands, the time for us to get what is rightfully ours has come! You, my people know that I have fought for you in the past; and over the coming months, I will challenge for Chief of The Tribunal! These reservation lands are ours and here is where we should be proud of and prosper, but if you must move away from here, you must first learn how to survive in the white man's world. Nobody has ever taught us these important things, which is why so many of us die out there, once we have left the reservation. No more should we lock ourselves away from the rest of the world, but we should teach them also, what it means to be Mohawk! To those of you who are selling us out to the outsiders, your end of days is coming, for there exists no worst Indian than you! With your support we will bring changes to our village and stop the whites from taking everything that belongs to us!"

"Yeh, yeh, yeh… Kane, Kane, Kane…," cheered the crowd of residents, who lifted him and his pups off the ground and walked about parading them!

Kane felt added jubilation when he realized all his comrades from the Mercier Bridge hijacking were present. News of his interest to lead their people into a new era was accepted with great joy, because the Mohawk trusted he would always put their best interests first. The excitement and celebration went from the jailhouse and continued on the Esquada property, where the locals brought all the necessary items and held a huge cookout. While most of those present attended to show their support, there were a few haters who opposed Kane and hypocritically went to acquire damaging information. Amongst the crowd of people gathered were two female employees of Cheval Ohuna, who despised the Esquada family and had his sights set on the position being sought by Kane.

That same night while Kane slept, he received a rare vision of his father and mother, who were both extremely proud of him and advised him to be cautious because of those who wished to do him bodily harm. After all the disappointments caused by the youngest Esquada, hearing his parents professed their approval of him motivated the rude boy Indian, who knew most importantly their warning was nothing to take for granted. As he walked away from his parents in the dream, Kane looked back over his shoulder and saw his brother who smiled at him.

When the Mohawk warrior arose from his night's rest outside was still dark and both his new pups were beside him on the bed, so he got up and assembled some supplies then went training in the hills as he used to do with Danny and Kevin. While fine tuning his shooting skills, Kane thought of his brother and past friends who were all horrifically taken from his life. Eagle had taught him the fine art of setting traps be it for food or prey, therefore as added protection he climbed a tree and hacked away several branches. After collecting enough wood, the Indian sliced off pieces of bark from the tree and sharpened wooden spikes, which he then tied to long pieces of branches and built several death traps throughout the property. Each trap was strategically hidden with its individual trigger and could not be disarmed once sprung, thus Kane ensured their heights were out of the reach of his pets. With his eliminate trespassers traps set, the Mohawk warrior collected dried wood from around his property and built several barn fire stacks of wood at the edge of the treelines surrounding his house. Any unwelcomed intruder who refrained from using the driveway stood the chance of falling into one of Kane's death traps, intended solely to exterminate its victims.

Life changed for Kane who embraced his friends that genuinely cared about him, hence he became more community orientated and less withdrawn. Even though Kane had publicly stated that he was considering challenging the head of the council, he had to make known his ambitions to the committee members in person or writing. The Aboriginal Ceremony of The Ancients, during which his community members commemorate their ancestors, life and the richness thereof was in six days and his first chance to personally address the council. Most of the local Indians expected Kane to announce his plans to become the next council chief, as they would prefer him as head of their committee instead of Cheval Ohuna.

The night before the Aboriginal Ceremony of The Ancients, Kane entertained five guests at his house until late into the night. Because of their host's discipline to abstain from the consumption of alcohol, none of his companions brought any form of liquor, yet they smoked Marijuana and had an enjoyable gathering. The group of Indians played cards and reminisced about some of their experiences, such as the mission where they ambushed the motorcycle mounted bikers or captured the Mercier Bridge and held it hostage to get their voices heard. Every Indian in attendance held Kane and his family in the highest regard; and each spoke of their experiences as if those moments were the pinnacle of their existence.

A black Chevy Suburban pulled up along a back trail on the north-east edge of the Esquada property, where seven armed men dressed in complete black outfits dismounted. All seven men carried high powered assault rifles and wore ski masks that they used to conceal their faces. The group of men were all members of law enforcement and aimed to exterminate Kane Esquada for the damaging information he possessed. With their mission objectives already discussed, the group of men moved onto the property and proceeded towards the Esquada house. The terrain was rugged and extremely dark, but the group of assassins came prepared with Night Scopes that allowed them to see clearly.

By the time most of Kane's visitors left it was almost 2 AM, but two of his friends decided to spend the entire night. The two friends who decided to stay were Jason Kahn-Tineta and Achak Degonwadonti, both of which were vehicle-less and lived in the opposite direction from those who had departed. An hour after the friends left all three men were asleep around the television inside the living room, when one of Kane's pups got up and started growling. Seconds later a loud scream came from the woods outside the house, when an intruder stepped on one of the traps and got killed. The intruder's sigh alerted the other pup which jumped up barking and eventually awoke everyone else. Once the rude-boy Indian awoke he grabbed for an AR-19 Automatic Rifle, that he stored behind his living room sofa and snuck to the closest window where he peeked through at the surrounding woods. Achak thought his friends were overreacting to the noise and stood curiously in the middle of the room, as Jason crept to a window on the opposite wall.

"Ahhh," shouted a second intruder from the woods, who had fallen prey to another of Kane's traps!

"Who the hell is out there," Achak questioned?

"I still can't tell, so get down," Kane responded!

"Any other guns in the house," Jason enquired?

"There is a shotgun in that closet and my handgun is in the nightstand drawer in my room," Kane instructed, while protecting his puppies!

As soon as Achak started moving towards the bedroom the intruders onside opened fire and began shooting up the house. Kane and Jason hid beyond the window ledges as bullets bored through the windows and unfortunately struck Achak three times. To show the intruders they were heavily armed Kane pointed his assault rifle through the window and callously fired off several rounds. Jason crawled on his stomach over to the closet, where he waited for a brief pause in the shooting before he opened the door and retrieved a 12 Gauge AA Semi-Automatic Shotgun with a box of bullets. Once he armed himself Jason crawled towards a window, through which he tried to distinct who they were up against. There were three other people shooting at the residence from two sides of the house, but Kane's primary concern was whether they were being flanked from the other two sections.

"Jay, make sure nobody come through the back rooms," Kane shouted, as he rose to one knee and fired several rounds in the direction of a shooter!

Two of the intruders had made their way around the back to Eagle's old room, where they broke the window pane and snuck into the house. The continuous barrage of gunfire from their comrades gave the home invaders the cover they needed to sneak into the house undetected, with Kane and his associates' attention focused elsewhere. Even though Kane compassionately held onto his pups they fought to escape and were agitated by something in the adjacent room, but the warrior Indian was more interested in protecting them from unnecessary injury. Jason repositioned himself and moved towards a backwall seconds before the two intruders began making their way towards the living room. Neither Jason nor Kane heard when the men snuck in, but the pups knew they were under siege and grew much fiercer as a result.

Jason had three dogs at home which gave him a much better understanding of the animals' behavior than Kane, hence he suspected the pups were attempting to warn them of eminent danger. With the intruders inside the house unsuspectingly sneaking up on their target, one of the pups escaped Kane's grasp and charged at the assassins. When the leading intruder sighted Kane and readied himself to execute the warrior Indian, the pup rushed in and latched its small teeth into the man's calf. The assassin frightfully missed his target and pierced bullets into the wall above Kane's head, stopping only after he struck the ceiling and regained control of the weapon. Instead of putting himself in the line of fire, Jason pointed his shotgun down the short hallway towards Eagle's old bedroom and fired. The shotgun blast struck the front assassin in the hip and sent him crashing to the ground, to which his companion panicked and began callously shooting. Kane frightfully reacted by pointing his rifle towards the hall then opened fire, even though there wasn't anyone in sight to shoot. With the injured assassin raving in pain and his companion backing away to safety, Jason selected another bullet to the buckshot's firing chamber and blindly fired another shot down the hallway. Having successfully saved his master the little pup stood his ground against the other assassin, who contemplated shooting the disruptive animal but decided against it. The injured assassin was silenced following Jason's second disburse, which also struck his partner who could be heard staggering into the room.

Kane felt relieved that Jason was there with him or the intruders would have successfully ambushed him alone. The second intruder inside the house got struck with a buckshot that extended from his right bicep up to his neck; and was forced to transfer his firearm to the left hand that was less effective. Neither Kane nor Jason knew the extent of the intruder's injuries, but they assumed he was tragically wounded once he stopped returning fire. Inside the bedroom the wounded assassin dropped his automatic rifle and leaned against the wall with his hand pressed against his neck, before he ripped off the mask covering his head and slid down to the floor. The home invader telephoned one of the gunners outside the house and could be heard pleading for them not to let him die and rescue him. While pleading the assassin could be heard strenuously coughing until he went silent, but the combative Indians were not eager to assume anything.

To scare the gunners outside and offer themselves more lighting, Kane fired at two small bottles he tied to two stacks of dried wood on the edge of the treeline. Both bottles were filled with gasoline which exploded and caught the wood piles on fire, thus frightening the assassins who hid in the bushes under the cloak of darkness. The piles of died wood shot huge extensions of flames in the air and could be seen from miles away, but most importantly exposed the assassins' positions. For the first time since the altercation began Kane and Jason could see the people they were up against, as they exchanged bullets with the surviving three assassins. Their exchange continued for another three minutes before the intruders accepted the fact their plans had failed, plus they were developing a shortage of loaded magazine clips. With their target hunkered down inside the house and the faint sound of emergency personnel on route, the last three assassins eventually disappeared into the woods and abandoned their mission.

When the fire department, the police and ambulance technicians arrived on the scene, Kane and Jason were sitting in the front yard unarmed. They had checked to ensure the second shooter inside the house was deceased and were surprised to uncover the person's identity. The unmasked home invader and his hallway partner were Constable Jack Quiere from the Shamattawa Reservation Police Department; and an unidentified male who also carried a Manitoba law enforcement badge. Moments after emergency services arrived locals began flocking onto the Esquada property to check the developments and lend their support if necessary. Within an hour the number of spectators grew to a large crowd, as most Indians attended to ensure their beloved advocate was not mistreated or harmed. A female reporter from the local tribunal news arrived some twenty minutes later and was crucially criticized by some in attendance, for not getting there sooner to show the world how the Indigenous people were treated at times.

The darkness of night still covered the province and at least half the traps on the property were intact, so to avoid further catastrophe Kane led the crime scene investigators to the locations where the other two bodies were killed. Investigators photographed, documented and recovered the corpses, but abandoned tasks such as evidence gathering until daylight. After checking the assassins' identifications investigators determined that all the men involved worked for two separate police departments in Quebec and Manitoba, none of which did business together although officers everywhere considered themselves family. A short time after it was reported that all the assassins were police officers, representatives from three other government branches arrived on scene, which was quite unusual. Even though all the evidence told the story of what occurred, Kane and Jason individually had to give disclosures to a group of men from agencies such as the Royal Canadian Mounted Police, Crime Scene Investigative Unit, Police Disciplinary Committee and the Native and Indigenous Bureau. Following their disclosures, the RCMP senior officer on scene offered Kane and Jason police protection, but both warriors refused and opted instead for protection from their own peers.

The solidarity between Kane and his supporters was a movement unlike anything the government officials had ever seen, considering the number of people who left their homes at such a late hour. Every resident on the reservation knew that their local law enforcement officers wanted Kane dead, but viewing the corpses of assassins sent to kill their controversial advocate drove more Mohawks to supporting him. Once the investigators were finished with Jason and Kane the crowd of spectators swarmed the assassination survivors and took them away to allow the investigators freedom to do their work. Both victims were brought to a nearby property where they could rest, although with such adrenaline it was impossible for either man to sleep. To protect Kane from whoever wished to harm him, nineteen Mohawk warriors went home and retrieved their personal rifles, then returned to guard their Indian's Rights Advocate.

Their monthly Aboriginal Ceremony of The Ancients usually began with a prayer from their council chief over the proceedings, but there were no citizens to pray for at the commencement of the gathering. For the first few minutes the council members, their medicine man and elderly citizens were puzzled about the whereabouts of their community members, until the cheering sounds of a huge mob slowly came into view a slight distance away. The mob of Indians looked like they were conspiring to conduct a revolution against their tribal committee, as they marched towards the celebration grounds. When the Mohawk Indians reached the night's event it was impossible to distinct who or where Kane was, as the locals kept him submerged amid their humongous crowd.

"What is happening here," asked the elderly Council Chief?

The crowd parted, and Kane walked forward. "I Kane Esquada am making my intent known, that I wish to be appointed the next council chief!"

"You are too late; the council chief has already appointed me as his successor," Cheval Ohuna jumped up and yelled out!

"Then I will fight you for the honor," Kane suggested!

"We are not barbaric Indians who live without rules and order! We have a system in place to get things done and that's how we live," Cheval declared!

"With all due respect Chief Council, since he claims we are not barbarians, why not have a vote amongst the people and let them decide who they want as

Bloodshed Never Ends

your successor," Kane asked?

"That is not the way that this is done," Cheval shouted!

"Wait... maybe the young Esquada has a point! Maybe it's time we change some of these old traditions," said the Chief Council.

"No, you can't do this! You already promised," Cheval lamented!

"All in favor of Kane Esquada as your next council chief, move over to this side of the field," the Council Chief shouted, at which nearly everybody move to the side indicated!

There were three individuals standing in support of Cheval, who angrily walked away and went to his vehicle.

"Ladies and gentlemen, I present your new Council Chief! Now let the celebrations begin," said the retired council chief!

"Yeh-yeh-yeh-yeh-yeh," continually shouted the Mohawk locals who knew Kane would appropriately represent them!

When the festivities began Kane snuck away moments later and pretended he was going to urinate. Cheval was still sitting inside his vehicle on his phone in the parking area chatting with a colleague about ways to get rid of Kane. The rude-boy Indian snuck behind Cheval's vehicle and unexpectedly climbed into the unlocked rear door behind the driver. Kane startled the council board member and stuck his knife to his neck, thus rendered his victim paralyzed with fears of getting his throat slashed.

"I want you to inform your friends that business as usual will be coming to an end on the Mohawk Reservation! Listen to my words Ohuna, if ever I find out you are involved in the crimes that go unpunished on these reservations, I will find you and finish the job of removing your head," Kane threatened, before he released his victim and exited the car!

The instant Kane exited, Cheval started his car engine and sped away faster than a F1 driver. Kane smiled to himself even though his was dead serious about what he would do to Cheval, as he walked back to their native celebration.

Part 41

Don Valentino Salvatorè was one of two Cocaine suppliers on whom Lass depended to maintain his drug empire. The sixty-one years old Italian supplied several top dealers across the (GTA) Greater Toronto Area and would provide his Montreal client with a minimum of four kilos each month. The Cocaine smuggler lived in the Little Italy area of Toronto and was a crude businessman, who legitimately ran a real estate agency with three branches across the province of Ontario. Monsieur Salvatorè owned several rental properties such as living residents, shopping plazas and industrial buildings, yet made most of his earnings dealing Cocaine. Unlike Lass who took more of a hands-on approach with his drug business, his Italian supplier had a network of workers who handled his drug affairs. While Monsieur Salvatorè took care of the financial aspects of his drug business, his younger cousin Filipe managed the packaging and the delivery process.

The drug lab and packaging facility from which the operation was ran was located at a warehouse in North York, Toronto. To deceive the public and law enforcement alike, the businessman placed a furniture store at the front of the facility and used the basement portion for his illegal enterprise. The delivery trucks used to transport the drugs were the same used by the furniture store, thus, to conceal their product each parcel got prepackaged in disposable antique statues or furniture. Don Valentino had a work crew of three females who packaged the imported drugs, two armed guards, his foreman Filipe and two tradesmen who hid the packages inside the disposable items. There was no form of drug deals done through the furniture store or directly from the drug lab, to abstain from attracting any unwarranted attention.

***

Under Kevin's tutelage Gilbert Stephano made their intel specialists develop a profile on Don Valentino Salvatorè, which he then brought to Jim Bartello at his home for the biker leader to execute. The Rough Rider leader had never argued or enquired why the person whose information was inside the envelopes was marked for death; therefore, likewise he simply looked at the photo, nodded in agreement and placed the package on the table. The people who the spokesman represented were concerned about Jim's recovery, thus Gilbert was relieved to receive a positive review on the biker's progress from the caretaker. Both men sat inside Jim's living room by the artificial woodfire over cups of coffee and cigars; and had the most lengthy and heartfelt conversation they ever had about everything from life to the death of loved ones. Jim was brought to tears when discussing his murdered girlfriend whom Gilbert also had fond memories of; and thus, found himself wiping away tears empathically. They surprisingly sat for nearly two hours, before the spokesman bided his host "au revoir", summoned his chauffeur and departed.

Following Gilbert's departure Jim telephoned Lil Wasp and had him pass by to discuss the assignment with three of their gunners. Lil Wasp showed up fifty minutes later with Sting, Low Key and Auger, who all sat with Jim inside his home office. Whenever Jim had members of his biker crew over an assortment of drugs was always available on a table for anyone who chose to indulge, but none of the bikers who accompanied Lil Wasp paid any attention. Contrary to his benevolent companions Lil Wasp headed directly to the drug table, sat down and used a card to shovel away a gram of Cocaine from the pile. While the three bikers focused their attention on their injured leader whom they had not seen in some time, Lil Wasp created two lines, rolled up a $100 bill and snorted the powder up both nostrils. There was no way that Lil Wasp could join the strike force being assembled with his pending legal troubles, therefore he relaxed into the sofa and closed his eyes.

"I have a cancelation mission in Toronto that the clients would like to look clean! You fellows think you can manage that," asked Jim, who passed the three assassins the file?

The men took the pictures and began looking through, but one specific photo of the target, his wife and their three grandkids stuck out. Don Valentino Salvatorè and his wife Megan were with their grandsons Eric and Christopher, and their sole granddaughter Martha, who was the spitting image of Auger's girlfriend Marie-Claire.

"We sure can, at a matter a fact we already know how we will do this," Auger exclaimed!

"Good, there is a hundred-thousand-dollar purse attached for you guys when it's done, Jim stated!

***

Don Valentino was a very popular individual throughout his neighborhood on Montrose Avenue where he had lived for over forty-six years. Unlike most of his neighbors who had adapted to the times and upgraded to modern day technologies such as video surveillance, Don believed he lived in a safe part of town and did not need such security. Two days after the bikers received the contract a tinted Porsche Cayenne pulled up on the Salvatorès driveway at 10:49 pm. The neighbor who lived next door had gone out jogging and was just returning home when she saw Mrs. Salvatorè hugging a female in the doorway to their home.

The Salvatorès were winding down for bed that Sunday evening when the doorbell rang, at which Megan got up and attended to the visitor. The couple's maid usually answered the door, but she had left the Saturday evenings and would take Sundays off to visit family, before returning to work on Monday morning. When Mrs. Salvatorè looked through the peephole she saw a female she believed to be her granddaughter Martha and thus opened the door. Megan had drunk five glasses of wine since the afternoon, so her vision was slightly blurred in addition to the darkness outdoors.

"Martha! Don come and look at the wonderful surprise! It's Martha," yelled Megan who hugged the female she opened the door to!

The jogging neighbor went into her house as the door closed behind the Salvatorè couple and their presumed relative. The second the door closed the female visitor withdrew a 38 Special, shoved Megan to the floor and pointed the weapon directly at Monsieur Salvatorè. Neither of the home occupants could believe the female was not their granddaughter, due to the astonishing resemblance. Once she had gotten the couple under control, Marie-Claire phoned her accomplices outside in the Porsche and had them enter.

Auger, Sting and Low Key joined the party, where they brought the couple into the living room and forced Don Valentino to crab his wife around the throat. The businessman did as ordered while pleading with the intruders who then sat him down and had him watch while Low Key strangled his wife. The team of assassins were incredibly unified and worked with gloves, ski masks and even covered their shoes with plastic to avoid leaving prints of any kind. Marie-Claire had a backpack from which she withdrew a noose and passed it to Sting, who tied it to a hanging light fixture. The bikers overpoweringly brought Monsieur Salvatorè to the noose and placed it around his neck, then watched as his neck broke under the strain.

Once they were through, Marie-Claire used disinfectant to clean the entire area around which they worked and even wiped the floors before they exited. The Salvatorès bodies were discovered by their maid the following morning, but the police's initial report stated, "deaths by murder suicide". When the deceased couple's children found out about the report, they immediately hired an investigator to look further into the matter, as they were convinced their parents did not die in such a manner. Following the outcry of family members, business associates and neighbors, law enforcement officers changed their preliminary assessment and opened a murder investigation.

***

Lass had a secondary or emergency Cocaine connection from whom he could acquire a much smaller quantity, whenever products on the market got scarce and Don Salvatorè failed to respond. The dealer's name was Ben Winthorp aka Rudy and his primary hustling turf was located south-east of the island of Montreal, across the regions of Brossard and Longueuil. Rudy ran a much smaller operation than Lass and smuggled his inventory into the country with the use of human traffickers, who would swallow and transported the drugs inside their stomachs. Unlike Don Salvatorè it was only possible for Rudy to provide up to a kilo for sale each month, because of the much smaller quantity in which he imported. To settle the developing war between the Jamaicans and the Rough Riders, Kevin went to Rudy's condo in Longueuil where he lived with his wife and two children. The children were away at school when Miss Nutcracker knocked the door and jammed her Glock 9mm in Rudy's pregnant wife Jeneel's stomach as she answered. Jeneel was then pushed back inside the dwelling where they went to the kitchen and made warm beverages to drink. Miss Nutcracker phoned Rudy during the tea preparation and ordered his wife to get him to return home immediately.

"Hello," answered Rudy!

"Ben, I want you to come home right now," Jeneel stated!

"I can't get there right now honey I'm on my way to deal with something! What's wrong is it the baby," Rudy said?

"I don't care what you have to do, I want you to turn around and come home right now," Jeneel commanded!

A moment's silence fell over the phone as Rudy became concerned there was some serious issue Jeneel was withholding.

"OK, I'm on my way! Let me get off the phone so I can call this guy and cancel," declared Rudy, who then disconnected the call!

When Rudy arrived home nine minutes later, he frightfully ran into the condo expecting to probably rush his pregnant wife off to the hospital. Jeneel and their uninvited house guests were seated inside the kitchen around the table, relaxed as if they were long lost friends enjoying each other's company. The sight of his wife smiling with a pleasant glow was indeed reassuring, but Rudy failed to realize she was incredibly terrified they might get killed.

"Honey I got stuff to do, what is it? I was halfway to my destination and had to turn back for what," Rudy yelled?

"Don't mistake our laughing and good humor for pleasantries! Matter a fact, come in and hold a sit," threatened Kevin who placed his firearm on the table for Rudy to see!

Kevin's long dreads shielded his face until he threw them to the back, at which Rudy became excited to have a person of his stature inside his home.

"Oh, snaps it's Kevin! Babes, why didn't you tell me we have a living legend inside our condo," Rudy stated, as he moved to shake hands?

"We met before," asked Kevin?

"Not really, but you a legend in the streets man! Right now, the whole city about to go to war over the same policies you fought to protect! Them bikers on the same shit you broke down; but niggers getting ready to break that shit right down again," Rudy exclaimed!

Kevin politely gave him a fist bump and had him sit for them to talk, in the presence of both females.

"We can't have no war like that in the streets of Montreal again! Besides, this youth Lass and who so ever him have with him will get annihilated," Kevin declared!

"Yow my man Lass got plenty of soldiers across the city who he deals with; them bikers don't know who they fucking with," Rudy stated!

"I don't business how strong Lass and his people think they are, like I said this war can't happen," Kevin insisted!

"I don't think anybody in the country can stop this war right now Big G, not after all the people shot and killed already! I heard Lass got like a hundred shottas around him well armed! There is even a rumor that the two sides might agree to meet somewhere like you OGs did it," Rudy reported!

"As exciting as all that sounds, none of that's good for business! And at the end of the day, it's all about business," Kevin said!

"I for one understand that Big G, but what am I to do about it," Rudy asked?

"Your business client Lass will be getting in touch with you over the next few days. Whatever him want, you can't help him right now," Kevin declared, as he collected an envelope from his female companion and passed it to their host!

Inside the Manilla Envelope were photos of every person involved in Rudy's trafficking scheme, from the drug boss, Falco Ramon, who sold them the Cocaine to his cousin Jake Winthorp, who bought and packaged the drugs, in addition to several of his swallowers who transported the products abroad. As the drug dealer began passing the photos to his wife, her mouth fell wide open once she realized who the people were. The documents given to the Winthorps were compelling evidence that Kevin could have destroyed them by turning them over to law enforcement, therefore they became much more inclined to show him loyalty.

"I had several options how we could have dealt with this; I could have come in here and killed you, your lovely wife and your unborn child, turned this information into the police or kill most of those people in the pictures, which would either way put a stop to your whole operation. But I believe that every man must eat, so you get the last option possible," Kevin threatened!

"How do you know all this shit," Rudy argued?

"Ben," Jeneel cried out!

"Ah, what did you say you want me to do again," Rudy timidly asked?

"Whether or not you answer your phone when Lass calls, either way you have nothing for sale," Kevin instructed!

Part 42

Two hustlers from Saint-Vincent-and-The-Grenadines who lived in Ville-Saint-Laurent were broke and needed to earn some money. While conspiring about their next heist, Terrence Beckford and Evan Bittle thought of a plan to rob the bikers, without getting implicated in the robbery. Their plan needed a female to be successful and for that they brought in Evan's cousin Jackey, who considered herself an entrepreneur willing to do anything necessary to get paid. Jackey had danced as a stripper in several night club throughout the city, during which her side hustle was dealing powder cocaine and marijuana to the other dancers; prostituted herself, trafficked drugs as a mule with the package inserted inside her vagina, shot after a female rival and a list of indecent things not becoming of a lady. The idea was to rent a motel room and have Jackey telephone the Rough Rider's drug line to place an order, then robbed the delivery men whenever they arrived. With word in the streets heavy on the ongoing drug war between the Jamaicans and the Rough Riders, the Vincy hustlers expected everyone to blame the obvious candidate.

They tried their idea for the first time at a Best Western Hotel on Papineau-Avenue, where the manager allowed Jackey to rent a room without the use of a credit card, because he was one of her regular sex clients. When Jackey called the biker's delivery line the dispatcher sent over twenty-four years old Vegan, who had a tattoo on his chest that read, "The only meat I ever ate was pussy". Vegan was a horny little bastard who wished he could have intercourse every second of the day. As a single man who lived alone, Vegan's television was always on a porno channel, plus he kept a box of Kleenex and a bottle of Baby Oil next to his bed for masturbation purposes.

Before the deliveryman arrived the gang of thieves plotted when, how and everything necessary for their success. Terrence and Evan then left the room and phoned Jackey's cellular to listen in on the conversation inside the room. Both Vincy thieves planned to enter unexpectedly when given a code word by Jackey, who had to get the dealer comfortable and trusting. The instant Vegan knocked the door and Jackey opened it, his mouth dropped to the floor at the sight of the stallion before him. Jackey enticingly wore a silk robe with white bra and panty, and barely exposed her proportionate figure, but her huge plump breasts and a sizable backside raised Vegan's pulse level instantly.

"Hello, you are Jackey right," Vegan asked!?

"The one and only," joked Jackey!

"I am sure I never served you before, are you a cop working undercover," Vegan asked?

"Ha-ha, me an undercover, yeah right! Wanna see my badge," laughed Jackey, who then took off her robe and did a twirl?

Vegan's eyes nearly popped out of their sockets and drool was almost falling from his mouth.

"So how come a lovely girl like you here alone," Vegan asked?

"I'm working," Jackey responded!

"Oh, so what did you want," Vegan enquired?

"Some Ecstasy please, and an eight ball of powder and some of those blue pills for some of my clients who need help getting their shit up," Jackey ordered?

"No problem," said Vegan, who then opened his jacket which had several hidden pockets underneath! "So how do I get some of you?"

"What do you want," Jackey questioned?

"I'm a woman devourer, I want everything," Vegan declared, as he removed two packages from two separate pockets and gave them to Jackey!

The female tossed the drugs on the bed and stepped closer to Vegan who immediately grabbed her huge round ass with both hands and squeezed. Jackey grabbed the Caucasian's crotch which was hard like a baseball bat, then used her other hand to caress his body as he kissed her neck and earlobe. While rubbing her hand all over the biker, Jackey felt his handgun shoved into his waist but neglected it and continued without hesitating. Vegan was overly eager to get at the appetizing dark chocolate in his grasp, thus he hoisted her off the floor and tossed her on the bed. The biker's spontaneous actions amused the female, who giggled at his sense of adventure. As Jackey fell to the bed, Vegan plunged his face between her legs and simply slid her panty to the side to perform oral sex.

Even though Jackey had Vegan in a compromising position, he was still capable of retrieving his firearm at a second's notice and could ruin their plan, thus she neglected to utter the code word for her partners to enter. As the female entrepreneur laid on her back and stared up at the ceiling, the nervousness she felt at the beginning of the operation slowly subsided, until she was left trying to pull every hair follicle from the Caucasian's head. The biker did such an exquisite job that the only thing Terrence and Evan heard for the first eight minutes were the passionate moans from Jackey who was on cloud nine. Once she was given a bit of reprieve, Jackey sat at the edge of the bed and started unbuckling her client's belt, therefore he withdrew his Colt 45 and placed it on the night table. For such an excellent performance, the stimulated female aggressively dragged Vegan's pants and boxer-briefs down to his ankles, then passionately stroked his penis before she performed fellatio.

While Jackey worked her magic the Rough Rider's dispatcher began ringing his phone to enquire if he was on route to his next delivery assignment. If Jackey felt like she was on cloud nine during the deliveryman's performance, Vegan must have been floating in space, because he simply looked at the number and ignored the call. Knowing he would have to leave quite soon; the drug trafficker interrupted the best blowjob he ever received and affectionately spun his partner around on the bed. From the biker entered the hotel suite he spoke English fluently, however, once his penis entered his captivating partner the French language was all Vegan spoke.

"Oh my god, my god; I now arrive in Heaven! Oh my god, take me dear lord," repeated Vegan, who began slapping Jackey's huge ass with excitement!

"Ah… Come get it daddy," said Jackey, who unknowingly called in her partners in crime!

Jackey had some coitus secrets up her sleeve and began quinting her clitoris, which increased the level of stimulation and compelled the single biker to personally apply for several undisclosed positions.

"Oh my god! Whatever you want I give you my number, just phone me! I pay for your bills, take you shopping, drive you where you want to go, whatever you want! Oh my god," shouted Vegan, as Evan and Terrence used their door pass to enter the suite!

When the armed Vincy thieves walked in Vegan was almost naked and could only manage to throw his hands in the air. The robbers threw the biker face down onto the bed and hog tied him as he was, without offering him the dignity of getting dressed. Evan and his partners tried their best to sound like they were Jamaicans, to trick the Caucasian male into believing they were from the Reggae tropical island. The trio stole everything from the biker and even took his car, which they sold to a chop shop for an additional five thousand dollars. Vegan was not found until the maid service came by the following morning to clean the room, at which he was able to disclose what happened to his biker peers.

***

The audacious Caribbean thieves used Vegan's stolen credit card and reserved a suite for the following day at a Holiday Inn on Boulevard Lacordaire. They made a grand total of twenty-three thousand dollars from their first heist, primarily from the array of stolen drugs and believed they could do better or equal their earnings next time out. Prior to their decision, Jackey spoke with her client at the Best Western who told her that no complaints or police were notified after the maid found Vegan; in fact, the bikers paid the maid a thousand dollars for her silence in the matter. The knowledge that the Rough Riders would never involve the police emboldened the gang of thieves, who planned to continue taking the bikers' products until they found another worthwhile heist.

The bikers protectively changed up their delivery routine and started sending two traffickers to each transaction instead of one. When Jackey phoned the delivery service line that evening the dispatcher sent over Ibrahim aka (Big-Rig) and Pierre-Leon aka (Terror-X) to the location provided. News of the past evening's robbery placed all the biker's work crews on edge, wherein everyone began carrying concealed firearms and drove about in larger numbers. The Holiday Inn was bigger and much busier than the Best Western Hotel and allowed for their customers to park underneath their underground parking facility. When checking into the hotel both Terrence and Evan were unhappy with the parking arrangements, but there was nothing else available at assigned areas around the building.

Informer 3

Moments before the bikers arrived the Vincy males exited the room and left Jackey to work her magic. Evan and Terrence were worried they might lose phone connection if they went too far away from the room, so they took an elevator to the floor above and waited there. When the bikers arrived, they parked their BMW-M illegally in a handicap parking slot and hurried up to see their client. Jackey attended to the door and was shocked to find two men, who both entered and were a lot more business orientated than Vegan was.

"You Pauline," Terror-X asked?

"Yes, I am, thanks for coming by! Any of you guys want a drink, I like have a bottle of Hennessy to myself," responded Jackey, who had a glass of liquor in her hand and the bottle of Hennessy on the dresser table? Unlike Vegan who was all over her at that point, the new deliverymen pretended as if they did not realize their client was half naked and flirting sexually.

"No thank you, what did you wish to order," Terror-X demanded?

"Oh! Sorry, I'll take a dozen Ecstasy Pills and an eight ball," answered Jackey, who thought that they must be gays to not attempt anything?

As Big Rig reached inside his coat pocket and began withdrawing a huge Ziploc Plastic Bag that contained his delivery supplies, the door flew wide open and Terrence and Evan walked in. Both Vincy thieves were armed with 9mm hand pistols and aimed them at the bikers, who were initially suspicious of Jackey and thus not as friendly as they customarily were. Terror-X had his hand on his HK-P30 9mm Luger inside his pocket before the male thieves busted in; and spun around to face them with his gun at hand.

"All you raise your blood-clatt hands in the air," instructed Evan, who tried sounding like a Jamaican but was slightly off key!

"Fuck you motherfuckers, you have to kill us tonight but we not getting jacked, fuck that," warned Terror-X, who then tried to back away from the intruders that he assumed were loafers!

Big-Rig who was a bit chubby, started reaching for his ZEV-Z19 Spartan 9mm Automatic Handgun that was shoved into his waist, when Terror-X began raising his firearm at Jackey's accomplices.

"Yow don't move man! Yow, yow, yow, yow, yow," shouted Terrence, who found themselves up against a pair of stubborn bikers who were totally unreasonable!

"Bam, bam, bam," sounded Terrence's firearm, to which Terror-X squeezed off two shots that struck the floor and the wall!

Jackey screamed out with fright having never contemplated a scenario as such occurring. Big-Rig stupidly pulled his 9mm instead of surrendering and got shot twice in the back by Evan, who thought he was about to shoot their female partner. The entire deal went sour before anyone knew what happened, as a result the thieves had to hurry and exit the premises before the police showed up. There was no doubt that the people going about the hallway and some inside their suites did not overhear the gunshots, so Jackey was forced to dress and grab all her belongings while her male partners grabbed the drugs and whatever valuables they found.

Within three minutes they were through the door and on their way to the elevator, that brought them down to the basement parking. Nobody said a word after they left the suite, and everybody stared blankly ahead as if they knew they had fucked up. When they reached their vehicle the three accomplices loaded all their belongings and drove to the exit, which opened to a sea of blue and red flashing lights. Police officers had gotten word that the people involved in the reported shooting were attempting to flee the scene and created a road block at the hotel parking exit. There were officers everywhere with their weapons aimed at the crew of thieves, who were taken into custody without further incident.

Part 43

There was a premature report given by one of the arresting officers at the Holiday Inn shooting, who told a Gazette reporter, "that presumably Jamaicans robbed and killed the bikers involved." When word reached Jim Bartello, he was none too pleased about the developments yet thought of what Gilbert Stephano told him and decided against responding to the matter. Everyone who called Jim regarding the killings wanted blood in return; and several close associates to the deceased even threatened to settle the matter themselves if he did nothing. Peer pressure from his comrades forced Jim to reconsider his position, at which he frustratingly ordered Lil Wasp, "to locate Lass' layer for them to send an eradication squad to wipe them all off the face of the Earth." Jim had made dramatic improvements with his recovery and could walk with the aide of a cane, but still had a long way to go. Because he was unable to lead the charge Jim selected Lil Wasp as leader of the squad, which would not include a designated area overseer.

To acquire volunteers Jim Bartello had his aides put out an emergency alert to their biker brothers across the island; and at a moment's notice received three hundred and eighty-nine acceptive participants. The call to duty alert simply stipulated that gunners were required; and all interested parties should be at their newly reopened Blues Bar in Verdun by 2 PM the following afternoon! Even though the intricate details of their mission were never preannounced, by 12:20 PM the specified day, vehicle loads of bikers began arriving at the designated spot, some carrying humongous bags. Majority of the bikers were owners of handguns that they concealed beneath their shirts, but those with much large rifles had no choice but to transport them as such. Inside the Blues Bar eventually resembled a weapon's fair, with bikers loading, cleaning and checking their weapons. With such a large group of bikers, plans had to be developed on who did what for them to succeed at their mission, therefore they broke the assassination force down into six teams. The largest team assembled was Lass' assassination gunners, however their plans were geared to covering every aspects of the mission, from dealing with the emergency response teams, to their escape strategy from the scene.

Jim oversaw the invasion plans and even inserted some of the schemes used by Kevin and the Alliance versus Martain Lafleur, which he believed might be effective. The most difficult task in their mission was expected to be Lass' execution, whom Lil Wasp learnt had significantly increased the security personnel around himself. To discard with the police during their escape, Jim arranged for some of their gunners to be stationed on several rooftops and balconies along the selected route. The bikers planned to use dump trucks and block three streets that led to lass' location, then place armed gunners across each boundary to impede the police's intervention. Transportation and uniforms were prearranged by the biker leader, who knew they would need to disguise themselves at certain junctions. With each stage of their mission and every possible surprise debated, Jim wished his assassination team good luck and told Lil Wasp to provide him with timely alerts as they sat out to execute Lass and his supporters.

***

It was pouring rain across the island of Montreal and the Canadian National Meteorologist issued warnings that they expected the downpour to continue well into the night. Lass was seated around a dining table with three other Jamaicans eating Dumplings, Boiled Yellow Yams, Boiled Bananas, Sweet Potatoes and Ackee with Salt Fish, when the lookout at the window started reveling about some Bentley that was being parked outside. The chef who had been sharing out plates of food for the other thirteen gunners, curiously ran to the window with several others to check out the cause for the excitement. When

Informer 3

Miss Nutcracker exited the vehicle and began moving towards the rear door, most of the stunned gunners began cheering and hounding like dogs although she could not hear them outside. The female opened a huge umbrella and used it to shield her client from the rain, and thereby unintentionally blocked Kevin from the spectators' view.

The NDG drug boss had two rented apartments on the building, one on the first floor from which his dealers sold their products and a second on the third floor where they hung out. Contrary to the residence on the third-floor, the first-floor apartment was positioned towards the back of the building and allowed for the Jamaicans to have a full view of everything approaching from the rear. There were buildings on either side of the residential structure, therefore the lookouts had less with which to be concerned. As Kevin and his bodyguard approached the front door a tenant exited and politely held the door open for them, therefore they simply walked in without having to seek entry. The unexpected visitors knew exactly which apartment Lass was in at 307 and proceeded to the door, where Miss Nutcracker stepped forward and knocked. While they waited for someone to open the door, Kevin and his female companion could hear the people inside shuffling about like pawns on a chess board. After nearly a minute the door swung open and a short little man stepped between the door frame.

"Can I help you," asked the man?

"Yes, can you please inform your boss that Monsieur Kevin Trudeau would like to have a word," Miss Nutcracker declared?

The little man snuck his head back into the apartment and looked at Lass, whose eyes widened like a fortunate child on Christmas morning. The boss emphatically nodded his agreement at which the doorman stepped aside and allowed their guests to enter.

"Mi General Kevin, the legend himself, welcome big man," Lass exclaimed as the rude-boy and his bodyguard walked in!

Both men shook hands at which the other gunners realized who the male visitor was and moved in to show their respects. Kevin shook every man's hand as if he was a Rockstar and was even offered a small plate of food, which he accepted then sat and ate with Lass and friends. Miss Nutcracker refused the food offered to her and stood by Kevin's right hand throughout the men's talk. There was no chance during supper to discuss the business for which Kevin had gone to see Lass with the amounts of questions showered at him by his adoring companions. Lass' gunners wanted to hear the whole story of what transpired between the Alliance Crew and Martain Lafleur's bikers, so Kevin took time to give them the correct details of the war. Following the stories Kevin asked to speak with Lass privately, to which everyone exited and allowed them to have the small kitchen.

Bloodshed Never Ends

"It was important for me to make your boys understand that I could easily not be here right now! I fought against Martain and him riders with the true owners of Canada, and you see those native people even though them bitter for getting their lands stolen, them know them don't need much to live, cause them no fussy, but them willing to fight for what's theirs! Because of what we did hustlers especially in this city get to deal with which ever supplier them want; and that policy will never change," Kevin exclaimed!

"Rumors in the streets is that you joined the bikers, after everything you guys gone through, why," Lass declared?

"There is joining the biker club, and then there is running the biker club, don't get the two confused! At the end of the day I know that them corrupt and prejudice, but as long as I have a say in what they do, every other culture must prosper in this blood-clatt country to," Kevin stated!

"So, what you saying Genna," Lass questioned?

"Why you in the hustling business," Kevin commented?

"To make some money of course," Lass responded!

"Everything good with your connects," Kevin asked?

"Bam-bam-bam," sounded the door, at which Slim peeked through the peephole then opened the door!

Dull-Boy and two other hustlers who had gotten assigned to the first-floor drug base rushed in carrying a container with the illegal substances they peddled from the apartment and their weapons at hand. "There are bikers like fuckery climbing over the back fence and hiding in the yard," yelled one of the drug dealers!

"What," said Kevin and Lass simultaneously as they leapt to their feet!

Lass withdrew his Wraith 9mm Luger and aimed it furiously at Kevin, as his cellular began ringing with a neighborhood informant calling to alert him about the bikers.

"You brought those fuckers with you," Lass blamed Kevin, as he looked to see who the caller was!?

"Do I look like a fucking informant to you," Kevin responded?

"Don't be stupid, if you have to shoot your way out of here, we will have to shoot our way out of here also," Miss Nutcracker declared!

Everyone who had been showering Kevin with praises were stunned at the accusation and focused their attention at both men. The female Pigeon of The Order walked over to the front window and look outside, where she saw Lil

Wasp organizing a gang of bikers. All the gunners were descending from a pair of yellow school buses that pulled up directly in front the building. To avoid alarming the neighborhood residents, the rifle carrying bikers brought their weapons in backpacks and other bags to disguise them. The alarming sight startled the female bodyguard who withdrew a pair of Uzi Mini Assault Rifles from beneath her rain jacket, that were attached to her back in holding cases. Kevin and Lass' dispute quickly became secondary, as the audience of gunners turned their attention to the sexy looking female.

"Pussy-clatt, there is like a hundred bikers out front," frightfully described the lookout at the window with Miss Nutcracker!

"Where the blood-clatt them come from," yelled Lass, who responded to the caller on his phone?

When Lil Wasp and Jim Bartello's assassination unit arrived at Lass' location, they used a Mack Dump Truck to block the top of West-Hill Avenue at the corner of Sherbrooke Street, to stop all commuters from entering their strike zone. The bikers also placed a second Mack Truck slightly below Madison Avenue on Boulevard de-Maisonneuve; and a third Mack Truck at the corner of Benny Avenue and Boulevard de-Maisonneuve. There were fenced in train tracks at the opposite end of West-Hill Avenue that would create its own problems, however the bikers had everything prearranged. Each biker assigned to the road blockage unit wore uniforms that belonged to the city's Sanitation Department to deceive both the police and pedestrians. The Rough Rider Bikers were ordered not to brandish their weapons until they were confronted, therefore they initially left their weapons inside the truck.

A police cruiser was parked three buildings away from Lass' location that sat vacant, yet the bikers ignored the vehicle and proceeded with their assassination plans. The assault team was split into two, with one team attacking from the building's rear exit, while the other went through the front entrance. One of the buses used to transport some of the bikers was placed strategically at the corner of West-Hill Avenue and Boulevard de-Maisonneuve, to block people's view of the incident from the opposite side of the train tracks. It was still pouring rain and with such a large group to command, Lil Wasp was seen pointing and talking on his phone.

"If you agree to buy as little as two keys from the bikers each month, I might be able to stop them," Kevin stated, but Lass had already gotten rid of the informant on his phone and was too focused on trying to contact his detective friends?

"What you want us to do boss," Pickard demanded, but Lass seemed just as lost as they were?

"We can't allow them to come up to the top floor, so everybody pack the staircase," Kevin instructed, but instead of moving the gunners all looked to their boss for confirmation!

Lass tired to phone the detectives he made the protection deal with, but the phone rang without answer. With a handful of gunners, weapons and bullets versus an army of assassins, Lass was speechless and had no strategies to ward a defensive stance against the much larger and organized bikers.

"Boss, boss, what should we do," Slim asked?

Lass was in shock and could not speak, therefore Kevin repeated his instructions. The Jamaicans knew they were terribly outnumbered and did not stand a chance unless they controlled the field of battle. Knowing Kevin had survived his share of gun battles, the gunners began taking heed and snuck out into the hallway where they aligned themselves against the walls and waited for their opponents at the top of the stairs. While all their gunners prepared for the showdown, Lass and Kevin moved to the window and watched the bikers below as they began entering the building.

"You would rather a shootout that might kill us all than making a deal that will benefit you and your business," Kevin asked Lass?

"Sorry, my mind elsewhere. Did you say you could do something to get rid of these fuckers," Lass enquired?

"If you agree to do business with these people, I might can call them off," Kevin suggested?

"Due to unforeseen circumstances I need a new supplier, so I will buy a thing from them! You have my word Genna," Lass agreed!

Kevin withdrew his cellular phone and called Monsieur Gilbert Stephano, who was in the company of several elderly Frenchmen. The Secret Cult's spokesman excused himself from the group of men and found somewhere private to chat. The Jamaican rude-boy explained their situation and instructed Gilbert that he had indeed secured the business contract with the N.D.G drug boss, whom they had spoken about. With the gun battle on the edge of sparking the spokesman quickly telephoned Jim Bartello, who had Lil Wasp on the other line providing him with timely alerts.

"Monsieur Stephano, such an unexpected surprise," Jim responded!

"Mister Bartello, I had neglected to mention that our aides had secured the business contract with Mister Lass of Notre-Dame-de-Grace. But it has come to my attention that your bikers are on location and apparently threatening to endanger our business venture? If you fancy your position sir, I would suggest that you call them off immediately," Gilbert warned!

"I'm sure there must be some misunderstanding sir, but I'll see to the matter right away," Jim said, as he quickly changed over and spoke to Lil Wasp on the other line! "Wasp cancel that fucking attack now, I repeat cancel, cancel!"

The Rough Rider assassins were on the second floor cautiously approaching the third floor's staircase, where they expected to get met with extremely stiff resistance. Lass looked at the faces of several of their shottas and noted the nervousness they portrayed, knowing the size of the monster they were up against. It was evident that they were in for the most turbulent experience of their lives and none of them might survive, in part to a disagreement which had nothing to do with any of them. Amongst Lass' crew of shottas aligned in the hallway was Miss Nutcracker who was close to the frontline and would face whatever judgement his gunners did, therefore the N.D.G drug boss felt confident they were all in against the approaching forces.

"Shhh," said Miss Nutcracker to two gunners grumbling behind her, as they listened intently to hear if the bikers were still approaching.

The timid shuffle from the bikers who were cautiously approaching the third-floor staircase suddenly seized and then silence. Lass who had his eyes focused outside the window noticed the bikers retreating from the premises and directly back onto the yellow buses.

"It sounds like they are backing away. Is there another way to get up here through an apartment or something," Miss Nutcracker whisperingly asked?

"No, only by the steps," whispered Slim.

"Then where the fuck are they," Miss Nutcracker questioned?

"They are leaving… They are leaving," Lass shouted, as the bikers reloaded their busses and drove away!

Officer Stan Shefford was heading east bound on Sherbrooke Street when he came upon the traffic holdup that was caused by the bikers closing the residential road. When the officer got closer to the incident and realized what was happening, he threw on his flashers and parked to help defer motorist from trying to disobey the workers' road sign. The bikers who were fiddling around as if they had road work to do, began getting nervous once Constable Shefford exited his cruiser and began walking towards them. The driver of the Mack Truck was high off LSD and seated behind the steering wheel, with his fingers tapping a T91 Assault Rifle laying on his lap. Since they blocked the roadway numerous motorists had expressed their anger by shouting and signalling illicit things that only managed to increase the tension. So, the officer's arrival came at a time when the bikers were expecting to keep everyone away with the use of force.

The constable walked up to two of the bikers who appeared to be revising some blueprints just standing outside the dump truck's door. Officer Shefford had no idea there was another biker inside the truck's cabin and stood enquiring, "how long the work was expected to take", when the biker began aiming his rifle at the officer. Fearing their plans might get exposed the biker pulled the trigger and was startled when the weapon neglected to fire, due to the safety switch being activated. As the biker inspected the weapon and activated the switch, one of his associates shouted out, "Let's get out of here, our job just got cancelled"! At that all the bikers climbed back aboard their transport as Officer Shefford guided traffic back to normal. Bikers at the other locations stopped whatever activities they were doing and got back into their vehicles and vacated the scene without any altercation. Kevin, Lass and everyone involved breathed a huge sigh of relief, as some of the dealers even hugged each other and cheered. Even though the female bodyguard was also elated, she simply smiled and made her way back to her boss' side which was her primary duty.

Part 44

With slumping approval numbers in the polls for Prime Minister Mathew Layton, the opposition parties believed they found the perfect platform with which to defeat the incumbent Canadian leader. The none punitive report released by the Ethics Committee on the Prime Minister's conduct, forced the other party leaders to call for a general election. Even though Mme. Teressa Lablonde's report sighted that they concluded the Prime Minister's response was attributed to National Security matters, none of the opposition leaders concurred with their decision.

 The Ethics Committee's office which had a new commissioner following Mme. Lablonde's resignation, issued a statement where they defended the findings of their former division head, who had been fighting for her life in a Cancer treatment center. Regardless of Teressa's life threatening status, Minister David McNeil of the People of Quebec National Party and other opposition leaders smeared her name in campaign advertisements aimed at defaming the Prime Minister. Even with her failing health Teressa Lablonde remained trusting of her doctor Deborah Spooks, who hypocritically remained her caregiver despite giving her patient her second dose of Cancer. The political smearing of her name in addition to the spread of the disease took its toll on Teressa, who died some two months before Canadians went to the polls.

***

Marceau Demerit got wheelchaired into the prison that housed his sister Marolina and her husband Andrea Veronovichi. Maurice Demerit pushed his brother with tears in his eyes knowing fully what their own sister had done to them. There were four lit torches about the chamber, where their frail skinned sister and brother-in-law were tied to hooks on the ceiling. Neither of the couple had the physical strength to look up at their relatives after five weeks of a grueling diet, where they were served a slice of bread twice weekly and water once daily. Kevin barely kept the Veronovichi couple alive for leverage and walked in behind the Demerit brothers, who both took a long stare at their sibling. As the glares of the torches flashed against the prisoners' bodies the evidence of their torture became quite clear, yet neither brother felt any compassion to help their sister. After staring at their betrayers for a few minutes, Marceau picked up a H&K VP9SK Semi Auto 9mm Luger off his lap and pointed it at them; but could not bring himself to pulling the trigger. Reluctantly, Marceau passed the handgun to his brother who still had tears rolling down his face.

Marolina heard her sobbing younger brother and slightly lifted her head to see who it was. By then Maurice's right hand was trembling as he slowly lifted the weapon up and stopped as their eyes met. Andrea was still passed out and didn't hear a word despite his close brush with death, however he seldom coughed as if he had contracted Pneumonia. Kevin was interested in seeing what would happen when they finally confronted each other, therefore he stood over in the corner and watched.

"Go ahead and kill me. I'm already dead," Marolina grumbled.

Maurice's hand fell to his side with the weapon, as he also could not bring himself to murdering his own sibling.

"You are both banished from Canada from this day forward! We didn't kill you because of love and family, but if you ever step one foot back in North America, the next time I will kill you, sister or not," Marceau threatened!

Maurice then turned his brother's wheelchair around and walked from the room, following which four men entered the room and released the prisoners from their bondages. Kevin walked out with the Demerit brothers who both appeared extremely angry and refrained from saying anything. When they reached the main floor of the mansion Kevin and Marceau met inside an office alone and had a productive discussion. While both cult brothers spoke in private Maurice waited for his brother outside the residence, where he puffed on a Regius Double Corona Cigar to ease his nerves.

"I must thank you for not killing my sister… and leaving her final judgement up to us," Marceau declared!

"You're welcome! And my sincerest apologies for your father," Kevin answered!

"Unlike my sister Mr. Trudeau, I have no ill-feelings towards you regarding my old man! I understand that he was beloved amongst his peers, but the fact of the matter is he was a mean drunk who would beat the crap out of my mother before she died! So, I don't feel all this compassion my sister does," Marceau stated!

"You are a very compassionate man Mr. Demerit. I don't know if I could ever show that amount of restrain," Kevin responded!

"I might be condemned to this wheelchair for the rest of my life Mr. Trudeau, so humility is one thing I have to start accepting," Marceau said!

"So where does things stand between us," Kevin asked?

"All water underneath the bridge as far as I'm concerned! Although by now it is possible that some of our board members may have heard about this, so your problems could just be starting," Marceau exclaimed!

"I'm always ready for whatever," Kevin muttered, as he withdrew a Marijuana joint and sparked it ablaze.

Marolina and her husband were dragged from the chamber where they had spent their last few weeks; being starved and tortured for conspiring with Kevin's adversaries. The couple were so weak that neither of them could walk when they got transported by ambulance directly to a waiting private jet inside a hanger at the Pierre-Elliot-Trudeau Airport, on which a medical doctor and nurses offered them medical treatment. Even though they were safe and being sent to a place they also considered home, Marolina wept throughout the flight knowing she had been exiled from her own place of birth and would never see her siblings again.

When the couple's-chartered flight arrived at Leonardo-da-Vinci International Airport in western Italy and rumors circulated about their return, dozens of news media flocked to the airport for a report on what happened to them. Because the kidnapping happened in a foreign country the couple was not first subjected to answering questions by investigators, instead they were given the option to speak with detectives at a later date if they chose to. Every hostage analyst speculated that some sort of ransom must have been paid for the couple to be released, but no formal comments were ever released from the camps of either victim.

Both Marolina and Andrea had to be wheelchaired off the plane and were transferred to waiting ambulances that rushed them off to the hospital. The instant the first ambulance exited the runway access gate, the technicians were bombarded by paparazzi and news reporters who brought the vehicle to a slow crawl. Instead of sharing the ambulance ride to the hospital where both victims were instructed to go for EX-Rays and further checkup, Andrea chose to ride solo and demanded a separate emergency transport. At the time many critiqued the husband's decision and accused Andrea of many unjustified claims, however, confirmation of the broken marriage came the following day when the Italian filed for divorce. Marolina would later move to France where she settled down outside the town of Saint-Sulpice-le-Gueretois. The exiled female bought and lived luxuriously in a vintage eighteen century mansion, from which she rarely departed and surprisingly remained unmarried.

***

The Secret French Cult held its private annual gala for its presiding members to loosen up and enjoy each other's company. The event was held at the Rideau Carlton Race Horse Track & Gaming Facility in Ottawa, Ontario, which they rented out for the private occasion. With never any expense spared for the pleasures of its governing members, the racing facility was separated into several eventful sections. None of the committee members were allowed bringing dates and the ladies and men present were only there for their pleasures, therefore from the moment they entered the building everything was designed for their enjoyment. For those who wished to gamble the casino was available with slot machines and card games, as was the live horse races, the International Buffet restaurant for dining, a lounge for relaxing attached to a party room and a massage area where everything sexual was permitted.

Sleeping accommodations were prearranged at the Airport's Hilton Hotel, which was a few miles away from the racetrack. The scheduled start time for the event was 3 PM, thus the cult flew each of its members into the city earlier that morning. Limousine service was given to all the designated guests, who all arrived at the gala wearing their black cloaks to hide their identities from possible long-ranged photo capturing paparazzi. Commuters travelling along Albion Road must have thought the event was being attended by government officials only, due to the amount of well-attired security personnel about the facility's grounds. There were absolutely no weapons allowed inside the venue and to enforce their rules the committee placed a metal detecting device at the entrance. None of the security guards monitoring the arriving guests were permitted to physically touch any of the members, therefore there were no guarantees that any weapons got smuggled in.

Kevin and Marceau had developed a mutually respectful relationship, therefore they both shared the limousine ride to the gala. Marceau's motorized wheelchair was a bit too wide to pass through the metal detector, therefore he was allowed in through a separate door. Being they hadn't eaten and planned on drinking heavily while enjoying the evening, both members decided to first visit the dining lounge for a proper meal. The racing tracks were right outside the window and spectators could bet on the races while they chilled inside the restaurant, so Kevin and Marceau started placing large amounts of money on the races. The food was splendid and by the time they exited the dining lounge, Marceau was sixty-four thousand dollars richer while Kevin lost thirty-eight thousand.

Before going to the casino both cult members decided to partake of a cigar and went to the lounge area where nine other members were doing the same. While every other member's cloak featured the same symbols, Kevin's cloak had a special emblem that signified he was the Chancellor. The committee provided everything for its members, including five of the most expensive cigars in the entire world. After selecting the cigars of their choice, the two men went to the opposite end of the lounge, where they sat and spoke as the puffed away. As soon as they sat down the waitress walked over and took their orders, then brought the unlikely friends their beverages and returned to her station. When Kevin selected his seat, he chose a position from which he could see the entire lounge, thus it was not long before all the other occupants started walking over towards the isolated drinkers.

The group of men were none too shy to show their intentions, hence halfway across the floor two of them visibly withdrew a pair of knives. The men intended on holding Kevin firmly while others stabbed him to death, therefore they separated into two groups and started moving towards the rude-boy. Marceau who could barely maneuver felt helpless and watched as their cult associates slowly moved in. Kevin sat puffing away on his cigar as if he hadn't a care in the world, while the gang of assassins crept closer and closer. When the cult members got within three feet of him, Kevin stood up and bit onto two pins attached to grenades and pulled the out. With the safety pins removed from the bombs, Kevin spat the pins onto the table ahead of him and held them high for all to see. The female waitress got scared and ran from the lounge fearful they were going to kill each other, as the cult members all froze and stopped their attack.

"Where the bold-clatt y'all think you going? Any of you ready to die," Kevin threatened?

"We heard rumors that you killed our fathers," said a member grumbled!?

"I don't know anything about your fathers; but take one more fucking step and we all will be visiting them," Kevin lamented!

With everyone at a standoff, Monsieur Gilbert Stephano walked into the lounge with two men behind him. Marceau sat in the middle of the commotion with his eyes closed tightly, expecting the worst outcome to transpire from the situation.

"Gentlemen, gentlemen! If you men are through behaving like boys, we have some serious business to discuss," Gilbert stated!?

As soon as the members calmed down and allowed cooler heads to prevail, the men who entered with Gilbert started going around the lounge with search devices to detect bugs or other recording devices. The other members joined the group while the search technicians checked about, until they finished their inspection and exited the lounge. With the doors closed behind them the cult members began a small debate, as Marceau assisted Kevin with the pins' replacing into the grenades.

"Gentlemen, as soon as we return to Montreal, we will be having our next meeting to discussing the upcoming general election; and our strategy to get our candidate to win the Prime Minister's office," Gilbert declared!

Part 45

Falco Lamon was a Cuban National who lived in the Rose Hall district of Montego Bay. The Cuban owned a tourist souvenir shop on the beach strip across from Doctor's Cave Beach, yet sold and trafficked cocaine abroad to four different countries. Three days after the Montreal biker debacle, Falco was driving home from work one afternoon at 1:37 PM when he came across an exquisitely voluptuous light skin female who appeared to be having car trouble. As Falco approached the distressed female who was on her phone and hunched over into the trunk of her BMW 335-I, he noticed there was no one else present and decided to pull over and offer some assistance. When Falco's Mercedes Benz 550 pulled over behind the parked BMW, the female spun around and looked who the person was. At first sight the Cuban was happy he pulled over, expecting to receive much more than a simple thank you for his services.

"What seems to be the problem, lovely senorita," Falco asked?

"It seems like I have a flat tire, but I'm having some trouble getting this spare tire out," exclaimed the female!

Falco looked at the rear tire and noticed that it was indeed deflated. "Let me help you with that lovely lady! By the way me, I'm Falco!"

"Hi Falco, I'm Holly nice to meet you," said the young beauty!

The imperiled female moved to the side and allowed the good Samaritan to assist her. As Falco bent over into the truck to remove the spare tire, the female withdrew a Dan Wesson 1911 Valor Commander 9mm Semi Auto handgun from her waist and shot him in the back of the head. Falco fell forward into the trunk of the car, therefore the female hurried and lifted him fully into the car. To avoid leaving any evidence the assassin searched for and picked up the spend bullet shell and placed it inside her pocket. There was an electrical pump beside the body's legs which the female took out and plugged into an electrical socket, then attached the connection to her tire. With the tire refilling with air the female used her phone and dialed a number.

"Hello, Holly my dear," Kadeem responded!

"That business was taken care of," Holly responded!

"Excellent, I'm wiring the remainder of your funds as we speak," Kadeem stated!

"I appreciate your confidence Don Killa! You already know me and my friend's dunce without reasoning, so anytime you have any contract bout here, please give us a link," Holly exclaimed, as she finalized her tire dealings and drove away?

While his paid assassin fulfilled the mission, Kadeem was on a forty-five feet yacht anchored out at sea with two female guards, a female server, the boat's male captain and six luscious females, who were snorkeling in the nude and partying about the boat. Everybody except the captain was high and intoxicated, as they bathed beneath the golden sunshine. A pair of the females were trying to inspire Kadeem to joining them, while they kissed and fondled with each other on the deck's furniture. Kadeem who was smoking a huge Marijuana joint with a glass of Basil Hayden's, Kentucky Bourbon at hand, phoned Kevin at his home in Quebec and got connected after the second ring. Kevin was on the other line with Kane in Kahnawake and connected all three friends to the conversation.

"My brothers," said Kane immediately as they connected!

"Family! My real brothers, what's good," Kadeem asked?

"Blessed," Kevin responded!

"Couldn't be better my brothers," Kane answered!

"Kevin by the way, when I meet up with your boy's relative later tonight, we'll set up the new business venture! But the opposition already deleted, so I don't foresee any objection," Kadeem said!

"Nice, more business more money Brav," Kevin joked, as he walked into the games room where Kevin-Junior was playing some virtual video game with friends! "Hey, your uncles are on the phone!"

"Hey Uncle Kane and Uncle Kadeem," Kevin Junior shouted, yet still his attention never wavered from the game!

"Hello nephew," said Kane!

"What a gwan," shouted Kadeem, before Kevin exited the games room and walked to the humongous widows in his living room, where he looked out at his huge estate while puffing on a cigar?

"Yow my Mohawk brother, what's new in Kahnawake," Kadeem asked?

"Nothing much brothers, I was just made the new Tribal Council Chief," Kane declared!

"What, congrats my brother that is more than well deserved! I know nobody loves your people more than you," Kadeem declared!

"Congrats my brother, I read about you in the Gazette! Eagle and Danny would be very proud, plus you know that I am," Kevin exclaimed!

"Thank you, both my brothers! I have lots of people to expose for their dirty dealings all these years; and lots of corruption to clean up, but I'm ready for the challenge," Kane stated!

"When it comes to exposing people, you know you better start watching your back brother," Kadeem reasoned!?

"My haters have tried to kill me many times already! They might succeed one day, but before then my only wish is that I could fuck them one time like they have fucked my people all these centuries," Kane responded!

"Then write a book or something," Kadeem suggested!

"That's a great idea brother! Thanks, I believe I will," Kane stated!

"Always think one step ahead of the opposition little brother. I'm driving out to visit Miss Emma with Junior and show him a bit of nature out on the reservation in about a month; so, we'll get to really sit down and celebrate your new position," Kevin declared!

"Looking forward to that brother! By the way Kadeem, sounds like you at a party out there," Kane joked?

"Pretty much brother, can't wait for you guys to come down to the islands for a vacation! Big yacht with nuff beautiful ladies around partying in the nude; life sweet brother! But I must holler at you gentlemen later, business calls! So, one love and keep safe," Kadeem stated as he disconnected from the conference call and joined the tempting females!

"One love brothers," said Kane!

"One love," Kevin added!

THE END

Personal Thoughts

This trilogy was inspired by my upbringing from Jamaica to Canada, in addition to my numerous visits to the United States of America. My primary goal in writing these novels was initially to provide my readers with dynamic reading material, but I also realized the platform I obtained to help guide youths who find themselves in dangerous situations. It was indeed a pleasure putting this work together and I already miss the process I underwent daily to create such works of art. When not tangling with the material during writing, I was always eager to get back to the pages of these novels; and now that I've reached the grand finale, I already miss everything that came with the creation process. While some people have chastised and scorned me for the unjust things I've done in the past, they failed to realize that without knowledge there would be nothing to put between the covers of my novels. Therefore, I encourage anyone with a dream or a goal to pursue yours and ignore the side noises, because success at anything only comes with dedication! My sole hope for youths has always been for the misguided to one day reach a greater plateau than their former self; that they might become like the wiseman and teach the next generation.

Special Thanks

{Photographer}

Janet Flowers

{Book Cover Design}

Clyde Williams at: www.graphiquemezza.com

Informer 3

CPSIA information can be obtained
at www.ICGtesting.com
Printed in the USA
BVHW071013170521
607542BV00002B/115